Road to Salvation

PURGATORY PREP ACADEMY
BOOK THREE

KERRY KELLER

LYNX PUBLISHING

Cover by: Leanne Brown at Sirenic Creations

Formatting by: Yours Truly-KK

Developmental Editing: Cassie Hurst with Inked Imagination Services

Editing by: Kellie from CreativeLee

Proofreader: Jillian of Locke & Key Proofreading Services.

Road to Salvation is a full-length RH/Why choose novel, which ends in a ✎ small cliffhanger (it's not a bad one... promise). It has graphic sexual scenes and foul language that has a tendency to cause a ruckus.

While there are fallen angels and the mention of Hell and Demons in this book, it's not intended to be read as commentary on, or criticism of, existing faith and traditions.

Once again please do not eat or drink while reading this book. I cannot be responsible if you choke to death. I'm too broke for the nonsense

If you're ready for your trip into Hell, continue at your own risk.

You've been warned. 😉

Road to Salvation is a full-length RH/Why choose novel, which ends in a ⬚ small cliffhanger (it's not a bad one... promise). It has graphic sexual scenes and foul language that has a tendency to cause a ruckus.

While there are fallen angels and the mention of Hell and Demons in this book, it's not intended to be read as commentary on, or criticism of, existing faith and traditions.

Once again please do not eat or drink while reading this book. I cannot be responsible if you choke to death. I'm too broke for the nonsense

If you're ready for your trip into Hell, continue at your own risk.

You've been warned. 😉

To my Betas for sending me encouraging words, memes, dirty only fan pics, tweets, and sweet drool-worthy Tik Toks to keep me going when I wanted to give up.

Prologue

Cain

Patience. They have always stated that patience is a virtue. Ha. It isn't a way of showing high moral standards; it's a necessity. A way of wills, some call it. I, for one, call it my salvation.

I tried to break free from my damnation multiple times before, and each attempt failed time and time again. My punishment was being doomed to live in a pit, which is a bleak understatement of suffering. I have done my time and should be free. Since my jailers won't release me, I've found my own way out. Possessions have gone wrong, and Demon summoning to Earth never panned out. Nothing had worked until I signed a new oath. A promise—as it were—to work for a greater cause to free ourselves from the slavery of the chains that keep us bound. Rebels they call us. Ha. They only call us that because we refuse to bow to conformity. We should be free to cross over to Earth and back as we want.

Over the years, I've found a way to attach my essence to Necromancers, feeding off of their power. They might be rare, but they are powerful in the aspect that when they raise the dead, they pull dark magic naturally without the side effects within themselves and feed it back into their creations. The darkness that crosses between them and the creatures they raise has a strong connection and keeps them both balanced. Without the darkness coursing equally through that connection, Necromancers lose their minds—physically and mentally —weakening them and causing memory loss. Let's not forget: the monsters gain their freedom, the power slips free, and it can raise an unimaginable amount of the dead. The creatures themselves can run amuck as they gain their freedom. They're tethered to the Necromancer's mind, and as the tether weakens, they can break free, which in effect causes the Necro's mind to shatter. The perfect storm for me to gain the darkness and energy I need to escape.

But instead, I've seen eons pass me by. It's taken an age to siphon portions of darkness from one Necro after another, to gather enough power to break free, but nothing has been sustainable. The darkness I'm able to pull from a Necromancer always depletes when their powers fail or they are caught and terminated.

The most promising Necro was Inez. When she raised that battlefield of monsters, it was the most power I was ever able to pull at once. Yes, it was a mistake when I had fractured her mind to do it, but I thought we could get away before the mob reached us. Instead, they put her down like a rabid dog, and I could only keep hold of whispers of her power while I waited for another Necro to take her place.

It had been a slow process, storing what little power I had from one Necro to the next. It wasn't until I found Ezekiel, someone who had their own store of power inside of them. Unlike most Necros, he had his own battery of darkness that didn't affect him. Yes, Ezekiel was different—stronger—more resistant, yet I was able to get what I needed from him.

I didn't scramble to pull scraps of darkness from him—like a trickle of water from a faucet. Instead, I received a flow that resembled a fire hose, even when the smallest of animals was resurrected. The problem with Ezekiel was convincing him to actually raise the dead. Fear held him back, but once Rez broke his heart, it was nothing to encourage him to let the pain take over. That was my ticket to gain the power I needed to break free of the curse placed on me eons ago. Now I just need the right moment to step free. Even though I'll be filled with power, my body will still be weak until I can rest. If I step free now, who knows what Zeke and his brothers will try to do to me.

"Quick, extinguish the light," Ryker says, and Levi flicks his wrist, casting the group into darkness.

Perfect.

I pull all the darkness I've been storing up in Ezekiel and gather it to my center, preparing to make myself whole. Will this kill my host? No clue, but since there is so much darkness in him, ask me if I care. I've attached myself to dozens of Necromancers in the past for this type of power, but now it's mine.

Heat swells as my power increases. I feel Ezekiel jerk, and his body becomes locked as I easily take over. I chuckle to myself as I think of the poor young man. He thought he could keep me contained.

I was just buying time, dear boy.

Glowing lights appear from the dark tunnels, but they have yet to reach the group. This is as good a time as any as I whisper my incantation and feel electricity flow through Ezekiel's body.

Boom!

The mountain shakes from the force of my shackles breaking. A rush of air swooshes past Ezekiel's body, bringing up dust particles from the seventh level of Hell, which was where

3

my body was contained. They swirl in a fast array as they solidify. A smile crosses Ezekiel's lips as I feel the vessel for my essence come to completion for my essence to return to my true form. It seems like it takes several minutes, but in reality, it's done within seconds. I take a wobbly step away and into my own body once again, finally leaving behind my Necromancer vessel. Screams ring out as the ground opens up and swallows the group while I quickly make my way over to one tunnel and slump against the wall.

Well, I definitely didn't see that coming.

I watch as part of the ceiling collapses in on the hole.

At least I don't have to worry about burying the bodies.

One of the cloaked figures walks over to me, their hand glowing with a spell at the ready. As they get closer, I see a man, his brows furrowed, and he frowns before opening his mouth to either yell or demand something. But once he gets a good look at me, his face drains of color, and I take great pleasure in the sheer fear I can inspire.

I know what he sees now that I'm back in my immortal body. A six-foot-six frame with midnight black hair and storm gray eyes, which will glow in the dark once they become acclimated. But that's not the most intimidating of my features, or at least that's not what's grabbed this man's attention. It's the mark of Cain, the one I bear that marks me as the original murderer, the first curse. It's a long line down the middle of my forehead, with arcs and symbols branching off. Most people have no idea what it says or what it means, but either way, they've all heard stories. No matter what potion or illusion I've worn, it still shows. So why not wear it with pride and marvel at the fear it causes?

"Take me to your leader." My voice comes deeper than I remember, but I find it pleasant. The tiny man nods quickly and motions for me to follow.

The darkness lightens as we walk down a few tunnels and

my night vision finally adjusts. The man leading me keeps giving me glances over his shoulder—no doubt wondering if the rumors are true. I'm tempted to see if I can make him wet himself just for fun. I dismiss the idea when we walk into another cavern-like structure. This one, though, is twice as big. A woman with long brunette curls is chained to a wall behind an altar, and a throne is carved into the wall across from me.

Walking in from another tunnel is a woman dressed in a long black robe with red lining. She turns to look at me before a smile slowly forms on her face, and I see identical storm gray eyes to my own.

"Ahh, Cain. I see you finally got here," the woman before me says, opening her arms wide.

"Thanks." I give her a smirk. I knew that someday I would be free, even if it came down to freeing myself. Of course, most people doubted me, even the one standing before me.

"Come, give me a hug," she insists.

Feeling somewhat awkward as this woman's body is unfamiliar to me, I lean down and pull her into a quick and gentle hug.

Beaming up at me, she tips her head. "Come, sit." Taking her own seat on the throne, she motions to the chair next to her. "Now, tell me what you've learned," she purrs as I watch the Rebels tattoo come alive along her jaw.

I give her a predatory smile of my own before I sit and shake my head at the foolishness in front of me. "I'll be glad to, Dad, but first, take off that face. It's making me uncomfortable. I haven't seen you in forever."

CHAPTER 1

Booby-Trapped Mind

Lynx

E ver had your ass lit on fire? Or maybe struck by lightning? Well, consider yourself lucky that you haven't, because that's what it feels like when I wake up with a jolt. One big, disorienting shock, like ice water being thrown on you to get you up and out of bed. If I was wet, I would think I slept through my alarm and my mother was tired of screaming at me, so she sent my father in to wake me up. He's already over it and brought out the big guns.

Is that a memory, or is that something I've seen? I have a vague memory of my mom and dad, but for some reason, it's a fleeting thought. *Huh. Is that the last thing I remember of them?*

I'm pretty sure the last thing I remember is a tear. Yep, that's the best way to describe it, a tear that turned into butterfly kisses. Isn't that how that song goes? Feeling little flutters all over my body before my eyes crack open to see a young woman with beautiful gray eyes disappearing before me with a soft, sad smile lingering on her lips. I don't know why, but she seems like she should be familiar to me.

That's the lamest wet dream ever. She could have at least given me a show.

Shaking off the thought, I glance around the room. It looks to be nothing but a hollowed-out hole and is completely empty except for me. *Definitely not the penthouse I should live in.* Pulling myself up from the rough stone, I stretch out and notice I'm only wearing pants.

Shit, maybe that lady did get freaky deeky with me and I don't remember.

I don't feel any aches or pains except for the lingering pain from the shock of waking up. No hunger or weird smells besides the musky scent of the surrounding ground. I have no fucking clue where I'm at or how I got here, but I don't seem to be severely hurt, so that's a plus.

I don't know what happened to the rest of my clothes, but at least I have clean jeans.

My tanned skin seems to illuminate from the inside out, but I feel like I've been through a full body massage and soaked in buttermilk for hours. Even running my hand through my hair, it feels like it's been freshly washed and conditioned, yet it's a little longer than I expect. I don't think I like it this long. Pulling the waistband of my jeans out to inspect the goods, I make sure I'm my magnificent self.

Yep, I still have my elephant cock, so all is good there!

Walking out the cracked wooden door, I find what looks like a somewhat familiar medical room. There are bloody tools lying around, unplugged medical equipment, and the stench of old blood that makes me feel nauseous. Though, I still have no clue where I'm at. *Should I know this place?* Going to the only other door in the room, I allow my eyes to focus as I walk on silent feet down the tunnels. Something inside of me—

which I can only assume is my instincts—is screaming at me to take my time and listen to my surroundings as I continue to walk down the winding tunnel.

As I come up to a fork in the tunnel, I pause long enough to assess which way to go. Voices seem to trickle in from the left, and I can see a slight glow from the end of the tunnel. To the right is only darkness and who knows what else? *If I go left, I'll find people and I'll at least get some answers to what the fuck is going on.* As I take a step in that direction, I'm punched in the gut, which knocks the wind out of me. My lungs freeze as my body cramps up slightly until I stumble back to the right.

Shit. Fine... I get it. That was the wrong direction. Just say so next time.

With my new course set out, I step into the darkness. I creep along the edges, trying to minimize any sounds I might make while moving as quickly as I can.

When I reach another fork in the road, I softly chuckle to myself.

I'm onto you now, fuckernuts.

I stick my foot in a direction, waiting for it to cramp to find out which way to go. I think it's less invasive than throwing my entire body down a tunnel and having to flop around like a dead fish on the ground to backtrack. When nothing happens, I make a turn down another tunnel. I pause when I hear voices up ahead and see a faint blue light.

Well, fuck. I guess the nut fucker has the last laugh after all.

I thought I wasn't supposed to be getting close to people for some reason. I start to backtrack and turn when I see a flicker of light coming down the tunnel behind me. Fuck! I'm trapped, like a constipated shit! Now, which way am I supposed to go?

"Quick, extinguish the light," an oddly familiar voice says.

The blue light in front of me disappears, and it gives me an idea.

With the light finally off, I can sneak around them and possibly find another way out.

"We've got you surrounded now," someone cackles behind me.

Shit.

I guess my instincts aren't the bomb, and they were tailing me after all. I scurry as fast as I can into the cavern, looking back once as I get close to the group of people huddled around a girl. *This might actually work, since my instincts have been pushing me toward this group.* A hooded figure appears—from the tunnel I had just left—with glowing red eyes, but before I can back up behind the group further, I feel the ground lightly vibrate as an earth-shattering *boom* resonates and the floor drops out from underneath me.

The fall is disorientating as I tumble through the air, but luckily it's over in a matter of seconds. I don't know what I land on, but something softens my landing to where I'm only coughing at the dust that flies up from the soft material. Rolling to my feet, I quickly get up and take in my new surroundings.

It seems to still be a cavern-like structure, but instead of being plunged into the darkness, the area where my night vision was useful, this place is covered in a red sheen. There's a river of red liquid flowing off to the right and left, that I would bet my left nut—no, I would never bet Bert. Maybe my right nut, Ernie—that's where the heat is coming from. Glancing down, it looks like I landed on some sort of pet bed. Stepping off of it, I finally notice a desk off to the side and a few chairs with wicked finials higher than the backrest beside me.

I would have looked pretty skewered on that.

"Damn, temptress. Twice now," someone moans, pulling my attention to the group I was hiding amongst.

"I'm so sorry, Ryker. I didn't mean to. I thought we were going to die," the hottie with the body says as she helps a guy up.

Unsure about the group of men and worried about what I've just stumbled into, I wait for fuckernuts to punch me in the gut, but I get nothing as I look at the group. Maybe I was meant to find them. They don't look armed, rather more or less lost like I am as they cough and try to brush the debris off of themselves.

If I had to guess, I would say we're in an office, but I don't see a door anywhere.

"Where are we?" I ask no one in particular as I brush off some debris and ash off my jeans.

"Hell," a couple of the guys say simultaneously.

I glance over in their direction. Something flickers like recognition, but I can't place their names. I think I know them or have seen them around, but before I can react, the woman I saw earlier flings herself at me. Without thinking, I catch her in my arms as she squeezes me tight.

"Lynx! Oh my God, I've missed you so much. How did you get here?"

I can hear the relief and happiness in her tone, but I'm completely dumbfounded at what the fuck she's going on about. How does she even know me?

She pulls back and looks up at me for a moment, and a sob breaks from her as I wet my dry lips in a panic.

"Uhh. Sorry. Who are you?" I ask as my brows pull down in confusion, and I frown. "I mean, you sound familiar, but I don't know you."

She shakes her head for a moment before squinting and pursing her lips. "Oh stop it, Lynx!" she laughs. "You're such an ass. I'm Rez, your best friend, duh. Stop playing." She smiles up at me and playfully smacks me on my firm chest, making my pecs pop. I know it's a serious situation, the fact I can't remember who she is, but I can't help but flirt with her. She's drop-dead gorgeous.

"Sorry." I shrug. "But you can smack me around any time you want, though, beautiful." I wink, hopefully lessening the blow. "That doesn't change the fact I don't remember you. Everything is a blank slate," I point to my head. "Don't take it personally. Until I get my memory back, I'll just have to take your word for it." I give her a sly smile as I lean back and take in her outfit, letting my eyes travel up and down her body. "So, *best* friends, huh? The kind that's there for each other and *rubs* all the problems away?" I say with a smirk. "You know what? I have this *huge* problem right now. I don't seem to remember what it feels like to come. Wanna help your *bestie* out?"

She reels back as if I slapped her for a moment and blinks her owlish gray eyes at me before giving me a sly smile. *Damn, is she really going to get nasty right here? I mean, I'm all for voyeurism.*

"Oh, I would loooove to help my bestie out," she purrs and runs both her hands up my shirtless stomach and over the ridges of my abdomen. My muscles flex under her warm touch, and I can't help but wonder how her hands would feel roaming over the rest of my body. Feeling her delicate hands caress my body like a lover awakens something primal inside me and sends electricity straight to my cock, hardening it.

Fuck.

Her hands slowly curve over my pecs, and she applies pressure right where it makes me weak. *How the fuck does she know what makes me feel good?* I'm about to moan as she reaches my nipples, but the titty twister she gives me is anything but sensual.

"Oww. What the fuck?" I pull back and cover my sweet nips. "You should savor these like strawberries, not rip them off like a condom wrapper. What's wrong with you, you heathen?" I yell at the gray-eyed beauty posing as the devil herself.

Note to self, this woman is dangerous, but freaky. I like it.

As one of the guys pulls her back and whispers into her ear, I get the feeling that I care for this woman. Thoughts of ripping her out of his arms plague me. Why is she giving him attention when it should be me? I shake my head in shock. *Where did that come from?* I can't be jealous that she's in another man's arms when I don't even know who she is. But there's something that's just out of reach as to why I'm bothered that some other male is whispering to her so intimately.

"Well, at least we're all okay and no one got hurt. I would hate to think of what would have happened if they would have caught us. Who were they anyway?" A redhead speaks up.

"Nothing good, and I can only assume, given their dark attire, they were Rebels," a man in a muddy suit replies.

"Well, it looks like we finally found Lynx," a tall male with black and blue spiky hair comments, checking me out.

Yeah, buddy. Take a picture... It will last longer. But it won't *keep you warm on those cold nights.* I wink, knowing he can't hear my thoughts.

"I would, but my phone is dead," the guy says, holding up his phone and giving me a wink of his own

"Well fuck me, a mindreader?" I ask, enjoying the possibility of that. Talk about a way to fuck with someone. I could have so much fun with him.

"Yep!" he replies.

"Well, great. We found him, but what happened to him?" the redhead male speaks up.

"Him is right here last time I checked, blood bag," I snark back, looping my thumbs through the hoops on my jeans. It pulls the material down lower, and I don't miss how several sets of eyes travel down to the edge of my pants. Not just Rez, but a few guys as well.

Yep, I still got it.

I look over the bunch. Most of them look familiar, but I don't remember them. "So, it appears you all know me, but I have no clue who any of you are," I announce, giving them the go-ahead to start this pony show.

"Well, no matter what has happened, it appears we need introductions. I'm Leviathan," the man in the muddy suit says, leading the charge. He's tall with blond hair and hazel eyes. A couple of dimples pop like deflated balloons when he smiles at me, leaning forward to shake my hand. By the smell of him, he's a mage, but I don't know what his affinity is. I'm sure I'll sniff it out of him soon enough.

"He goes by Levi," Rez's shoulders slump as she addresses me. "And you would already know that if—ugh." She deflates, throwing up her hands and shaking her head at me. "How in the Hell did both of us lose our memory of each other, only for me to gain mine back and yours to be completely gone? This is unacceptable." She stomps her foot, looking all cute. "Someone's head needs to roll for this shit!" she growls before her gray eyes swing in my direction once again. "I need you to get your memories back because I can't lose you again. We've been attached at the hip since I was six. You're the yin to my yang, so let's find a way to pull your head out of your ass and put it back on your shoulders," she says, stepping into my bubble and pressing her hand against my chest.

"She's kinda cute when she's angry, huh?" I say with a smirk, and a few guys nod while her back is turned to agree. Although as soon as she spins around, they quickly wipe the smug look off their faces.

"I'm Zeke, the blood bag," the redhead one says, leaning over Rez to shake my hand. As I reach for his hand, I get a whiff of him and cock my head at the smell.

"Are you sure you're just a blood bag?" I question,

quirking an eyebrow. He pulls away without taking my hand and pops a fang to prove he's a vampire. "Then why do I smell decay and death on you, like a Necromancer?" The entire group freezes and tenses up as they look at each other. "I take it that's a secret?" I ask, and it's Rez who answers.

"Lynx, you've never been able to smell something like that before. What's changed?" Taking my silence as an answer, she shakes her head, mumbling nevermind before continuing. "Ah yes, Zeke is one. That knowledge just stays within our group, though. People would either try to kill or enslave him if they knew," Rez mentions, and all I do is shrug. I only have her word to go off of since I can't remember shit right now. It's no skin off my back to take their side and go along with their rules for now.

"So, I have something on you guys then, huh?" I joke, rocking back on the balls of my feet, but they give each other nervous looks.

I see they don't have a sense of humor then. Well, shit.

The guy with black and blue spiky hair walks forward and pulls me into a side hug and slaps my back. His smell is intoxicating, but I can't really place him. He seems to be a hybrid, but I don't know well enough to distinguish yet. "Well, Lynx. It's good to actually meet you as a human, finally. I'm Jacques Pierre, or JP, whichever you prefer. Who knew the cat or rat-looking thing I was cooking for was actually a human? A pretty good-looking one at that." He winks before stepping back and giving my body another once over.

Did he just flirt with me? Wait... What did he just call me? A cataract? He was cooking for me? How well does this guy know me? What the fuck was that about? I wonder, and I hear a giggle in my head before a beautiful voice follows.

'Haha. Yeah. I think he did, but that's normal for him, Lynx. I think he's a bigger flirt than you. And you're a Shifter.

15

Your main form was a lynx or a martin.' I hear Rez's voice, and in sheer panic, my eyes go wide as I seek her out in the crowd.

When our eyes meet, she has the widest smile on her face for the briefest moment before I slam down the connection I didn't know we had.

Fuck!

Her smile turns watery as I break eye contact before another guy comes forward to introduce himself as Knox, if I heard him right.

"Ox? Is that what you turn into? That would not surprise me by your size. You're fucking huge. Like a boulder or a mountain. Maybe you're the one that broke the floor and caused us to fall in here."

The Shifter in front of me frowns and tenses up, until Rez pats his arm and calms him. Another spike of jealousy hits me out of nowhere for a moment.

Why would I be jealous of her showing concern for the Shifter? Ugh, why am I being an idiot? You don't even know these people!

I get the sense he's not my favorite person, but I don't remember why, so I make a mental note to find out and push him to the breaking point. I wonder how far I can push before this giant explodes into a million pieces.

The last guy is covered in tattoos with a permanent smirk. By the smell of him, he's part Fae and part Demon.

"I'm Ryker," he says and extends his hand.

When we shake hands, a bolt of lust hits me, and the fact I need to adjust myself in my pants solidifies the fact that Ryker is an Incubus.

Well, this just gets better and better.

"Well, I guess I'm Lynx. Now, does anyone know why I'm named that instead of something cool?"

I see Rez bristle as all eyes turn to her.

Well, fuck me. It doesn't look like I'm winning any points here at all.

CHAPTER 2
Welcome to Hell

Rez

I wonder if I kicked Lynx in the balls if that would make him get his memory back. Never in my wildest imagination did I believe I would find him again, but without his memory. Speaking of which, how did I lose my memory of him in the first place? One minute I was thinking of him—even found him in the dreamscape, or whatever it really was—and next... His memory is gone. Poof. Like he never existed.

My feelings are all over the place. I feel like shit that I forgot about him, even for a moment. Yet, I'm livid that someone did this to us. Did those horrible things to him. Killed him? Looking at him, though, he looks like nothing has happened. If I didn't know our link still works, I would think he's an imposter. I'm so confused. I'm trying to be positive and focus on the fact that he's alive and here with me, but all I see is the huge problem in front of me. How do I get my Lynx back?

Is there a manual for this? A potion? A magic eight ball?

My chest is in a vice grip as I watch the guys properly introduce themselves to my best friend and mate.

This isn't how I expected this meeting to go. Maybe something more chaotic, or funny even, but not soul-crushing to the point where I'm left fighting to understand the emotions cycling through me. One moment I'm devastated, feeling as though I've lost Lynx all over again even though he's standing right before me. In the next, I'm fucking pissed. How in the hell did this happen? Whose ass do I need to kick? And how the fuck do I fix this? Horror overcomes me at the thought that this can't be fixed. *No, I refuse to believe that.* I didn't just get him back to lose him.

I must zone out for a little while, because the next thing I hear is Lynx asking how he got his name and why he didn't get a cooler one.

"Jesus flipping Christ," I curse under my breath and a spurt of lava jumps up near us, making me squeal like a stuffed pig. "Shit! Watch out for exploding lava. Where are we again?" I ask, not having really paid attention in the first place.

"Hell," Levi deadpans.

Well, shit on my bed with lava. This is just great.

How in the world did we end up in Hell without dying? Is it like Purgatory, where I didn't have to die to pass over to this plane? Did a door bring us here? I didn't see one; though it's great that I remember how we got here this time.

"Just to clarify, we're not dead, right?" I ask no one in particular.

Ryker chuckles, grabbing my attention. "No, we're definitely not dead. But I have no idea where we are *in* Hell," he states.

Great, that answers that question at least! The rest can wait, I guess. I turn back to Lynx's questioning gaze.

"To answer your question, Lynx, I named you, but you have to give me a break. I was six, and you showed up as a small furball on my doorstep," I recap as he gives me a blank look.

Lord have mercy, I'm going to lose my mind trying to help him gain his back.

Another spurt of lava leaps. "Are you kidding me?" I grunt out a sigh. Picking up on my thoughts, JP chuckles as he moves over to me.

"I guess it's true what they say. Using any heavenly words or thoughts is a sin in Hell," he explains, looking at the lava as another spurt pops, giving off more heat in the tiny office.

My clothes are going to melt off of me if this keeps up.

"So, you were the only one responsible enough to name me? Why didn't your parents give me a proper name?" Lynx questions, giving me a doubtful look.

Bringing my attention back to Lynx, annoyance flares once again at his question. I don't care if he's my mate or not, I'm gonna make sure he can never reproduce! I hear Knox chuckle beside me, obviously picking up on my feelings. As I push back my jacket sleeves, I take a step forward in preparation to sock Lynx when the floor shakes and a god-awful sound screeches in the room, making us cover our ears at the intrusion.

Turning toward the noise, we back up next to Lynx as the wall parts and a yellowish light spills into the room. A silhouette steps in front of the glow, blocking it from filtering through and effectively cutting off our escape.

The creature standing in the doorway is at least seven-foot tall, I'm guessing, but he's definitely wide enough to be blocking the freaking door. He's taller than my guys, but not as tall as the Giant I was hanging off of a few days ago.

Was it really only a few days ago?

Something flares behind him, and suddenly my throat feels dry and I find it really hard to swallow. It shifts, and light illuminates something in his hand. I realize it's a machete resting in his palm.

Okay, it's official. I'm not a badass. I thought I was, but my magic doesn't always work, and I'm not sure if it could put up an adequate fight against whatever the hell he is.

My heart rate speeds up, and I quickly wipe my sweaty palms on my black jeans as the creature ducks and walks into the room. Knox's fingers lightly wrap around my waist as he tries to gently move me behind him, but I'm not having any of it. Prying his fingers off, I give his hand a squeeze in thanks, but hold my stance. Fire ignites in the creature's palm, and he throws it between our group. It casts shadows around the room, lighting it further than the red and purple hues we were getting used to.

I quickly take in the creature, or I guess Demon, in front of me. Sepia skin, just like my own, a bald or shaved head with two black horns sprouting from his skull, and a five o'clock shadow along the hard planes of his jaw. He's shirtless, with a massive tattoo over his chest. The tattoo is of two wings, two skulls facing each other with a sword running between them, and underneath, it spells out L.A.M.B.

What's a L.A.M.B.? Does he have a thing for cute little white fluffiness on four legs?

I snort laugh but quickly stifle it so he doesn't kill me.

Something flutters behind him that catches my attention. Wings! Black, feathered wings flicker along his body, tearing my eyes away from his impressive length, not realizing that's where I was staring. He looks over the group, and when his eyes land on me, I swear my breathing stops. There are actual flames in his chocolate pupils as he stares at me. It's like if I dare move, it will allow him to crack me open, study, judge, and punish me in one blink of an eye. And I don't mean in a good way.

He gives me a half nod, as if he finds me acceptable, and

turns his attention to Lynx, squinting his eyes as he inhales deeply.

"You smell familiar," his rough voice rings out, causing goosebumps to appear on my skin.

"And you look like shit, but you don't see me complaining," Lynx comments, and it brings a small smile to my face until I see the look of confusion crossing his.

It's as if a small part of him is still in there, demanding he act like his normal self, but he doesn't understand. I wish there was an easier way to help him. I look back at the Demon before us, and it looks as if he's debating skinning Lynx alive as he grips his machete tighter.

It's not until Levi speaks up that he breaks eye contact with Lynx.

"Hello, Beelzebub. How did you find us?" Levi questions. I might be wrong, but I think I detect a hint of fear in his voice. I don't blame him, though. The Demon in front of us is terrifying.

"Leviathan," he grunts, nodding his head in greeting. "Wards went off. Come. I have something that might be yours," Bee—I'm not calling him that long ass name—turns before walking out of the room, expecting us to follow him. Yes, Bee sounds appropriate. He stings like a bee but seems to have more than one stinger.

"Come on, Rez. He's a gentle mass murderer. He won't harm a hair on your pretty little head," Ryker says as he wraps his arms around my shoulders and guides us after the so-called "nice" psychopath.

Yeah, that's what I want in my murderer... A gentle touch.

"He's part of L.A.M.B.," Ryker continues.

"L.A.M.B.?" I arch a brow. "You mean that tattoo doesn't mean he loves little baby sheep?"

Ryker chuckles. "Not at all. L.A.M.B.: Lucifer, Astaroth, Murmur, and Beelzebub. Together they rule Hell."

Aww fuck me.

W
e walk out of the cavern-like office and into a wide hallway. The walls are lined with abstract art, the kind you would find in a museum. We come upon a window and I pause, glancing outside. There's a blood-red moon hanging low in the sky, highlighting a massive gate and structures that look like scarecrows just inside of them. The few stars that are out shine a bright orange and blue. This can't be Hell... Isn't it supposed to be full of blood and fire or something like that?

Are we still in hell, or did we just switch realms or something?

We walk into an open concept area, which reminds me of a fucking palace. The room is massive, with towering ceilings, and even though it's an open area, it's divided into sections, separated by various arrangements of black leather furniture.

Directly in front of us is a sitting area with an L-shaped sofa, a love seat, and two armchairs. An enormous decorative fireplace is embedded into the wall to the right. It's fucking big enough for me to walk into without slouching. A morbid idea flutters into my head, and I can't help but wonder if our sweet mass murderer ever has his victims walk into that for a quick clean-up.

Across the room from the sitting area is an old-fashioned L-shaped bar with a coffee machine in the corner, and a poker table is to the right. *Fancy.* My eyes travel to the far-left corner, where a floor-to-ceiling bookshelf catches my eye. It is filled with books and tchotchkes. I wonder what secrets it holds. To my immediate left is a small game area with a set-up chess table and a few stacks of games, waiting to be picked.

There are three exits off this room, not including the way

we came in, and massive white marble pillars line each archway. The walls are painted light gray, and the floors are gray marble with black marble swirls. Thick white rugs are placed around the room, giving it a somewhat lived-in atmosphere, but the fact I'm standing in Hell is doing nothing to calm my already frazzled nerves.

"Sit," Bee demands as he walks around the sofa and to the back of the room. He looks back at us as the guys make themselves comfortable before he pushes through a set of swinging double doors, leaving us alone.

A squeak leaves me as hands grab my waist, pulling me down onto Ryker's lap. I watch as the guys settle in, but it's obvious who's been to Hell and who hasn't. Levi sinks into the armchair like it was made for him, but JP shifts in his seat like it's irritating his skin. I don't blame him. My best friend's memories are blank; I don't know where Moni's at or if she's okay; Knots is still at the school, which is currently under attack; I have no idea how to reach him or if he's okay; and to top everything off, I'm in Hell, where a homicidal Demon keeps grunting at us.

"Relax," Ryker whispers into my ear.

"I can't," I confess, and Knox gives me a concerned look.

"I'm sure I can *make* you relax," Ryker whispers. His breath tickles along the rim of my ear, causing my skin to break out into goosebumps.

"This is hardly the pla—" I jump out of Ryker's lap as I hear a commotion in the room Bee has disappeared into.

"What was that?" I ask and look around so someone can give me an answer.

"I'm sure it's nothing..." Ryker says, reaching out for my hand. But I pull away when I hear a small *boom* going off in the back room. And before I can say anything else, I hear the best sound in the world, propelling me around the sofa and toward the back of the room.

"Then get out of my way, Goliath!" Moni shouts angrily, flying through the swinging door in the back of the room, looking all red and flustered.

"Moni!" I yell, running to her and pulling her tight to me. JP comes up behind me but waits while we have our moment. "Are you okay?" I whisper low enough for her to hear.

"No!" she wails as she pulls back and looks at me as she turns a light teal, showing her worry. "I don't know where Chester is. He was with me one minute, and the next, a dirty Demon got his hands on me and assaulted my tail. My tail, Rez. And worst of all, they have no beans! They only have decaf. I can't live on decaf, Rez! I need my *sweet nectar of life!* I only have a limited amount in my socket pocket," she cries as she grabs her tail and rubs it against her rapidly changing blue cheek.

Not knowing what to do or what she means by socket pocket, I look over my shoulder at the guys, and they all have a look of pity. JP pulls Moni into him and starts whispering words that slowly calm her down, and her skin turns back to her standard green color. I walk back to the group and sit down next to Ryker as Zeke slides over and leans in to whisper.

"For some creatures, their tails are very sensitive and can be a direct stimulus to certain body parts. Luckily, Moni's tail doesn't directly affect her reproductive organs, else she just went through the equivalent of sexual assault on humans. Though, what she experienced wasn't pleasurable at all," Zeke informs me. I swivel to look back at her as my heart breaks for another reason besides her missing her mate.

Bee comes back out of the room with a purple body shuffling after him. *What the hell is that?* The creature is no bigger than a toddler, or a four-year-old. *Dammit, I wish I was better with measurements.* It has large purple ears with earrings dangling from the side of its head. White hair sprouts from the top of its head along with two small lighter purple horns. He's dressed in all leather, but his midrift is bare. Big clunky boots with spikes around the soles, I'm sure, weigh him down and add to him shuffling instead of picking up his feet. His head swings our way, and I'm taken aback at the sight of him. His cat eyes glow a slight orange as he takes in our little group. He has two small fangs that pop out over his lower lip. The only normal thing about him is his cute button nose.

JP and Moni sit down on the chair and footstool in front of us as Bee leans against the wall, looking our group over. The little purple dude walks over to join him, barely coming up to his knee.

"Did you find the intruder?" A husky voice rings out from across the room. I peer around Ryker to find another Demon walking through the archway by the bar.

Damn. He's yummy.

JP catches my eye and arches an eyebrow my way. All I do is shrug and say, '*So? He's hot! Sue me.*'

JP chuckles and cocks his head to agree with me.

Bringing my attention back to the new Demon, I let my eyes travel over his form, and a part of me is disappointed that he's wearing clothes. At least the tight white Henley shirt is form-fitted, showing off his broad chest, and his black jeans are tight around his thighs. Red and black leathery wings are pulled tight against his back, and I follow them down to where a tail in the same color as his wings swishes behind him. I'm surprised that the thick black boots make no noise along the marble flooring as he walks in. His long strides remind me of a panther stalking its prey. It's hard to make out his eye color from here, but it's easy to see that they are definitely unique and bright, to the point of glowing.

As he reaches Bee's side, I realize he's as tall as our first captor, even with his ram horns curling around the side of his head. I admit I'm a little jealous of how his long, light-brown hair seems to float around his shoulders as he walks. *Is that a power thing, or is that just a trait he gained? Would it be rude to ask?*

"Just kids," Bee answers and nods in our direction.

The newest Demon motions for the little purple guy, and the toddler jumps to attention.

"Go get the boss, Trometh," he instructs, and the purple guy nods before running out of the room like his ass is on fire.

The hottie turns toward us, where I can get a closer look at his face. Those glowing eyes almost put Lynx's to shame. There's a yellow flame glowing in his light-blue eyes, and if it wasn't for the intensity with which he's staring at us, I would find them gorgeous. His full beard only highlights his plump lips, which are currently pulled down in a frown.

"How the fuck did you get in our vault?" the Demon demands, his eyes traveling across our group.

"That's Astaroth, the original Wrath Demon," Ryker whispers to me, and suddenly, my mouth goes dry again.

"That was a vault? Looked more like a mausoleum to me," Lynx answers, giving the Demon a bored look. I appreciate what Lynx is trying to do by attempting to lighten the mood, but I doubt Astaroth will see it that way. Both Demons have their arms crossed over their chests while staring down at us.

Astaroth's tail whips out in the blink of an eye, and a small boom cracks, making us all jump. Welp, guess I don't have to worry about Lynx missing his memories. He's not going to live long enough for it to be an issue.

"I see we have a funny guy in our presence," he says, taking a step in Lynx's direction. "Do you know what we do with funny guys?" he says, his voice dropping an octave.

"Take lessons? Because you should. I doubt you know how to take a joke," Lynx replies easily, and he gives me a wink when he catches my jaw drop.

Astaroth gives Lynx a cruel smile that makes my heart race,

and the lump I am trying to swallow gets stuck.

Fuck, we're dead.

"Bez. Want to get the table ready? I'm thinking about making you a new holster for your machete, and I just found a volunteer," he says as he slowly prowls closer to Lynx.

Bez? Well, dang it. That's better than Bee.

The atmosphere around the room becomes tense as the guys shift uncomfortably. Lynx smartly stands up and moves to put the chair between him and the approaching Demon. At least he has some sense of self-preservation.

What the fuck is going on? Is this about to turn into a bloodbath? I haven't gotten to the Demon chapter yet in class. I know they have an entire month dedicated to them. Surely we can't be held responsible for falling into a private residence when it wasn't our fault.

I can't be the only one that feels like I'm being judged or fucked with, and it's confirmed when I hear a familiar voice come from behind Bez.

"Astro, Bez, will you stop tormenting our guests?" I would recognize Lilith's purr anywhere. Her hand wraps up and over Bez's shoulder, making the massive Demon's muscles melt under her palm. She smiles up at him before turning her attention in our direction. Her eyes go wide as her mouth drops slightly. I would find it comical if it didn't send Bez back on high alert as his hand conjures up a ball of flames.

So that's where the flames came from when we were in the vault. This guy can conjure up fire.

She steps out from behind him, and I do a double take as I take in her outfit. She's dressed in a light-blue 1950s sundress with white pearls around her neck with a blue flower pinned in her curled hair. I swear, I'm looking at a real-life Stepford wife, but in Demon form because she no longer looks human. Her skin is a bright burgundy color—the same as her hair— and there are beautiful white glowing tendrils lining her hair-

line and falling down her cheeks. Her black spider-webbed wings lay against her dress, and her tail swings down by her Jimmy Choos.

Tears pool in her eyes as she looks at the guys sitting around the room. "Boys! My babies! I'm so glad you're safe." She rushes to Levi and pulls him up from his chair, wrenching him into a fierce hug. She runs her fingers through his hair, messing it up, then brings both her hands around to his cheeks, pinching them together and making him do duck lips.

Ryker snickers, and Lilith quickly kisses Levi's cheeks before she tackles Ryker, doing much the same but rocking him back and forth a few times. Letting him go, she proceeds to a very shocked Knox, who just freezes as Lilith approaches.

"Oh stop it, you big lug. I used to wipe your ass. Now, give your mother a hug. I've missed you so much!" She scolds Knox and pulls him into her, and instead of pushing his cheeks together like she did with Ryker and Levi, she just gazes up at him longingly before running her fingers over the tops of his ears. "Are you ticklish like you were when you were a baby?" she asks, and Knox shudders, drawing a laugh out of her.

"Yep, like father like son, I see," she teases before looking over at Zeke. Zeke looks like he's about to bolt but doesn't know where to go.

"Don't you dare, Ezekiel. The doors are locked, and I'm getting my hug. I'm not chasing you around the room like your toddler years anymore either, so come and get it over with. I've missed you." She leaps and lands right in front of him. He turns bright red as she points out his thoughts and pulls him in for a hug.

She pulls back, looking at all of us with her hands on her hips. She claps her hands, "It's so good to have you all here. We have so much to go over. Oh! Let me make dinner tonight!" She turns to walk around the sofa when Astaroth speaks up.

"Lil, they were found in the vault. I don't care who they

are to you; they need to be questioned," he says, his tail whipping out with another little boom.

Does he do that when he's frustrated?

Lilith whips around, and her face darkens in a second. "Those are my children and their friends. If you lay one claw, tail, or *point* a dagger in their direction, I'll force you to be my male model and go shopping with me for the next century," she says, giving him a cruel smile.

"I'd rather have you cut off my balls and hang them from the chandelier for a century than do that," he growls out, backing away from us with a pout.

"I know," Lilith sings as she flips her hair. She turns back around and walks toward the back of the room, stopping short to look at Bez. "Oh, Bez, can you show them to their rooms so they can clean up? I'm so excited to have guests... and for them to be my boys! Ah! This is turning out to be a marvelous night!" She claps excitedly and exits the room.

I look between the stunned group and see I'm not the only one confused by that exchange. Levi, Zeke, Ryker, and Knox are all wearing perplexed looks, and JP looks like he's about to burst out laughing.

I'm sure he's reading all of their thoughts, so it's not surprising he's so entertained right now.

"Is this what our dads were talking about when they said she needed to heal?" Ryker asks.

"It seems she needs more than just healing," Zeke mumbles as he stares at the spot he last saw her at.

"Um, is that normal?" Lynx asks, looking around the group.

"Is it normal for you not to have your memory?" Knox grunts.

"Wouldn't know," Lynx replies.

"Ditto," Zeke confirms.

"Come," Bez commands as he turns to leave. A sort of

combined shuffle and stomp precede Trometh before he comes into the room, stopping next to Bez. He grabs his chest and gasps for air.

The room pressurizes and my ears pop before Bez can say anything.

Suddenly, in a puff of silver smoke, a creature appears before Bez wearing a black tailored suit. I can make out his white-feathered wings laying against his dark outfit and his messy dark blond head as he straightens out his jacket.

"What was in the vault?" a smooth, silky voice asks, and I shift from the reaction he causes. He sounds like pure sex, and I notice Ryker and Knox glancing in my direction, picking up on my lust.

This dynamic of them knowing when I'm turned on is gonna suck.

I can't help it if I get excited. I know this is something I'll have to bring up with them later. I'll probably have to mend their egos later, assuring them that this delicious man meat before me doesn't compare to them, but now is not the time.

Bez juts his chin in our direction, and I'm met with piercing blue-green eyes from a model. He's too gorgeous to be a Demon. His tanned skin seems to glow against his black pin-striped suit, and his five o'clock shadow only defines his angular jaw. His white feather wings remind me of a Sprite, but it's not until I spot the two delicate horns protruding from his hair that I realize that this is indeed another Demon. *Fuck me!*

"Hey Rez, you seem to be drooling right there," Lynx calls out, bringing my attention to him. He points to the side of his lip. "You might want to get that before you slip on it and break your neck." Lynx chuckles.

'Are you fucking kidding me? You're supposed to use this link for embarrassing shit, Lynx,' I send back to Lynx, but he doesn't respond, which only makes me somewhat sad and

desperate to get him alone to make him understand what we had.

"Good to know you haven't lost your ability to embarrass me. Thanks," I deadpan.

"So, kids wound up in my vault?" the Demon asks with wide eyes.

"Not just any kids. Recognize any of them, Lucifer?" Astorath urges as he walks over to the other two.

Wait. Did he just say Lucifer?

"The L in L.A.M.B.," Ryker whispers into my ear, trying to be quiet, but the Demons smiling at me is a sure sign that he failed.

"Lilith's brood," he confirms, nodding his head. "How in the name of Hell did you guys get in my vault?" He places his hands on his narrow hips as he glares at us.

I'm getting really tired of people asking the same fucking question. Don't they know that if we fucking knew, we would be glad to answer so we could get the hell out of here?

"If we knew how, we would tell you," I say, standing up. *We did nothing wrong here. In fact, falling into Hell was a godsend.* Fire erupts in the dead fireplace, making me shriek, and Moni faints with a plunk. JP reaches down to pick her up off of the footstool she was sitting on, moving her to the loveseat.

"Please don't take *His* name in vain. Hell doesn't tend to like it, as you can see," Lucifer says with a dull tone and points to the fireplace. There's now a long black scorch mark along the marble wall that was once white.

"Oops. But wait, I just thought it; I didn't say it," I argue.

"Same thing," Lucifer counters, giving me a pointed look.

"Sorry," I say, biting my lip until Lucifer waves it away.

Levi stands and tries to straighten out his clothes. Soon enough, though, he gives up and just curls his lips in disgust when he sees the extent of the damage.

"Lucifer, we do not know how we ended up in your vault. We were escaping the Rebels when the floor opened up, and instead of falling to our death, we somehow went through a portal and ended up there. We apologize for any inconvenience," Levi says in an eloquent and professional tone.

I know I wouldn't have been able to pull that off. Now that the emotional rollercoaster has slowed down, the main thing I feel is irritation. I'm also frustrated that Lynx doesn't seem to remember anything, and I want a change of clothes and maybe a damn shower.

"Well, that's not good enough. There has never been a break-in into my personal rooms; it's impossible. They are spelled, and since you've saved me the time in having to track you down, we migh—"

"No! I'm tired, hungry, and still have dried cum in my ass crack." I tick off with my fingers. "I need a fucking shower and clean clothes. You can interrogate us later, *after* we have cleaned up and eaten some food. We've been through... well, Hell... before we got here, and I need to decompress before I explode." I ramble on, and it's not until I take a deep breath and look at the Demons that what I just admitted hits me.

"And you say I'm the one that should use the link for embarrassing shit," Lynx says before bursting into a laughing fit while my friends join in, except for Knox.

He comes up behind me and wraps his big arms around my waist and nuzzles into my neck. *Yep, he's winning brownie points with me today.* The Demons all drop their eyes from me and bite either their lips or the inside of their cheeks to keep from laughing at me. I swear, if I was Moni, I would *boom* them all to kingdom come.

Boom.

The fireplace shoots fire along the wall once again, making me jump into Knox's arms.

Well, that's one way to shut them up.

CHAPTER 3

Road of Hard Knots

Knots

'The word is anxiety, Knots. You should know that by now,' Willow reprimands me as I pace across the living room.

'*Are you sure? It feels twice as bad now that I'm able to move outside of my door,*' I point out.

Well, maybe outside of my door is wrong, considering I can't step outside of this dorm room, which I'm now stuck in. At first, I started out just being a little worried as it started sprinkling outside, and I hoped Rez, Moni, and Chester didn't get too cold. Then, when the rain started to downpour, my nerves skyrocketed, making my gut clench. I tried to distract myself by watching TV and working out, but that was a lost cause when word came through the Door Knights about the imminent Rebel attack.

'*Yes, I'm sure,*' she replies. If I could see her, she would roll her eyes at me.

I glance out the window and see lightning flash across the sky, putting me on pins and needles. Before I return to my pacing, movement on the ground catches my eye. There, between the shadows and highlighted by the lightning, are Rebels walking out of the woods and heading toward the school.

It's an evening of phenomena I've never seen before. We've had rain here, that's a given, but the vicious winds, lightning, and rising sea levels—judging by the swells down at the beach—have never happened before. Now the school is under attack, and the only things I care about are my wards and their safety. I can't do anything to help them unless they are *here*.

Why did I allow them to go? I murmur to myself.

'Because you were thinking with your knob, literally,' Willow teases me, knowing there's nothing I can do and trying to lighten the mood.

'Yes, I suppose so. I should have fought harder,' I begrudgingly admit.

'Knots, you can't keep a woman like that tied down. She needs to be free to make her own choices. You've gained your body back during a time when women no longer need a man's permission to do things. All you can do is give her advice and make sure she has what she needs. I know it's hard for you, but all you can do is be there for her when she needs you and try to support her where you can.'

Damn.

Willow once again hits me where I least expect it, my pride. She's right, of course. She's been one of my best friends for as long as we've had our posts in the doors, and she hasn't steered me wrong yet. It's still a hard pill to swallow, though.

I've always had a soft spot for my wards. It's my job to protect and watch out for them. It's been different with JP, Moni, and Rez. I guess you can include the furball into that group as well, even though he tried to piss on me and threatened to cut me. They have become more like family, including me in their talks around the dinner table or when they're all watching TV together, even back when I was just a Door Knight to them.

It's hard to adjust to this different role of... whatever I am to each of them. Fuck, this anxiety is killing me. Walking into Rez's bedroom, I head out onto the balcony, trying to see what's going on with the Rebels.

Cloaked figures rush into the fray but don't attack the building like they should for a proper attack. They launch a few fireballs into the sky, but with the downpour, they are quickly extinguished, covering the grounds in smoke. *Hmm.* Why not use the hotter fire spells to do damage? Why use weaker spells? Unless they are just a distraction?

For the first time, I wish I had one of those cell phones. I smack myself in the forehead and thank the Fates no one is around to see my foolish behavior.

Note to self: Ask for a phone and learn how to use it.

Withdrawing from my surroundings, I open my communications with the other Door Knights.

'Urgent! Rebels are using weaker spells. This could be a distraction. Reinforce the portals, entrance ways, and doors, and pass along to any leaders close by. Again, this might be a distraction.'

Multiple acknowledgments echo back to me as I pull myself back to my surroundings and focus on what's before me. A flash of silver catches my eye. A silverback gorilla is using the cover of darkness to run to the woods, where the rebels are waiting.

My jaw drops as I recall whose animal is not only a gorilla but a silverback. What is he doing running into the fray without backup?

Banging on the door pulls my attention away from the Rebels down below.

"KNOTS!! Let me in," Chester yells.

Not knowing what's on the other side of the door with

Chester, I pull my sword free, mentally unlock the door, and decide to meet him in the entranceway. I find him leaning against the wall, and since no one is rushing in behind him, I allow him to enter and lock the door before sheathing my sword to refocus on him. He's a mess, wearing Moni's satchel on his back, covered head to toe in mud and debris, and drenched from the storm outside.

"Where is she?" he says in a panic as he holds the back of his head.

"Who?" I ask, my shock mirroring his own.

Chester pushes his crooked glasses dotted with water droplets back in place before shoving off the wall and walking past me.

"Moni." He drops his hand from the back of his head, revealing a dark matted spot of hair as his head swivels around looking for her.

"Is that blood?" I ask, reaching out to grab his shoulder.

"Yeah," he brushes me off and starts down Moni's hall. "MONI!"

"Hey, why are you bleeding? Why aren't the girls with you?" Grabbing his shoulder, I whirl him around and push him against the wall.

"Where the fuck are the girls?" My fear spikes, making my voice come out harsh as I get in his face.

"I don't know," he yells back, shaking his head. "Moni and I got separated from Rez in the Ever Woods and found ourselves surrounded by Fericrocs."

Shit

"Moni fainted after she knocked them out with her sonic boom, and I carried her back here as fast as I could. I... I was so worried about getting her back here safely that... that I didn't notice my surroundings." His voice chokes as he throws his arms into the air before he looks down at his chest in defeat.

Placing my hands on his shoulders, I lean down to make eye contact with him.

"Breathe, Chester. I need you to take a deep breath and tell me what happened. Where's Moni?" All I really want to do is shake this man before me, but I know that won't help. He's already admitted that they lost Rez out in the moody ass woods in this horrid storm, but I might be able to still help Moni if I know what's going on.

A sob leaves him as he looks up at me, his bottom lip trembling. "I don't know. I was jumped by someone at the edge of the woods. I woke up and found her missing. I was hoping she ran here."

I let go of Chester's shoulders, and he crumbles to the floor, his matted hair leaving a bloody smear on the wall. I step back until I feel the wall against my back as my mind tries to process what this possibly means.

Okay, so Moni is missing and was likely taken if Chester was knocked out. Rez is alone in the Ever Woods, with no backup or weapons, and her magic isn't guaranteed to work.

Fucking fantastic.

When I see her again, I'll take my chances of her threat to castrate me and say I told you so.

I reach back out to communicate with the other Door Knights. *'Does anyone have eyes on the Princes or JP? I need them urgently.'*

'I did have eyes on them, but you won't be able to reach them now, I'm afraid,' Birchman, the Administration Door Knight, answers.

'How come?'

'Anwen took them,' he answers matter of factly.

Fuck! Why does she have them?

'Thanks,' I say begrudgingly.

I grind my teeth as I fight back the frustration at not being able to reach the people I need. For once, I feel completely and absolutely hopeless in my duties as a DK. No, that's a lie; I've felt this way before when I didn't catch the spell in Rez's room, which was meant to kill her. But at least I was there to help dispel it. I'm stuck here helpless, with Moni's bloodied mate and a communication system that has finally failed me.

Opening my eyes, I find Chester's brown ones staring up at me as though I have all the answers.

"Did you find out anything?" he asks, and it kills me that I'll have to break the hopeful look upon his face.

Reaching out, I grab his hand and pull him to his feet. "Let's get you cleaned up," I say, leading him down to the bathroom. "You have a nasty gash in the back of your head I need to fix before Moni finds you and blows up the dorm with her worrying. Un—"

"Oh, so you know where she's at?" His voice takes on a hopeful tone. I'm hoping his passive nature makes him easier to handle when I break the news to him.

"I was hoping to find the guys and have them look into Moni's disappearance. It seems that Anwen—one of the Fates —has stepped in, so we will go with Plan B."

"What's Plan B?" Chester asks warily as he pushes up his glasses and steps into the bathroom.

"Keep you here until it's safe and then get a search party out to look for Rez and Moni."

Chester's eyes go wide as he looks up at me for a moment. I let out a sigh as he stands up straighter and clenches his jaw when he sees me kick the door closed.

Of course, he would pick now to grow a backbone.

"I'm doing this for your own good, Chester."

"I'm sure you think so," he says with a growl.

This is going to be a long night.

CHAPTER 4

Ring Around the Answers

Lynx

After the fireplace exploded for the second time, Lucifer allowed us to leave to get cleaned up, but not without a warning: that he will get his answers one way or another.

'I still can't believe I just met the *Lucifer. He's a fucking celebrity! The original OG. The Smooth Operator. I wonder if I can talk him into teaching me his ways. He can be my Obi-Wan Kenobi and I can be Anakin Skywalker.'*

'You know Anakin went bad, right?' Rez shoots me a cocky smirk over her shoulder.

'Fuck! Get out of my head!' I shoot her a glare but smile when she sticks out her tongue, showing off her piercing.

'Actually, you reached out to me on that one. So, you're the one that's in my *head.'* She blows me a kiss before turning her attention back to the guys on either side of her.

Ring-a-ding-ding. Look at that tongue ring. I wonder if she knows how to use that. If not, I volunteer as tribute for her to learn. I catch her eyes darting back to me briefly as she smirks. Hmm. There might be a benefit in having this connection with her, especially since it seems like it's just between us. It can be my way *in* with her.

Beelzebub leads the way down a few halls decorated with scenes I can only guess are from Hell and its occupants over the years. The lake of fire is a nice touch, and a few burnt corpses for portraits really set the tone. There are a few pictures from a time when things looked uncomplicated, with gravel paths and simple buildings. No telephone wires, industrial buildings, or lavish homes are pictured. A picture of a moss-covered hill and a rock formation against it draws my attention. A distant memory is right on the edge of my grasp before it's gone, and I shake my head to dispel the fog before catching up with the group.

"These will be your rooms during your stay. You have an hour. If you need anything, call for Trometh. He's our assistant, and he's been with us for over three centuries." He indicates the purple nurple dude standing next to him before continuing. I swear, the little guy looks like someone took him out of World of Warcraft and gave a kid a marker telling him to go nuts on him. Who ever thought to color a Demon purple, dress him in miniature biker leathers, and make him shorter than my knee? Bez clears his throat, pulling me back to him as he sends a glare to our group. "Don't keep Lilith waiting. She's in a fragile state," he warns before turning and walking away.

Now, he's one scary fucker.

Everyone looks at each other with wide eyes. I'm sure we're all thinking the same thing: What the hell did he mean by that?

"Well, temptress and I are off to get cleaned up, so excuse us," Ryker says, grabbing Rez's hand and pulling her to the closest room to the left.

"Nope." She pulls her hand free while giving him a soft smile. "I think it's best for Moni and me to stick together right now," she says, pulling a blue-looking Moni to her side. *Hmm. Now she's an interesting mix. She smells like coffee and chaos. Caffeinated casual chaos. Yep, all bundled up in a pixie package.* Moni visibly melts into her hug as they move off to the room on the right side. "See you guys in about an hour," she calls over her shoulder as she opens the door and guides both of them into their temporary digs.

JP reaches for Zeke's hand. "Come, *mon amoureux.* Let's get cleaned up." Zeke smiles as they take a room further down the hall together. My eyebrows raise at his meaning. *Hmm. So, they are a couple?* How does that work? A couple within the bigger couple? I shrug, not really caring. As long as everyone is happy, love is love, right? Doesn't really surprise me with that JP fellow. He's a delicious flirt, one I should learn from. Levi and Ryker soon follow the guys but go into the room opposite JP and Zeke.

"Well, I guess that leaves you and me, huh, tough guy?" I clap my hands and go to open the door across from Moni and Rez's room when Knox—or the stubborn ox—steps in front of me with his arms crossed.

"Nope. You need to go in there." He juts his chin in Rez's direction.

"Now, why would I do that?" I grab his shoulder and push him out of my way, which doesn't go as planned. We end up in the middle of the hall, glaring at each other, after he spins me around with him.

"She's your best friend—" He pushes me toward her door.

"I don't remember that—" I spit, pushing him back.

"—and she wants to talk to you and try to understand what happened." He places both hands on my shoulders and forces me against her door.

"—there's nothing to understand," I growl out, mirroring his stance and placing my hands on his shoulders.

He knocks on her door. "Well, then you can tell her that to her face," he growls.

Oh, hell no. That's it!

I push the ox back, and he chuckles like I fucking tickled the oaf. We get into a pushing/wrestling match until I finally get close enough that I open the door to our room.

"Stop being a pussy," Knox growls as he grabs my arm and pulls me back into the hall next to him.

"You're confusing me with someone else. I *eat* pussy, I don't have one," I reply, putting my hands on his chest and pushing him into the wall. "I don't need you telling me what to do, you overgrown caveman." I pull my arm free, roll my shoulders, and stare daggers at my unwelcoming roomie.

Knox smirks and meets my gaze, which only gives me a strange urge to piss on him. *Is that normal?*

"What the fuck are you smiling at..." I say with a sneer. *Why is he smiling?* Turning my head, my jaw drops slightly at what has caught his attention. Rez is leaning against the doorframe of her room with her arms crossed and an amused look on her face. "Oh Rez! Hey, sexy! I was just thinking about coming over and spending some time with you." Turning to fully face her, I beam in her direction, I shove my hands into my pockets, and rock back on my heels.

"Oh really? It looked like you were trying to learn how to wrestle with an overgrown *caveman*," she says, giving me an innocent smirk.

Well, fuck. I guess she heard that, huh?

"Nah. I was just asking Knox for some privacy—" A door closes, and I look over my shoulder, only to find said Shifter gone. "Well, that wasn't so hard." I give Rez a smile that's somewhat forced.

"So, let me get this straight. You were wrestling with Knox because you wanted privacy?" she mocks, trying to call me out, but I won't let her.

"Yeah," I admit, raising my chin and continuing to rock on my heels.

Her eyes drop from my gaze as she slips her bottom lip between her teeth and bites down through a smile. *Is she trying not to laugh? At me?*

"Oh, my Lord, Lynx—"

"Ahhh!" Moni screams, and I quickly look into their room to find flames jumping in the fireplace and Moni fleeing from that side of the room.

"Fuck me," Rez says under her breath.

Would love to, I silently answer.

"Fugly Furry Baby Bottoms, Rez. You're going to kill me," Moni says, sporting pale white bark as she flies up to us. I can't help but wonder if anyone has taken the time to create a glossary of what all her colors mean. Whoever would think to do that would be a genius.

"I'm so sorry." Rez bites her lip once again as Moni catches her breath. "I didn't mean to."

Moni gives her a small smile as her bark goes back to green. She pulls a massive cup out of thin air that oddly smells like coffee. "I think I'm going to go find JP. I'll see you in a bit," she says, waving as she moves down the hall. She quickly zips down to a door opening and JP pokes his head out, without her knocking. *Did he read her mind? I need to remember we have a mind reader in this group.* He glances at us and yells, "have fun," before winking and closing his door.

Was the wink for me or Rez? I mean, I know I'm sexy, but I'm pretty sure I don't swing that way.

I turn back and find Rez smiling up at me. "Well, it looks like your wish came true. Come on." She walks into her room and grabs a bundle of clothes at the end of the bed.

"Wow, these rooms are snazzy," I comment, looking around the space. There's a window across the room, but the curtains are drawn, so I can't see what's out there. Then again, it's night, and I'm not really expecting a seaside view in Hell. Black and gold furnishings decorate the room, and the bed—which is bigger than a king—is in the middle, draped in white and gold bedding with matching nightstands. There's a vanity, an armchair, a fireplace—which has already made itself known —a full-length mirror, and two doors. One looks to lead into a closet and the other into the bathroom. Plush rugs cover the entire floor in shades of white, black, and red.

"Didn't you get to see your own room before you and Knox had the wrestling match?" Rez asks, and I take in how big the bed is. I bet it has to be this huge because of the Demons and their wings.

"Nah, that overgrown pussycat told me to get my shit together and knocked on the door before you opened it." I turn and find Rez walking through one door. "Is there more of it?" I ask, following behind her.

"That's what I'm going to find out."

Well, shit!

Who knew coming to Hell would find you standing in a bathroom that's covered from head-to-toe in white marble. Embedded into the black countertop along the wall to my right is a large mirror and sink. Rez sets her clothes down there as we check out the rest of the room. By the door, there's a small closet filled with bath towels and shower products. A large shower sits behind a partitioned area with multiple shower heads and a wooden bench for placing towels and clothes. The toilet is behind a separate door for privacy.

I lean against the sink as Rez turns on the shower, grabs a few towels and shower items, and goes back to the bench inside the shower.

"What are you doing?" I ask, giving her a curious look.

"What does it look like?" Rez huffs and rolls her eyes. "I need a shower, and you wanted to spend some time with me," she points out, not looking at me. Instead, she concentrates on undoing her boots, kicking off her socks, and throwing off her jacket. *Damn.* "So, get comfortable while I shower. It's not like you haven't seen it all before." She peers over her shoulder with a smirk before she rips her shirt off over her head and shimmies out of her pants in front of me, showcasing her matching lavender underwear.

I force down the lump in my throat and shift my stance to hide my growing erection.

Aww yeah, a peep show! Why does this feel familiar?

She sways her hips before she disappears behind the partition. *Aww.*

"Lynx. What do you remember?" Rez asks as I hear her drop the rest of her clothes and step into the water.

There's a part of me that wants to strip down and join her since she feels so comfortable with me, but I know deep down it would be wrong, and I just can't do that to her. Or to me, to be honest, so I hop up on the countertop and swing my feet as I think about what I do know.

"You mean when I woke up?" I ask for clarification.

"Yeah."

"It was probably just a dream, for all I know," I say, shaking my head. "It was all fuzzy, but the only thing I remember is watery gray eyes and a tear. At least, I think it was a tear."

"That doesn't give us much to go on," Rez replies over the noise of the running shower.

My fingers curl around the edge of the countertop so hard my knuckles hurt.

"It's so frustrating not knowing anything. I woke up in a strange smelly place, and it was like my instincts kicked in," I admit. "I ended up following different passages until I ran into your group, where you all said you knew me." A barrage of emotions suddenly arise, and I pause, swallowing them back down as I try to relax my muscles. "It's the most surreal feeling in the world, to have a bunch of people look at you and say they know you when you don't even know yourself. And to top it off, I have a best friend who I can only assume knows everything about me." I try to control the trembling in my voice, but it's hard. "So, please, if that's true, can you give me a rundown on the basics? Family? Friends? How old am I? Where were we together last, and how the fuck did I lose my memory?"

I stare at the partition in front of me, my feet swaying slightly as I wait for answers with bated breath. *If she can't answer those things, then who can?*

Rez

My heart breaks for Lynx, listening to the anguish in his voice as he asks for any answers about his past. Thankfully, I have some. While I scrub the dried cum from my ass crack and wash away elements of the Ever Woods, I fill him in on our basic past. I start at our beginning, telling him about how he's a Storm Shifter and he came to find me when I was six, but that this was recently revealed to me since my mother had spelled him the night he came to find me.

I also tell him we normally use the link because, for the longest time, that was the only way we *could* communicate.

And back when he could change into a real boy, it was our secret.

I admit I don't know much about his family except that he told me he was an only child and his parents were still alive and are also Storm Shifters. We didn't have many friends until we came here, but that didn't bother us since we always had each other. I skip the details of my mother's death but explain that my father disappeared the night Lynx showed up. Though, one of the Fates told me he's alive.

I explain that we're now... Well, we were in Purgatory because Diablo pulled me there to help the Supernatural world, which I'm still trying to figure out. I go on telling him how we were only at Purgatory a week before the Rebels attacked him and I thought he was dead. I was ashamed to admit how I acted and curled within myself while I mourned instead of tearing down the place and kicking ass and taking names. I didn't know he was still alive until I learned about the Dreamscape and that it was real.

I admit I saw the signs of him possibly losing his memories when I visited him during a nasty experience. I tear up as I recount the moment I found him tied up and tortured. At least I get him to chuckle when I tell him how I threatened to castrate Knots when he wouldn't let me leave to go find Lynx after I found that magical trail. The Abuhuku was a whole horror story within itself, but I got through that too.

By the time I come to the part of me being stuck in the cave by the storm, I'm dressed and walking around the partition, reattaching my magic bracelet to my left wrist. I'd brought in my clothes, a purple tank top and black pants that include a thick sheath for my knife and pockets for my USB and dead phone. Lynx is sitting on the counter cross-legged, leaning back against the mirror and looking down at his hands.

"You okay?" I ask, startling him as his head pops up with wide eyes.

"Uh. Yeah. It's just... a lot to take in, you know?" he says, shifting his eyes away from mine.

"Yeah. I guess." I force a small smile to my lips before reaching into the bathroom closet once again for the familiar container of the green goop that JP gets for me back in Purgatory. *This stuff works miracles on my hair.* I hear a distinct swoosh in the other room, and I bet the fireplace just exploded with brimstone. While applying the stuff to my wet locks, I continue my explanation. "So, where did I leave off?"

"After the Abuhuku," Lynx says with a visible shudder. "You stopped at the part where the thunder stag saved you, gave you shelter, and then you ended up trapped there."

"Oh yeah," I say, combing through my hair and leaving it down. "I was trying to follow the silver trail back to you and got sidetracked by the Abuhuku, and I ended up in the cave where you found us. But before that, I had lost my memory of you. I think it's because of what happened the last time I saw you in the Dreamscape."

With a nod, Lynx propels himself off the counter and walks towards the door to the bedroom.

"Don't you need to take a shower?" I ask, a little perplexed.

"Nah, I feel as good as new," he says, looking down at his body. "I guess I could use a shirt, though, unless you like staring at all of this sexiness. Maybe I'm a distraction that you *want*." His lip curls up into a cocky smile before he steps out, and I follow him.

Ugh. I forgot how insufferable he could be on two legs, but I still love him.

"I just don't understand," I say, changing my mind and pulling my hair up into a messy bun.

"What don't you understand?" he retorts, cocking his head.

"Lynx, when I saw you last in the Dreamscape, I'm pretty sure you were dead. It wasn't until I saw you again after we fell into Hell that I got my memory of you back."

Well, that's one way to wipe the cocky smile off of his face.

CHAPTER 5
Voices in my Head

Knox

I can't help but grin as I hear Lynx stumble over his words to Rez as I lean against the door. I could feel kitten's anxiety over Lynx's memory loss and figured it would be best to give them a few minutes to talk. When I hear Moni mention checking in with JP, I know I've done the right thing. Pushing off the door, I take in the room as I go to find a closet for some new clothes.

I've never been to Hell, but this isn't what I expected. I pictured fiery pits of brimstone and Demons hopping around with pitchforks. Nowhere in my wildest dreams did I think there would be a palace with marble flooring, elaborate decorations, and bedrooms this fucking big. I guess the only things that are spot on are the heat and the subtle smell of brimstone.

Damn, it's hot. Pulling off my shirt, I feel my animals shift as I throw it on the bed.

'It's a furnace in here. How is one to get comfortable?' a stuffy posh voice rings out.

My eyes go wide as I stop in my tracks.

What the fuck?

My eyes scan around the room as I listen for the intruder. I could have sworn there was no one else here. Satisfied that I am indeed alone, I shake my head before continuing on, opening the first door to find a bathroom that is indeed also unoccupied.

The heat must be getting to me if I'm hearing shit.

'Can you ask the bell staff to turn down the heat? It's doing a number on my feathers,' the pompous voice complains.

I stumble over my own feet and slam into the closet doors.

'Cheer up, buttercup... Maybe this heat will sweat the sour out of your bones,' a rough voice responds to the first with laughter.

'Do me a favor and go dig a hole and bury yourself, will you?' the sourpuss retorts.

I quickly open the closet doors to get the jump on the people talking without my presence being known and find it empty.

'Give it a rest, featherbrain. I'm the one with a damn fur coat on, and you don't see me complaining. Just think of it as a sauna or a day out in the sun!' the bubbly voice says.

Running my fingers through my hair, I lean against the doorframe. *Okay, Knox. There's no way you're losing your mind. Just think. You've swept the entire room and no one is here, so what does that leave?*

It takes a minute before it hits me. Holy Shit! Are those... my animals?

'Baron? Wolf?' I ask hesitantly.

'At your service,' the pompous voice says. So that must be Baron.

'It's Fluffers, not Wolf,' another voice growls. *'Oh! Let's go running!'*

A snort leaves me as I feel the pull to go running from... *Fluffers.* Why do I picture him like Dug from the movie *Up* when he says 'squirrel?'

The reality that I'm finally hearing Baron and Fluffers causes me to do a little shuffle in front of the closet. The constant rage that darkens my soul lifts for a moment, showing me what other Shifters feel. For once, I feel somewhat complete as my lips curl up in a slight smile.

For years, I thought there was something wrong with me. Depression added to my anxiety, and, of course, that only exacerbated my anger issues. I've listened to other Shifters talk about their animals, and I figured I was defective somehow. Maybe the reason I couldn't talk to them was because I had more than the normal two shifts, and it was the Fates' way of keeping me grounded. Hell if I know. I just knew I wasn't normal, and it has always festered away inside of me like an infected sore that would never heal.

Shutting the closet doors again, I conjure up cooler clothes to change into. Even though I'm ecstatic that this has finally happened, I still don't know what sparked it.

'How is this possible? You've been dormant for my entire life, and now, *of all times, I hear you? What's changed?'*

'Don't be so daft,' Baron says, and I get the distinct feeling he's sticking his beak up in the air while staring down at me.

'It's not like we got to choose him, Baron. Give him a break... beakbrain.' He snickers. *'He's slow on two legs.'* Fluffers snorts out a laugh.

Grabbing my clothes, I head into the bathroom, where I set my stuff down and turn on the shower. I strip down and grab stuff out of the small closet before stepping under the stream. I'm slow in my movements as I contemplate this development, before realizing I am literally confirming their assessment of me and speed up my actions to a faster pace.

'*Slow? How do you figure?*' I fire back. Maybe being able to talk to them is not such a blessing after all. It's a double-edged sword. I finally get to know what they think, but their condescension and mocking aren't helpful at all. I start lathering up my body to wash away the sweat and grime from the cave system.

'*Well, my simpleton,*' Baron instructs. '*You simply haven't figured it out yet. That's why we finally agree on something.*'

'*That's not true,*' Fluffers' singsong voice sings out.

I purse my lips as I think about what he means, and it's a quiet moment before Fluffers starts cackling in my head.

'*Look who's a dog with a bone, now!? Oh, I'm loving this.*' Fluffers laughs in my head. A picture of the black wolf rolling around with his tongue lolling out of his mouth flashes in my mind.

Well, that's definitely new.

Since when do vivid images of my animals come to me?

'*What's wrong, Knox? Cat got your tongue? Are you a... birdbrain?*' Fluffers laughs so hard he coughs, and before long, he's choking, which is so violent, I worry he may actually die.

Is that even possible? And where is my Stardust Kitten? Will I hear from him?

'*Amateur, really,*' Baron says, as I see a picture of him rolling his eyes. '*What is it you see in that walking carpet? Anyway, think about it, Knox. What has changed recently?*'

I swear, my animals hate me. Why torture me this way? Can't they see that I'm stuck and have no clue what they are talking about? Everything has changed. I'm in Hell. I've met the infamous L.A.M.B.—minus Murmur—whom most of us have heard horror stories about since we were kids. Lilith looks like she's Betty Freaking Crocker. Levi is about to permanently tie himself to Emer on Sunday. *Shit. That's only three days away.* I wouldn't wish that on my worst enemy. The Rebels are—

'It seems I have to spell everything out for you.' Baron lets out a sigh. *'You have a mate!'*

'Oh! That's what was keeping me from hearing you guys?' I ask, confused. *'That doesn't make any sense. My peers don't have mates, and they can hear their animals.'* I grab the shampoo and wash my hair as I listen to Fluffers continue to cough up a lung while Baron berates me.

'There you go, being silly once more. They are not your peers. They might be around your age, but we are superior to them; that is why your power comes in different forms,' Baron informs me.

'Yeah. What he said,' Fluffers adds when he finally catches his breath.

I rinse and dry off, wrapping a towel around my waist before going to the bathroom counter to brush my teeth and fix my hair.

'What do you mean, my power comes in different forms? I'm a little lost here.' I admit.

'You're more than lost. You're like Little Red Riding Hood, and the Big Bad Wolf is stalking your ass,' Fluffers chuckles at his pun. All it does is ruffle my... well, shit... feathers.

'Okay, you mangy mutt. If you don't help me, then you're practically not helping yourself. Ever think of that?' I picture Fluffers' eyes going wide as that comment sinks in, and I laugh, knowing that I finally got the upper hand.

'You're going to have to trust us. You won't find out anything about your powers in a stuffy old book or by mimicking your so-called peers, as you call them. You are more powerful than you know, and judging by the space inside of you, we aren't the only powers you will have,' Baron says, giving me an all-knowing look only he could pull off, the fucker.

I lean against the counter and look at myself in the mirror as a sigh escapes me. My black spiky hair is a little longer than I like, but it's my green eyes that catch my attention. They seem brighter than usual, yet there's something else different about them. It's as if there's a darker ring around the irises.

'Do you know what the power is?' I ask, hoping that someone has an answer. Instead of Baron elaborating, I get an image of him rolling his eyes, like he can't be expected to spell everything out for me, before he straightens out a few feathers.

'The birdbrain is done talking. It's his preening time. He'll be at it all night. I swear, with all the time he spends on it, I'm surprised he's not a naked goose. Oh! Do you think Lilith will have fowl for dinner? I'm starving!' Fluffers says, and my stomach growls in agreement.

Well, that was a lot of help, same goes for the fucking shower, I'm still burning up.

'If you would just ask, I would be glad to regulate our body so it's not so hot,' a meek voice speaks up in my mind, causing an embarrassing squeak to escape me.

'Who's that?' I ask, thankful that no one was around to hear that unmasculine noise leave my lips.

'Well, no one has named me yet, but I'm your smaller form. So, I guess until you name me, I'll go by Dusky, your Stardust Kitten.'

The thrill goes through me at the fact that I could give him another name. I wouldn't know where to start with so many prospects to choose from. Hell, it almost seems like magic that Kitten came up with Baron and Fluffers. Though, I sense Dusky is wise beyond his years, so I'll keep the name he chose.

I smile at my fierce little guy. He's always been in the background and he hasn't come out of his shell in the time that he's been active, so this is a real treat.

'Well, it's nice to officially meet you, Dusky. I didn't know you could control our body that way. Thank you,' I say in relief as I feel the heat slowly dissipate from our body.

'It's no problem. I'm loving this recent development of being able to communicate with you. You can get to know us better as

we teach you more. But for now, since I'm more comfortable... I want a cat nap.'

I look over at the clothes I had picked out and scoff. Now that I'm not burning up, I walk back to the closet to get my usual black on black outfit.

Now, to just survive dinner.

CHAPTER 6

The Mad Hatter of Hell

Rez

Shortly after I get dressed, I show Lynx how to use the closet. I'm ashamed to say it took longer than it should have because he had to do an '80s fashion montage. It amazed me and had me cracking up that he could remember that decade but didn't remember me. He walked out with more gold around his neck than Mr. T. I think I died for a few seconds when he came out wearing leotards and did a short Jazzercise routine. After the double denim phase, I begged him to find some clothes so we could eat. He finally settled on jeans and a white tank that said: *Kiss me, cause I'm Lynx*.

Afterward, we meet up with the others in the hallway, heading back for dinner. Levi is back in his usual attire: a sharp gray suit with a black shirt and tie. Zeke is wearing a red wife-beater and black shorts which compliments JP's blue t-shirt and black jeans. Knox is in a fresh pair of jeans and a wife-beater, black as always, while Ryker wears a white casual long-sleeve shirt. But Ryker doesn't do anything simple. The sleeves are rolled up, showing off his sexy forearms, and since only the bottom three buttons are closed on his shirt, his tatted chest is on full display. The only one that isn't wearing shoes is Lynx, and I can't help but smile to see his personality showing through; he's always hated foot prisons.

Him wearing shoes when we were younger was practically unheard of. Hell, because of Lynx, some stores we used to frequent put up signs saying: *No shirt, no shoes, no service!* I remember one time we got kicked out of a store for his lack of shoes. I turn to share that memory with Lynx, only to be hit hard by the fact he wouldn't remember. It makes me feel sick. *Fuck, this sucks.*

As our group walks back to the parlor, I observe how Moni's wings and tail wrap around her blue body. JP pulls her into a side hug, making her smile as her bark lightens to green. Knox gently pulls me into him, and I melt against his side as he wraps his arm around my shoulder. "Did you work anything out with Lynx?"

"I explained a little about his past and tried to fill him in on the main points," I say with a sigh. "I wish I knew how to help him remember. I've missed him," I confess. He squeezes me to him when I lean my head against his chest.

"We'll figure something out, kitten. Just take one moment at a time. Don't downplay the fact that this is a win."

Well shit. He's right. I should see this as a victory. He hasn't told me he doesn't believe me, and besides the memory loss, he's here. He's alive. I much prefer this to the alternative.

"Thank you." I smile up at him and feel his happiness and comfort through our link.

"Anything for you." He leans down and gives me a kiss, leaving me feeling breathless and a little dizzy.

Damn, can that man kiss.

We walk back into the room we met L.A.M.B. in, or at least some of them. If I went by who we've met so far, I'm missing the M in the name. We stop before the leather seats, right as Lilith walks out from the back with a heavily loaded covered tray in her hands. My stomach growls at the thought of food. *When was the last time I ate? This morning before class? Is it even the same day?*

"Ah! There you all are!" she beams. "Come now. You are all just in time for dinner." She walks past us and goes down the hall between the bar and the poker table.

"I swear, we're in the twilight zone," Zeke says, turning and walking backward as he follows her.

"That I definitely agree with." JP steps up next to Zeke and turns him around before pulling him into his side as they trail behind Lilith.

"At least it's better than where I've been recently," Moni whispers and visibly shudders.

I reach over and squeeze her hand, silently giving her my strength and reassurance. I need to make sure we have some girl time soon, so I can check in with her. It can't be easy waking up to Demons and being assaulted, let alone without your mate.

"Maybe this is that *fragile* state Beelzebub was talking about," Levi points out.

"So, is Lilith still possessed?" I ask Levi because the last I heard, the council was working on a way to help her.

Levi's eyes go wide before a slight blush touches his cheeks, and he fiddles with his cufflinks. "Sorry, things have been kind of hectic lately, else I would have told you earlier. It turns out she's unpossessed, but our fathers only told us she was staying with L.A.M.B. until she healed. I guess this is her healing," he says, straightening his already perfect tie.

"Okay then." I smile with pursed lips and wide eyes. *This should be fun.*

We follow Lilith down the hall as she carries her tray and through an arch into the next room on the left, which looks to be a dining room. The marble theme extends into this room as well, but the floor is more of a dark brown. The walls are a dark gray, with gold curtains draped along the walls and old tapestries depicting gruesome battles. That seems to be a theme within itself around here. In the middle of the room is an already set, rectangular table with high-backed chairs. The thing is big enough to seat at least twenty people comfortably.

Bez walks out of the swinging door in the back of the room, and I catch a glimpse of a large kitchen.

"Um..." I start.

"Lilith, why—"

Lilith slams down the tray she was carrying hard enough that the lid flies off the table and turns to glare at Zeke. Fire radiates from her eyes for a moment, until I realize it's actually the glare of Bez's fireball in his hand. The question, though: Is that for us or Lilith?

"What did you call me?" she growls.

Zeke's eyes go wide as he backtracks. "Um... I mean... Mom?" Lilith's eyes suddenly have unshed tears as a watery smile appears on her face. "Why walk all the way around carrying food if the kitchen is right there?" he points behind her.

Opening her arms, she approaches Zeke and pulls him into her chest, smothering him as she answers.

"Oh, my dear boy. How else would I be able to see you when you come in looking for a home-cooked meal?" She leans back and smiles sweetly at Zeke as she rubs her thumb along his cheek. "Momma has to take care of her boys now, don't I?" Pulling back, she looks up and her eyes go wide, seeing all of us staring at her in shock. "It's my first family dinner with all of my boys together." She claps and holds her hands against her chest for a few minutes as she takes in our group. "Well, come on. Have a seat. I've made some favorites for all of you. Let me go get them. Bez, will you help?"

"Of course," he says, extinguishing his fire and following her out, leaving us alone in the dining room.

"Does anyone else feel like we should be armed?" Lynx asks, pulling out a chair.

"Nah. It's just Lilith. Now if all of L.A.M.B. was to join us, then yeah. I would advise you to sharpen your claws," Ryker says, taking a seat and pulling me close to him as Levi pulls out my chair.

With Ryker on my left, Levi ends up sitting to my right at the end of the table. Lynx and Knox sit on the other side of Ryker, while Moni, JP, and Zeke sit across the table from me. The kitchen door swings open as we get comfortable, and my stomach clenches when I see Astaroth stroll through with a covered dish. Trometh clip-clops his way in shortly after with fruit and sets it on the table before disappearing into the kitchen again. Footsteps sound from the hallway we just came through, and Lucifer and a blue Demon I haven't met yet walk in to join us.

"Ah, I see our intruders have had no problem making themselves comfortable," Lucifer says, smiling, though it doesn't reach his eyes. He walks to the other end of the room and takes a seat at the head of the table. "How are you liking my hospitality so far?" He looks at all of us as he straightens out his cufflinks and his wings flutter. If I didn't know better, I'd say I'm looking at an older Levi with his mannerisms.

"Well, I wasn't going to say anything, but since you mentioned it, the host's demeanor could have been nicer. Overall, I would give the hospitality three out of five stars so far, but I'll wait to do my full review until after dinner," Lynx quips, grabbing a napkin and placing it in his lap.

Ryker leans over to Lynx. "You should probably start sharpening your claws now."

Oh my God! We're gonna die in Hell! Lucifer himself is going to smite us.

I silently thank whoever decided not to have a fireplace in here. Then the room shakes violently. Lucifer's piercing eyes focus on me, and I wish I had Moni's ability to shrink as I force down the lump in my throat, leaning back to hide behind Ryker's frame.

"Well, I can see they are a lively bunch." The dark blue Demon laughs, leaving a seat between him and Lucifer. *Is that a British accent I hear? I definitely have a thing for accents.*

"That's only the half of it, Murmur," Lucifer says, cocking an eyebrow in our direction.

Hmm. Murmur. What kind of name is that?

The blue Demon glances over our group and smiles once his eyes come in my vicinity. "How's it going Ry?"

His skin is like Mystique's color in the X-Men franchise, and I wonder if it allows him to change shapes as she could. His brown hair is cut short on the sides, but it's longer and shaggier on top and doesn't seem to hide any horns. He looks like he rides a motorcycle, since he's decked out in a leather jacket and black pants. His black and blue wings look like leather too as they lay against his back, but what really grabs my attention is the blue monstrosity that is his tail. As he grabs his napkin and tucks it in his shirt, his tail whips out and grabs the pitcher on the table, pouring him a drink. *Handy.*

"Aww, you know. Accidentally fell into your vault and now we're being accused of doing it on purpose. Same old shit." Ryker shrugs.

Murmur snorts and lowers his head to hide a slight smile.

Lilith walks in carrying a pot of what looks like Mac n Cheese, and Astaroth, Bez, and Trometh follow with other dishes. The door opens again once everyone is seated, but this time, I don't see anyone walk in.

Am I seeing things?

I glance around the room, but it's not until something brushes up against my leg that I see a red grubby hand reaching for my cup, and I scream, "Fuck!" I scramble out of my seat, bumping into Ryker's chair before plastering myself against the wall. A commotion of noise erupts—silverware clattering along with chairs scraping—before Fluffers' growl rises above it all, but I can't tear my wide eyes from the creature I'm focused on. "What in Hell is that fucking thing?" I scream, pointing next to my chair with a shaky hand. My heart is pumping so hard that my vision waivers for a second. Levi is in front of me in an instant, blocking out the creature.

His hazel eyes take up my focus as his hands become a familiar weight on my shoulders. "Breathe, Rez. It's okay; that's just an Arte Demon. They are all males, harmless, and are normally used as servants if they are lucky. Most of them are used as chew toys for other Demons. You are safe." His insistence and reassurance calm me enough that I can take a deep breath. I slowly let it out while shaking the tension from my body. I feel Knox's, or maybe it's Fluffers', frustration through our link. Nodding my thanks, I smile tightly before he steps away, and I look up to find Lilith giving Levi a look of pride. All of L.A.M.B. gives me curious looks and heat rushes to my cheeks as I blush over causing a scene.

Movement catches my attention as Knox shifts back to his human form and picks up his chair from the floor. He shoots me a questioning look, and I feel his concern through our link. With another deep exhale, I give him a small smile and send back reassurance that I'm fine.

"Sorry," I mumble as I notice multiple Arte Demons in the room going about their chores before I slowly go back to my seat. Not even a mother could even love an Arte Demon. The nearest one stands at knee height, covered in layers of wrinkly red skin while it moves on its two hind legs. A stubby red tail lashes behind it like a cat, and it has two small leather wings, which look like they can't possibly hold its weight. My theory is proven correct when it hops up and grabs my cup off the table and its wings flap wildly, only to slow its descent to the ground. It fills my cup with what looks like Fae Wine and hops back up to replace my drink. Each hand and foot has four digits, and it looks like it has little suckers at the end of its fingers and toes. I've seen some crazy things since coming to Purgatory, but this one caught me unexpectedly.

"Thank you," I say, not sure if it even understands what I'm saying, but my mom didn't raise me to be rude.

The Demon looks at me, and I flinch as I finally get to see its face. Its ET-shaped head is like a mega peanut with two bull-like horns coming out of the skull. Gigantic eyes take up most of its face. I don't even know how to explain its mouth. Think of a snout with teeth that are way too big, and it looks like it's missing its lower jaw—or it's just so small that I can't see it from this angle. Either way, I'm not about to ask to see it. It has two holes on the snout that I can only imagine is the Demon's nose.

The creature's tongue flicks out and hits an overly large eye, sticking there as it observes me. Cocking its head to the side, it watches me before quickly bowing and making a sound in the back of its throat like a growl or a toad choking. I stand upright again, noticing its tongue is still stuck to its eyeball. It blinks before stubby arms frantically swipe at its tongue, trying unsuccessfully to dislodge it.

Um, gross.

Glancing around the table, everyone is busy with their own servers and getting settled that they aren't paying us any attention. Inwardly groaning, I quickly whisper, "Sorry," before pulling its rough yet slimy tongue free and wiping my hand on my pants.

"Hrmjc oep."

"Huh?"

"It said thank you," Levi interrupts. "Here, give me your hand so I can clean it." He grabs my palm and mumbles a few words, leaving my hand tingling as the saliva washes off me. When he finishes, Lilith stands to gain the room's attention. She hasn't addressed me the entire time I've been here, which, gratefully, hasn't been long. I don't find that a hardship at all, though, since we didn't have the best relationship to begin with. Besides, if what Levi said is true, which I have no reason not to believe, she wasn't herself then, and now, she's making up for lost time with her boys.

"Look at my boys! All grown up and in the same room with their momma. You guys mean the world to me—" Her voice catches, and she lightly dabs at her eye before continuing. "I finally get this second chance to be your mother, and I get to start that the right way by preparing your favorite meals and having our first family dinner together. The only way this would be more perfect is if your fathers were also here, but sadly, they are still at the academy, taking care of things. They are dealing with a lot, and if you all go back tonight, you might be in the way. So, I think it's best if you stay. Hopefully, they can join us tomorrow morning for breakfast." She smiles wistfully and looks over the table again. "Let this be our first of many family dinners! Dinner is served," she announces and waves her hand.

The lids on the food trays suddenly lift and fly into the kitchen, unveiling a smorgasbord of food before us. Some I've never seen before, but a few look familiar—like the mac n cheese and tullë strips. I'm about to ask Ryker if he can pass down a bowl when the trays levitate and slowly start moving around the table on their own, like a carousel.

What the hell?

"Now that's what you call presentation," JP says in awe. One tray lays a piece of meat on his plate before adding a clear liquid to it. Then a flame appears out of nowhere, searing it to a toasty finish. "This is impressive. Thank you, Lilith."

She smiles and nods as she takes a bite of her own food. I

sit back and watch as the Beauty and the Beast live-action dinner party meets the Alice in Wonderland tea party and plays out in front of me. The only thing missing is freaking music. I lean over to Ryker and whisper, "Is this normal?"

He scoffs as he reaches out and plucks one of the flying bowls out of the lineup. "Not at all. First, she's never cooked for us. Second, this flying circus"—he points up to the flying food—"I didn't know it was a thing," he confesses, as he scoops what looks like a piece of chicken onto his plate before offering me the bowl. "Want a piece?"

Movement catches my eye, and I focus on Moni as she pours milk into her Sparks gallon cup and desperately shakes it. Her bark turns periwinkle, a color I've never seen on her, and I'll need to ask JP about it. I suppose the milk is her way of rationing her coffee. I don't know how long that's going to last.

I give my attention back to Ryker, saying, "Sure. Thanks." I grab the bowl and help myself to a piece, too. At least, that's what I'm going to tell myself. I gently raise the bowl, mimicking the others, and snort when I feel it leave my fingers and join the other floating serving bowls.

You'd think with the revelations of coming to Purgatory, learning about Supes, and getting some powers of my own, things wouldn't surprise me anymore, but that's definitely not the case.

Bring on the dinner. I'm hungry, and nothing in this godforsaken place is gonna stop me from eating. The room shakes violently, and I hear a groan and cursing from Lucifer's end of the table.

Okay, so nothing is going to stop me from eating unless it's an untimely death by L.A.M.B.

CHAPTER 7
Nightcap in Hell

Zeke

Dinner wasn't too bad. I mean, no one died, so I consider that a win. The food was edible, and Lilith had some O blood in the fridge that she served, chilled. It wasn't the shake that I normally get from JP, but it did the trick. Toward the end of dinner, one hovering plate crashed into a gravy boat and the Arte Demons rushed to clean up the mess on the table. Unfortunately, that just caused food to go flying and half of it landed in Rez's lap. Thankfully, Levi swooped in and saved the night by casting a spell to clean up her and the table.

Too bad our night hasn't ended there, though. I was hoping to get Rez alone once more, but Lilith—oops, I mean Mom—wants a nightcap in the Parlor so we can catch up on things. Honestly, by the way we are all dragging, we'll probably pass out during this nightcap since Moni will never share her coffee. I need to find out why they don't have coffee beans. Even the most depraved should have coffee around. Maybe I'll ask tomorrow at breakfast. I know I'm feeling my energy drop, but I need to know how the hell Mom went from a mother figure to our real mother and how she now has this proper, smothering persona that's giving me the heebie-jeebies. I guess it's better than the dark feeling I've had in the past, which I find weird.

Speaking of which, I haven't felt my entity since the cave when he took over for a minute, not even an inkling of him. I feel lighter, happier, as if there's no darkness residing in me. That can only be a good thing, right?

As we shuffle in, there appears to be extra lounge seats and footstools placed around.

Rez gives the fireplace the side eye before sitting in the furthest seat away from it, which places her on the sofa. I put on a burst of speed, knocking Ryker out of the way and sliding in next to her. She rewards me with a giggle.

"Smooth," she says, leaning into me.

"I know," I agree, wrapping my arm around her shoulder and kissing her forehead.

Slurping noises pierce through everyone moving around, and I eyeball Moni. She frowns as she looks under the lid of her cup before shoving it behind her. Within seconds, she pulls another Sparks cup out of thin air and she starts drinking.

"Is that a new one?" Rez whispers, and Moni pauses long enough to nod. "How many do you have left?"

"Only four more. I don' t know how I'm going to function tonight to be honest," she replies before going back to her drink.

Rez melts against me, and I take a moment to check on her.

"Are you okay?" I ask as she hides a yawn behind her hand.

"Yep. It's just been a long day," she admits before gracing me with a smile.

Ryker grumbles as he sits down between Rez's legs, then shoots me a dirty look. All I can do in response is smile and stick out my tongue. Rez shifts and pinches my tongue between her thumb and pointer finger before whispering in my ear.

"You know, if you keep showing off the goods to everyone, I won't feel special." Rez pouts when I pull my tongue free and smirk at her.

"Whenever you want to sit on my face, spitfire, my tongue is all yours."

She bites her bottom lip as her eyes turn molten. *Aww yeah. I still got it.* Ryker leans his head further back, opening Rez's legs wider and inhales deeply.

"So intoxicating, I swear. I'm addicted," he mumbles, but it's enough to make Rez turn bright red.

"Oh my God. Your mom is right there," she shrieks, pushing Ryker's head away from her crotch, and jumps when the fireplace shoots up with brimstone.

"You know, I might just have to charge you for the damage you're doing to my abode," Lucifer says in a bored tone.

I swing my head in his direction and find him over at the bar while Murmur pours drinks.

"Oh hush, Lucy. It's not her fault that she's smitten with my boys." Mom silences Lucifer, or "Lucy," in this case.

I try to hold in my snicker, but it slips a little. A fireball flies by my head, heat almost singeing off my eyebrows as my eyes go wide and a lump gets stuck in my throat.

"Fuck me," Ryker whispers as he looks past me, and I shakily turn to see Bez with a cruel smile on his face as he blows on his fingertips.

"Bez! That's enough. These are my boys and their friends, so please treat them like family. They are my family; therefore, they are also yours," she chastises.

"No family of mine," Astaroth says as he picks up a drink from Murmur. He sits down on a footstool and leans against the wall, kicking out his long legs so they are stretched out before him.

The tension in the room is heavy and someone needs to break it before it comes crashing down on all of us.

"About that. How in hell are the guys related to you anyway? I mean, I know I'm new to all of this, but even history has to be right, saying that you didn't have kids. Yet here you are claiming them," Lynx asks. I'm not sure if he's brave or fucking suicidal; though, I'm grateful he's the one asking.

"Thank you for asking." Lilith beams as she sits down in a lounge chair. She holds out her hand for a drink, which Lucifer passes her before he takes his own seat in a wingback leather chair next to her.

For the next couple of hours, Lilith—my mother—tells us the story of how she was betrayed, possessed, and then blamed for the murder of our birth mothers. She goes on explaining how we were dying and how, with her magical essence, she saved us, changing us in the process. Nothing is for certain, but she's sure that we are more than the normal species of Mage, Vampire, Shifter, and Fae. Already she's seen some changes in us, but she was barely able to do anything until now because of the three Demons that were in her body for decades.

Realization finally hits me that Mom might be the only person who truly understands what it's been like for me my entire life. Having this entity inside of me, not even feeling like myself completely some days, has made me feel more alone than ever before. I don't know how to explain it, but I feel as if that dark entity has either locked himself up so tight that I can't feel him anymore, or he's disappeared entirely. *Maybe coming to Hell has saved me.*

"So, the entire time we've known you... You weren't yourself?" Knox asks, running his fingers through his hair.

"Yes, my dear boy. It's been heart-wrenching to only see bits and pieces of you throughout the years, only being fully present for small parts of it," she admits.

"How do we know this is the *real* you now?" Levi asks, his calm exterior giving nothing away. Throughout her story-telling, he sat back in his chair, swirled his drink, and occasionally took a sip, but he has mostly stayed quiet.

"I am so sorry, Leviathan. You, out of all my children, have been treated the worst," she says, getting up from her seat and walking to him. She drops to her knees before him and lays her hands on his crossed knee. "I don't know why they sought you out more than the others, but I can only imagine it was because you, out of everyone, would be able to subdue me, or at least see through the charade once you were tired of obeying."

She sits back on her heels and bows her head. "I know you have no reason to believe me," she says, her voice sounding thick with emotion. She reaches up with her hand and grabs her pearls, twisting them in her hand before looking back up at him with moisture in her eyes. "But all I can do is assure you that this is the real me and open myself up for you to read without any barriers between us," she says, waiting a moment before getting back up and going back to her chair.

"All I ask is that you give me the same chance that I asked of your fathers. Don't cut me out of your life. Allow me to make it up to you all. Please," she begs, looking at all of us.

I shift uncomfortably in my seat, and Rez reaches down to grab my hand, giving it a squeeze.

"What's the matter, Ezekiel? You look confused," Lilith comments.

"It just blows my mind that our dads are your mates. That means they are old as hell," I say, trying to keep the disgust from my tone.

"How did you break the possession?" Rez bravely asks.

I'm curious as well, as are all the others, and we all lean in to hear the amazing tale.

"Oh, that's an easy one to answer, Rez." Mom smiles at my woman. She turns back to us, though, to answer. "Once your fathers figured out what was wrong, they looked up the old prophecy. They got it in their heads to come together to help me," she admits, a blissful smile slowly crossing her face, making me squirm even more.

Maybe I don't want to know.

"Still doesn't answer my question," Rez murmurs, but it's loud enough for Lilith to hear it.

"Oh, sorry dear," she says, reaching up and grabbing her pearls before twirling them in her hand. "They *fucked* the Demons right out of me. HmmMmm. Just like old times. Gangbanged like a pro. You would have never guessed we'd been apart for so long."

Well, that's one way to add shock value. I'm left speechless while I try not to picture the image she has just dropped on us, and Knox gags immediately, while Ryker laughs. Levi is stoic as usual, except for wide eyes. JP also laughs as he waggles his eyebrows in my direction, and Moni cackles like a damn hyena until she falls off the stool she's sitting on. Rez's jaw has hit the floor.

Bet she wishes she didn't ask now.

"Well, damn," Lynx says, leaning forward more. "Do you think you can teach me a thing or two?"

Lilith's laughter fills the room until she looks over at us and her face drops. "Oh! I still have to give you guys the *talk*. There's so much for you all to learn."

"Ugh. No, Mom. We're good," Ryker says, shaking his head with a smile.

"Oh!?" She looks at Rez with shocked amusement. "Well, I see you've already tamed them then, huh?"

"Ugh. Just kill me now. Why can't the floor just swallow me up?" Rez moans and tries to cover her reddening cheeks.

"Since when are you embarrassed about your sexuality?" Knox provokes.

"Since we're talking about sex with your mother." Rez gives him a pointed look. "How do you like talking about sex in front of your parents?" she fires back and does that cute like neck roll that sends her loose strands flying around her head.

"Ugh. Gross," Ryker groans, wrinkling his nose.

"I concur," Levi says, pursing his lips.

"Yeah. No thank you. Now all I can picture is Dad's wrinkled ass," Knox announces.

"Oh no. It's not wrinkled at all. It's quite firm, and tight in all the right places," Lilith confirms and looks back at Rez. "You have some very good-looking men, if I do say so myself. Only the best."

"Hmm. How do you know—"

"Oh, because of the bond. And I remember you very well, Nerezza Taylor. The *human* with the familiar—" She cuts off as she looks over at Lynx and cocks her head, but I'm not focused on that. I'm still lost on the bond Mom was talking about.

"Wait. What bond?" I ask, and I feel Rez stiffen next to me.

"Well, that's not good at all. Who have you pissed off?" Lilith asks Lynx.

"Huh? What do you mean?" Lynx asks, shifting and pulling his knees to his chest.

"Is he your familiar?" she asks Rez.

Lost for words, Rez's jaw moves up and down for a few seconds before answering. "Um. Yeah, kinda. I mean one of his forms, but it's more complicated than that."

"Clearly," Lilith deadpans.

"Can someone back the fuck up and tell me about this

bond that you seem to be picking up that the rest of us are missing?" I ask, getting frustrated the more I have to wait. Rez tries to grab my attention, but I brush her off as I stare at my mother.

"Wow. This is like one of those soap operas that Earth is always playing on TV," Murmur comments, sitting down on the floor before he digs into a bowl of nuts. He frowns as he crunches on a handful and throws the bowl over his shoulder. "It's not the same without popcorn," he whines as Trometh rushes to clean up the spilled nuts. *Where did that creepy little guy come from?*

"Agreed," Astaroth says as he hands Murmur a bowl of popcorn and sits down next to him, looking in my direction.

What the fuck? When did he get up and get popcorn? And since when did my life become a soap opera?

"Ezekiel, calm down. I'm simply talking about the mate mark between Rez and Knox. Now that the Demons are out of me, it's easier for me to pick up the aura surrounding them, proving that they're mated. It also explains that I know something is up with you, dear boy," she says, swiveling her body to look at Lynx. "What happened to you?"

Lynx bristles from the attention but plasters on a smile and answers, "Well, that's easy. I don't remember shit, so I'm guessing my memories took a vacay, and they didn't leave a time frame for when they were coming back."

"Is this how he was when he was in his cat form?" Lilith asks Rez.

"He's a little rusty," she admits sheepishly.

"The nerve..." Lynx scoffs as Lilith gracefully gets up from her seat and walks to stand in front of Lynx.

I lean over to Rez and whisper into her ear. "You decided to mate with Knox?" I ask, feeling a little insecure.

We spent the night talking about mate marks and the guys when they found me underneath my altar yesterday. Shit, was it really yesterday? Man, this has been the longest day ever! Either way, it's not a complete surprise, but I wasn't expecting it to happen this soon. She seems to have made progress with everyone else except me, and I can't help but feel a little hurt by it.

"It happened when we were stuck in the cave during the storm, Zeke. It doesn't mean my feelings for you are any less," she promises, lowering her voice so only I can hear. She grabs my chin, turning it and planting a heated kiss, yet all too soon, she pulls away, making me chase after her lips. I still want more time with her, but her kiss reassured me a bit.

She chuckles as she leans into me and draws my attention back to Lilith.

Mom moves across the room and places her hand on Lynx's forehead. They both let out a yelp of pain, and Bez jumps to his feet, a ball of fire in his hand.

Talk about being a little trigger-happy there.

"Ow." She shakes out her hand. "Well, I should have known better, given the aura. You, sir, have grabbed someone's attention enough that they found you a threat." Her eyes look over Lynx's body in a calculating assessment before swinging towards my spitfire. "Or maybe it wasn't you they were worried about. Either way, we can restore your memory easily enough once I have the ingredients. It will just take some time to get them."

"Are you serious?" Rez jumps from her seat and looks at Lilith like she's an angel coming to deliver us from Hell.

Fire shoots up from in the fireplace and I groan, throwing my arm up in the air. "It was me... sorry." *Talk about a bad habit.*

"I'll help," Rez says as she walks up to Lilith and grabs ahold of her hand, bringing it up to her chest. "Please, let me help. He's my best friend, and it's my fault he's this way," she pleads. "I'll help in any way that I can. Washing bowls, getting ingredients, grinding leaves, whatever you need. Just please tell me you're not joking with me. I don't think I can take it."

I knew Rez cared for Lynx, but it's painfully obvious that she loves him more than life itself. If I didn't know any better, I would say she didn't have any more room in her heart to love all of us. But I've seen how she pushes back against Ryker, calms down Knox, gives Levi the firm hand he craves, and goes along with JP's flirtatious yet caring ways. Us, though, well... We are still working on us. I just want to have more one-on-one time with her.

Lilith cradles Rez's jaw with her other hand as her eyes search her face for a moment until she finds what she's looking for. A sad smile appears on her face as tears gather in her eyes. "You remind me so much of her," she says, and Rez visibly jerks back as if Lilith slapped her.

She lets go of Lilith's hand and steps back, studying her with furrowed brows. "Talk about déjà vu. A friend of mine told me the exact same thing once but didn't say who."

"Oh? Who was that?" Lilith asks, taking another seat in her chair.

"Anwen," Rez says, bringing her chin up, daring Lilith to question her.

Maybe Murmur had a point about this being like a soap opera. I kind of wish I had popcorn too.

JP comes over and sits down in Rez's seat, handing me a small cup of popcorn. *Where the fuck did he get that from?* I didn't even see him move. I look over to where Murmur is, and he lifts the bowl in a salute. *Oh. That makes sense.* I raise my cup with a small smile and throw a warm, buttery piece into my mouth.

This is much better with popcorn.

Lilith's smile widens hearing the Fates name. I'm still in awe that we've met her. It's considered an honor to meet a Fate, let alone see their face. "She's a wonderful friend, and of course she would say that to you. She was the closest to your mother."

"My... mom?" Rez asks, her shoulders dropping as she takes a step back. "What do you mean?"

"Liliwen. Isn't that your mother? Anwen and Liliwen were best friends until she was taken from us. Didn't you know that?" Lilith cocks her head as she analyzes Rez's reaction.

Rez's mouth parts slightly as her eyebrows shoot up to her hairline. "Um... noooo! I think you might have some wires crossed." She drops her voice. "No offense," she says, backing up.

Lilith waves away Rez's comment. "No offense taken, Nerezza. I know new information is hard to take in like this, so I understand you must need to digest it all."

Oh shit. I know I'm not a mind reader, and I don't have a connection with Rez like Knox does, but even I can read her.

"Excuse me!" Rez says, taking a wider stance and putting her hands on her waist.

"Um, does anyone else feel like we need to take shelter?" Moni whispers, flying over to land on JP's shoulder in her small form, her coffee absent.

"You have a point, Tweedle Dee," JP replies, keeping his voice down.

"I'm sorry. I know you're going through a lot right now with the new adjustment of the mate mark, your familiar losing his memories, and now, the news of your real mother, but the fact is—"

"You're wrong!" Rez says matter-of-factly. "My mother is Jillian Hunter; she's human... or she was." She chokes up on the words as they get caught in her throat and starts pacing before Lilith. "I don't know who this Liliwen person was, but obviously she meant a great deal to you and Anwen, and for that, I'm sorry. I'm truly sorry that looking at me reminds you of someone that you lost who was dear to you, but she was not my mother. I have pictures at home and birth certificates that prove Jillian is—was—my mother," Rez says, stopping to face Lilith.

"Yes, but as my story just proved, they can be falsified also," Lilith says, before calmly sipping her drink.

Tears begin to build in Rez's eyes, and I set down my drink to reach out to her, but JP stills my hand before leaning over.

"She wants to be alone to process. She would just shrug off your touch," he advises, and I look at him in question, to which he just points to his head and shakes it. *Ahh. She must be screaming her thoughts and not shielding.* Nodding that I understand, I slump back against the couch, defeated and hopeless. But there's not much to do besides watch as Rez gets heated and clenches her fists.

I don't blame her. If I had a mother that I grew up with my entire life and someone accused her of not being mine, how would I feel? I would probably tear their throat out for even suggesting it.

"Just because you got your body back and you're free to say and do what you please, doesn't give you the right to actually do it," Rez says, pointing her finger in Lilith's direction. "You have no idea what I or your boys have gone through while you've been preoccupied." She points to herself and back at us before continuing. "So maybe, while you have the freedom to speak, you should follow the golden rule, and if you don't have something nice to say, don't say anything at fucking all. Think of what it will do to others and their *happy* family. So, I take great pleasure in saying that you're *fucking* wrong, Lilith," Rez spits out, and flips her the bird. Not looking at anyone, she starts walking out of the room. "I'm going to the bathroom," she says over her shoulder as she leaves the room.

"Well, that went better than I expected," Lilith states, clenching her jaw.

"More popcorn?" Murmur asks the room, indicating his empty bowl.

"Sure, I'll go grab us more." Astaroth gets up, taking the bowl with him.

"I'll help make some for the room, sir," Trometh adds as he follows Astaroth into the kitchen.

"I'm pretty sure I saw Jillian at the cooking competition," Ryker hesitantly says. "So, I doubt that this Liliwen is Rez's mother."

"That's impossible, Ryker," JP states, leaning forward and placing his elbows on his knees.

"No, I did. She even warned me that I needed to keep Nerezza safe and that there were more players on the field than what our parents knew." Ryker implores us to believe him with his wide eyes, and I must admit I do.

"No. You. Don't. Understand. Ryker. Rez said her mother was murdered. There's no way you saw her a few weeks ago." JP shakes his head. "Whoever you saw had to be a doppelgänger or wore a really convincing facade."

Ryker snorts and shakes his head. "It would have to be a pretty good glamour to get past me."

"Well, let's ask Lynx. He might know," I try to supply helpfully as we all turn to look at him.

"Don't look at me," he says, raising his hands up in the air. "Rez filled me in on our highlights, but the only parents I seem to remember are my own."

"How is that?" Levi asks, cocking an eyebrow and lacing his fingers over his chest.

"Maybe we should wait until Rez comes back to discuss that so we don't have to go over it twice," I suggest, feeling the need to change the subject. Plus, it's making my stomach curl that we're talking about Rez without her being here to defend herself.

"That's a good point, Ezekiel," Lilith purrs. "So, boys, tell me what I've missed while I've been away."

This is going to be a fucking long night.

CHAPTER 8
Bringing in the Knight

Rez

The stinging tears push me to get to my room quickly. I don't want to be caught crying in front of anyone. For now, I just need to be alone. I couldn't stay in that room anymore, listening to what else Lilith was saying. It's great that the guys finally get to experience their mother for the first time, but that doesn't mean I need to stick around and let the memory of *my* mother be tarnished.

Really? Lilith is practically saying that my mother isn't my mom. Who the fuck does Lilith think she is? How the fuck would she know? Was she there when I was born? It's not her face in the picture holding me as a baby, so she should keep her fucking mouth shut and only talk about shit that she knows.

I finally make it to my room, but I don't stop there. Closing the door, I continue into the bathroom and lock it. When I close myself off into a corner, I feel better, so that's what I do. Instead of crawling underneath the counter and making myself as small as possible, I go behind the divide and sit on the floor on the other side of the bench. Feeling somewhat protected and blissfully alone, I let go, allowing myself to fall apart.

Tears flow like an endless river down my cheeks as thoughts of my mother flood me. Yes, she wasn't perfect, that much is clear, but she was mine. She raised me and taught me to respect all life forms.

The thought of her not being my mother is... it's... I can't —no. I won't entertain it. This has all been a mess. Ever since I lost my mom nothing has made sense. Now I have Lynx back, but he doesn't remember me or our history.

Rocking back and forth, I think about what a clusterfuck this all is. An ancient evil is back; the Sulks; the Rebels are uprising again; Lynx somehow died but is back with no memory; Levi has to tie himself to the Queen Harpy herself on Sunday; Lilith is, for all intents and purposes, the guys' mother; Knox and I have a matebond, where we can feel each other's emotions sometimes; Zeke has an entity; L.A.M.B. looks like they want to skin us alive if given the chance; Moni is missing Chester if her blue coloring has been any indicator; JP has a water Nyx form he can turn into; Knots is free of his door but trapped in the dorm; and apparently I'm Ryker's Viagra. Did I miss anything? Oh, yeah! We're in Hell!

All of my muscles in my body seem to tense up as I curl into a ball, thinking of the emotional drama my friends must also be going through. Empathy, that's what I'm feeling—and I can't contain it any longer as it flutters to the surface. But it's too much combined with all my stress. With a vicious yell, I scream out and beg for relief at the top of my lungs. But nothing changes. I know that's not how it works, but at least it's cathartic in its own way. Letting my body slump against the wall, I sob onto my knees.

I just want someone to hold me and tell me that things will be okay. Why can't I have Knots here to wrap me in his arms right now? He helped make me feel safe when my life was spiraling out of control and I believed Lynx was dead. He would gather me in his embrace and just hold me, not having to fill the silence between us.

Out of nowhere, the room jars slightly, causing me to brace myself against the wooden bench as a loud crack reverberates on the other side of the partition.

Crack!

An onslaught of coughing starts on the other side, and I freeze, my heart racing as I hold my breath.

How did someone get in here with the door locked?

"Ugh," someone groans. "Shit. I think I broke... Are we in a bathroom? Why is it so hot?" a voice squeaks.

"Hush. I was pulled here for a reason," a familiar yet gruff voice says. White flames glow along the wall as heavy footsteps come closer to the partition. Within seconds, a figure steps out and into my view. This time, I let out a sob for a different reason.

"Rez?" Knots' eyes widen slightly before his sword extinguishes and disappears. He swoops down to pull me into his chest. "What's wrong? Are you hurt?" He quickly assesses me before I can get a word out.

"Rez?" I hear something heavy hit the floor. "Rez is here?" Chester's blond mop of hair peeks over Knots' shoulder. "Are you okay? Is Moni with you?" His eyes dart around the room. "Where's Moni?" he asks, his voice jumping an octave, ending in a squeak.

"I'm not injured, Knots," I assure him as I lean back and peer into his brown eyes, gently patting his chest. "I'm just upset," I say before turning my attention to Moni's mate. "Chester, Moni is in the living room with the others. I can show you the way in a moment... I just have to clean up." I sniffle and try to wipe my tears, but it's a little hard with Knots pressed up against me.

"No need. I'll find her," Chester says, and before I can stop him he disappears from my sight.

"He's going to get lost," I mumble against Knots' chest as he pulls me into another hug.

"He will be okay. He's been frantic without Moni. You have to remember they are mated; he will be able to feel his way to her. Or at least, he should be able to. Now, tell me what's wrong." He gives me a big squeeze, and I break down in his arms. I don't know how long I ugly cry, but Knots allows me to do so silently—exactly how I was wishing for—until all that's left is sniffling and the occasional tears.

My body relaxes against him as he rocks me against his chest. Sweetly, he pulls my hair tie loose from my hair and starts massaging my scalp as tears coat his shirt, soaking the skin underneath.

'Shh. I'm here now,' Knots says against my heated forehead.

'How are you here? I thought you couldn't leave the dorm?' I ask through our link, pulling myself tighter against his muscled chest. The tears that have already drenched his shirt now cool my heated cheek as I press myself against him, hearing his soothing and steady heartbeat. *He's here. He's really here, holding me just like I needed him to be.*

'I thought I couldn't leave either, but apparently, you're the key. I was restraining Chester from leaving the dorm when I felt a pull and we popped up here, so if you want answers... You need to ask yourself that.'

I let out a frustrated sigh that only adds to my tears as I pull back my hair over my other shoulder.

'We can work this out together. What were you thinking about before I was pulled here?' Knots shifts so we're sitting side by side, and he runs his thumb up and down my arm. Goosebumps pebble along my skin, but I lean into him more, his familiar touch soothing me.

'I was thinking about how much I wanted you to comfort me and just tell me things would be okay,' I admit.

'So, there is something wrong.' Knots sits up and glances around for any danger.

'No... I mean... Isn't there always something wrong?' I say as I lay a hand on his chest.

He sighs. *'So, what must we conquer this time?'* He gently caresses my cheek before smiling down at me, and I can't help but release a sigh.

I give him a watery yet sarcastic smile. *'Well, we're in Hell, specifically in L.A.M.B.'s residence.'*

'Oh! *I heard they are pleasant to be around. Did you find Lynx?'* he inquires.

'Yeah, we did bu—'

'Well see? All is well; no one died.'

'Lynx did!' I cry out, releasing another bout of tears.

Knots rears back as if I've slapped him and gives me a deer in the headlights look. *'Um... what? Say that again.'*

"Lynx died and came back to life, but he doesn't have his memories of me, of us," I pronounce each word slowly, shaking my head before I bite my lip.

"Okay. That's a problem. Anything else?"

"I'm not Lucifer's best friend right now because of my holy, or rather unholy, thoughts."

"What do you—" He's cut off by the whooshing sounds from the bedroom through the door that Chester must have left open. "What was that?"

"Oh, the fireplace shooting brimstone because of my sentence. That's why I'm not his favorite." I tuck my head down and smirk as Knots lets out a boisterous laugh.

"This is perfect! Talk about some built-in entertainment." He grabs my chin gently and lifts it. "But do not worry. You have my life and shield. I will protect you wherever I can follow," he declares, and I fall for him a little more.

"Thank you. Think you can also take out Lilith?" His eyes go wide at my words, but I just brush it off. "I'm kidding. Kinda. It's just... She's finally been relieved of her possession and is acting crazier than the Mad Hatter in Wonderland. Plus, she said that Jillian isn't my mother."

"I don't know how the Mad Hatter is in this Wonderland you mention, but why would she say that?" he inquires as he stands and holds out his hand for me to take.

"Because I remind her of someone," I confess, letting him pull me up.

He smiles down at me as he pushes a few strands of hair out of my face. "It does sound like you've been through a lot in the short amount of time you've been out of my sight. Is now a good time to say..."

I squint my eyes at him in warning. "I swear Knots... I still have my knife on me," I growl out as he pins my arms against my body.

"But you really don't know how to use it properly." He smirks before he nibbles on my bottom lip. "And you *need* me now. So much that... I told you so!" he yells before letting go of me suddenly, making me lose my balance.

"KNOTS!" I scream as I catch myself on the wooden shelf.

He runs around the partition and into the bedroom, screaming like a little girl. I can't help but laugh at his antics as I run after him. I quickly hop over the broken pieces of the marble counter, which Knots must have landed on when I pulled them here, before running into the bedroom.

Knots is opening the door when he spots me and screams again, running out and laughing. This crazy man, he cracks me up. I end up catching him when he gets to the fork at the end of the hall. Left leads to God knows where, and right leads back to the parlor room.

The room shakes, and Knots grabs a hold of me with wide

eyes while I sigh and throw my head back. "That was me," I confess. "I can't wait to get out of here so that stops happening."

"Dirty thoughts?" Knots' eyebrow raises in question.

"For Hell, it was." I laugh.

A scream sounds from the left, and we turn to find a naked Chester running out of a room. When he sees us, his expression turns hopeful.

"Knots! Get your sword! Kill it! Kill it," he screams. My eyes—I don't know where to look, at Chester or the ceiling, but I don't want to miss what he's talking about. Hopefully, Moni will forgive me for getting an eye full of Chester's manhandle. Behind Chester is an Arte Demon waddling after him with a pile of fabric and a green satchel.

Knots pulls his sword free of wherever he hides it, but I grab his arm. "Wait! Trust me. It's harmless."

Chester slides behind Knots and white knuckles his biceps, screaming at the top of his lungs for him to kill it now.

"Chest, it's harmless. See!" I point to the ugly ass Demon.

"Harmless? There were hundreds of them in a room, and as soon as they saw me, they started to swarm. The only way I could get out was to shift and climb the walls and ceiling to get here. Then that one has been following me the entire way. Kill it!"

Sighing, I pat Knots' arm and step forward to meet the little guy, who's wearing shorts... He kinda reminds me of Alf and Pete the dragon if they had a damn baby. Kneeling, I take the fabric and sack the Arte Demon hands me.

"Thank you," I say, trying to smile.

"Oep'gl lbseal." It nods and starts waddling back the way it came.

I hold up the items in front of me, and Knots throws his head back, laughing as Chester turns bright red, everywhere. He approaches me and takes his clothes and glasses back. I turn to face Knots, giving Chester some privacy while he changes into his clothes.

"This looks a little girlie to be your bag," I say, observing the dirty green sack with faded flowers dotted along it.

"That's because it's Moni's emergency pack," he explains in a muffled voice while he pulls on his shirt.

"What would she need in an emergency?" Knots questions, sharing a look with me. I shrug but relinquish the bag when Chester motions for it.

"Thanks," he says shyly as he throws the bag over his shoulder.

"You're welcome," I tell him, patting him on the shoulder as I pass, keeping my eyes locked above the equator even though he's completely dressed now.

Knots pulls me into a quick hug as Chester adjusts his glasses.

"What did it say to you?" Chester nervously asks as he looks briefly down the hall he came from.

I shrug. "I have no idea, but I assume it said: You're welcome." The guys give me incredulous looks, so I explain how Levi had to interpret a small conversation between me and one at dinner.

"That makes sense," Chester agrees, pushing up his glasses.

"Ready to see Moni?" I ask, giving him a smile.

"You bet. I should have waited like you suggested. I guess our bond isn't that strong yet," Chester admits as his shoulders drop.

"You're also in Hell. I don't expect it's easy on the senses either, so don't beat yourself up." I smile and start walking toward the Parlor. "Let L.A.M.B. do that. Apparently, they're itching to do it," I mumble under my breath.

CHAPTER 9

Hell's Angel

Rez

We don't even get within five feet of the archway when Chester goes running into the Parlor. I probably should have gone in first, to tell them about Chester and Knots, but I'm feeling a little salty at the moment, so I let it play out. I pull on Knots' arm because I'm sure things are going to blow up. L.A.M.B. is still in there, and if they see Chester running in, they might get defensive with a strange man running into their home. And with Moni being protective of Chester, well, that's probably not a good outcome.

To be on the safe side, I wait a bit and am not disappointed. Within a few seconds, I hear Moni yell out Chester's name while Bez asks who Chester is, followed by a scuffle of activity. I make out JP and Zeke's voices as they yell "stop" right before Moni's shockwave hits the wall, blocking us.

Groans and moans reach my ears as we walk into the Parlor and find everything in disarray. The seats that most of L.A.M.B. and Lilith occupied last are overturned, and the occupants are quite dazed themselves. I do a little internal dance as Lilith pulls herself from the floor and tries to straighten out her hair.

Levi is using his magic to restore the room, starting with the knickknacks that fell from the bookcases and then the chess pieces from the back area. Knox cracks his neck before sitting back on the sofa, and Ryker helps Zeke off the floor. I find Chester and Moni in a tight embrace, paying no one else any attention, and I don't blame her.

JP pulls himself to his hands and knees and glares directly at me. "You did that on purpose," he accuses.

"I'm not dumb enough to upset Moni, but I knew L.A.M.B. would be," I admit as I chuckle. The asshole I heard push Moni too far pulls himself off the ground and retakes his seat. Bez gives Moni an assessing look, and for a moment, I find myself worried about my best friend. That is, until I find Bez giving her a small nod and his eyes turn thoughtful.

Lucifer straightens out his jacket and runs his fingers through his hair before facing Moni and Chester. "I apologize. I did not know he was your mate." He looks glaringly over in my direction, and I blink my innocent eyes at him. "Nor did I feel him or your companion come through any of my wards."

"Wow. You must need to get your wards fixed. Sounds like a you problem," I say, pulling Knots along with me to the sofa.

"Hello, Knots. Nice to see you outside of the dorm," Levi says as we pass him to sit on the sofa.

"Same. I've always wanted to travel," Knots jokes.

"Hey, Knots. Nice to officially meet you, man!" Zeke says, holding out his fist for a pound. I sit down next to Zeke once more on the sofa, but this time JP is between Zeke's legs while Ryker moves between mine, and Knots sits next to me.

"So does this mean all Door Knights have real life bodies like you?" Knox asks, handing me a bottle of water. I give him my thanks, and he sits down, leaning against Levi's chair. I'm curious to know the answer myself.

"To be honest, yes. But I had thought we lost our ability to be pulled from our doors until Rez here pulled me out." He shifts a little as he answers honestly. Picking up on him being uncomfortable talking about himself, I try to sway the attention from him and bring it back to the room itself.

"So, what did I miss while I was away?" I ask, trying to act like I didn't run off like a scared little girl. Yes, I needed the moment to myself, but that doesn't mean I want to revisit the reason I ran off in the first place.

Ryker clears his throat and turns to face me. I go taut as he looks up at me, and I watch his Adam's apple bob in his throat.

"Rez, that day you went flying with Knox and most of us went to the cooking contest... I think I ran into your mother. I didn't think much of it until, uh, Mom and you got into it."

I gasp as I stare at him and slowly pan the room. No one is laughing or trying to hide secret smiles, so... *fuck.*

"JP said that can't be true since you said she was murdered, but I can see through glamours and this person didn't have one. She resembled you." He reaches up and grasps my knee, lightly squeezing it. "She even said she knew me and told me to keep *you* safe, specifically, and that her body wasn't her own."

"Why didn't you tell me before?" I squeak. I'm not sure what to believe or think right now, but I feel like I should at least be asking questions.

"When we got the call that you and Knox were hurt and were in the hospital, I had completely forgotten." He bows his head. "We wouldn't bring it up with you right now if we could avoid it, especially after the whole emotional upheaval, but Lynx couldn't remember your mother, only his own parents. I'm sorry," he admits.

"It's okay." I smile down at him before taking a moment to breathe. "It's not your fault. We've been through a lot lately.

And to be honest, I really doubt it's my mother. Unless a Necromancer went to Earth and reanimated her, she's at rest 6 feet under." Knots squeezes my hands, and I give him a reassuring smile before turning to Lynx.

"Just to play the Devil's advocate," Levi says and looks to Lucifer. "No offense."

"None taken," Lucifer waves it off with a bored look.

"Then why would this random lady warn Ryker to protect you and tell us there're more players on the field than what we know?" Levi asks.

I grind my teeth together as his words hit a sore spot for me, and I let out a frustrated sigh.

"I don't know. I came home one day and found my mother dead. Just a few weeks ago in Familiars class, I slipped into Lynx's mind and relived that memory. I saw her murderer in a black cloak. So if she's alive, then you tell me." I look around the room and throw my hands out as I get frustrated, on the brink of tears once again. "How is that possible?" I demand.

"Maybe she had a sibling?" Zeke says helpfully.

I know what they are trying to do, but it's a moot point.

"I have an aunt, but they don't look enough alike for you to have mistaken her. Look, I appreciate you guys trying to work this out. I think she would have come to me and explained everything if she was alive or reanimated somehow. As it is right now, all this is doing is upsetting me," I confess.

Knots leans in and wipes away a tear on my cheek that I didn't realize had fallen. I feel all the energy seep out of my body as I lean against him, but I know I can't leave it there.

"I realize how stubborn I sound, and I do hear what you're saying. So when it comes down to it, someone is either playing a horrible trick on me and my mother's alive but doesn't want to see me. Or she's dead, and someone has a skill that's so strong they can trick Ryker's ability to see through the glamour. Either way, I'm here without an answer and with more questions than I care to think about. Speaking of which," I look over at Lynx. "You can remember your parents but you can't remember anything about me? How is that possible?" I ask, lost at the logistics of that.

"Now that I can answer," Lilith speaks up with a smug smile.

I repress the urge to roll my eyes at the she-devil since she's about to shed some light on my bestie and finally getting the subject off of me.

"There's a common memory loss potion that we Demons use when we strike deals with humans that summon us to their plane." My mouth drops at her admission. "It's a loop-hole, dear. That's the only other way Demons can cross over to Earth without the Doors. Although, it's a short amount of time we can stay. It's normally only the duration of the summoning spell the humans use."

"Wait. There are actually humans out there who know spells to summon real life Demons? I thought that shit was just in movies and TV shows?" I snort, finding this unbelievable.

Lilith gives me a salacious smile, and I hear all of L.A.M.B. snicker off to the side. "Darling, ever heard the saying: Myths are created to only hide the truth?" My silence is my answer, and she mumbles, "What are they teaching children these days?"

"The education system is lacking, Lilith. We all know this," Lucifer speaks up, and I shoot him a dirty look. He winks and raises his glass to me before he takes a sip.

That smug asshole.

"Well, nonetheless," Lilith says, pulling my attention back to her. "Ouija boards, pentagrams, crystal balls, and certain mirrors have the power to summon Demons if you have the right words. There are rare occasions that people with enough passive power play around and accidentally summon one of us. Typically, we break free of their puny circle of containment, but that's a different story. The point is, there are plenty of ways for Demons to cross over; we just can't stay there very long that way."

I shudder at the thought of what Demons who don't take the proper way to travel are up to.

"Simple enough. Most Demons carry around memory spells that will act as an eraser, but for short-term memory." She turns her attention to Lynx, and he shifts under her scrutiny. "Now, what appears to have happened here is a little more complex," she says, getting up and once again getting close to Lynx, though keeping a safe enough distance.

'Don't tell her you died and came back,' I urge him, praying he's not blocking me out. I still don't trust her or L.A.M.B. Knowing my luck, they would use me as a science project and not let me leave here.

His eyes dart to me. *'I won't.'*

I let out a shaky breath and allow my shoulders to relax as I bite back a smile. I think I'm more excited that he replied to me through our link than anything else.

"My guess is they took you to the brink of death and added in a spell in hopes of manipulating and controlling you, possibly to bring you to their side. But who, or for what purpose, are questions I cannot answer." She looks deeply into his eyes. "Can you?"

"It was the Rebels," I blurt out. I don't know what Lilith is capable of doing or what L.A.M.B. will allow her to do. We aren't her kids, and I'm not about to bet their protection extends to Lynx and me, so I try to pull her attention back to me. "They took him. You're right about your theory. They went after him because of me. I received a letter telling me to leave Purgatory or they would go after my Familiar," I confess and suddenly it hits me, sitting here in front of Lynx and everyone... This is all my fault.

Yes, I'm glad I got Lynx back. We've been through all types of shit together, but the only one at fault for this mess right now... is me. "I am so sorry, Lynx." My voice catches as my vision becomes blurry. "If I had known sooner, or if I knew how to get us out, I would have left in a heartbeat so they wouldn't have had the opportunity to hurt you."

Hands take hold of me as image after image of his time in the dreamscape flash before my eyes. The marks, the candles, pentagrams, the blood, the knives, ropes, chains, and the final picture of him dying takes up all of my vision.

"Mà cherie!"

I feel my cheeks being squished together and my vision clears, but instead of seeing JP in front of me as I expect, I see Lynx's turquoise eyes staring at me.

'You have nothing to be sorry about. I can see how much this is tearing you apart, but look at me, I'm pretty hot. I would fuck me. I wonder if that's possible... wait... is that masturbation?'

I can't help it; I laugh and smile.

'The point is, whatever happened, it's over and I'm here now. Yes, we have a slight hiccup with my memories, but like the Bat Queen over there said, she'll be able to help get them back. I'll be good as new, and you can get back to giving me all those wonderful handjobs besties give each other.' He winks, and I push his shoulder, making him laugh.

Not a word is said out loud and everyone gives him a weird look as he sits down, but it means the world to me that he took the time to talk to me, and through our link. I know there's a part of my Lynx deep down in there somewhere.

"Eek!" Moni squeals and flies across the room to her emergency bag. Chester must have dropped it when he came in, and Levi must have moved it while he cleaned up.

Moni hugs the bag to her chest as she flies back to Chester

and gives him a look of admiration in her eyes. "You saved my bag?"

"Of course I did. I know how much your emergency bag means to you. And since we're in Hell, it might really come in handy." Chester runs his hand along her cheek.

"What's in your emergency bag anyway?" Knots asks, breaking the moment.

Moni gives Knots a bright look before reaching into her bag and pulls out a cup of coffee. "The only thing I need in an emergency. The sweet nectar of life." She cuddles with her cup before digging into her sack some more.

A throat clears, and my attention swings back to Lilith.

"Well, I know of someone who might help us shed some light on all of this, but that will have to wait until tomorrow. I have my own Demons to torture tonight, and I'm sure you guys need sleep. It's late," Lilith announces, standing up and walking out without another goodbye. I look over and see Lucifer, Astaroth, and Bez stand, but I don't see Murmur.

Where the hell is that blue Demon?

Speak of the Demon, and he shall rise.

Murmur walks in with two big bowls. One is filled with a variety of nuts and another with popcorn. "The party's over?" he questions with a pout. He sets down the bowls on the table and his jaw drops as his eyes go wide when he notices I've joined the group again.

"Kanotiel? Is that really you?"

"Mur?" Bez says, pausing and glancing back at us. I can't help but squirm under the attention. Lucifer and Astaroth also turn around and look in my direction, but I soon realize it's Knots they are looking at, not me.

Knots and everyone else around the table tense up. "Umm. I'm sorry, but what?"

"Kanotiel, it's me, Muriel, but I go by Murmur now," Murmur explains. He turns back to his friends. "Guys, bear with me. Just picture our old attire and his hair longer, tied back in leather."

"Holy Hell, how did I miss that?" Lucifer says, and fire shoots up in the fireplace.

I jump up out of my seat, point my finger in his direction and yell, "Ha! See? You did it that time!"

He turns his icy stare toward me, and I pantomime zipping my mouth and sit back down. *Okay, Lucifer is sensitive apparently.*

"I don't know who you think I am," Knots begins, standing up to move around the table before us. "But I'm a Door Knight at Purgatory Prep Academy, and these are my wards, s—"

"Not all of us," Moni speaks up, and I find her being rocked in Chester's arms as she continues to hold her bag to her chest.

Awww.

"You are right, Miss Moni. You and JP are my wards. Rez is my woman, and the princes are my friends, along with Chester and the furball, when he gets his memory back," he says, looking over at Lynx before addressing L.A.M.B. once again. "The point is, I don't have time to play around, so make your point or swallow it and don't bring it up again." Not an ounce of fear shows in Knots' expression as he stands about three feet in front of Murmur, looking every ounce the knight that he is.

The blue Devil starts laughing. "Mate, you crack me up," he says, slapping his knee. It all happens within seconds. Murmur's long-ass blue tail whips out and grabs Knots around the waist, pulling him closer. Knots pulls out his glowing sword and brings it up to Murmur's throat simultaneously.

I hear a plunk and look over to Moni's prone form before Chester scoops her up. We all jump to our feet but pause when Murmur starts laughing. "I see you still have Alexis."

Knots pulls away his sword from Murmur's throat and gives him a scowl. "How do you know about Alexis?" he whispers in awe.

Murmur unravels his tail and gently pushes Knots' arm down and away from his face. "Simple. We knew you before we fell and went with Lilith."

Holy shit! Does that mean... Knots is an Angel?

Boom! Boom!

"Can you blame me, with that bomb of information?" I throw out my arms when Lucifer glares in my direction once again. *Lord have mercy, we're gonna need it.* I bite my bottom lip and scoot away from Lucifer when the fireplace takes another beating.

He clenches his jaw but pulls his glare from me. "Okay. I see. We've had enough excitement for the night. We will pick this back up tomorrow morning. It's good to see you again, Kanotiel. We will catch up later."

"I go by Knots, please," Knots says as he sits back down beside me as Bez and Astaroth leave the room.

"Very well," Lucifer says. "Just in case you didn't figure it out, you can change your rooms around by thought. Just like the closets." He turns to leave with Murmur following him out. "Don't destroy my place."

"What did I miss?" Moni asks as she looks around the room. Chester leans in and whispers in her ear. The fireplace erupts as her eyes go wide and her bark goes glitter bomb.

"Wow!" Moni says, looking at Knots with astonishment. She quickly shakes herself out of it, and with Chester's help, pulls foot stools up to the table so we're all sitting in a circle around the coffee table.

"Does anyone else feel like they've been on an emotional roller coaster that we didn't sign up for?" I ask as my mind whirls with so much information. "I mean, we just got an information dump from hell. I feel like my brain is about to malfunction just to keep everything in."

"Just a little," Moni agrees, sporting her natural green color again.

"Yeah. At least the good news is, you found Lynx," Chester chimes in. "And Lilith can restore his memory."

"Lynx doesn't seem to be the only one that needs it," JP says as he peers over at Knots. "You okay, man?"

Knots slowly shakes his head back and forth as if he's in disbelief before he takes in our expressions of worry and astonishment. He runs his hand through his hair as his voice chokes slightly. "I knew I was missing pieces of my past, but I had no idea that—I—they have to be wrong," he chuckles and looks at me. "I think I would have remembered if I became one of the fallen. I just don't understand." A worry line appears between his eyes as he shakes his head again. "It's just too much to handle right now."

"It's okay, Knots. We'll figure things out later," I say, reassuring him.

"Well, that was delightful," Levi says, leaning forward and grabbing a handful of nuts.

Lynx looks over at Moni and Chester. "Who are you?" he asks, cocking his head to the side. He gives Chester a once over and a bland look, blatantly unimpressed.

"I'm Chester. Moni's mate," he replies, pushing up his glasses and grabbing Moni's hand.

"Who names their kid Chester?" Lynx snorts, and I consider junk punching him on principle.

"Who names their kid Lynx?" Knots whispers, leaning into me as I roll my eyes.

"Me. I named him when I was six. Give me a break." I laugh when he blushes and gulps audibly.

'It's a wonderful name. Really!' he backtracks, and I think it's adorable.

"Well, it's actually Chestnut. We have a tradition in our family to name your child after the first nut thing they eat," Chester admits, pushing his hair back from his eyes. A faint blush rises on his cheeks, and Moni swoons against him.

"Oh. I see. So let me guess. Chestnuts are your favorite nut," Lynx says and pushes the bowl of nuts on the table toward Chester.

Leaning away from the bowl Chester stammers. "Umm. Act—actually, I'm allergic."

The room goes silent as we process that information.

"That's good to know, from my standpoint. Any other allergies I should know about since I'm the resident cook of this group?" JP asks, trying to lighten the mood. He throws up some popcorn, and Zeke playfully catches them out of the air before JP can with his mouth.

"I'm allergic to stupidity," Knox growls.

"I think everyone is in this group," Ryker chuckles.

"Got that right. Anyone else finding this extremely weird?" Moni asks, holding her tail against her.

"What do you mean?" Levi asks, giving Moni his full attention.

"Well, think about it. How did you guys get here? I was stolen and Bez saved me and brought me here. Chester and Knots were pulled here, and you guys fell here. Isn't that a little weird?"

"She does have a point," Lynx agrees, picking out chestnuts and smiling at Chester before throwing a few into his mouth.

"Not to mention how we've been looking for Lynx and he just suddenly shows up out of the blue, just in time to fall into Hell with you all. It's just too much." Moni's coloring starts to cycle through dark gray, white, and blue, and without missing a beat, Chester turns to her and plants a kiss on her that leaves her melting into his hand.

"What the fuck?" JP shrieks. "That's my sister!"

Chester pulls away and blushes while Moni sports the biggest and dopiest smile on her face until she focuses on us and then laughs. "Now you know how I feel when I see you and Rez kiss."

"Lord have mercy, my heart can't handle this," JP says, and the fireplace erupts once again.

"And with that, maybe we should call it a night. It's beyond late," Levi suggests, standing up and fixing his jacket.

If only erupting fireplaces were the least of our worries.

CHAPTER 10

Unbelievable Bully Secrets?

Rez

"Are you alright?" I ask Knots as we trudge back to the hallway where our rooms are.

"Yeah, it's just a lot to take in." Knots sighs.

"That's what she said," Lynx chirps, walking past us and snickering.

"Are you sure he's lost his memory because I swear, he's not acting like it," he comments, squeezing my hand.

"That depends. Are you annoyed or amused that he's not acting like it?" I ask, giving him a small, knowing smile.

"Both. It would be nice to pick up where we left off, but it's unfair if he doesn't remember," Knots confesses. "So, are you sure?"

"Oh. I'm sure. But you heard her; Lilith said she can help with his memories. Do you think maybe she can help with yours?" I say hopefully, trying to cheer up my sour Door Knight.

"Maybe." He sighs.

Zeke slows his steps so we can catch up with him. "Hey,

Rez... Knots," he says, giving us a small smile. "I was wondering if you would mind staying with me tonight, Rez? Or should I be asking to stay with you tonight? I'm not sure how that works with our rooms," he admits, running his fingers through his ginger faux hawk.

Aww, my Vampire is nervous, and somehow, it makes him more vulnerable right now. Coming to a stop in front of my room, I turn toward Knots because I know he's lost and confused. I, for one, understand how that feels, and I don't want to leave him feeling that way. "Will you be okay?" I ask, worry evident in my tone.

He smiles as he pulls me into his embrace. "I am your protector. You shouldn't be worrying about me."

"I can't help it. I worry about everyone I care about," I admit, squeezing him back.

"I'll be fine. I'll shack up with the hairball tonight and promise not to skin him until he gets his memories back," he jokes, giving me a lopsided smile. "I'll have a good night's sleep, and we can tackle all of this in the morning, okay?"

"Okay." I reach up, and he gives me a sweet kiss on the lips. While my eyes are closed, he gives me another on my forehead. I smile as I feel him walk past. "Oww!" I shriek, turning around to find Knots running down the hall, laughing.

That little bastard just pinched my ass!

He follows Lynx into a room, sticking his head out to yell, "Told you so!" before slamming the door.

"What was all that for?" Zeke questions with a smile.

"He told me not to go out looking for Lynx by myself because I would get in trouble," I admit, opening my door.

"Ahh. I see. A man after my own soul." Zeke chuckles as he walks past me and looks around my room.

"Sure, if you want to be a man who's going to be castrated soon." I smile, looking over my shoulder. "I like you the way you are, though," I say, turning around and leaning against the door.

"Oh, you do?" Zeke looks back at me and smiles slightly, popping a fang out.

I bite my bottom lip and push off the door to walk over to him. I'm glad he took the initiative and asked to spend time with me. I haven't had any one-on-one time with him since the first day of school.

Shit, has it really been that long?

I walk into his arms as he lightly grips my hips as I wrap my arms around his neck. "Yeah. Just a little," I say. Before I can do anything else, Zeke lets go of me and sits on my bed with his hands between his legs. I'm a little disappointed at the sudden shift, but curious as to why.

"It's kinda awkward between us, isn't it?" he asks, not making eye contact with me. "I mean, since I confessed my love for you. Or is that just the sexual tension I'm picking up?" he asks, finally looking at me with a vulnerable expression yet trying to make light of it.

Leave it to Zeke to not beat around the bush. I really respect that, and I don't hide the smile that he brings to my lips. Walking over to the bed, I hop onto it, making us both bounce. He smiles at me, which was my goal.

I turn so I'm facing him while propping one leg under me and hanging the other off the edge before I reach for his hands. He turns to mirror my position. "I have a confession, Zeke," I begin, lowering my head and quickly licking my chapped lips. *God, I'm so nervous.*

Swoosh! The fireplace shoots fire into the hearth, and Zeke and I both jump with nervous laughter.

"Man, that's a bad habit of mine," I say, pushing my hair behind my ear.

"Yeah, you'll be lucky if Lucifer doesn't kill you," Zeke jokes.

"Well, if you think about it, if I died now, I probably have a lot of sins and I'll be in Hell for eternity, where I would be saying all sorts of things. Probably ruining a lot of fireplaces," I snort.

"Oh man." Zeke shakes his head and then he stiffens. "Wait, so technically, you're probably exempt from going to Hell!" he exclaims, and then laughs with me.

"Well, you definitely know how to break the tension," I admit.

"I do what I can," he admits. But his cheerful expression slowly melts off of his face as his green eyes focus back on mine. I take in a deep breath and let myself be honest as I begin again.

"Before everything fell apart at the beach party, I was falling in love with you," I confess. "What we had felt so natural and carefree that I didn't think anything of it. You just came out of nowhere and swept me off my feet. So, when I saw that video, a part of me felt ripped apart. I won't lie. I closed down and pulled away from those I became closest with."

Zeke tucks his head to his chest, and a part of me wants to stop and comfort him and say sorry, but I can't. I need to get this out if I want to heal and get past all of this. I want to be with Zeke. I've forgiven Levi, and hopefully we will work on our relationship. But Zeke and I haven't had this chance to talk, for me to express myself, and for him to be forgiven.

I swallow around my dry, swollen throat, but I push to get out the next words. "Then I lost Lynx, and I didn't want to live anymore."

Zeke's head snaps up at my admission. His eyes turn glassy as he squeezes my hands. "But with the help of JP, Moni, and Knots, I pulled through enough to stand on my own two feet again. The thing is, even though it might look like I've gone leaps and bounds with the other guys, it's been a slow process. You've just been gone for weeks, and this is our first time together since you ripped out my heart."

"Rez—"

"When I heard you were missing, I didn't want to hold a grudge against you anymore. But I also knew that we wouldn't be able to continue where we left off. So, can we start over?" I ask with a shy smile.

"I think it depends on what stage we're starting from." Mischief flashes across his expression, and he returns my smile. "I'm Eziekel, but call me Zeke. I think you know my brothers and little sister already. My father, you've had the displeasure of meeting. And I really like you."

The mention of his father has my eyes going wide and my mouth dropping. "Oh my God!" Fire shoots up in the fireplace like clockwork, but I'm too busy pulling the USB out of my pocket. "Zeke! I totally forgot. I did see your father, but on more than one occasion. He came to check on you while you were resting in your room yesterday," I confess.

His eyebrows pull down in question. "Really? That doesn't sound like him."

"He did!" I say, bouncing again on the bed. "He even apologized to me."

"Okay, so now I *know* it wasn't him." He laughs before getting up. He makes a pass across the room before stopping in front of me and running his hands through his hair.

"No, I'm serious." I sit up and grab his hand, pulling him back to sit beside me. "He said he was sorry the council's decision had affected my relationship with all of you guys. He also explained that you're stubborn"—Zeke smirks at the comment—"and that I shouldn't have blamed myself for you getting hurt," I admit and lower my head, not able to look him in the eyes.

"Now that I agree with," he says, as I feel his thumb under my chin. He lightly lifts it up so I'm looking at him. "What I did wasn't your fault, Rez. I hope you know that," he tells me, and my heart feels a little lighter as we talk this out.

"I do. Plus, like I said, having your dad explain things helped, and I think he gave me a peace offering," I say, holding up the USB between my fingers.

"What's that?" he asks, taking the small black device.

I shrug my shoulders. "I'm not really sure. Your dad just said it was the security feed from when they found me at Diablo's door and when they questioned me."

"Are you serious?" Zeke's voice jumps an octave as he gets excited. "This is amazing. I tried to find that information right after I heard about the meeting, but I never found the footage. Do you mind if we share this with the guys?"

"No," I tell him, still a little shocked by how this is turning out. "But I don't see a computer or anything around here to upload it," I mention as I look around the room.

"Leave that to me. Just go grab the guys real quick before they pass out."

"Okay," I say, dashing out of the room.

. . . . .

While I was out rounding everyone up, which was hard given the late hour, Zeke had completely transformed the room to a mini theater. The fireplace is gone, and in its place is a TV screen, taking up the entire wall. Two smaller loveseats are sitting in the front, and a longer couch is toward the back. Off to the right, Zeke is sitting at a computer desk, where he looks right at home behind the monitors.

Zeke and I are the only ones still dressed in our day wear. Moni was dressed in a light-yellow baby doll until JP screamed something about going blind and threw a robe at her. So now she and Chester are wearing matching silver robes and are cuddled up in one of the loveseats. Levi is dressed in, I kid you not, blue suitjamas that match JP's silk pants. They would make another cute couple if they were cuddling in the other loveseat in the front. My shirtless men, Knox, Ryker, Lynx, and Knots, are on the big sofa with an opening between Ryker and Lynx, which I happily squeeze into.

Once we're all seated, Levi addresses the room. "Okay, since we're all here now, can you please inform us why you've summoned us?"

Internally cringing, I realize I might not have told them anything besides to hurry up and get to my room, stat. I do appreciate the fact that he doesn't make me feel bad for not waiting to do this in the morning.

Zeke clears his throat. "Oh yeah. We can do that. Rez?" He gives me a cocky smile as he throws me under the bus.

That little ass!

I can't be all that mad at him, though, so I stand back up and head to the front of the screen, trying not to drool at all the yummy male flesh in front of me. Levi gives me a small smile and his dimple pops out in his cheek. Without fail, Ryker's eyes flash that electric blue, and I know he's picking up on my lust. *Okay, Rez, get your shit together.*

I look over at Moni, and my lust dies like ice water being thrown on me, especially when I see her yawn.

"I'm sorry to pull you guys here when it's so late, but I had forgotten what happened while Zeke was recovering." Knots gives me an inquisitive look that flashes with suspicion, and I throw out my hands, trying to calm down the situation before my knight comes to my rescue when I don't need it. "Before you go off the rails, just listen, okay?"

Reluctantly, Knots gives me a nod and relaxes back in his seat. "The reason we brought you in here is because Zeke and I want to look at the USB that Mayor Abernathy gave me as a more or less peace offering when he visited Zeke. He apologized for my treatment and his involvement in asking Zeke to spy on me, and he asked for my forgiveness." I look around the group while they all give me blank stares, like I'm daft, and out of nervousness, I bite my bottom lip. "Okay then. Any questions?" I ask as I clap my hands and rock anxiously back and forth.

"Are you sure it was Abernathy? Like the real Abernathy?" Ryker asks with wide eyes.

"It was the same one that was in the apartment that day when you walked by," I answer.

"What's a UBS? Unbelievable Bully Secrets? Is that what we're going to find?" Moni asks, bouncing up and down in her seat.

I can't help but chuckle. "Moni, I love you."

"It's a USB. It stands for Universal Serial Bus, and it holds digital information. Supposedly, it has video footage of Rez coming to Purgatory and her questioning, so we're going to watch together," Zeke explains while I take a seat.

I get comfortable as Zeke fiddles with something. We hear a sizzle, and the lights flicker and Zeke cusses. "FUCK!"

Simultaneously, everyone asks if he's okay or if he needs anything.

"Nah, I'm fine, but it looks like we're in for a treat, though."

"What do you mean?" Chester asks, pushing up his glasses and pulling Moni closer into his body.

"It looks like the USB is spelled. Levi?" Zeke beckons him over.

Levi runs his hands over the device as I watch his lips move soundlessly, nodding his head before walking back over to his seat. "It's an immersion spell, so it looks like we'll be seeing at least part of this from your perspective, Rez, since I picked up on your resonance coming off of it," he explains before taking his seat once again.

"How is that possible since I don't remember any of this?"

I say under my breath. Thoughtfully, Lynx takes my hand and squeezes it as Ryker places his hand on my thigh.

All Levi can do is shrug, and the action looks so foreign on him.

Well, ready or not—bring on the VR experience.

CHAPTER 11
Bonfires Lead to Dust

Rez

Do you know what the best feeling in the world is? It's not being body slammed into the ground by a fucking gorilla, that's for sure. I mean that literally.

"Stop resisting and stay down," a gruff voice yelled.

I just knew going to my 'Welcome Home' party and drinking the night away was a bad idea, but it was my first time to really let loose after leaving my grandparents' house. Drinking around the bonfire with old friends the weekend before college was supposed to be relaxing and fun. You know how it goes: letting your hair down, doing things you wouldn't normally do, and blaming it on liquid courage.

"I'm not resisting. I'm just saying you've got the wrong girl," I argued, my voice coming out in a jumble of grunts as I tried to find purchase for my hands in the gravel underneath me, only cutting myself in the process.

Oof.

I felt air swoosh out of my lungs as I'm slammed back down and a knee is jammed into my back. Rocks bit into my skin as *tears swell in my eyes.* Well, this isn't what I was expecting when I agreed to drink.

"You are hereby in violation of Order 12-4: Trespassing in an unauthorized travel zone," a feminine voice says, while my arms are pulled sharply behind me, causing me to flinch. Cuffs locked around my wrist, cutting off all circulation to my hands. The motion pulled at my shoulders, and I heard a pop.

What the actual fuck?

The weight disappeared suddenly from my back, allowing me to lift my head and take a deep breath, only to break out in a coughing fit.

"Who are you, and why are you here?" a nasally voice demanded, and I can't help but laugh between coughs. It's a feat I don't recommend. The person sounds like a double-stuffed chihuahua that was found in a twatwaffle!

Footsteps crunched across the rubble, and suddenly, I'm lifted off the ground to where my feet dangle in the air. I desperately tried to get my hair out of my eyes by shaking my head, huffing and puffing, trying to move the offending curls with no such luck. Black, thick fingers pushed my hair out of the way, and when I saw what was waiting for me, I quickly dropped my head back down.

Nope. Nada. Not today, Satan.

I suddenly fall and crumble to the rocky ground with a groan. FUCK! I struggled to sit up when I heard a chuckle and look back up. The fucking gorilla was laughing at me. A seven-foot-silver looking gorilla was chuckling at me as he scratched his monkey balls. Yeah, you heard that right. Big old hairy monkey balls were staring me in the face before I looked away in shock. For a moment, I wondered if Lynx would have claimed his were bigger, but again, I was given another shake and caught them jiggling with a sway out of the corner of my eye.

I quickly gaze back up at the nightmare, and the damn

mountain of a primate just showed his teeth in what I could only hope was a smile and not a precursor to be eating me.

Wait? Do they eat meat?

Dammit! I guess I should have paid more attention in biology class.

He lumbered off, leaving behind what I would expect a fantasy world to look like in a post-apocalyptic world.

A huge black marble door looked broken in half from the top down, and it was standing in the middle of the construction zone. All around it stood what can only be described as a fairy tale from the Grimm Brothers' book. I'm talking about creatures that towered over me, and not all of them were pretty or wearing clothes.

I tried to take it all in, but honestly, I was losing it. This wasn't real. *I tried taking in a deep breath, but my lungs refused to work. Panicking, I decided to focus on one object, any object, as my eyes bounced around.*

The door!

My eyes swung back to the black door, and I swear I saw red eyes looking back at me right before the world started spinning and blissful blackness called me under.

·｡·＊·｡·

The others around me gasp as they come out of the immersion. I wasn't expecting to hear my own thoughts like that. I thought I would just see what I saw at the time or maybe truly just have the VR experience, not live it! Or is it re-live, since it's a memory, even if I can't remember it?

"Damn. Did anyone else feel all of that?" Ryker asks beside me.

"Yeah, that was enlightening," Knots says, clearing his throat.

"I could actually feel the gravel along my body. Is that normal?" Chester asks in awe.

I stare at the blank screen as Knox kneels and pushes against my legs. I open my thighs to allow him closer, and he lays his head on my belly. Instinctively, I run my fingers through his hair and mumble, "I'm okay. It was just weird. That's all."

"Wow, bestie. I never knew you had so much to say! It's like you have something that holds you back all the time," Moni says in awe, before looking at Chester with concern.

"It's called a filter. Some people have it. But I think Rez might have been too shocked to bypass hers. She doesn't seem to have a problem turning it off most of the time," Lynx laughs.

Moni looks at Chester with concern. "Should I have one, or was she just broken?" she asks.

Chester, without missing a beat, wins the best boyfriend award tonight. "You're perfect," he says, kissing her on the forehead.

Zeke clears his throat, grabbing our attention. "Are you ready for the next file marked Human Council?"

"Do we know whose mind we will be in?" Knox asks. The question is meant for Zeke, but he keeps his eyes locked on mine. His expression is a mix of sympathy and determination, and I can't help but attempt to iron out the crease between his brows with the pad of my thumb before kissing his forehead. *He so has my heart right now.*

"No clue. But I have a good idea that since it says council, it will be a council member and not Rez this time," Zeke answers with a shrug.

"I'm okay," I reassure Knox and lean forward to give him another kiss. "Thank you."

"Anytime, kitten."

After everyone gets settled again, I look over and find Zeke looking at me with sadness in his eyes. *Shit. I really need to work on my relationship with him.* I give him a smile, and he brightens slightly before Levi clears his throat to get our attention.

"Before we continue, did everyone see Diablo's eyes at the end?" Levi asks "Does anyone have any guesses as to why he suddenly woke up?"

Fuck!

I guess since Lynx lost his memories, I'm the only person who knows the real reason I was brought to Purgatory. I haven't had a chance to have a pow-wow with everyone, so I might as well come clean.

"I might have the answer to your question," I confess. "The first day I met Knox, I needed some time to myself." Knox jerks back, knowing that I meant the day he played that prank on me. But I quickly give him a soft smile, letting him know there're no hard feelings and continue. "So, I found a little glade, and Anwen came to me. She showed me how supernaturals were formed from the Four Horsemen before they became Diablo. Anwen showed me a scene where Diablo sacrificed himself to end the resistance. She then explained how Purgatory worked on a fine line of checks and balances and how it's been out of whack lately. Then she showed me the image of me lying in the rubble before anyone showed up. I just didn't know that was what I was looking at." I go on, telling them that Diablo apparently pulled me here to help restore balance to the realms, but I have no clue how I'm supposed to do that.

"Shit, now that's heavy," Zeke comments, slowly shaking his head as his eyes go glassy. It's as if he's imagining what it was like for me.

"Well, that would explain why you were found by Diablo and why he's dormant again," Levi murmurs to himself as he rubs his chin. I swear his mannerisms are so much like Lucifer's.

Knox pulls himself tighter against me as Knots gives me a contemplative look, and I catch Ryker's fleeting look of worry before he winks and gives a sly smile.

"Such a badass," he says.

Knox gives me one more tight squeeze before moving back to his seat next to Ryker.

"Aww yeah. That's how my bestie does it. She doesn't do anything easy. She makes you work for it. Can't do anything easy. No handjobs. No blowjobs. No quick fixes for the world. Let's just save all the realms." Lynx winks and does a little wiggle in his seat.

A sigh escapes me at his antics, along with a giggle. He's just too crazy.

"Don't worry, bestie; that's why we're here. We won't let you fail. We're Batman to your Robin," Moni cheers!

I think it's the other way around, but who am I to ruin her vision?

"Either way, you're stuck with us, ma chérie," JP says and blows me a kiss.

"Thanks," I reply, looking over at Zeke once again. "Want to start up the next clip? I know I'm ready."

"Everyone else ready?" he asks before sending us back into the Matrix once again.

CHAPTER 12

No big Deal, Only History Repeating Itself

Rez

Nodding to a few students as I passed, I quickly made my way to the medical building.

"Good morning, Dean Caldron. You're the last to show up," the redhead receptionist said as a greeting. "If you'll follow me?" I nodded in thanks, and she escorted me back toward the observation wing. Reaching the hall, she buzzed me in where there were guards posted at the other end.

Hmm, that's unusual. Maybe this really was an emergency. Since when do we need guards around the school?

Carl popped his head out of the door to my left, pushing his dark-rimmed glasses up on his nose before waving me over. I walked into a decent-sized room with all white walls and hardly any art, besides a calendar with a picture of a kitten that said: "Just hang in there." There's a filing cabinet against the far wall, and a frosted window embedded in the wall to the right of the door. The rest of our rag-tag group was already seated at a long wooden table in the middle of the room.

Daniel sat in his impeccable three-piece suit, with his auburn hair slicked back, His assistant, Jeffery—who was furiously writing notes—was left standing behind him. As Mayor, he'd already taken his seat at the head of the table.

Even without seeing his face, I would have noticed Jessup and his shiny shaved head a mile away. His fury rolled off of him in palpable waves while he was berating a few guards in the corner. My instinct was to diffuse the situation, but I knew better than to get between the Chief of Police and his men. He'd been on edge lately. I needed to make a mental note to make sure he was shifting enough for the release.

Lilith had even joined us—for whatever this was— and was seated to the right of Daniel. Her four assistants stood surrounding her, which was over the top in my opinion, but she'd taken to needing the extra attention over the last few centuries. Each of them held tablets filled with the latest designs and fabric choices, waiting to hand them off when she motioned. Well shit, if Lilith isn't at her design table or in Hell, then things are serious!

She'd been spending a lot of time at the office or in Hell, and I'd been grateful for that. Why did I have to be the one to bear the hassle of watching her? Scratch that; I knew the reason. This was the only time my powers became a curse; I was the only one who could read her. She hadn't been the same since her imprisonment in Hell. Though there were still moments when she was her old self, the one I mated with and loved more than anything, and the others saw it too. Over time, those appearances had lessened, and it wasn't enough. So, I'd been appointed "the man" she'd be seen with and the one to keep an eye on her.

Carl would have jumped at the chance, but with her being so different, we got him to see reason. We agreed to allow her around our children and be the mother figure they sorely needed, but until we all agreed and felt the same, we were being cautious. We wanted to trust our mate, but something was obviously wrong with her, and we still hadn't figured out what.

"Thank you for coming so soon. Please have a seat." Carl motioned to the table, and I took my seat next to Lilith, nodding my head in greeting toward the rest of the room. Glancing at the frosted window, I noticed a blank TV monitor up in the right-hand corner I hadn't seen from the room's entrance. Carl moved to the center of the window, grabbing my attention. Watching him pace for a few moments while he gathered his thoughts, I observed his appearance and feelings. His salt and pepper hair was disheveled, and his short beard was untrimmed. His pristine lab coat barely hung on his tall, thin frame. On any given day, it could be normal, except for his eyes. Yellow flecks shined through his chocolate brown eyes, betraying his nerves and excitement. What is he excited about?

After another lap, he stopped his pacing and faced us with his fingers laced in front of him. "We had a breach in the wards as of thirty minutes ago," he stated.

Gasps rang out around the room, and the looks of shock mirrored my own.

Anticipating our reaction, he gave us a moment before he continued on. "Obviously, this is a serious matter and the reason for this meeting," he said. As I watched, I noticed his eyes flare once again with excitement.

This is a fucking disaster, not something to be excited about, I thought to myself.

We haven't had a breach in over 3000 years, not since the Rebels last attacked.

"What do you mean, the wards have been breached? That's a mistake, surely," Jessup roared, slamming his fist down on the table. Everyone sat up straighter in their seats, including me. Having a short fuse on a good day made Jessup a loose cannon.

Since he was already agitated when I first walked in, this reaction made him downright lethal.

The last thing we needed in this small, crowded room was a pissed off Shifter. Sitting back, I watched as he fought to contain his temper. I had to agree with his outrage, though; the reports must be wrong.

Clearing his throat, Carl continued his pacing, while fidgeting with his glasses. I wondered why he even wore them since he'd never actually needed them, but the fidgeting was a nervous habit that I've told him a million times he needed to work on.

"The wards detected activity from Diablo. The guards were notified, and they found a young woman unconscious in the rubble." He motioned to the officers in the corners. "Captain Brooks and his team detained her and brought her in for me to check on her injuries. From my initial observation, she's human." A few murmurs went up around the room, but I didn't miss the accusatory glare from Jessup to Captain Brooks.

"Human? Here?"

"That's Impossible."

"This has to be a joke."

I couldn't tell who was talking with the state of chaos that erupted, but my attention turned to the window in front of me when it changed to opaque. "I ordered a blood test, and I'm awaiting the results." Carl's voice carried over the dying murmurs.

The monitor flickered to life, showing a picture of a young woman. The sounds of shuffling feet accompanied my own as we all moved over to the window for a closer look.

The young woman looked like she was in the middle of a nightmare, her body convulsing and twitching as we watched through the window. What's going on? Is she hurt?

"To keep her from waking, I called Delvin. He placed her in a heavy Tranqspell. Even though she seems human, she

continued breaking through his lesser spells," Carl said, answering my internal question.

"So," Lilith spoke up. "She has strong mental capabilities then if you had to call in Delvin to subdue her. No one's been able to surpass his Tranquil spell before; well, except you, Matthew," she purred, giving me a look. A smile crept onto her secretive lips as she turned back to assess the young lady. My stomach clenched just thinking about her last 'project' in Hell. She'd always loved the strong-willed types and often enjoyed the challenge of breaking them, slowly. The Demon couldn't help herself; it was in her blood. It was one of the reasons we had our own chasm between us. If this human girl had already caught Lilith's attention, then no pits in Hell would keep her safe.

Murmurs started back up among the assistants, trying to offer solutions. A bunch of brown-nosers if you ask me. That's why I'd only stuck with Abs, and that relationship started out as friends at school.

"Lock her up," one of Lilith's stooges threw out.

"Just kill her," Jeffrey said flippantly, before going back to his scribbling.

"Why don't we just wipe her memories if she has any, kick her back through the gate, and reinforce the wards so she can't pass back through?" Captain Brooks asked, quickly snapping his mouth shut when Jessup sent him a look.

"I wish it were that simple, Captain," Daniel said, walking over to the window and peering at the young woman. "You forget, she has already crossed over. The only way to get her back to Earth is for her to obtain the ability to cross, or if Diablo sends her back himself, but why would he so soon after bringing her here?" Quirking an eyebrow at the captain, he asked, "You were there shortly after she came through; is Diablo fully functional now?"

The young male, being Captain Brooks, stepped up and shook his head no. "Dormant, sir."

"That's what I thought," Daniel continued. "That means he brought her here for a reason. It's not the fact that our wards are weak. It means our oldest and most powerful gate, which we thought was destroyed, woke up and allowed her access."

That fact alone mesmerized me. I pressed my hand against the window and traced her outline with my fingers, intrigued by the mystery surrounding her.

"Diablo stopped working thirty centuries ago, after the rebellion, so there has to be a reason she's here," Jessup said in a gruff voice. I already knew what he was thinking, that she was a spy for the Rebels somehow. It wouldn't surprise me to know they were taking extreme avenues to topple our system. But there's no way that Diablo would allow her to cross if she was.

I peered at the monitor that showed the young woman's face. The surrounding conversations faded out, becoming background noise as I watched her for a few minutes.

Her long, curly brunette strands fell into her face and her nose scrunched up like she smelled something foul. Beauty marks run across her nose and along her cheeks.

I wondered if Levi or one of the guys would notice her. She seemed to have an inner beauty that even normal "humans" didn't have. Could she be more than human?

What brought you here? Why did Diablo finally wake up and drop you on our doorstep? Narrowing my eyes, I focused on her aura but came up blank, like a blanket was dampening her somehow. What are you?

"Is it possible to question her without hurting her? If we can do it without her knowledge and nothing goes wrong, then we wouldn't have to take drastic measures in the first place, right?" I asked. I felt eyes on my back as I gazed at the monitor, but I kept looking at her anyway before turning around to find Carl. My question must have given him a lot to consider, because he continued to stand there with his hand under his chin, looking thoughtful.

Daniel cleared his throat to draw everyone's attention back to where he sat at the table. "If she's burning through Delvin's Tranqspells, there's a good chance my thrall won't work on her. Maybe adding the white cuffs while another spell is cast will allow us to gain information before we make any hasty decisions."

Carl brightened up. "Yes! That's an excellent idea," he said, then mumbled incoherently for a moment. "I've never done this with a human, but let's get this interrogation started," he called over his shoulder while walking out the door.

A chill ran down my spine at that word, and I flinched.

Interrogation.

It seemed such a harsh word for such a young woman, but I understand the caution. However, we needed her to trust us, and interrogating her for merely showing up unconscious was a huge red flag saying: "Hey! We can't be trusted." We needed that trust more than anything.

A few weeks ago, the earth's world leaders received hints they weren't alone out there. There was a fine line to balance if we indeed came out of the proverbial closet, especially when politics were involved. The movies, books, and entertainment that featured us lately should have softened the blow, hopefully.

Right now, though, we were still in the shadows, waiting for our time. Presumably, we would have a better outcome than we did a few hundred years ago. The Salem Witch Trials were still a sore subject for the magic users after all this time. I should know; my grandparents were among them.

The monitor crackled to life as I watched Delvin, Carl, and two guards step into the room. They propped her up against the bed, handcuffing her with white dampening cuffs, and then inserted a syringe of orange liquid into her arm.

Carl pulled up a chair and took a small tablet out of his lab coat to start his questioning. A guard rushing into our room *pulled our attention away from the window, and I immediately picked up the sense this guy was petrified.*

"Speak," Dan commanded.

"Sir, what should we do with her pet?" he asked, practically shaking as he pointed to the girl in question.

What pet?

This time coming out of the immersion is easier, but that might be because we were in Dean Caldron's head. It was weird yet refreshing to see things from his perspective, and it lines up with what he had told me from before.

"Man, that was trippy," Lynx says, shaking his head.

"Yeah, tell me about it," JP agrees.

"Isn't that how your talents work when you see people's experiences?" Ryker asks, leaning forward to rub his temples with his palms.

"Pftt. Not at all. It's like watching a movie, like I'm right behind them or next to them," JP says, getting animated as he moves his hands around in front of him. "It's not as if I *am* them, and I definitely don't hear their inner dialogue either," JP retorts, shaking his head in surprised confusion. "Oh, wait, I do," he laughs. "It's just different. I don't know how to explain it."

"Who's Delvin?" I ask, wondering who the guy is and why he seemed so important.

"Delvin is... or was a high mage, only second to my dad," Levi answers.

Was?

"Was? What happened to him?" Lynx asks, picking up my question and running with it.

Levi sighs and rubs the bridge of his nose, but it's Zeke that speaks up.

"We've been trying to get that information. Your interrogation was actually the last time anyone saw him," he supplies. "I've been trying to track his last movements, but after he left the hospital, it's like he disappeared. Poof. Gone! So I don't know if the Sulks got him, the Rebels, or what."

I sit, somewhat devastated that one of the strongest and most powerful mages just up and disappeared right after seeing me. How did that come about? If it wasn't for everything else that's happened during my time in Purgatory, I would just call it odd, but I can't let it go. It can't be a weird coincidence. The room goes quiet as we all take in what we've learned in this short amount of time until Moni speaks up out of nowhere.

"I knew Matthew couldn't have been on the side of evil. He's just too sweet. But that Jeffrey guy has to be bad news to say Rez needed to die. That's my bestie he's talking about," Moni says, standing up on the sofa cushion.

"Easy there, Moni. I'm sure he just didn't know any better and wasn't thinking." Chester tries to calm Moni down while pulling on her arm.

"Well, I say we go shave him bald and leave him outside for the butterbees!" she demands, throwing her tiny fist in the air.

What is her fascination with those damn bees?

"It's not Jeffrey we have to worry about," Knox says, catching my attention.

"What do you mean?" I ask, giving him a worried look. This is the first I've heard about needing to worry about anyone before.

Knox stands up and pulls out his wallet from his sleep pants. *Who keeps their wallet in their sleep pants?* I mean, I guess since we're in Hell, we really don't have anything that's ours. My knife and phone are on me as well, but I'm still in my day clothes. To each their own, though.

He hands me a scrap piece of paper.

"What is this?" I ask, looking at a list of scribbles.

"I found that right after I caught Brooks snooping where he shouldn't be," he confesses. "Remember when we... ugh... got stuck together?" he asks, his cheeks turning a slight pink.

I snort at how cute he sounds.

"Yeah. Our first time," I say and squint up at him. "What does this have to do with it?" I ask.

"Well, I was on my way to have my appointment with Dad, but I ran into his secretary instead. He left me a letter since he had another meeting he had to attend. That's what I found on her desk that didn't belong."

"Wasn't that like Tuesday morning?" I ask, making sure I had my days right.

"Yeah. Two days ago, almost." Knox nods.

I look over the paper while Ryker and Lynx lean over my shoulder and take in the list of my actions. It looks like whoever wrote it did it so fast that it's in what my mother called chicken scratch.

> Got roundabout opposite princes
> Hanging around Princes, befriending them?
> Grandparents cut her off
> Rumors are successful about the Human
> Showing no powers so far
> No idea of her species yet
> Unsuccessful attempt to grab target at Lilith's ritual
> Lyrical was successful with blood sample

What. The. Hell?

"How do they know my grandparents cut me off?" I ask, stunned that whoever wrote that knows about something so personal. "The only person who knew was Lynx." I point my thumb in his direction.

"It had to be tapped," Zeke supplied. "Before we get our phones, they normally sweep them for bugs and hook up the internet through the IT department. Question is: why would they need to bug your phone?" he asks.

I don't know, but I don't feel like carrying it around anymore if the damn thing is being traced. I pull it out of my pocket, and Levi hands it off to Zeke for me.

JP reaches over the back of the loveseat and gently grabs the paper from me to see it for himself, and Moni and Chester move over to look as he shows Levi. "How did Lyrical get your blood? I thought you were going to wait for Steinbeck?" JP asks, giving me a look of shock.

"I did wait," I explain. "At least I think I did." I think back to that day and what happened leading up to it. Lynx was missing and presumed dead, the dorm room was trashed from the fight and my meltdown earthquake, and everything was crumbling around me. I'm not even sure how I functioned that day, but I remember the visit with Lyrical, and I know it was Steinbeck who took my blood the next day.

"Levi, are you able to find the magical imprint off of that?" Knox asks, pointing to the paper.

Levi takes the paper and rubs it in his hand for a moment before handing it back to JP. "Yeah. I should be able to do it in a few days. If we can get the ingredients, I could do it while we are here."

"Thanks, man."

"Here you go, Rez. I got the tracker," Zeke says, holding up a little silver capsule. I wouldn't have guessed that to be a tracker if I saw it lying around the room. He hands me back the phone and gives the device to Levi. Holding it between his fingers, he whispers a few words and the device changes to dust, falling to the floor.

"Thanks." I give them a weak smile as I slide the phone back into my pocket when the memory hits me, and I bolt upright in my seat. "JP! You remember when you answered the door that morning and the movers came in?" I ask JP and he nods his head, probably wondering where this is going. "Well, I felt a pinch on my arm while I was distracted by the door, and she apologized, saying she didn't mean to scratch me. Maybe she took my blood then?" I offer, hoping that helps answer that question.

"That could have been it. You had different nurses that came in and checked on you, right?" JP confirms.

"But the question is: why would they even want Rez's blood? What is the purpose?" Lynx asks, his brows pulled down in worry that somehow dull his turquoise eyes.

"It can be used for a lot of things, depending on how much they took, or how strong your powers were at the time it was taken," Levi says, giving me a thoughtful look. "It can be used for anything as mundane as seeing what species you are, looking for genetic markers like your birth parents, or used in different awakening spells that use blood so the caster doesn't have to use their own."

"What's the atypical uses for taking her blood?" Knots asks.

Levi swallows audibly and doesn't meet my eyes for a moment. I already know I'm not going to like what he has to say when his hazel eyes meet mine and he has a worry line between his brows. "Tracking her movements, sending her to her closest kin, regardless of differences in both time and space, to slowly corrupting her blood for the spellcaster's purpose."

Well, I'm up shit's creek without a fucking paddle.

There's a bump at my closet doors that causes me to pause and give it my attention. The doors are slightly ajar, though I remember closing them. Zeke gets up and fully opens them.

129

Knox quickly joins him when they walk inside. I hold my breath for the few seconds they are gone, and Zeke walks back out, holding up a small gold earring.

"Missing an earring?" he says with a clenched jaw.

My ears are pierced, but I haven't worn earrings since I got here, and Moni hasn't either.

"Whose is that, and how did it end up in my closet?" I ask.

"Trometh, by the smell of it," Knox answers as he walks back in. "And I have no idea. There's no door or signs of a secret passage that I can find," he growls out. His frustration slams into me, making me gasp. I send soothing vibes down our link as Knox closes his eyes for a brief moment to calm down. He takes a deep breath and slowly exhales before returning to his seat.

"You okay?" I ask, and he simply nods before swinging his attention back to Zeke, who lays down the lone earring on the desk. Zeke leaves the closet doors open and turns back to face us, shrugging.

"I don't know what to make of that," he confesses before sitting back down at the computer desk.

"I say we take it for what it looks like. Someone was trying to eavesdrop, and it was either Trometh or someone who wanted us to believe it was him," Chester helpfully speaks up.

"Agreed. Either way, we can confront him with that earring tomorrow," Levi instructs.

Great. Now I have to worry about the purple nurple Demon dude.

CHAPTER 13
Satanic Deals

Rez

After the eye-opening files, we agreed that there was obviously more at play than possessed Lilith just trying to help me with my bind and said our final goodnight to everyone. Zeke puts the room back together, leaving the earring on a nightstand, and we *finally* change into night clothes. We talk for a bit about what we want to do together once we get back to Nova until we pass out with him being the big spoon. Honestly, it's perfect for me.

The next morning, I wake up with a start as a bulldozer bangs on our door. It looks like we managed to get about five hours of sleep before Bez yells that it's almost time for breakfast and we better not keep Lilith waiting. Since he doesn't give us a time limit, we opt to just brush our teeth and get dressed as fast as possible. It's kinda nice to get ready with Zeke, even though we're in a rush. It reminds me of what a "normal" relationship would be like. It's the little things, like catching him smiling at me. Or the other way around, and he catches me doing the same, making my stomach flutter at the domestic bliss of it all.

Zeke wears a green tank top and black shorts, which bring out his red hair and slight scruff, along with his green eyes. Damn, he looks yummy. I dress in a lightweight gray shoulder crop hoodie top, and gray and pink leggings with a pocket. I make sure the material is light enough to combat the heat down here.

Since I still don't know what to do with my knife, Zeke suggests a holster that I can attach to my thigh until we get home. Impressed with the simple solution, I have him conjure one from the closet to add to my wardrobe as I turn to grab Trometh's earring from the nightstand, only to find it missing.

We look around the room for a few minutes before giving up.

"Did you find it?" I ask, straightening out my clothes from looking under the bed.

"No. Someone probably came in and took it while we slept. There's nothing we can do about it. Just keep an eye out and tell everyone that it's gone." He shrugs and hands me the holster for my knife.

Once I have it secure, he gives me a heated head-to-toe perusal, and I return a smug grin as we head out to the hall.

"You should stay armed because you never know when you'll need it down here. Plus, it's sexy as hell," he remarks.

Ryker gives a wolf whistle in agreement as he exits his room, and we make our way down the hall.

"Just so you guys know, the earring we found last night is gone. We looked and couldn't find it. We think someone took it while we were sleeping," Zeke tells the group.

"Oh no! Do we need to set up booby traps?" Moni asks, her bark turning pale white as she takes a sip of her coffee.

"No. But it means we have nothing to confront Trometh with," JP explains.

"Or a way to find out who set him up," Chester adds.

Knots leans in to me as he passes. "You look sexy with that knife attached to you."

"I don't even know how to use it. I just got one to look badass while looking for Lynx," I admit shamelessly.

"I don't mind teaching you," Ryker offers, smirking as we walk into the dining room. I'm sure he doesn't mind *teaching me,* but I doubt he's thinking about knives at all, since his eyes glow an electric blue.

"Teach her what? How to wash her mouth out with soap?" Lucifer butts in.

"Now, where's the fun in that? I was just going along with that saying, you know, How many curses does it take to crack the foundation of Lucifer's mansion?" I smile sweetly at our host as I sit down in the seat Knots pulls out for me. If I'm not mistaken, Lucifer's lips slightly twitch; I'm taking it as a smile.

Knots sits down next to me as JP smoothly slides in on my other side. Levi takes his normal seat at the end, but Ryker stands by me for a moment. Zeke slides into the seat across from me and gives me a smile before putting a napkin on his lap.

"I was offering Rez lessons in how to use the knife," Ryker helpfully supplies.

"You? With a blade?" Astaroth quirks an eyebrow as he comes in and places a platter of cooked eggs down before us.

"I'm trained in knife combat, yes," Ryker says with pride.

"Hmm. We'll see. I want to see you in the training room after breakfast," Astaroth says as he takes a seat.

Ryker nods his head and leans down to give me a brief kiss, but I move past his lips and whisper in his ear, "Is this where I kiss you goodbye and say it's been real?" I try to hold back a giggle as he gives me a cruel smile.

"Nah, temptress. It's where I get a goodbye quickie in the hallway bathroom, where I bend you over the counter and take that wet cunt over and over again until you beg for mercy." His words have my pussy already begging, but not for him to stop... The greedy hussy wants a trip to the bathroom. Ryker's eyes glow an even brighter blue as he inhales deeply, closing his eyes. While he exhales, a shudder runs through his body before he licks his lips and leans back to whisper in my ear. "Then Astaroth will hand me my ass. But at least I'll enjoy the appetizer. You're delicious," he says before playfully biting my lip.

"Ryker! Didn't your mother teach you not to play with your food?" Murmur teases, walking in from the kitchen.

Ryker slowly stands up and gives him a saucy smile. "No. She didn't," he says as he walks to an empty chair.

"I'm pretty sure I did. But then again, you don't always follow the rules," Lilith says, walking in with a smile.

Today she's wearing head-to-toe black. Black jeans, a black tank top, and black boots.

"What's the occasion?" Levi asks, putting his napkin on his lap.

"Oh! I have a wonderful meeting planned with your fathers, and my ex-husband. We have a few questions for him, especially since he was the person behind my possession. We need to know why," she explains while sitting down and unwrapping her utensils.

Trometh shuffles in wearing the same clothes from yesterday, which I'm beginning to think is his uniform, and hands Lilith a yellow paper. I glance at his ears, and he's not missing an earring. So either he conjured up a new one, came in and grabbed it last night, or someone set him up, but I can't imagine who would do that. As it is, I don't know which explanation I prefer. "Thank you, Trometh," she says before opening the letter and reading it. Her face falls the more she reads until she throws it up in the air and it disappears into dust. "Well, it seems your fathers won't be joining me after all. They have to stay behind and work on the aftermath of the attack at school," she tells us with a clenched jaw.

Shit! I forgot about the school.

She looks at us, waving off our concern. "No one was hurt, just some damage to buildings. They'll be arranging the repairs and setting up better defenses. That's all. Nothing to worry about. You are better off staying here anyway. Today's classes have been canceled, so just think of it as an extended three-day weekend," she says flippantly as she fills up her plate. Noticing no one else is eating, she waves her hand, sending the dishes off in another carousel like she did the night before.

"At least until Sunday," Zeke murmurs.

"What's on Sunday?" Bez inquires with his mouth full. I'm so tempted to point out that he needs to work on his manners but I highly doubt the friendly murderer would appreciate that.

"Levi's ceremony," Knox supplies.

"Huh?" Knots asks, his bite of food dropping off of his fork.

Fuck, did I not tell him?

All the dishes freeze as Lilith looks up at Levi. "You're taking your oath this weekend and you didn't invite me, your own mother?" Lilith looks at me, and my jaw drops as my hands come up in defense.

"Woah. First of all, if we were taking that oath, I would have invited *everyone,* even my new male bestie, Lucy," I say, giving him a hesitant look.

"Watch it, kid," Lucifer growls, but he doesn't smite me, so I'm calling it another win!

"So don't look at me. It's my evil nemesis that's trying to steal my man," I say as I look at Levi. He gives me a sad smile and reaches over to squeeze my hand before addressing his mother.

"It has come to my attention that... I have certain obligations that I need—"

"Oh cut the crap, Levi," Zeke says, looking at him in annoyance. He turns and looks at Lilith. "He's being blackmailed."

"By whom?" Lilith demands with fire igniting in her eyes. Her jaw clenches tight, and I catch her tail twitch along with the slight extending of her wings.

Wait, how did I miss a tail? She has a tail?

I elbow Knots and point to the plate of scrambled eggs in front of him. There's no point in not eating just because she's getting caught up on our drama. We start manually passing around bowls of food, and once I have tullé strips, fruit, and eggs on my plate, I dig in.

I'm actually surprised he didn't mention any of this when I ran away after dinner last night. You would have thought they would have had a mother–son moment, but, oh well. I guess I wasn't gone that long.

"King Elverson," Knox growls. Well, there's no question how he feels about him.

"Alrin Elverson? As in Emer's father?" Lilith asks, looking at us. "Why would he be blackmailing you?" she says, her words deliberate and cautious.

"It seems Princess Emer didn't appreciate the word no," Levi grumbles while pouring himself some juice.

"You know what? She did mention at our training class that once she had you bound to her, it was only a matter of time before she had the others. Do you think she was just after my harem?" I question, and Lucifer and Bez both snicker.

I snap my head in their direction. "What's so funny?" I ask with an attitude. If my eyes could flame like theirs, they would absolutely be sparking right now.

"Harem," Lucifer says mockingly. "Harems are mostly for

strong, powerful females, sweetheart," he says conde-scendingly.

"Shows what he knows," Lynx mumbles, but we all hear him.

Before anyone else can chime in on my behalf, I give him my own smile and begin singing in my head: *"Jesus loves me! This I know, For the Bible tells me so; Little ones to Him belong; They are weak, but He is strong. Yes, Jesus loves me!"*

The room starts shaking and something in the kitchen falls with a shatter. Murmur jumps from his seat and runs into the other room as Astaroth and Bez jump up to hold various pictures along the wall. My guys reach out and grab the food to hold it steady, and all I do is look at Lucifer as he stares right back at me.

Never the one to back down for obvious reasons, he smiles, and in the blink of an eye, my body is airborne. I'm whipped around until my back hits something hard and my lungs give out an *oof* as all the air leaves me.

A hand closes around my throat, cutting off any sound I hope to make as my eyes pop open wide. Lucifer's blue-green orbs stare into mine from less than a foot away as I fight for breath. He leans into me while loosening his grip slightly, allowing me to take in a shallow breath, and I can't help noticing my chest is rubbing against his.

Dear Jesus, why is this so fucking hot?

I hear the swooshing of the fire from where I'm up against the wall, but I can't see it. The room is black, except for a red haze, yet I can clearly make out Lucifer's face. Gone is the dining room and everyone else. It's just me and the devil.

Hot damn!

"You, Nerezza, are testing my patience!" he growls. His sweet smelling-breath runs across my skin, and I almost melt.

"You... love... it... though," I wheeze out.

He steps back, tightening his hold on my neck, and my

arms fly up to my throat, trying to release his grip. I kick out to no avail; it's hopeless. My lungs burn as they fight to take in oxygen, and my heart's beating so fast, I'm surprised it hasn't already jumped ship. Black dots creep into my vision, and I panic. Again, I kick both legs out and twist my body in the air to turn, relieving some of the pressure and bring my hand out to knock his hand away from my throat, but it's clear that he allowed me to get that far.

"Not that easy to disarm, am I Nerezza?" he says in a bored tone. In a flash, he slams me into the rock wall, twisting my arm into my back.

"Fuck!" I scream.

"It seems that not only are you dead set on trying to bring down my house, but you're completely untrained," he spits, then lets me go.

I spin around and try to take in my environment, but it's hopeless. I still can't see shit besides Lucifer's face; though, I can hear some kind of river. Other than that, I can't make anything else out.

"I'll make a deal with you," Lucifer says, practically daring me.

"Nah-uh!" I say, shaking my finger proudly, unaffected. "I know better than to make a deal with the Devil."

"This one is more or less going to benefit me," he says. Stepping closer to me, suddenly his wings flare out as they ruffle in a gust of wind that comes by.

If I didn't know better, I'd say he was protecting me.

"I'm already bored," I say, keeping a close eye on him.

"You stop deliberately trying to tear down my house, and L.A.M.B. will train you," he says, throwing back his shoulders like that should mean something to me. The longer I stay in this room, the more my eyesight begins to accommodate. At least I can make out more of Lucifer, or maybe it's the fact I'm picking up on his inner glow.

I arch an eyebrow at him and blink a few times until he shifts his stance. *Ha. I made the Devil uncomfortable. I still got it.*

"First of all, what happens if I accidentally slip and use curse words or those *bad* words down here? I'm not perfect; I'll think them or say them occasionally. It's a part of me. And second, what's so great about L.A.M.B. and your training?" I cock a hip and place my hands on them. I'm not sure if it's false bravado or real, but hey, fake it till you make it.

Lucifer looks at me for a moment and laughs. Straight up belly laughs to the point he almost falls over, and I go slack jawed. His laughter is hypnotic, and I can't help but start laughing with him just because you have to admit this is a crazy situation.

"Nerezza Taylor. You are a unique... creature," he says, shaking his head.

"Is that a good or bad thing?" I ask the ruler of Hell.

"I haven't made up my mind, yet. Although to answer your question, your accidental slip ups will not count against you, but no more of the shit you just pulled in the dining room." He stares at me.

"Okay!" I say sarcastically and throw in an eye roll.

"Let me give you a brief lesson on L.A.M.B. We are the original ones that fell. The first fighters. Astaroth is our weapons smith. Bez is our vengeance Demon—he knows how to control and wield HellFire. Murmur knows too much shit about mental fortitude and shields. And I... Well, I handle the rest. When you have time. I will teach you what they can't. Actually, I know Matthew well and can arrange for you to come down here for your specials to get your training."

"Well, that almost sounds too good to pass up. So..." I chew on my lower lip to look like I'm thinking. "I'm gonna have to pass unless you sweeten the deal," I say, raising my eyebrows.

Lucifer mimics my expression but his is from shock. "WHAT?" he shouts. "No one has ever said no to any of my offers before."

"Well then, I guess my name is now No One, because I am."

Lucifer's eyes blink a blood red before he closes his eyes and takes a few deep breaths. I fight the urge to tell him he would have better luck with his stress if he were to get into child's pose. Something tells me he wouldn't appreciate my suggestion, but yoga really might help him. Aww fuck it.

"Aww. You know... yoga might help y—"

Lucifer's head jolts up as he gives me a wide-eyed stare. Anyone who's ever been in trouble knows that stare. The one where your parent is on the edge of snapping, and all you have to do is breathe and that straw will snap, and it might be the last thing you'll ever do.

"Nevermind," I whisper as I shrink back into myself.

He closes his eyes once more and goes back to doing his Lamaze, or whatever technique he's trying, while I take in the room. I still can't make anything out, but my stomach rumbles, reminding me of what I was doing when I was so rudely interrupted and brought here.

"What would sweeten the deal?" he asks while his eyes are still closed.

"Throw in the option to train everyone in my party, help me figure out my powers, and you got a deal," I say, holding out my hand.

CHAPTER 14

Kiss the Booboo

Levi

The room suddenly stops shaking, and a few of the guys laugh.

"Just like the one that landed us here," JP chuckles nervously.

"Or the earthquake we felt a few weeks ago, huh?" Ryker jokes.

"Yeah, but we at least know wh—"

"Where's Rez?" Knots asks, jumping from his chair.

"Should we be worried that Lucifer is gone too?" Moni asks as her bark cycles through a light teal and pale white.

Chester reaches for her coffee and coaxes her to drink it. Once she takes a sip, her bark returns to green.

"Nonsense. He probably took her to a private room to talk. Continue eating," Lilith says.

I look at my companions and easily pick up their unease, but there's not much I can do. I've been to Hell before, but I've never been to L.A.M.B.'s. residence, so I wouldn't even know where to look for her. Unfortunately, we have to trust

Lilith and hope she understands how much Rez means to all of us.

"Did I miss anything while I was busy with my little nuisances last night?" Lilith asks as she cuts up her food.

"By nuisances, do you mean the destruction of the Demons that possessed you?" Lynx flat out asks.

I swear, he's got a death wish.

"Why yes. It's a great way to relieve stress. If you ever want to learn, I don't mind teaching you." She looks up, smiling at Lynx. "For some reason, I was outvoted on the council to teach that at the academy, so instead, I fill in to teach where I can."

"One of the things we talked about was how I found a note saying that they were unsuccessful at acquiring a target at Lilith's ritual," Knox says before taking a bite of his biscuit.

He does it the smart way, just throwing it out there to see what happens. I've already talked to Lilith about this, and she said hooded people came in and attacked them, but let's see if her story has changed or if there's any new evidence.

"Is that all it said?" she asks frantically. "It's been driving me nuts, not knowing what happened." Lilith's eyes dart back and forth between Knox, Bez, me, and her plate.

"Lil... calm down," Bez says, grabbing one of her hands.

"NO!" she yells and stands up. "You don't understand what it felt like, to be there with your children or helping a student and then all of a sudden, black out. Or to wake up and find blood on you, not knowing what the fuck you did!" Her entire body shakes as her wings flare out.

Bez stands up and conjures a fire ball, holding it in front of her. "Lilith, look at the fire. Concentrate on the fire."

"I don't want the fucking fire, Bez! I want the truth!" she roars, throwing her hands up and knocking the fire out of his hands. Bez quickly extinguishes it before it catches the room on fire. She starts pacing the short distance at the end of the table as her tail whips manically and her wings flutter about, making it hard for Bez to get close to her. "I should have made those fuckers suffer more. I should have gotten the answers I needed." She turns around to leave but stops suddenly as the room pressurizes, making my ears pop.

Silver smoke appears, and Lucifer is standing in front of Lilith, blocking her way.

"Calm down, Lily. We will get answers. But first, let us have some breakfast before we go skinning, okay?" Lucifer coos.

I hear muffled words coming from behind me, so I get out of my seat and look out the door. Down the hall, Rez is stomping her feet as she mumbles.

I pick up frustration, anger, and amusement from her as I jog up to her. "Rez?" I ask, getting her attention.

"Oh, hey!" she says, smiling up at me.

"Are you okay? Did he hurt you?" I ask, checking her over anyway to see if I can spot any damage. Her hoodie shifts briefly, and I catch discoloration around her neck. Reaching up, I move her collar and fury takes over. There's a bright red mark around her neck that wasn't there a few moments ago.

Without thinking, I turn around and march back into the dining room. Rez yells something, but I pay no attention as my thoughts are set on Mommy dearest's best friend. As soon as I walk into the room, Lucifer stands up at the head of the table, fixing his jacket while everyone is still seated.

I feel Rez come up behind me, pulling on my arm to stop me, but my thoughts are locked on the Devil himself. My first idea is to freeze the fucker. He doesn't get a chance to move, just like he didn't give Rez a chance to get out of his choke hold. Lucifer's eyes go wide in shock, and I feel him pushing against my hold. I'm not even questioning how I'm able to control him without touching him, but I'll take whatever I can right now.

Slowly, I start to pull his arms away from his body. His arms are stretched out completely, but I keep on pulling. I'm going to rip his arms out of their sockets. I'm so focused on hurting him I don't see the blue fist heading straight for me.

"If you would have just listened to me, Murmur wouldn't have needed to deck you," Rez says as she gently places a cooling ointment around my eye.

I hiss and try not to flinch, but that blue fucker can pack a punch. Rez managed to talk me into sitting on the kitchen counter, where I have her between my legs applying healing ointment over my soon to be black eye.

How is it that I've gotten two black eyes in one damn month already?

"I hate to say it, Levi, but you kinda deserved it with how you just marched in there and tried to kick Lucifer's ass," Rez says, kicking me while I'm down. She doesn't say it out of spite, just stating the facts. "I mean, I know why you did. But really, he didn't hurt me too bad. Yes, he held me by my throat, but I tried to fight back because I didn't want to be pinned, and he saw how I wasn't trained." Rez gives me a shrug. "Turns out that was his bargaining chip. I don't purposely take down his house, and he offers to train us." She looks around and sees that we're still alone before she bites her lower lip and glances up at me under her lashes. "I have to admit, though; what you did was kinda hot." Her voice turns husky as she leans further into me.

"Really?" Liking the sound of that, I place my arms on her hips and run my fingers along the exposed skin between her hoodie and jeans.

"Yeah. I mean, to see you come in guns blazing like that. I

didn't know you had it in you. And to see that you would do that for me... It was pretty sexy," she admits.

She blushes, and I can't help but take pride in knowing that even though I got sucker punched, my girl finds it hot.

"Do you know what would really heal your eye right up?" she asks, putting the lid back on the canister.

"What?" I smirk down at her as I slide off of the counter.

"Kiss your boo boos away. But since you have goop all over those, you'll just have to settle for a different type of kiss," she teases as she wraps her arms around my neck.

"Yes, ma'am," I whisper excitedly. Anytime I can get kisses from Rez, it's a good day.

She wraps her arms around my neck and slowly pulls me down until her lips meet mine. I assume she's just going to give me sweet kisses like you would for a boo boo, but... oh no. Not my Rez. I should have known my woman is anything but predictable. I swallow her moans as she presses her body against me and my rapidly growing cock.

Breaking the embrace, she lightly runs her tongue along my bottom lip as we inhale each other's breath. She softly nibbles on my bottom lip. "And it's Mistress... my little pet," she says before biting a little harder on my lip. Not enough to draw blood, but enough to make my dick jump in my pants.

I don't think I'll be able to handle this teasing and walk back out there in front of my family, sporting the world's largest tent ever. Rez slams her mouth back to mine, and I forget all about my current worries. She spins us along the counter a few times, sending us deeper into the kitchen. Our tongues explore each other as she walks me backward until I'm pressed against something firm. Pulling away, I notice we're tucked into a corner behind a massive fridge.

"What ar—"

"Nuh-uh. What kind of boys get rewarded?" She lets out a breathy moan as she runs her hands over the length of me, over my slacks. I try my best to control my breath, but I end up panting as my cock pushes against my zipper.

"Good boys," I manage to get out. I remember how to play this game, and I so want to be good right now.

She gives me a smirk before she licks her lips and reaches for my zipper. Stepping into me again, she licks along my jaw and up to my earlobe.

"Did you enjoy the last time I had you in my mouth?" she whispers, and I nod. *I don't dare answer without her permission.*

"Do you often wonder what it would feel like to come down my throat?" I bite my lip so fucking hard, trying not to answer. My hips buck on their own, pushing my hard-on against her belly, and she gives me a breathy laugh.

If she keeps this up, we won't have to worry about her swallowing anything. It will all be in my damn pants.

"I guess that's answer enough," she says, dropping to her knees. The sound of my zipper falling sounds extremely loud in the quiet room, and that reminds me we're not alone. I quickly mumble an incantation and a silencing bubble surrounds us, and with that settled, I look back down at this goddess on her knees before me as she pulls out my hard shaft.

Her soft hand strokes my cock up and down a few times before she slowly leans in with her tongue out. I'm completely mesmerized from the moment I feel her warm breath hit my slit as she licks up my pre-cum. Her tongue swirls around the head, and I feel her tongue stud run along the edge of my sensitive dick, causing my legs to shake.

She's worked me up so much from just this little tease that I have to squeeze the edge of the counter to keep myself from bucking my hips. I want her wet mouth on me, and I'm willing to do anything she asks just to feel her again.

Her hooded gray eyes look up between her brunette curls, and she smirks while she strokes my length. "Be good and don't make a sound, and I'll swallow everything you give me," she promises. My eyes go wide as I take in what she just said.

Shit, really? I've never had a girl swallow. I've always had women say it's below them to ever do such a thing and I should never even ask.

I quickly nod my head like a lovesick fool, and she rewards me with a smirk before swinging her hair off to one side, slowly licking up my shaft. That first wet lick sends vibrations straight down my spine. My breath hitches as she takes me as deep as she can until I can feel the back of her throat. *Fuck!* Legs shaking, I'm grateful I'm already holding onto the counter, else I might actually collapse onto the floor from that alone. She slowly pulls me back out while sucking and licking as she goes, and all I can do is watch with hooded eyes as she bobs up and down on me.

It's almost a sensory overload when she lightly rolls my balls in her palms. Overcome, my head falls back as she lightly squeezes my base and sucks a little harder, increasing her pace. *Fuck, it won't be long with what she's doing.*

My hips slowly rock as she leans against me, and I feel my pending release as the tingling reaches down to my toes. Rez must know I'm about to come because she simply looks up at me and winks, then starts humming.

"Fuuuuuuck!" I moan as I explode in Rez's hot mouth, and the waves of my cum shoot down her throat. I almost slip against the counter as she continues to keep her promise and takes everything I give her and then some. Once I'm spent, she licks my cock clean and puts me gently back into my pants, zipping them up for good measure.

"Damn. You're fucking gorgeous," I say, reaching for her face.

"Levi." She laughs, pulling away. "I just swallowed your cum."

"And it was hot as hell," I tell her, slamming her mouth

against mine. I taste my salty self on her lips, but I don't care. It drives me crazy that she thinks I won't kiss her just because she spent the time worshipping me in that fashion. She deserves the world, and if all I can do is kiss her right now, then so be it. I try to deepen the kiss, but Rez playfully nips at me, so I take the hint and lean my forehead against hers.

"I wish I had time to repay you," I gasp, still coming down from the high.

She giggles as she shakes her head and smiles. "It was your reward; no need to return the favor. But if you want to help me out, I could really use a cleanup spell on my underwear." She runs her tongue ring over her lower lip before continuing. "They're kinda wet," she confesses.

CHAPTER 15
Imposter Syndrome

Rez

Thankfully, Levi's spell saves me from needing to change my underwear, but it does nothing for the wetness between my thighs. We walk back into the kitchen like nothing happened, but a quick peep at Knox and Ryker proves I'm not as slick as I think I am. Ryker's brilliant blue eyes lock on me as he licks his lips and rubs his tummy, confirming he's been fed.

As I sit down, I notice Knox raise his chin slightly and inhale deeply, giving me a knowing smirk. If only I could kick him under the table, but lucky for him, I feel his humor through our link, so I give him a wink.

"So what did I miss?" I ask as I pick up my drink and take a sip.

"Besides most of breakfast?" Chester says before Moni elbows him, and he mumbles his apology.

Lilith gives a small clap and pulls everyone's attention, graciously giving me a break and getting us all back on track. "It seems we have a lot to do in a short amount of time. We need to work on at least one memory spell, and possibly two; that is, if you want one as well." Lilith looks at Knots, and he does a half-shrug move she takes as a yes. "And we have a time limit to get you all back to Purgatory by Sunday for Levi's oath," she adds, choking on the last word.

Well, I guess they did a good deal of catching up while I was occupied.

She touches the pearls at her neck, trying to hide that she just threw up in her mouth. It's comforting that she feels as disgusted by the idea as we all are. This new Stepford Lilith is probably harder for my guys to adjust to than it is for me, having not spent much time with her before she was unpossessed. If it weren't her saying things about my mother, I probably wouldn't have many reservations toward the Demon. "Also, with the new information that was brought to my attention this morning"—I give JP a questioning look, and he nods, letting me know he'll explain later—"I believe Adam, but there had to be a bigger player behind my possession, including the attack during my ritual with Rez. So, that only gives us today and tomorrow to get the ingredients, so while you were attending to Leviathan, I decided to speed things up. Though you might have to come back after the ceremony to complete the spell. "

With a quick glimpse around the table, I'm glad to see I'm not the only one lost. "Excuse me, but Adam?" I question.

"Oh, yes," Lilith chuckles. "Remember that first day of class when I told you Adam was my first husband and was currently strapped to a table, having his skin flayed from his body?"

The memory is faint, but I nod, getting a queasy feeling in my stomach as I wonder where she's going with this.

"That's the Adam they are bringing," she explains, her lip curling up into a smile. "The backstabber who took decades from me, my loves, and my sons."

Before she can say anything further, one of the Arte Demons approaches her and bows.

"Speak," she demands. Once the Demon says what it needs to, Lilith smiles. "Ahh, it seems he's here already. Come. Let's have some fun. You will all get to see the art that is torture." She claps giddily with excitement, her eyes alight with an unholy fire that makes me like her even more.

We get up to follow her, but not before grabbing a few more pieces of tullé strips off my plate and shoving them into my mouth. *Don't judge me. A girl's got to keep up her strength.* Moni shrinks down and sits on my shoulder to whisper in my ear. "Where were you earlier?" she asks.

"Striking a deal with the Devil," I admit, knowing very well she meant to ask what I was doing with Lucifer, and immediately run into Knox's back.

"What deal?" Knots asks from over my shoulder. I'm now pinned against Knox, with Chester by my side, Knots at my back, and the wall to my right.

"L.A.M.B. is going to train us if I promise not to turn his house into rubble," I say, shrugging. Knox throws his head back and laughs before continuing on, and Moni's awestruck as she looks at me.

"Really? We get to train with L.A.M.B.?" Her eyes are as big as saucers, and her bark lights up like a glitter ball. "They're like superstars!" she says and swoons, falling off my shoulder. Chester easily catches her before giving me a shy smile and following Knox.

"That's all he wanted from you?" my Door Knight asks as he grabs my hand and we continue walking.

"Yeah. Why?" I ask, wondering if there was something I should be worried about.

"I've never heard of him offering to train someone before, that's all," he confesses.

"Well, he did say I was growing on him." I smile up at Knots, and he shakes his head in wonder.

We come to a stop as soon as we turn down a short hallway and find Lilith and L.A.M.B. at a door at the end.

L.A.M.B. heads through as Lilith remains until we're all caught up to her.

"Ready for some fun?" She walks through the door with her eyes alight.

Entering the dark room, a chill runs down my spine as I take in the dim surroundings. The ceiling and marble floors are gone, and in their place is black and red stone. If I look closely, the red seems to move like living lava. *Is that brimstone?* The room is lit up by the red liquid, but it seems significantly cooler than the other rooms.

"Why is it so chilly in here?" Moni asks, shivering and leaning into Chester. It's sweet how he wraps his arms around her, rubbing her arms. The half hoodie I'm wearing makes me grateful for JP's mind-reading as he walks up behind me and does the same.

"Can't have our guests be too comfortable now can we?" Lilith crows as she leads us to the back of the room. There's an alcove where stairs lead down to a lower level. Astaroth motions for us to stay on the landing while Lilith heads down the stairs. Candles suddenly come ablaze one after another around the circle-like pit, showcasing hanging equipment I can only guess are used before on their *guests*.

A group of eight Arte Demons—led by Trometh—waddle into the room, half carrying, half dragging a body between them and plop it on the metal table in the middle of the pit. The thump of the body hitting the table echoes around the room, and Lilith squeals with joy as she steps closer to the table.

"Oh, Adam," she says in a singsong voice. "It's time to answer some questions." She goes directly to one of the walls and starts looking at the knives, muttering eenie meenie miney mo. My stomach clenches at the thought of watching this so soon after breakfast.

I mean, I can handle a lot of things—blood, vomit, gross shit—but I don't know if I have the stomach for torture. I think it takes a special type of person to stomach that. I turn into JP's embrace and shield myself between his neck and my hair.

Bez walks to the other side and easily flips the body over. The man lying on the slab is barely dressed. I can only just make out the blond matted hair and crusted beard. "Lil?"

It's so surreal to know that's the real Adam. The first man to live on Earth. I feel as if I'm not real and this is all a dream or a movie that I've somehow gotten a glimpse into. Why do I feel like it's more like a curse to see this, though? He looks so... weak. Nothing like I would imagine.

She lets out an exasperated sigh. "What, Bez? Can't you see I'm trying to find the right tool?"

Bez walks away from Adam's prone body and gives the rest of L.A.M.B. a look and a slight nod with his head before stepping next to Lilith. The motion of the rest of the guys jumping down into the pit pulls Lilith's attention away from her wall of horrors.

"Wh—What's wrong?" Her eyes go from questioning to demanding within a blink of an eye as Lucifer walks over to the body on the slab.

"He's dead?" Murmur asks as he lifts Adam's head and lets it fall. The crack is deafening in the silent room.

"Impossible," Lilith says, grabbing the first thing off the wall she can reach, which happens to be a very long spike. She walks to his body, and with a scream, drives the spike into him and straight through the table.

I jump from the sight and sound of the impalement, but the body doesn't move. Lilith's eyes go wide and her lips part.

Since there's going to be no torture, I pull away from JP and move closer to the edge, where there's a railing to keep us from falling into the pit. *Who knew they cared about the observers' protection?*

"No. This is wrong." The words pass through her parted lips as she jostles her head. Bez comes up and gently tries to pull Lilith away from the body, as Zeke tries to comfort his mother from where we watch above.

"It's okay. There are other ways to get answers." Zeke sends her a reassuring smile as she fully turns our way.

"You don't understand." She chuckles, but it just gives off a creepy vibe. The sound reminds me of a movie where someone is on the verge of insanity.

"Adam. Can't. Die," she spits out and throws her wings in the air, throwing Bez off of her.

I look at the body of her ex-husband as she does. When my eyes travel down to the spike in his chest, something catches my eye. It's a small cyclone of inky black color that starts at the edge of the spike and slowly brightens to white the further away it goes. I look behind me, but JP is no longer there, only Lynx and Ryker.

"Do you guys see that?" I ask, leaning into them and pointing.

"Where?" Lynx asks, leaning in toward me to line up his eyesight.

"By the spike," I say, swallowing the bile that suddenly comes up my throat from thinking about what organs the spike went through.

"The ripple?" Ryker confirms.

"What's a ripple?" I turn to look at him.

"It's the remnants of a spell or a potion that's been penetrated; you're seeing an edge of it." He smiles down at me. "Good job, temptress," he says, giving me a kiss on the forehead before rushing down the stairs.

"How much do you want to bet he's gonna take all your glory?" Lynx whispers to me.

"Our usual?" I can't help but fire back, hoping he will miraculously remember.

"What was our usual?" Lynx asks as Ryker calls out to the group.

"Normally you would ask for a belly rub in your cat form," I explained. "So, let's make it a backrub. Loser gives it."

"Deal." Lynx gives me a cocky smile and crosses his arms before we give Ryker our attention.

"Hey!" Ryker yells out. "There's a ripple by the spike. Rez caught it. Someone tampered with the body."

When Lynx's head falls back on his shoulder and his arms fall down by his side, I can't help but gloat. I throw him a cocky look as I run my tongue over my upper teeth and brush the dirt off my shoulders. He throws me a glare before shaking his head.

'You better not act like a sore loser. Do you know how many times I've lost to you?'

'No, I wish I did. I bet those belly rubs were purrrfect.' He waggles his eyebrows, and I giggle, bumping into his shoulder.

Even though it's sad that he doesn't remember, at least he keeps it light, and that's one of the many reasons why I love him.

"Rez!" Ryker's voice calls out

I look up and find L.A.M.B., Lilith, and Ryker looking at me. *Oh shit!*

"Sorry. What?" I ask, giving the room a slight smile.

"I can't see it from here. Do you think you can show her?" Ryker hesitates slightly, pointing to the body.

Taking in a deep breath, I nod and hurry down the stairs. The last thing I want to do is get on Lilith's bad side when she's this close to... doing whatever Bez implied the other day.

"Sure," I say, squeezing between Lilith and Bez. I reach out next to the spike to point at the edge, but as I get closer, a film-like substance seems to lift slightly. Following my instincts—or more my curiosity—I glide my hand away from the spike and closer to the film. My mouth drops in awe as the layer ripples like water over rocks as it slowly draws away from my hands and I guide it away from myself. A few gasps and murmurs ring out around the room as I continue to move up the body, but it's not until I get to the face that all hell breaks loose, or more specifically, Lilith.

"NO!" Lilith roars! She reaches the body just as I uncover it, which doesn't look at all like the blond-haired man they had brought in. Instead, this is clearly a female demon with small onyx horns and a heart-shaped tail. Lilith throws her arm out with a growl, and the body rips free of the spike with the force she uses and flies across the room, slamming into the wall.

She raises her other hand, causing a candle to fly across the room and slam into the floor, where it twirls in an invisible whirlwind. After a few more candles join the terrifying dance, I notice the rattling in the room. Weapons that are lined along the walls start lifting before slamming back against the wall as if a magnet is switching off and on, and in the middle of it all is Lilith, screaming and cursing Adam's name.

Shit!

A blur of blue moves in front of me, and something grabs me around my waist before I'm airborne for a brief second. The room stops moving, and I'm back on the ledge with Murmur and Ryker.

"We need to get you all out of here before you get hurt!" he yells over Lilith's screaming.

We turn to move away from the pit when a glint catches my eye. My heart flies into my throat, choking any air from escaping as an ax rips free from the wall, along with a few other weapons. The ax spirals toward me, and there's no way I can move out of the way. I'm at the back of the group with

Murmur, so all I can do is put up my hands and hope Lilith's whirlwind will swing it off course.

Bang!

Cracking open my eyes, I have a déjà vu moment when I find my glittery force field up in front of me once again. Murmur turns toward me, looks down at the ax by my feet, and then back at my force field.

"How are you doing that?" he asks with a slack jaw and wide eyes. "I thought you were a novice."

"I'm a Rez! And I have no clue," I answer honestly with wide eyes.

"Well, that's not good." His nose wrinkles as he looks at my shaky hands. "Can you move with that?"

"I can try," I admit. My shield is doing a decent job of blocking some of the debris Lilith is causing from entering our little pathway, but I can't see if everyone is clear. From where I'm at, all I can see is the rest of L.A.M.B. dodging Lilith's chaos as they try to get close enough to stop her.

Murmur backs up and gives me a nod. "Everyone is clear," he calls to me, raising his voice to be heard over the noise.

I slowly take a step back, keeping my eye on my forcefield and as soon as I move my other foot, I feel it. Something inside of me that feels tight like a string is being pulled too far, and *pop!* My field drops just as another weapon heads my way. My lungs give a whoosh as something hits me in the stomach just as I get pulled back and out of the way.

"That was a close one, lil' bird," Murmur laughs as his tail unravels and sets me down next to him.

If I'm a little bird, then let's leave this shit for the bigger birds.

CHAPTER 16
Hell's History Lesson

Rez

After our near-death experience, Murmur ushers us back to the parlor room to wait until they get Lilith calmed down.

"Delicate state, my ass. Your mother is off her damn rocker," Lynx says, pacing in front of the fireplace. "No. I take it back. She never had a damn rocker. Instead of fucking building the damn chair, she's been waving around the sticks in the air trying to make fire."

"Lynx, you need to calm down," I warn him from my spot. Instead of being sandwiched between the guys, I grab a footstool and sit between Levi's chair and the sofa.

"Why?" he yells. "What's the worst that could hap—"

With a poof, Lynx is sitting in front of the fireplace... as a lynx.

'Because you used to change when you got too angry and weren't concentrating on your shape.' I sigh as I take in my best friend. *'I figured you would do it again if you didn't have your memory... I guess I was right.'*

'*What the fuck? Since when do I need laser hair removal everywhere?*' Lynx says, spinning around to see himself. Suddenly his head darts down between his front legs and he ends up sprawled on the floor after the most inelegant somersault ever executed by a person or a furball. '*Shit! Where did my dick go?*'

"Oh! LYNX!" Moni squeals and flies over to him. She grabs him by the neck and squeezes him. It's hilarious how she's treating him like a cat when he was a human just two seconds ago. His eyes are about to pop out of his skull in pure shock, and I can't stop the laugh that bubbles out of me.

"Did he just shapeshift?" Zeke asks, giving me a bewildered look. "How is he able to do that when he doesn't remember you?"

"He doesn't." I try to hide my smile. "He would always accidentally shift when he got upset."

Knots howls at my confession and hits the chess board, making the pieces jump.

"Hey, that's cheating," Chester whines, glaring up at Knots as he tries desperately to put the pieces back correctly. *Huh? Had they started a game? How long have we been here? When did they have time to start?*

'*Well, look who just turned himself back into fur boots,*' Knots says.

'*I have a sudden urge to piss on you. I knew I should have done it last night while you were sleeping,*' Lynx growls. Moni lets go of him, giving him a wide berth.

"Oops. I forgot." She blushes and turns a cute pink. "He's really a guy and I shouldn't be doing that, huh?" she asks, turning to me for direction.

I just shrug. "Honestly, if he's a cat, I treat him like a cat. If he's a human, I'll treat him like a human. For a long time, I just thought it was all in my head, so just go with it." I laugh.

Lucifer picks that moment to walk in and quirks his brows

as he looks around. If you'd blink, you'd miss the half smile that appears when he sees Lynx lifting his paw and retracting his claws.

"Well, I see you've kept yourselves occupied," he announces as he sits down before he conjures up some black licorice and takes a bite.

Moni lets out a squeak, and all eyes turn her way as she stares at the gross candy. "I just knew you would like that stuff." She nods to herself.

"Yes. I made it. I enjoy the taste," he admits. I wrinkle my nose at the admission, but quickly shake my head to address the elephant in the room.

"Is Lilith okay?" I ask.

"Astaroth is helping her calm down," he says with a pinched expression. It's easy to know he's concerned by the crinkled lines around his eyes.

Bez and Murmur come in and go directly to the bar, pouring drinks for themselves. Something tells me I might have to ask for something stronger than the water I got earlier.

"So, what's the deal with Adam?" Knox questions as he leans back against the sofa and sees the guys at the bar. "And will we need some of that?"

Bez and Murmur share a glance before they nod and start passing out drinks for everyone.

"Besides Adam being Lilith's ex-husband, there's a lot of animosity between them," Lucifer says, accepting a glass filled with dark liquid. Murmur's tail hands me a tall glass with a bubbly pink liquid that smells a lot like strawberries. I take a tentative sip and lose myself in the light and flavorful taste; it's so good that a moan slips out. Opening my eyes, I find everyone staring at me.

"Oops. Sorry. It's just really good," I say in my defense.

"I'll have what she's having," Moni says, and I stifle a laugh.

"You want a Four P?" Murmur asks, his eyebrows raising but giving her an appreciative nod before he makes her the same drink. "I'll add some Hatcha. It's Hell's version of caffeine." He gives Moni a wink.

"What's a Four P? Is that really the name of it?" I ask. There's no harm in knowing what I'm drinking because it's fucking fantastic. It's something I would definitely order again.

Murmur's slow smile makes me rethink my question, but before I can take it back, he opens his mouth. "Nah, that's not the real name. No bartender will know it by that. That drink, it's a Pussy Pounding Pleasure Pleaser. You're welcome!"

Yeah.. I might rethink ordering this drink in public.

He winks and hands Moni her drink.

She tentatively takes a sip, and immediately her barks turns magenta as her eyes dilate.

"Are you about to cheat on coffee?" JP smiles as he takes in Moni's gleeful expression.

"Never! But this is a close second," she admits before taking another sip and shivers in exhilaration.

"Um... so, yeah... um... Adam! Yeah, so why did Lilith say Adam couldn't die? Isn't he *the* Adam from Adam and Eve?" I ask.

'And I thought I had problems. At least I'm not bright red like a tomato right now.' Lynx laughs.

'Found your dick yet?' I snap with a cocked brow, but he rolls his eyes and doesn't reply.

"Simple. He can't. She took his innocence, therefore changing him unexpectedly. He gained immortality and can't die," Lucifer supplies.

"Does that mean our parents are going to outlive us?" Levi questions, appearing intrigued.

"Oh, bloody hell! Could you imagine?" Murmur's British accent shudders as he takes his own seat.

Bez hands off the last few drinks and takes his own seat, chuckling.

"I didn't ask what their sexual experiences were before they started dating Lilith, but if they were inexperienced, there's a good chance." Lucifer gives us a bored expression.

"The fact is: Adam has not been happy with his circumstances for quite a while, and his recent actions against Lilith have proven he is willing to act on them finally," Lucifer says, swirling the dark liquid in his glass. "It was probably around the time you boys were conceived. We found out that Lilith never made it to Earth and her mates—your fathers—were there without her, so we went searching, finding her in the 7th level of Hell with a knife in her back, which Adam put there. He somehow tricked her, then convinced your fathers that she wanted nothing to do with them and to move on."

"If someone says that to you, Chestie... don't believe them. You're mine forever. Okay?" Moni says, snuggling up to Chester.

I smile as he comforts her and promises that he won't let that happen. *Aww, so sweet.* Someone starts gagging, and I consider Lynx to see if he's coughing up a hairball, but it's JP that's making all the noise and rolling his eyes. My jaw drops, speechless, trying to find the words to berate his behavior, but there's no need. A small green shoe slams into the side of his head, stopping him.

"Stop it, you ass!" Moni shrieks.

JP's jaw drops, and he slowly turns his attention to his sister. "Did you just hit me with your shoe?" The incredulous look on his face is priceless.

"Well, it's the only thing I was willing to give up at the time," she shrugs.

Our group chuckles while Lucifer and Bez stare at us as if to say we're nothing more than immature children. They are older than dirt, so compared to them, we absolutely are.

"If I may get back to my story," Lucifer interjects. Moni and JP mumble sorry, and Lucifer gives them a nod. "Lilith was possessed by three demons, but we didn't know that at the time. Turns out they were Asmodeus' children. Needless to say, he probably won't be happy when we deliver what's left of their heads on pikes to him this afternoon."

This time there really is gagging as Chester runs to the kitchen with his hand plastered over his mouth. Moni is right on his heels, sporting a yellowish-green hue to her bark.

"You guys are going to need stronger stomachs if you plan on surviving in this world." Murmur shakes his head before throwing back what's left of his drink.

"Agreed," Bez says, getting up and following them into the kitchen.

'Do we have to survive? Can't we just coast... barely perish?' Lynx interjects.

'Still having problems over there, or did you give up and decide to stay furry for the rest of your life?' I tease.

'Well, at least this way I get out of giving you a back rub,' he teases and smiles.

'True, but it also means you miss out on good food, games, and looking at your dick again. Really want to pass that up?' I quirk my eyebrow, and when his eyes widen, I know I've won my case.

'Fuck!' he hisses.

"You said Lilith had three Demons inside of her. Is it possible to be born with a Demon already possessing you?" Zeke asks with intensity, leaning forward on the sofa.

Lucifer uncrosses his legs and sets down his drink next to him. "Now, that *is* an interesting question. Why do you ask?"

Propping his elbows on his knees, Zeke rubs his hands together in front of himself. JP rubs his back and whispers in his ear. Zeke gives him a friendly smile before taking a deep breath and refocusing on Lucifer.

"I've always felt a dark presence in me, ever since I was a kid. I just thought it was a part of my nature, until recently." He nervously licks his lips before continuing, and I'm proud of him for being willing to admit this secret. He deserves answers. "There was one time when I was trying to change a decision, and this *entity,* for lack of a better word, took over. He said 'I got it from here' and I could no longer control my body. In the end, I blacked out, and he took over. I was lucky enough that I had weakened myself to the point he couldn't do anything with me, and my family found me in time." JP pulls Zeke into a hug as Lucifer rubs his chin, then snaps his fingers.

Trometh and an Arte Demon dressed in cute red overalls run in—the latter wheezing—and stop by Lucifer's chair.

"Ve srlsc ej cmnj," Lucifer says, getting up and going over to the bar. The Demon runs off as fast as its little legs can take it while Trometh bows low and quickly walks away. We watch as Trometh easily catches up with the Arte Demon with his longer legs as we sit there in silence.

Grr. It's really frustrating that I don't know what the hell he's saying. I don't like the way he looks at the group when he doesn't think we're watching. It's just something about him, and we never found out about the earring that we found in my closet.

"Do you think there's a chance?" Murmur questions, making Lucifer another drink.

"A chance of what?" Levi asks, swinging his attention back to the Demons behind us.

Moni, Chester, and Bez come back into the Parlor looking better.

"What did we miss?" Chester asks, but Knox beckons him over and whispers in his ear.

"Oh!" Chester's eyes go wide, and he nods before playing telephone and passing on what he knows to Moni as they take their seat.

Lucifer turns to face us, leaning against the bar. "Demons can't possess someone unless their barriers have been weakened and the vessel they are introduced to is extremely powerful. I assume, in Lilith's case, the knife Adam shoved into her back weakened her enough for possession. I just don't know what he used to move the Demons. So, no. I don't think you were born possessed by a Demon," he says, and Zeke's shoulders drop.

"But I do think there's a chance of a group possibly trying to fuck with you. There used to be a few individuals that were capable of... influencing those... out of their direct presence. But only one remains, and to err on the safe side, I sent word to have someone check on him," Lucifer says. "I should hear back in a few hours." He picks up his drink, taking a small sip before he salutes Murmur with it and he takes his seat.

"This entity—has he ever told you anything personal about himself?" Murmur inquires, sitting cross-legged in front of Zeke, getting into his personal space.

"No. When he talked, he always used the pronouns us or we. Why?" his brows pull down and he shifts in his seat.

"No reason, just trying to help sort out who's messing with you." His eyes search Zeke's face before coming back up to his green eyes, and they suddenly narrow. "When was the last time you felt his presence?"

Zeke slightly squirms in his seat and audibly swallows as his eyes shift to Lucifer. "Right before we fell down here," he admits.

This is news to me.

"What?"

"Zeke!"

"Are you okay?" I ask.

"Why didn't you tell us?"

"QUIET!" Lucifer orders, and my body stiffens for a moment as I look at him like he's lost his mind. Maybe he has.

Obviously, he's never been around us, but this is kinda normal for us. Glancing back over at my friends, I find them frozen in place.

"Hey, unfreeze them, you pompous ass!" I stand up and point to my group of guys on the sofa.

"H—How are you not frozen?" Lucifer demands as he stands and eyes me up and down.

"Wait, you mean you didn't mean to leave me unfrozen?" I question.

"Told you there was something special about her," Murmur says in a cocky tone.

Lucifer blinks owlishly at me before shaking his head and unfreezing everyone with a wave of his hand.

My friends take in an audible sigh of relief but give Lucifer wary glances. I don't blame them; he just froze their asses with one word when all we did was express worry for a friend.

"How rude!" Moni says, and Lucifer's jaw clenches.

"I apologize. I didn't handle that in the best fashion, but this is my home, and I don't handle chaos well," he says, straightening his suit as he regards us once more.

"Haha! See, Rez! I did it! I'm no longer a cat!" Lynx cheers in triumph. His voice breaks the tension in the room. I'm a little disappointed that he's wearing clothes, but smile all the same because, either way, he is able to shift.

"See, it wasn't all that hard. Now you just have to practice until you can do it with ease," I say, shrugging a shoulder.

All he does is scoff as he heads to the bar. "Not before I get my own drinks. I need to catch up!" he says, doing a little two-step around the sofa.

"Amihlg! Irmwl jli!" The red overalls Arte Demon runs into the room waving his arms.

Well, that was quick.

"It's really annoying that I can't understand them," I mumble, and I hear a few people agree.

Growling, Lucifer snaps his fingers once again, but this time, the roots of my hair start tingling. The room tilts as a dizzying spell hits me momentarily, so I reach out and grab a hold of the closest thing, which happens to be Levi.

"Are you okay?" Levi holds me steady as I try to focus on him.

"Yeah, I think so," I nod.

"Speak," Lucifer commands.

"Master. A guard stopped me on the way and hastily asked me to deliver the news urgently that his body is gone." The Arte Demon shakes as it bows his head and slowly backs up. Trometh walks into the room, looking grim as well.

"It's true, sir. A guard was on his way to inform you. When they did their daily checks yesterday, they noticed his absence." His voice started out loud at first, but slowly loses its flare as he takes in the atmosphere.

Yesterday? Why wouldn't they notify him sooner than now if that was the case? I murmur to myself, but apparently, I didn't block my thoughts because it's Knots who answers me.

"Each level has its own time zone. The highest level has no difference in time, but depending on where this 'he' was kept, it could have been the equivalent of a week," Knots explains.

Fuck.

"That's not good, is it?" I ask, noticing how all the color is draining from Lucifer's face. *But it's pretty neat that I can now understand the Arte Demon. Does this mean I can understand Demonic, or whatever it's called?*

In a flash of silver, Lucifer disappears, and Murmur reaches out for Zeke's hands. "Can you feel his presence now?" he asks in an urgent tone.

Astaroth walks in and glances around with drawn eyebrows, but Bez quickly walks over, pulls him into a corner, and starts whispering to him.

"Um..." Zeke's eyes wander around the room.

"Concentrate, Ezekiel. Can you feel that dark entity in any of the recesses of your mind or body? Do you feel any different? Lighter perhaps? Happier?" Murmur presses.

"Yes, I feel lighter and happier. Right before the floor opened up, my body locked up and I couldn't control myself there for a moment, but since then... I've felt free, for the first time ever," he confesses. I smile, feeling happy for Zeke. He's finally able to get that gray cloud away from him.

"FUCK!" Murmur yells and spins away from Zeke. He runs his hands through his brown hair before slowly letting out a breath and bringing his attention back to Zeke. Pursing his lips, he tries to give him a smile, but it's a lost cause.

"Sorry," he says, collapsing his hands before him. "I'm happy that you're finally free of that entity, but it seems you were possibly used to free our version of the boogeyman," Murmur admits.

"Hey, I've heard that saying before when listening to talk about the Withering Sulks. So, who is the other boogeyman?" I retort, raising an eyebrow his way.

Astaroth snorts, bringing our attention to him as he comes to the front of the fireplace. "The Withering Sulks only affect the people on the ground in Purgatory. This boogeyman will tear down everyone, even those on Earth—if he gets that far—and yes... It seems Zeke was the vessel he used to break free of his shackles."

"Who?" Moni asks, leaning forward and completely enraptured by Astaroth's story.

"Cain."

"Cain, as in...?" Lynx asks, coming up behind me.

"Cain... As in the first murderer."

"Fuck," Lynx and I say simultaneously.

CHAPTER 17

99 Mistakes, but she Wasn't one

Ryker

"Are you sure you don't want to go eat lunch?" Rez asks, as I watch her ass sway before me. *What I want to eat for lunch is between those delicious thighs.*

After the revelation of Cain and Adam being free, Astaroth informed us that Lilith was more than likely going to be knocked out with a tranquil spell for the rest of the day. Lilith would not have the chance to go to the market and get the ingredients for the memory potion. Of course, this upset my temptress, so Bez—the big softy—compromised, deciding to show us where Lilith's workshop was. Apparently, the fragile state Lilith is in causes her to have extreme emotional mood swings. Obviously, that's not what L.A.M.B. said— that's just Rez's observations—but clearly, she's onto something.

"Nah! What you and Levi did this morning filled me up to the brim," I tease and watch Rez's cheeks blush pink. *I want to bend her over and make her other cheeks match in color.*

"You're just jealous," she spits back.

"Damn right I am. I know how good that mouth is when it's being wicked." I wink.

"Do you guys need a room?" Levi chuckles.

"Who needs a room? We have a wall," I point out.

Bez clears his throat, bringing our attention to the fact that we've stopped in front of a door. "As you don't want to wait, you need to find the spell and make an ingredient list," Bez says, and with that, he turns and leaves.

"He's really grumpy, huh?" Rez whispers to me.

"Nah. He's really a big teddy bear when you get to know him," I say following Levi in the room.

"Uh-huh," she says doubtfully. "Teddy Bear with claws maybe," she mumbles before entering the room. "Wow. Now, this is a workshop." Rez whistles.

The room has two full walls of bookshelves with tomes, loose pages, and jars. The other two walls have potted herbs, shelves full of crystals, dust, and things I do not know about. This is more Rez and Levi's wheelhouse. I'm just tagging along because I wanted to instead of going to lunch.

"Hello. May I help you find something?" a tiny voice speaks out, and I pause as I listen for the words again.

Am I hearing things?

Rez's head swings around quickly, glancing about and trying to find where it's coming from.

"Do you guys hear that?" Rez asks, bending down and searching underneath the table beside me.

"Um, Rez. Are you okay?" Levi asks before going to a bookcase.

"You mean you don't hear that?" she asks as she moves her hair out of her face.

"No." He shoots her a concerned look. "All I hear is the watering spell going off, taking care of the plants in the upper rows over there," he confesses, pointing across the room.

Well, shit. If he's not hearing anything, then how come Rez and I are?

I catch sight of something gold slipping underneath a shelf. Tapping Rez on the shoulder, I point to what I see.

"Yes. We need help," Rez answers, squatting down in front of the herbs.

"Fantastic!" A miniature Imp pops out from underneath the shelf, scaring Rez. She falls back onto her ass and scurries back until she runs into Levi's legs.

"Hey," he says, almost falling and dropping the book he's holding onto Rez. "What's wrong?"

This Imp takes on a different appearance from the normal upright Imps we see. Regular Imps are red or black and are usually a little shorter than Moni, with long ears like Elves. Taking a closer peek, this one appears to be more like a Chinese Dragon with a gold body and pink fringes along its side and around its mouth.

Rez shakes her head and gets up. "Sorry," she says, giving the Imp a small smile.

"Holy shit!" Levi whispers in awe, and the room shakes. The Imp stands up on its hind legs and waves its tiny arms in the air before a clear film slides over the shelves, holding everything in place as the room rocks. Levi blushes slightly. "Sorry. I didn't mean to do that. But she has an Illustrious Imp."

"What's that?" Rez asks.

"In truth, I'm one of the first Imps that were ever created. The common Imps that everyone is more familiar with are actually crossbreeds," she informs us.

"I've seen your kind before. Aren't you like the Chinese Dragons?" I ask.

"Umm. From what Lilith has told me of the outside world, not quite, but I'm glad to see you are trying to make the connection." She laughs, only it sounds like she's growling.

"Well, it's nice to meet you. I'm Rez, and this is Ryker and

Levi." Rez smiles as she introduces us, pointing to us respectively.

"Oh! Where are my manners? I'm Benevolent, Lilith's helper, but you can call me Benny. Was there something I could help you with?" She bows before crawling up one leg of the ornate mahogany table that's set along the back wall. Once she reaches the top of it, it brings her up to waist height.

"Yes. We were looking for the spell Lilith was hoping to use to restore my friend's memory," Rez relays.

"And if you happen to know if she has a spell for magical imprints, that would also be handy?" Levi adds, and I curl my lip at his request.

"It's to help find out who wrote the note that Knox found," he reminds me.

"Oh! Yeah. That makes sense," I murmur, turning to lean my butt against the table.

"Ah yes! I am familiar with those books. Come," Benny clicks her tongue and scurries back down the table and across to one bookcase.

Not really needing anything but not wanting to be left out, I wander over to a bookcase closer to the open door to study some of the spines. I've been to *Mother's* residence when I was younger, but I've never been to L.A.M.B.'s. It was always off-limits.

"Here you go." Benny happily points out. Rez pulls the book to her chest with glee and hurries back to the desk, opening it up and scanning the first page, no doubt in a hurry to get started. Levi is more subtle in his approach, but I know for a fact he's busting at the seams to get back to crafting potions. It's one thing he enjoyed in the little free-time he used to have.

I find a book on some unusual practices of sexual arousal and potions while I wait. Rez and Levi have no trouble writing the ingredients down, but what slows them down is needing

Benny's help in locating what's already here and what still needs to be collected. Hopefully, she can at least point us in the right direction.

Seeing that they're almost done, I put the book back on the shelf and decide to wait by the door. Levi leans over and whispers something into Rez's ear, and she sharply inhales, rubbing her legs together a moment before I'm hit with the sweetest smell in the world. Taking in a deeper breath to get another hit of her lust, a familiar scent mingles with hers right as I feel a slight brush at the back of my neck.

Reacting on instinct, I drop and reach up and across with my left hand, grabbing the arm that swings at the spot where my neck would have been and connect with a wrist. I roll forward, pulling the intruder at my back over my shoulder, while pulling out the knife that's concealed on my pants by my right leg. As we land with an oomph, my lips curl up as the knife presses against the pale-skinned Succubus underneath me.

"Didn't get me this time, Zissa," I chuckle. The Demon underneath me isn't concerned one bit about the knife that's pressed to her slim neck. She laughs as the blade knicks her skin and a trickle of blood drips down the side of her pale white neck.

"Oh, really, Ry?" she giggles. "Does that mean you don't feel this," she asks, and I feel a slight pressure against my balls that has my entire body clench up as I slowly, without moving my knife, peer down. My knees are pinning her arms down, but she still has a very long blade pressed against my balls.

"Tie?" I offer, smiling down at her. She rolls her eyes and lowers the knife from my precious jewels.

"Fine," she agrees, and I shift off of her arms and remove my knife. She grabs my extended hand as I help her up.

The slim Succubus has changed little since I last saw her a few years ago. Standing at 5'7 most people would underestimate the purple-haired beauty. But she's like me; she doesn't want to just rely on her Succubus powers, so she's learned another way to protect herself. It seems she likes the type of weapons that allowed her to be up close and personal with her target. Just glancing at her delicate facial features, icy blue eyes, and tiny ram horns, you would never expect her to be able to castrate you in two point five seconds.

Her painted black lips are a stark contrast against her white skin as she smiles up at me.

"It's so good to see you, Ry Ry. I've missed you so much." She squeals and throws herself into my arms, dropping her weapon in the process. Knowing her, she still has plenty strapped to her body, but I'm careful not to hurt her as I catch her and squeeze her back.

"Hey, Zissa! You're looking good." I lean back to release her. She turns and does a little spin, showing off her outfit.

She's wearing head-to-toe black leather and boots that travel up to her knees with leather straps connecting her boots to her itty-bitty shorts, and of course, her corset top. Sexy, I must admit. Her corset is long-sleeved and shows off her figure, highlighting her slight curves.

A throat clearing pulls my attention away from Zissa, and I turn to find Levi and Rez staring my way with various expressions. Levi's stoic as normal as he folds his piece of paper and deposits it in his suit jacket. Rez, on the other hand, has her head cocked to the side and that adorable eyebrow raised while her gray eyes bore into mine. Her lips are slightly parted as she inspects me before her eyes dart over my shoulder, reminding me of Zissa.

"Oh, sorry, guys." I chuckle. "This is Zissa, my best friend." I smile as Zissa waves. "Zissa, this is Rez, and you already know my brother, Levi, I think."

"Yep. Nice to see you again, Levi. You definitely haven't changed at all," she says, as she takes in Levi.

"I can say the same for you," Levi replies respectfully, always the prim and proper one of our group. His eyes don't even waiver to take in what Zissa is wearing before he focuses back on Rez. Speaking of which, I check out my woman and find her eyeballing me as if she's waiting for something. I have no clue what, since I had given the introduction already.

Rez's eyes seem to get bigger and bigger as time moves on until she finally withdrawals and goes back to normal. She lets out a scoff before her jaw wobbles slightly, and she vigorously grabs her paper before shoulder checking me on her way out of the door.

What the fuck?

My jaw drops as I spin to stare at the door and the table which Levi's leaning up against, his arms folded across his chest and legs crossed at his ankles with a smirk on his face.

"What?" I growl out, not liking the idea that Levi knows something that I don't. If he knows why Rez is upset, he better explain it, and quickly. I don't see why introducing her to my best friend would upset her so much.

He chuckles as he pinches the bridge of his nose.

"I swear, Ryker, for a self-proclaimed lady's man, you missed the mark on that one," he says, shaking his head.

"What's going on?" Zissa asks, moving to stand between Levi and me while strapping her knife back to her weapons belt.

"A few things have changed since you've seen Ryker, Zissa. The biggest is Rez," Levi starts.

"Okaaay," Zissa says.

"Our brothers and a few others, me included, are dating her. Plus, she has two mates that we know of, Knox and Ryker," Levi says and gives me a pointed look.

Zissa visibly jerks as if she's been slapped. Her jaw drops and her eyes go wide as she turns to me and slaps me hard on the shoulder.

"Oww. What the hell?" I ask, rubbing the sore area.

"Just feel lucky I didn't punch you in the fucking jaw! No wonder she ran out of here." She eyes me in disgust. "You're an asshole."

"What?" I throw out my arms, completely missing the point.

Zissa grabs my arms tightly and gets in my face. "Okay, Ry. I'm going to break it down for you," she says slowly. "We just had a short sparring moment, right?" I nod, staying with her. "Okay. Then we hugged it out, complimented each other, and you introduced me as your best friend, right? Are you sticking with me?" she says, nodding her head as she stares at me with wide eyes. *This can't be that serious, right?*

"Then you said... Come on, tell me what you said and really think about it," she prompts me.

"This is Rez and you... oh fuck!" I slump into her arms and squeeze my eyes closed at my blatant diss of my mate. *SHIT!*

Laughter has me slowly rising and glancing over at my big brother. "Do you want another black eye? You'd have a matching pair," I threaten.

"Sure. I'll make sure *my* girlfriend patches me up while she's pissed at you for *two* things," he mocks, walking over to us. "It's good seeing you, Zissa. I'll leave you two alone. Maybe you can help him. Hell knows, he needs it."

Turning around, he peers under the table. "Thank you again, Benevolent. I'm sure we'll see you soon."

"Bye!" Benny replies, waving earnestly.

I look to my best friend and sexual mentor for help. "Think you can help me fix this shit?"

She chuckles and shakes her head before sighing at me. "I'll try my best, but it all depends on what type of girl she is and what she knows about us. How do you actually have a mate in the first place?"

I run a frustrated hand through my hair before answering. "Quickest way to explain it is, Lilith is my biological mother. And apparently having a mate is one of her traits that I inherited," I explain, hoping that's good enough for her.

"Okaaaay. Okay. Yeah, that would explain it. So, what all does she know about us?" she asks again.

"Ugh. She knows nothing. What we had was in the past, and you're the only friend I have outside of my family," I admit. I know it's sad, but it's true. Everyone else that wants to hang out or come around is there because of my status and what I can do for them, and always in a sexual way. Zissa has been the only person who stuck around after Lilith asked her for help teaching me how to feed properly as an Incubus.

"All I know is that I'm excited for you and I would love to have a girlfriend, so you better not fuck this up," she pokes me in the chest.

"Well, help me get her back!" I yell, trying not to panic, but it's obviously not working.

"Okay, so here's what we're going to do," she regards the room with furrowed brows and shakes her head. "Wait, we need to go bigger."

Shit! What the hell have I gotten myself into now?

CHAPTER 18
Bartender, I Need an Upgrade

Rez

I wonder if you can upgrade shit at the market here in Hell. Or wherever I was going to buy these ingredients. I mean, we can do it back on Earth, so why couldn't we do it here? "Hi, I have an Incubus and his brain is malfunctioning, so I would like an upgraded model, and yes, I would like the extended warranty."

Rez. Just Rez. Levi is his brother, but I'm only *Rez.* Not his *girlfriend. Not his mate!* He'd rather play fight using blades with a hot chick in sexy leather—his "best friend," who I've never heard of—than admit that I'm something to him.

I guess I could have waited a little longer to see if Ryker was going to pull his head out of his ass, but honestly, I don't have the time. It's Friday, so I only have today and tomorrow to get these ingredients before I have to go back to Purgatory and watch Levi sign his life away to Emer.

The good news is while I was immersed in the book Benny helped me find, I found something that might help the guys if Emer decides to keep her promise. She mentioned she would make all the guys forget me, so I figure that's another memory potion she's going to use. So all I need besides getting the ingredients is a good charm or container to hold the potion.

Heading back to the parlor room, I'm on a mission to talk to my new bestie, since Lilith is out of action and currently resting. I'm so deep in my thoughts that I don't hear the music playing. When I walk into the room, I'm shocked to see Lynx, JP, Moni, Chester, and Zeke doing some complex footwork and dancing in front of the fireplace.

Murmur is leaning back against the bar with his eyes closed and a goofy smile across his face. Knox has a device and seems to be recording them, while Bez sits at the chess table sharpening his machete. Knots is laying on the sofa, watching, and Astaroth stares in my direction.

Well, that's not unnerving.

Murmur opens his eyes, and the music stops while everyone that was dancing breaks out in laughter.

"Wow! That was so much fun," Moni squeals.

"It's so weird not having control like that," JP says.

"But it's also freeing, though," Lynx adds.

"What did I miss?" I ask, walking into the room. Seeing them laugh helps get my mind off of my asshole mate.

"I was just showing them what high mental capabilities can allow us to do." Murmur smirks.

"So what type of Demons are you? I know Lucifer mentioned what your fortitudes were, but he didn't mention what type of Demon. Is that even a thing?" I ask, making myself comfortable as I go behind the bar to take a peek at the drinks. I don't even care that I don't know how to make special drinks. I just feel like I need one.

Murmur turns to keep me in his sight as he points to himself. "I'm the original Mischief Demon." He smiles and points over at Bez without looking. "The original asshole or Vengeance Demon." He smirks and points over his other shoulder at Astaroth. "The original bigger asshole, a.k.a. Wrath Demon."

I smirk at his comment. Murmur's tail whips out and catches a dagger flying in our direction. My surprise causes me to jump and drop the empty glass in my hand. "Fuck!" I exhale sharply as I take in how close that knife was to us.

Murmur laughs out loud and slams the knife down on the bar. "Your aim is getting pretty bad there, old man. Do you need to get your eyes checked?" Murmur teases as he turns back to me.

Astaroth's lips jerk up as his arm flings out, and I flinch in response. Once again, I hear a clang as something falls behind Murmur's back. Murmur turns, glancing down by his feet, then brings his head up to stare at me with wide eyes. Over his shoulder, I see my small glittery shield.

"Are you sure you don't know how you're doing that?" he asks, his tail dropping what resembles a weird throwing star on the counter.

"I'm sure." I swallow around the dry lump in my throat.

Murmur pulls out a few bottles with his tail and mixes them into a glass, not even needing to peek behind the bar before he slides the drink to me. Without question, I throw it back and hiss at the welcoming burn but nod my thanks.

"Well, you definitely should learn how to control that," Murmur encourages.

"Well, that's the least of my worries right now," I retort. "I came in here because I need to get these ingredients, but I don't know where to go, let alone have any money. Wanna help me out?" I lean up against the bar and bat my eyelashes at the Demon of Mischief.

He smiles, pouring himself a drink and shoots it back before batting his eyelashes back at me obnoxiously.

Brat!

"Oh, and can I also get a new Incubus while I'm at it?" I ask sarcastically.

"What's wrong with the last one?" Knox asks, turning to face me from the end of the sofa.

"Besides a hot Demon hanging all over him, or the fact he didn't introduce me as his girlfriend? Nothing, I suppose," I say, grabbing a towel and picking up my mess from earlier.

"What?" Moni shrieks, flying over and hovering above me. "No way are we going to let this stand! I say we tackle them and tie them up. No! What about beating them with a paddle and then gag them so we can't hear their cries!" she says with a firm nod. Pulling out a coffee cup, she tips it back and frowns when nothing comes out, setting it on the counter.

I give her a blank stare for a moment because I'm sure something will click here in a moment.

Her eyes go wide as she sits down on the ledge and regards me. "Rez! That might not work," she says adamantly, like it was my idea. "Because some people might consider that a turn on! Did you know some people are turned on by being tied up? I just found out last night when Chester and I—"

"Lalala!" JP yells. Moni yelps and falls, and I drop the glass that I was picking up to catch her.

"Fuck," I mumble as pain shoots in my palm.

"Thanks, bestie," Moni says, picking herself back up and popping over the bar. "That was uncalled for!" Moni yells, and I hear someone getting smacked. JP's yelp makes me smile.

I sit down on the floor behind the bar and check my hand that's bleeding. Damn. Taking another towel that's under the bar, I quickly dab at the cut before wrapping it around my hand.

"You okay, kitten?" Knox asks, his worry coming through our bond.

"Yeah, I'm good, just cleaning up the mess I made," I say

as I tuck in the ends and throw the glass and Moni's empty coffee cup into the wastebasket.

"So who was all over Ryker?" Zeke asks as I raise back up and lean against the bar.

Murmur peers at my hand as he pours another drink, then back at my face, but he doesn't say anything.

"Zissa." Levi's voice rings out as he enters the room.

"His ex?" Zeke asks.

"I thought they were best friends?" I retort, looking to Levi for answers. I know I should really be looking to Ryker for them, but I don't feel like talking to him. And for some reason, I feel like I'll get a more honest answer from this group than him right now.

My hand starts itching underneath the towel, so I cautiously pull away the fabric. There's only a faint pinkish white line, and I'm momentarily awestruck. *Nice! If fast healing is one of my powers, I'm all for it!* Momentary distraction over, I drop the dish towel in the sink and walk out from behind the bar, turning my attention back to Levi.

"They are now," Levi says as he watches me. He's probably assessing my mood. I narrow my eyes at him as he gets closer, wondering whose side he is on. "There's a history there between them, yes," he confirms as he rubs his hands up and down my arms, trying to comfort me. "But that's also not our story to tell you; though, I want to. I can vouch that they are only friends and have been for years now."

I purse my lips, deciding I have better things to deal with, like getting these ingredients. "Fine. I don't like it, but I promise not to go shopping for a new Incubus. Yet," I say and lean around Levi to stare at Astaroth. "But I still need some money, and to know where this market is." I give him a pointed look.

"Oh, I want to go. Maybe I can find some coffee there! I

only have two cups left. Not even enough for the morning," Moni remarks over my shoulder.

Astaroth gives me a blank stare, and for a moment, I contemplate repeating what I just said. "We will give you our brand that will allow you to purchase anything you need. As for finding the market, that is why I sent Zissa to find you," he says. I swear his eyes spark as he mentions the last line, and I bite my tongue so hard that I taste blood.

"Well, I don't want *her* help," I grind out between clenched teeth.

"You will need her for protection," he counters.

"Pfft." I roll my eyes and cross my arms over my chest. Yes, I know how childish this looks. I am well aware this is below the actions of a person my age, but I don't care.

"Bring your weapon here," Astaroth demands.

Dropping my arms, I turn to face the long-haired demon. "How do you know I—"

"I'm a weaponsmith. I can sense them. Now, bring it here," he commands, holding out his palm.

Deciding not to push the issue further, I pull my knife free of its holster and hand it, handle first, to him. I'm rewarded with a slight smile.

"At least you know the basics of how to hand over sharp weapons," he comments.

"My mother was a nurse, and on odd occasions, I had to assist her with needles, scalpels, stuff like that," I confirm, and he nods as he examines my knife.

He scoffs and shakes his head. "This is weak metal and poorly crafted."

I jerk back at the slight offense. *Damn!*

"Well, excuse me." I grab the knife back from Mr. Perfecto and put it back in its holster. "I conjured it up in my closet back in Purgatory, and it has protected me just fine."

"Pfft. That is why she's going with you. And when you return, we will start your training. Before *and* after dinner."

My jaw drops as I look at him, but he just stares back at me, no expression on his face. "Yeah, okay. Lucifer said—"

"I know what Lucifer said when he agreed that we would train you, which includes *me*. *I'm the A*—your weapons trainer. We need to find you the right physical weapon to train with, and then we can work on the other issues you have," he states in a no-nonsense tone.

My eyebrows disappear into my hairline for a moment as I take in the words that just left his lips. *Did he just... excuse me?*

'*Damn girl. You just got your ass handed to you,*' Lynx says. It's great that he's using the link, but now is not the time.

Oh, Astaroth wants to play that game.

Leaning back, I cross my arms under my breasts, purse my lips, and just stare back at Asstro. Yep, he's earned the name since he's being an ass.

"Do you really want to make me mad? A Wrath Demon?" he inquires.

I cock my head and really think about it. "I don't know. When people say that, I kinda wanna poke them to see how far I can go before they blow up," I say honestly.

He blinks at me, and then too fast for me to comprehend, he pulls me into a hug while he belly laughs. "I like you. We're going to have fun training." He chuckles before ushering me over to Bez.

Why do I have the feeling that him liking me isn't a good thing?

CHAPTER 19
Inferno's Black Market

Rez

I rub at the phantom pain in my left wrist. I still can't believe the brand that Bez drew into my skin isn't visible. They've assured me that when I go shopping, the keepers will have a way to know that I'm under L.A.M.B.'s protection and that my "money" is good. They didn't actually *give* me any money, though.

Before leaving for the market, Bez sat me in the seat across from him at the chess table, and he rubbed a cold liquid on the inner part of left wrist. It tingled for a bit, and I took the opportunity to take in what Ryker called the gentle killer. I guess I could see it. That was before he gave me a small, lopsided smile and said, "I take no pleasure in doing this." And then slammed Hellfire against my skin.

Gentle killer, my ass! Try sadistic asshole!

I should have let Fluffers tear him a new one. It was kinda funny, though, seeing Murmur and Astaroth try to hold back Fluffers, Knots, and Zeke from trying to kill Bez as I swore and cried out in pain. But after he finished burning their brand

KERRY KELLER

into my skin, you could barely see any damage. Before we leave, Trometh hands us a couple bags for the supplies and recommends a stall for us to go to first. I'm a little weary of it, but Zissa agrees, saying she knows the place.

When we stepped out of L.A.M.B.'s residence, we found ourselves on a hilltop, which they shared with another mansion. Levi helpfully pointed out that it was Lilith's residence. Both places and their individual lands were surrounded by gates and protection spells. When asked why they needed it, he shrugged and said he never got answers when he asked the same thing as a child.

It's a shock to step out and see Hell in the daylight. I'm not sure if the sun is actually red, or if it's just the world that's reflecting back making it look that way, but it's enough to throw me for a loop. They have grass just like we do on Earth and at purgatory, but with pale white mixed in with the green. Off to my right is an Arte Demon, cutting some with a sickle, and I have a sick thought and wonder if they're short because they've accidentally cut off their limbs using that. In the sky, I don't see any clouds, but I do observe winged creatures flying off in the distance and shudder to wonder if they are friends or foes.

"I don't like her," Moni whispers in my ear as she plays with a curl. Currently, she's sitting on my shoulder as we follow Zissa and Ryker down a well-lit cobblestone path past a cavern-like dwelling. Knots, Levi, and Knox are trailing behind me. I'm sure she would be sitting on Chester's shoulder if he was here. He asked to call his parents before we left to give them a quick update. Apparently, he checks in with them daily around breakfast and doesn't want them to freak out about his disappearance. So, he was led into an office where there was a computer he could use to call from.

Turns out, when he mentioned he was pulled to Hell after getting separated from his mate, his mom freaked because

186

someone dropped the ball and Momma didn't know Moni was his mate. So, Chester wasn't able to make his phone call as quickly as he wanted. I still chuckle, thinking of his "help me" look he gave me when Moni and I went to get him. He was so cute. Moni just gave him a kiss and said she would be back, and we left him there to suffer his mother's wrath with a thousand questions about Moni.

The good news is, he'll have company once he's done. Lynx, Zeke, and JP stayed behind as well, for a couple of reasons. One, it was less people we would have to "protect," Asstro's words, not mine. And Zeke wanted to update all of our rooms with outlets to see if we could charge our phones in Hell. JP had the urge to cook, and Lynx said he had other things to work on.

Before we left, Knots did promise Chester that he would keep an eye on Moni. She insisted she knew her plants and wanted to come help. So, who was I to turn down an extra pair of eyes to find the ingredients we need to find? The others are here for our protection, despite my protest.

"Are you saying you don't like her because of what I said, or are there other reasons?" I whisper, keeping my eyes on the two sex demons in front of us. I'm curious if there are other reasons I'm missing. Ryker tried to apologize to me earlier, but I wasn't in the mood to talk. At the moment, they are chatting and laughing away like best friends, but at least they're keeping a respectful distance between them. His furtive glances my way tell me he's thinking about me at least.

"Of course there are other reasons!" Moni screeches, and I hurry to hush her, but Zissa peeks over her shoulder at us, giving us a friendly smile. I find myself giving her a half-assed attempt at a smile, but Moni sticks her tongue out before she turns back around. "Rez. I've heard of Z before, but I thought he was a guy—not a hottie with an electric body."

Her words strike a chord within me, where my insecurities

run deep. *Does he not find me attractive anymore?* No, that's silly. He even said he can't get it up around anyone else but me. *But that was around the Harpies, and this is his... ex.*

A hand wrapping firmly around my bicep brings me out of my musings and face-to-face with a frustrated Knox.

"What are you thinking right now?" he demands.

"I–I... It's nothing," I stammer out.

"Really? Because that's not what I'm feeling from you," he admits and peers over my shoulder. I glance back and find our group waiting for us, and it makes me uncomfortable. "We'll catch up. Continue on," Knox says, and they all start walking.

"I think I'll catch up with you in a bit, Rez!" Moni says, and she flies out of my curls, catching Knox off guard for a moment.

"Look, I know it's driving you crazy not knowing the details about Ryker and Z. I can feel it here. You can't hide it, Kitten," he says, placing my hand over his chest. "But don't you dare start questioning your worth. That's my best guess at what you're feeling. Am I close?"

My breath just seeps out of me with his words, and I deflate against him. He pulls me into him and wraps his arms around me. "I just feel so... less right now. It's either that or I get pissed, but I'm not sure who to get pissed at, Knox. I don't know Z, so it feels easier to get mad at her because I don't want to be mad at Ryker," I admit. "But honestly, I'm more frustrated because I'm annoyed at myself for even feeling this way instead of manning up and just talking to them like the adult I am supposed to be."

Knox chuckles, and the gruff rumbling sound in his chest seems to calm my chaotic thoughts. He squeezes me just a little tighter, and his warmth reminds me of a warm blanket that you cuddle into when you need comfort.

"Kitten, it's okay to feel things, even anger. Consider us Shifters; most of the time all we feel is anger and frustration.

At least you know why you're feeling it, and you even know how to fix it. Those are the hardest roadblocks I think there are when trying to figure out your feelings. Or at least they are for me."

I lean against his firm chest and listen to his heartbeat for a few more minutes as I think over what he is saying. He's right. I either need to man up and face Ryker and Z, or just wait until later. But if I wait, I can't go around bashing myself or questioning shit when a simple conversation would solve everything.

I pull back enough to gaze up at Knox. "Thank you."

"Anytime, kitten," he says, and leans down to give me a sweet kiss that leaves me a little light-headed. Damn, I'm liking this dominating yet sweet Shifter.

W e catch up with everyone right at the entrance to Hell's Bazaar. It's like a farmer's market but with tents, furs, and questionable items that make up the stalls. The cobblestone path is gone, and in its place is a reddish brown dust that makes me grateful I can easily change my clothes. I can't imagine trying to get this crap out of my outfits. Bright strings of big lights are embedded along the walls and along the tops of the tents, highlighting their wares. Some stalls look like they've been permanent structures since the beginning of time, while others are clearly portable tents that were set up for this occasion. The stalls range from clothes, pottery, herbs, and food. There are even sections where food hisses and pops over open fire pits next to smaller pits of brimstone. The entire atmosphere is exciting, yet strangely nerve-wracking.

Demons of all shapes and sizes are yelling at each other, trying to get good prices. I spot a few other creatures that I've learned about from school prowling around, giving me some semblance of normalcy. There's a Gargoyle—

Oh my God. Since when do I think of any type of supe as normal?

Swoosh!

"Fuck! Astarte's tits, who's cussing around here?" a Demon by one of the fire pits yells as he tries to save whatever he was cooking.

Oops.

Whatever it was, I hope someone around here likes their food burnt.

Knots shoots me a knowing wink, and I roll my eyes.

'Knew it was you,' he teases.

'It's a habit. Sue me,' I shrug.

'They would do much worse than sue you if they found out it was you,' he reminds me, and a shudder runs down my spine. I had totally forgotten there for a moment that Knots and I could communicate this way. But in all honesty, being in Hell, I wasn't sure it was possible. I had thought it was only a Door Knight ability and he only had it since he was in the dorm. I'm definitely okay with this, though.

I lean up against my Door Knight and entwine our fingers. *'Are you okay? I noticed you were laying on the sofa earlier,'* I ask, worried about him still. It's so hard to keep up with everyone and make sure no one is feeling left out.

'Yeah, I'm okay. I've been feeling a little off, but I'm sure it's just from being pulled here and that I didn't know it was possible.' He gives me a reassuring smile.

'Are you sure that's all? You'd tell me if it was something else, right?' I persist.

'Promise!' he leans over and kisses me on the head. *'Now, let's find these ingredients so I can get my memories back, shall we?'*

Zissa stops in front of a stall where a couple of Goblins

pop up behind the counter. One is tall with a bluish hue, a pot-belly, and beady eyes, while the other one is short and fat with stubby legs. They kinda remind me of the Arte Demons.

"Hello. What can we do for you?" the tall, older one asks.

Levi steps forward and hands over his sheet of paper. "Do you have any of these ingredients here?"

"And Coffee," Moni piques up.

The Goblin studies the paper and, with squinted eyes, surveys our group. "How do you plan on paying?" he barks out with a gruff tone.

Well, let's see how this works.

I step up to him and immediately regret it as I choke back the impulse to gag. The stench of him reminds me of rotten fish. My eyes start watering as I try to breathe through my mouth.

"Well, come on, girlie. I don't have all damn day. Hand over your arm." He huffs and grabs my arm, yanking it toward him.

I yelp as his dry and calloused hand scratches my skin. "Oh, stop it. It doesn't hurt that bad," he mocks as he runs his other hand over my arm, turning it roughly, trying to find where my brand is at.

If the fucker would have just asked, I would have told him. I don't know what the fuck I'm doing.

I can tell the moment he sees it because he drops my arm as if it's burnt him, and he starts visibly shaking as he gawks back up at me with wide eyes. His jaw wobbles before his gray tongue comes out to wet his disgusting, cracked lips.

"I... I apologize... We'll get you what you want," he says, smacking his partner and handing him Levi's list without breaking eye contact with me. "I'm not sure if we have everything on that list, but... I–I'll double check." He turns and moves urgently behind his boxes. I assume to work on Levi's list.

Levi gently grabs my arm and looks at it. "Are you okay?" he asks, seeing the small scratches and droplets of blood pooling.

"Yeah, I'm fine," I reassure him. "Just scratches from his skin."

Zissa steps up and peeks over his shoulder to look intently at my arm before yelling over the counter. "What kind of Goblin are you?"

The taller one turns with a frown, but when he sees what the commotion is, he pales. "Ahh. I—" his eyes dart to the left for a moment. "I didn't think I broke the skin," he protests as he looks at me.

"Yeah, yeah. Answer the question," Zissa urges.

The Goblin eyes Zissa before he turns and darts out the back of his stall.

"*Shit*," Zissa hisses and takes off after him, with Ryker right behind her. Knots jumps over the counter and pulls his sword, bringing it up to the chunky Goblin's neck and clucks his tongue to make sure he doesn't try anything sneaky.

"Don't move, Rez," Knots instructs, while Levi still has a hold of my arm. *I wasn't planning on it.*

Moni pops up to her four-foot self and sits on the counter. "Am I missing something? We haven't gone over the Goblin chapter in school yet."

Yeah, I'm also lost.

"What type of Goblin are you and your friend?" Knots kindly asks as he presses the sword tip deeper into the neck of the chubby side-kick.

"Hercules," he hiccups, and tears stream down his face. "We couldn't turn it down. The price was too great," he sobs.

What the hell is going on?

"Since you're in a chatty mood, why don't you tell me where the antidote is," Knots presses.

"Why would we have the antidote?" he sniffles, and Knots

pushes the sword harder into his neck, causing the Goblin to lean back into the boxes behind him, toppling them over.

"Oh, shit!" Moni squeaks, raising up and floating up closer to me. "Are those dead bodies?" Her bark flashes pale white before she crumbles to the floor with a soft plop onto a tarp.

Laying between the stacks of broken boxes are two fresh Goblin corpses with their necks slashed and black veins along their arms.

"How much you wanna bet those are the real shopkeepers?" Levi mutters.

"I think you'd win," I hiss, focusing on my arm. Black veins are starting to appear where the Goblin scratched me.

"The poison and the antidote are both made from elements of your body, right? I know you guys make a killing selling it. So, where's your stash?" Levi asks.

Knots uses his foot to gently nudge Moni awake, and she shoots up like a rocket, immediately shrinking and focusing on the Goblin at knife point.

"Levi?" I ask, a little panicked now.

"Rez. Pay attention to me," he coaxes, and I bring my attention back to him. His hazel eyes warm me as he smiles as calmly as he can manage at me. "I need you to stay calm. Knox is going to help through your connection." Levi's eyes dart off to the side as I feel Knox come up behind me, wrapping his arms around me. "Moni, can you help Knots find their antidote?" Levi calmly directs her.

I love the fact he can easily direct all of us so calmly, because I would probably blow up, but as it is, I am able to focus on his kind eyes and feel Knox's steady reassurance flowing through our link. And I do my best to block out the heat I feel slowly crawling up my forearm.

I see a flash of red out of my peripheral as Moni zips back and forth, frantically searching for the antidote. Another crash makes me jump, and Knox squeezes me gently as I hear Moni get into her enforcer role.

"Don't make me *boom* you! I will! That's my best friend you're fucking with," she yells.

"You don't understand. If I help, they will kill my family," the Goblin cries out.

"Who?" Knots demands, getting into his face.

"I can't." He shakes his head before it drops to his chest.

The crowd that we've drawn starts moving away hastily as Ryker and Zissa walk up behind Levi. In between them, they have the other Goblin wrapped up with a whip, his face bloodied, and he's limping.

"Is that one talking?" Ryker calls out, nodding to the Goblin Moni is glaring at.

"Just saying he can't tell us about the antidote," Knots replies.

"Same, except we found this on him," Zissa says, throwing a medallion on the counter. It's tarnished yellow with a black sigil and two blunt horns curving up to meet in the middle by a Demon's tail.

'How are we supposed to know who that belongs to? I mean, the two curvy horns are unique looking,' I muse.

'Those aren't curvy horns, Rez,' Knots says. *'Take a closer view.'*

I lean in and gasp at my mistake. How did I confuse cocks with horns? Thank Jesus Lynx isn't here to rub that in my face.

I hear the cursing and the shouts at my little faux pas and feel heat crawl up my neck as I focus back on Levi.

"Asmodeus?" Levi questions, reading the sigil.

Ryker comes over to me, asking, "How bad did he get you?" I stare down at my arm, and his eyes follow. "Fuck!" he curses under his breath. He pulls out his knife and pushes it against the Goblin's throat. "Now, you only have two choices.

You either give us the antidote that we *know* you have, or we kill you and get it from your dead corpse. Which one would you prefer?" Ryker asks very calmly.

The Goblin gulps and nods. "Okay, but we need protection. He will kill us and our families since we've failed in the mission he gave us."

"Who? That Imodium guy?" Moni asks, curiosity getting the better of her.

"It's Asmodeus, Moni," Levi corrects her.

"That's what I said!" She pouts and puts her hands on her hips.

"No, you called him a medicine to treat runny poo," I state.

"Oh, so he's diarrhea? Can't he just wear diapers for that? I don't understand," Moni whines.

"You guys are crazy. We're getting off track. Give us the antidote and I'll have Ryker and Knox take you someplace safe," Zissa promises.

"Okay. It's in the golden vial under the countertop," he admits and hangs his head. The other Goblin just continues to cry that he's sorry, that he did it for his family.

My heart breaks for the poor guy as Moni hands Levi the vial. The vial is pretty enough, but the sludge inside makes my stomach churn just looking at it. It's a dark white, visceral substance, and when Levi pops the cork, it smells even worse than the Goblins.

"I have to drink that?" I ask, wrinkling my nose.

"Not all of it. Just a sip, and the rest will go on your skin over the black veins," Levi supplies.

"Oh, great... I think I'd rather die," I whine. Levi brings it up to my mouth, and I gag, almost throwing up. I physically can't do it, even with the heat increasing along my forearm.

"Sorry. I seriously can't do it, guys. Go on without me." I dry heave, catching another whiff of it.

Levi glances over my shoulder, and Knox's arms become a vice grip around me as I find myself restrained.

"Fuck! What are you doing?" I squirm, trying to move.

"Saving you, kitten. You'll thank us later," Knox says as he lifts me up so I'm plastered against his chest.

Ryker comes up next to me and pinches my nose, but I refuse to open my mouth. No way in fucking hell am I drinking that shit. I have no idea *what* part of his body it came out of.

"Rez, please," Levi begs while holding the vial right above my lips, ready to betray me once I open my mouth to breathe.

'Knots!! Help. Do we even know if it's an antidote? It smells like shit; it's probably going to kill me.' I try to get his help, but all he says is sorry.

My lungs start to burn and my body starts to twitch involuntarily. Great, my own body fucking *betrays* me. My mouth flies open, and Levi quickly pours some of the foul liquid down my throat before slamming his hand against my lips. Ryker releases my nose and whispers in my ear.

"Come on, baby, be a good girl and swallow. We know you can!"

I send him a scathing look, and he shrugs unapologetically. "The faster you swallow, the quicker the taste is gone."

Fuck, he has a point.

I swallow the liquid down, then start coughing as it burns. Levi quickly starts pouring the rest of the vial along my arm, and I hear it sizzling on my skin, yet all I feel is a slight cooling sensation. I watch as the veins start to disappear.

Knox releases me, and I turn on all of my men in attendance. "That's it... None of you are getting any sex!" I yell, pointing at all of them. Cheers and boos explode around us from the closest stalls, and I'm too pissed to even be embarrassed. All I do is turn to the closest Demons and say, "Don't you have shopping to do rather than watch my shit show?" I hiss. A Demon that takes after my own smartass self smirks and says "no" while peering at some cloth.

I turn back to study my guys and I huff, "I'm serious. You're not getting shit from me."

"We were only trying to save your life," Levi explains.

I turn to the blubbering Goblin that Knots is walking around the stall to join Ryker. "How do you produce the antidote?"

He sniffs and looks up at me with wide eyes. "What?"

"Where did that white secretion come from? Like what orifice?" I ask, knowing damn straight I shouldn't. I could have just walked away and believed it came from sugar and rainbows and unicorn farts delivered it, but I just had to ask.

He swallows and glances around nervously, as if waiting for someone to save him before he brings his attention back to me. "It comes from our armpits, ma'am. It's the sweat that's produced while our body warms to make the poison."

"Ugh. I think I'm going to..." Moni doesn't finish her sentence before she faints just as Knox reaches out to catch her.

Well, I'm glad he didn't say it was jizz.

I run to the side of the stall next to the Demon that didn't have anything better to do and give him a show. I mean, who doesn't enjoy watching a girl throw up armpit sweat?

CHAPTER 20

I Shall Call him Fluffy, and he Shall be Mine!

Rez

After the ordeal of purging my body of foul—I can't even go there—Ryker and Knox decide to escort the Goblins back to L.A.M.B.'s mansion. I'm sure they have more questions and creative ways of getting answers than we did in the marketplace. Thankfully, Moni gives me a small bottle of water to rinse my mouth out, else I might have insisted on going back with them. The only thing we discovered was they were told to kill the merchants, but the poison was taking too long, so they sliced their throats when they saw us coming down the path.

Levi, Moni, and I search through the stall and find a few of the items on our lists, but not all of them. Moni does a little dance when she finds a bag of coffee beans, but she says it wasn't the jackpot she was looking for. She was hoping she would find Sparks brand coffee.

"What do you still need?" Zissa asks, scanning the area as Levi finishes zipping up the last of the ingredients into a satchel.

"I have everything on my list. Rez?" Levi looks at my paper. "Why do you have two lists?"

"Because I found a spell that repels a memory potion, and I wanted to make sure that we are protected against Emer's threat. I just need to find a locket or container of some sort to hold the spell. Do you know of anything?" I ask, hoping that he's run across something in his studies. This is kinda outside my wheelhouse of knowledge.

Levi jerks back to look at me in surprise. "Really? You found a spell for that?" he asks, slowly cupping my cheeks. I try to nod between his hands. "Have I ever told you how amazing you are?"

"A girl does love compliments, so I would remember you saying so," I tease.

"I am beyond grateful to have you in my life, Rez. There are no words to express how amazing you are, still thinking of me even with everything else going on around you," he confesses. A little piece of me breaks at his admission. Of course, I would think of him. He's mine, and I don't want to lose him or anyone else. Before I can say anything, he pulls me in for a gentle kiss, our lips barely touching.

"I love you... so much," he whispers, before kissing me again.

I don't know if he meant for me to hear it, but I do, and I deepen the kiss before reluctantly pulling away.

"Levi, I love you too. And I refuse to let Emer take you away from me so easily," I say, while caressing his jaw. "So let's make sure that doesn't happen, okay?"

"You? You love me?" Levi looks comical, with his shocked expression. It's like telling him you just met the real Santa Claus.

"YES!" I shout, and Levi gives me a crooked smile before he picks me up and swings me around. "Now, put me down so we can work." I laugh. "You still need to tell me if you know of something that can hold a powerful spell."

"I do," Zissa speaks up. "But you won't find it here in this market."

Turning, I give her my full attention. "Really?"

"Yeah, but you'll have to promise me you won't tell L.A.M.B. we went or that you even know about this place." Her icy blue eyes bore into each of ours as she scans our group.

"Why?" Knots asks, as he climbs over the counter.

"Because it's forbidden for me to go," she simply supplies.

"Okay," Moni and Levi agree simultaneously.

"No, I want it from Rez," she challenges as she stands with her feet shoulder-width apart and her hands on her hips.

"Why?" My eyes narrow. *What's her angle here?*

"Because I want a girlfriend," she admits, and my eyebrows disappear at her confession. Her arms drop as she holds her hands in front of her, giving me a vulnerable expression. Her icy blue eyes soften as she worries her lip for a moment before she continues. "All the friends I have are males. Plus, I'm trying to help Ryker get back on your good graces. People think because we're Sex Demons that we should automatically be good partners, but it's a hundred percent the opposite. We have no idea how to handle relationships because that's never been a thing for us."

She sighs and glances down at her feet as she kicks a small stone for a moment before giving me her attention once again.

"Please, it would just mean a lot to me if you would promise and allow me to tell you my side of the story before you go off and decide to cut off Ry completely," she begs.

This was what I wanted, right? To know their past... or what their story was. And besides, I need those containers.

"Sure, no skin off my back," I say and give her a brief smile.

"Great, this way. Don't talk to anyone, or touch anything." She turns to move deeper into the market.

"Where are we going?" Moni asks as she shrinks down to catch a ride on my shoulder.

"Onyx's Mort," Zissa says, making a sharp turn and squeezing between a crack in the wall that I did not see.

"Black Death?" Knots questions.

"Sounds like a blast," I murmur as I slide in and start side-stepping along the rough wall behind Zissa.

"Hold me," Moni whispers, squeezing my neck.

Zissa gawks when a light appears above our heads. "Wow, that's never happened before," she says in awe.

Moni and I chuckle at her.

"What?" she snaps.

"Sorry, just never thought you'd be awestruck by something so simple as one of Levi's light spells," I say, smiling. "Thank you, honey buns," I say to Levi in a singsong tone.

Levi reaches out and squeezes my hand.

"Oh. Yeah. I should have figured that out. I guess I'm just nervous," she admits.

"You? Nervous? You're like Xena: Warrior Princess, and you're nervous?" Moni jokes.

"Well, yeah. I've heard some stories about you, though, Moni. You have an offense or defense that brings creatures to their knees. You, Rez, have some wild magic. Who knows what you'll be able to do once you've gotten control of it. If what Astaroth told me has any truth to it, you're possibly an Angel, Knots. And the guys, or the so called 'princes,' aren't just normal supernaturals either. And here I am, just a Succubus with *some* knife skills who's friends with one of them," she scoffs. "So, yeah, I'm nervous," she admits.

"How did you become friends with Ryker?" I ask, since she led me down the hole.

"Well, I did promise to tell you. It was a long time ago. Ryker was going through his change, or getting his Incubus powers. Did you know that as a Sex Demon we can easily drain and kill our partners?" she asks, waiting for me to answer.

"Yeah, I think I read that somewhere," I respond, not knowing where she's going with this.

"Well, Lilith brought him to Hell because she thought it best he learned how to feed properly from another Sex Demon. So she brought him to my doorstep. I was his teacher for a time, and he would feed off of me before I would bring in others for him to practice with. Afterward, we just naturally became friends and kept in touch. I turned into more of a mentor if he ever had questions."

"Oh! So you were his PIMP!" Moni shouts, and her words echo around the passageway.

Zissa laughs but nods as a light starts shining from the other end. "Yeah, after I had him first, I guess I was, in human terms."

Shit. Zissa was his first? I don't know how to feel about that.

"I guess I should thank you for teaching him all of his tricks, huh?" I deadpan.

"Oh not at all, Rez. From what Ryker told me, your relationship with him is different from anyone else's. You guys are *mates.* No Incubi or Sucubi has ever had one before him. If something were to happen to you, he probably couldn't feed like he used to. He might survive by living off of the sexual energy around big group outings—like parties where sexual tension is high—but what kind of life is that?" she asks.

Fuck. I never thought of it that way before.

"Not only that. From what he said, you can actually see his tattoos and his so-called 'tricks' don't work on you either. Now *that's* something that has never happened before. I don't know where I would be if I wasn't able to seduce and change for each of my partners." She looks back over her shoulder at me as we almost come to the end of the tunnel and smiles. "What you guys have is extremely special. It's unheard of in the Demon world," she confesses. "Plus, if there're any feelings between both of you like Ryker has hinted at, then that will play into your physical relationship too."

Talk about a mental slap. I didn't realize how important or unique Ryker and I were. Yes, I knew he said I was the only one he functioned around, but... *Shit,* this is a whole new level. My mind whirls as I think back to how I reacted, walking away because he didn't use a stupid title to introduce me. *A title he wouldn't be used to using, ever.* I sigh and drop my head. It dawns on me how stupid I was to expect him to treat me differently all of a sudden, when he was never raised that way.

Doesn't that make me a hypocrite? The guys had to ease me into the idea of multiple partners, and here I am, giving Ryker a hard time for something he wasn't used to. Fuck me... I'm a horrible girlfriend! Shit... I mean mate. Ugh.

When am I going to get this right?

We step out onto a small outcropping of land with planks lying over bubbling black liquid, which we have to cross before continuing. The atmosphere is completely different here. Instead of the noise of creatures trying to sell their items or haggling over prices, it's quiet. Creatures huddle against walls, alcoves, or around cooking fires. There are no lights along the walls or ceilings, creating an unlively ambience. I definitely see where they came up with the name Black Death.

We carefully make our way over the black sludge and onto the main thoroughfare. Following Zissa, we weave between a few shady characters and into a short but wide alleyway before we come to a stall with crystal vials hanging from the beams.

"Ah, I see you've come to the right place. Find something

that catches your eye? Or did you come for something darker?" The young Demon with solid black eyes and yellow skin asks Zissa as we approach.

"Yes," she says, and I place my list in her outstretched hand. "We need four dragon scales, a vial of moon drops, bat flowers, and"—she drops her voice and leans in closer—"Demstones." The Demon quickly backs up and nods, but not before I catch his sly smile. Hell, down here, it would pass as a sinister one.

"Oh, and can you see if you have Sparks coffee?" Moni asks with hopeful eyes.

"Yes, I'll see what I can do." He goes about searching through his supplies, so I take a moment to look around.

There's only a few people in this short alleyway, and the setup at the corner of the entrance catches my eye.

"Will this do?" the Demon asks, but Moni's screech grabs my attention first.

"Sparks!" Moni cries as she picks up a sack of coffee beans and hugs it to her chest. "Now I can make all the coffee in the world!" Happy tears gather in her eyes. A throat clearing brings my attention back to the Demon, who's giving Moni a bewildered look. She kisses the bag and gently places it back on the counter before patting it tenderly and shrinking down to her preferred size.

There's a pretty pink stone the size of a quail's egg with a yellow swirl in the middle sitting in his hand. "How many do you have?" I ask, thinking of all of my friends, including the ones Emer didn't mention. Knowing her and the way my luck is, she would fuck with me out of spite. "I need eight more."

The Demon chokes but tries to hide it with a cough, apparently talking shit in his demonic language as he bags up my other ingredients. "This crazy girl; thinks I'm daft. Nine Demstones? She doesn't look like she can afford her own food, let alone stones this powerful."

My mouth drops as I consider this Demon. I glance back at Knots and Levi, while Moni just chuckles in my ear.

"Excuse me, but I have no problem affording my fucking food, or a bath, or clothes, which you are sorely lacking." I point out.

Leave it to the Demon to not be ashamed that I called him out. He just peers at me over the counter and chuckles. "Listen, I like your spirit. How about we help each other out? I know where you can get some more Demstones. I'll give you the spot that I harvest them from, if you can bring some back to me. I don't care about the size or shape. I just want five, and you can obviously take what you need," he bargains with me.

I don't trust anyone, but I also know I need those Demstones if I want to protect my friends. "Why?" I ask suspiciously.

He chuckles. "Hmm. A smart one." He leans back and pulls his leg up on the counter, showing us that half of his calf is missing. "It's not exactly safe for an unarmed Demon, and I lost my partner on our last run. It's taken me a few months just to heal, to get back here to sell my stuff. I need to make a living, and you need Demstones. Plus, you'll be able to find your bat flowers there, so it sounds like a good deal for me."

"Sounds like a good deal, but why trust us?" Knots leans in.

"Because I know that if I don't play nice, you could easily send L.A.M.B. after my ass, and you still need the bat flowers, which I don't have," he confidently says with a pointed gaze at my left wrist.

"You can see that?" Shock races through me that he can see the brand from where he's at. He's not even that close, nor is he touching my skin.

"Of course, with our license to sell, we have the sight to see brands. I just don't always sell legal shit; that's why I'm here." He points out.

Well damn.

Zissa regards me and the rest of the group. I swallow around the lump that's stuck in my throat as I take her in, knowing that they are waiting on my call. "You wanted my friendship? Well, that needs to start with trust first. So, if you can get us there and back alive, you got it!" I tell her, and she smiles as if I just gave her the biggest gift.

"Deal. We can plan to go first thing tomorrow morning," she says, then turns back to the Demon. "Tell me how to get there and what to expect."

Moni flies over to Knots and starts talking about going on another adventure, but this time, it's in Hell. It's like a field trip! Levi listens intently to the Demon and adds my items to his satchel, but my attention goes back to the entrance once again.

Walking over, I spot a Demon sitting by a pen with a few animals moving around in it. He spots me approaching and throws the haunch of meat he was eating into the pen. The sound of ripping flesh and growls roar from the pen.

"What's in there?" I ask, trying to see but not daring to get too close.

"Hound puppies. My bitch had a litter, and I need to get rid of them. Want one? These are vicious as fuck and can tear through bone in seconds," he brags. As if to prove a point, I hear the snapping of the bone he had thrown in there. Then one pup looks up at me with beady red eyes.

"Ahh... I'm good," I say and start backing up, but a thick chain by his foot catches my eye. Following it, I peek at something that does grab my attention. "Wait... What's that?" I ask, pointing to the puppy that at a glance could only be eight weeks old. The closest breed it resembles is a golden retriever, but with short hair and two little nubs poking out behind his ears. *Are those the start of horns?* Runes glow along his front legs, and a short trail of fire runs from between his ears down to the end of his really long tail.

"Oh. He's spare parts."

"W-what?... What do you mean?"

"Exactly what I said. People will pay good money for Hell-hound parts, and that's what I'm going to sell him for," he informs me, and my heart shudders for a moment.

"How much for him?" I ask without a second thought.

"Which part do you want?" he asks, picking up a knife.

"NO! I mean him as in the whole dog!" I explain.

"You don't want this menace. Look at him! He ain't right. His tail is too long, his skin is funky, not to mention he's not vicious at all," he points out. "I wonder if my son dropped him as soon as he came out... Maybe that's why he's goofy acting," he mumbles to himself.

"How much are you selling your normal Hellhounds for? I'll pay the same price, but for him," I say adamantly.

He scoffs, shaking his head, but he gets up and walks over to the little guy and unhooks him. As soon as the chain is off of him, he comes running over to me, and I squat down to pick him up. He trips over his own feet and rolls to a stop before me.

"Good luck. He will probably cause you more heartache than he's worth," he says, then has a quick look at my arm. I hold out my left wrist, and he raises an eyebrow and nods. "But it seems you're already up for those types of tasks."

I pet the puppy and notice how his fiery mane is warm but doesn't burn... yet. *I wonder how to train him.* Standing, I'm happily surprised that the puppy starts to follow me when my friends meet me at the opening of the alley.

"Eek! He's so cute," Moni says, popping up to her normal size and bending down to pet him.

"You know Lucifer is going to kill you, right?" Zissa notes.

"He loves me," I retort, and glance down to where Moni is laughing.

"Look, Rez, he's giving me love nibbles," she adds as he chews on her fingers.

"Moni, he's using you as a chew toy," I tell her.

Shit, maybe Lucifer is going to kill me.

CHAPTER 21

Let the Bodies hit the Floor

Rez

O kay, so I don't have a problem admitting when I'm wrong, but I sure as hell wasn't going to admit it to the guy that was going to chop up my new pup. Making it back to L.A.M.B.'s residence is an easy trek after the first five Demons that we walk behind are knocked off their balance and fall to the side. It turns out I didn't have to worry about my puppy staying by my side, he heels just fine. His tail is the unruly one. It trips Demons, sending them falling over, and one even fell into a fire pit as we walked by. After that, they just scatter as we walk down the path.

I cringed after the first few accidents, but after the Demons turned and snarled at my apologies, I changed my attitude. *Fight fire with fire and a charming hellhound.*

He's so adorable how he growls at the small rodents running around. I even catch him chasing a small stone that the breeze moves down the pathway. He's so full of life and easily distracted when he runs around and grabs his extra long tail, rolling upon himself and forgetting we're moving along the trail. Oddly, it's so hard to come up with a name, but I'm hoping as I watch him interact I'll be able to come up with something soon. I just know I don't want to be too quick about it like I was with Lynx—but I was six then, so I don't think people should judge.

"What the hell is that?" Lucifer asks as soon as we walk into the parlor.

"Your new puppy? You seem so bitter; I thought you could use a little cheering up," I announce, giving him a big cheesy smile, but when he still stares at me with no expression, I give up. "Okay, fine. So, I got a puppy. They were going to chop him up into Hellhound bits, and I couldn't let them do that!" I explain. The sound of something sizzling pulls my eyes away from Lucifer and down to my feet. My pup had an hour walk back here, and he chooses *now* to piss on one of Lucifer's chair legs? And to make matters worse, his piss is eating away the metal and the fabric covering it.

My friends purse their lips as they scurry past me and down the hall to our rooms as I stand there to face Lucifer's wrath. Cowards. "So, um... You can fix that, right?" I ask as I point to his ruined furniture. "I have training to get to, and I don't want to piss off a Wrath Demon," I say, giving him a nervous smile. He closes his eyes, pinching the bridge of his nose, so I take my chance to run while he's not looking. With my puppy chasing after me, I can't help the giggle as I hear Lucifer yelling my name.

After quickly changing into a pair of leggings and a tank top, I meet Moni, Knots, and Levi in the hallway. "Does anyone have any idea how to get to the training room, or know where we're supposed to meet?" Moni asks as we walk back down our hall.

Zissa leans against the wall at the end and gives us a salute as we reach her. "That's my job once again. Come on," she greets us as she propels herself off the wall and heads down a hallway we haven't been down before. My puppy and Moni take off as they zip back and forth, playing tag down the hallway.

"What are you going to name him?" Knots asks, bringing my attention to him. He's dressed in casual light-blue sweats, his hair pulled back with a hair tie, and he's wearing tennis shoes. Damn! I kinda want to rip his clothes off, but I notice he's a little paler than normal.

"I don't know yet. Are you okay? You're looking a little pale," I ask as I put the back of my hand against his forehead.

He chuckles and pushes my hand away. "Yes. I'm just a little tired, that's all. Although, I'm sure I'll wake right up when I see your ass moving in that outfit." He smirks.

"Knots!"

"What? It's a beautiful ass. I can't wait to see it kicking ass," he teases.

"I'll more than likely be falling on it," I mumble.

"Well, you have plenty of cushioning back there to pad your fall." He laughs when my jaw drops at his words.

"Don't worry, Rez; I will be here at your every beck and call, ready to rub anything that's sore, including that wonderful backside of yours," Levi says, winning some major boyfriend points as he comes up beside me and cocks an eyebrow at Knots.

Knots, in fun, throws his head back and laughs. I can't help it, my mouth starts to water as I take in Levi's appearance. His gray basketball shorts and black tank top against his tan skin make him appear more down to earth, and I love how I can see those subtle changes. Like how his hazel eyes shine as he jokes with me and Knots. It's the first time I've seen him in shorts, and I wish I had a working phone, because I need a picture. I found a note from Zeke in my room with a charger on my nightstand, stating he got it to work, so my phone is charging in my room right now.

"There you are," Astaroth's voice rings out.

I'm so focused on Levi that I don't notice we've stopped in front of an archway leading into a massive room made up of dark wood and concrete walls. This is nothing like Mr. Weston's setup back home, where there are seats, a few mats, and a wall full of mirrors. This room also has mirrors, but they're toward the back, along with dummies like the ones at a shooting range. Punching bags, a boxing ring, and a range of weapons take up space along the wall too. There's a boxed off area that appears to be an office, and the floors are covered in... black wood?

'*Why would someone want black wood?*' I wonder.

'*To hide the blood,*' Knots supplies, and a shudder runs down my back.

Okay then.

Ryker, Knox, Zeke, JP, Lynx, and Chester are already off to one side, stretching on a set of mats; they wave at us. Moni comes riding into the room on the back of my puppy, and they skid to an undignified halt as they crash into Astaroth's leg.

"Oops," Moni squeaks as she hops off of my puppy and flies over to Chester.

Astaroth glances down at my puppy, who's running around grabbing his tail successfully, then coming back to me. "I doubt this was on your list. Has Lucifer seen him yet?" He quirks an eyebrow in question. He's shirtless, with a man bun and wearing black martial arts pants.

"Of course." I cock my head and proceed to walk around him to the mats where everyone else is sitting. "And I'm still standing," I say as I throw out my arms and walk backward, feeling bold.

"Maybe not for long," Murmur laughs, coming out of the office structure in the back with a long pole in his hand while wearing identical pants as Astaroth. "Make sure you stretch because you'll be landing on your ass a lot," he chuckles.

I give Knots a pointed look, and all he does is laugh as I sit down between Zeke and JP and start stretching. I hear everyone laughing as the puppy runs over to us, but he trips over his feet and tail until he reaches the mat and plops down to start chewing on the edge.

Well, that works too.

"I can't believe you got a puppy," JP says. "But I can't wait to spoil him."

"Thought of a name yet?" Zeke asks as he studies my hound.

"Not yet," I admit as I switch legs and get in a good stretch.

Murmur throws a small pole over by the mat, and it rolls to the back of the room, sending my puppy after it and out of our way.

"So, who here has used a Cudgel before?" Murmur calls out, and we all blink our eyes but say nothing. "Are you kidding me? What do they teach you in that school?" He sighs in frustration and runs his hand through his hair.

Moni raises her hand.

"Yes, Moni," he calls.

"We learned some defensive moves when we had a Death-weaver running loose," she helpfully says.

Zeke shrinks into himself slightly as his shoulders round, and I already know what he's thinking. I lean into him and grab his hand, whispering in his ear, "It's okay. We don't blame you, remember?" I give him a kiss on the cheek, and he seems to brighten up a little, giving me a small smile.

"Well... That's a start. Grab a partner and come on up and show me," Murmur coaxes. He places both hands on the end of his staff and rests his chin on it as Moni gets up in front of him. She makes eye contact with me and gives me a cheesy smile. I know that look. I let out a groan but join Moni front and center.

F ive minutes into watching me and Moni spar, Murmur wasn't having any of it. He called it all garbage and told us to forget everything that we had learned at Purgatory. Astaroth slipped in and said it shouldn't be hard since it wasn't much. *The nerve of him.* Murmur then gave everyone a bo-staff, paired us off, and got us to work. I've been blessed to pair up with the weapons master himself.

"Again," Astaroth barks as I lay on my back, trying to catch my breath. His freaking tail whipped out and distracted me, so he got the upper hand, beating me once again.

"I can't even feel my arms anymore," I whine, as I slowly get off the mat. He's been running me through all the blocks and basic attacks, repeating them until he's satisfied, to the point my arms feel like Jell-O right now.

"I thought you said you've had some training," he taunts, opening himself up for me to strike, but I'm not falling for it.

"Think of it as more like karate. I'm what you would call a scrapper. I know how to throw a punch and fight dirty," I insist. "None of this formal weapons crap," I huff out, leaning against my staff.

In one swift motion, his staff strikes the end of mine, sending me sprawling to the floor again.

"What the fuck?" I grind my teeth as I jump up without my stick and advance toward him. He just cocks an eyebrow, as if to mock me. "Why'd you do that?" I get in his face and I don't know what provokes me to do it, but I shove him—at least I try to.

He blocks my shove, and I go for a right hook, which he dodges easily, then brings his right knee up and lightly jabs me in the ribs.

Fuck!

Growling, I move in closer and send another punch his

way, and when he kicks out, I'm ready and block it with my own knee. But I'm not fast enough for the punch in my shoulder, which knocks me to the ground.

Walking over to me, he scoffs. "Is that all you have?" he questions as he gives me his hand, but I refuse it and roll out of his way. I size him up as we start to circle each other. *There is no way I can take on this guy, but I'm pissed and hangry. I want food.*

Finally eyeing something that I can use to my advantage, I smile as I meet his eyes.

"See something that amuses you?" Astaroth questions as he takes on a lower stance.

"Yep!"

"Want to enlighten me?" he jokes.

"Sure... in just a few seconds." I move in and once again throw a punch that he easily blocks, but I pivot on my back leg and do a two-step dance move—t*hank you, Mom, for a few dance classes*—that puts me at his flank, where I deliver two short jabs to his kidney. My heart is in my throat as he swirls to face me and his arm swings around to knock me in the head. I quickly duck and pivot, driving my heel down *hard* on his tail that I've noticed he likes to sweep over the floor when he moves.

"Fuck!" he bellows and stumbles, and I take my advantage by aiming for his inner thigh.

I'm not stupid enough to hit a Wrath Demon in his junk, but I'll show him I could have. He drops to his knee as his eyes flash silver, taking a deep breath and shaking his head. He studies me as I stand motionless while it finally dawns on me that maybe I should be running. But then a smile slowly appears on his lips, and I get cocky. "I totally got you!" I say, putting my hands on my waist.

"I was pulling my punches, but I see you have the talent to

note weakness. Who taught you that?" He stands, giving his inner thigh one last pat and considering me.

"Um... Taught me what?" I ask, pulling at the hem of my shirt in uncertainty now.

"How did you know to aim for my tail?" He walks over and picks up our bo-staffs, beckoning me to follow him to the end of the room.

"When you move, your tail likes to show off and draw my eye away from you. It's a distraction if I'm not careful, so I used it to my advantage," I admit, shrugging.

He opens the door and ushers me inside to what I thought was an office, but boy was I wrong. It's a weapon's stronghold. Along the wall are cases and underneath them are lines of open drawers. From what I can see, there are all kinds of small weapons here. Ninja throwing stars, brass knuckles with a knife protruding from the middle, free knives, something that resembles wolverine claws, and small Grim Reaper sickles.

"As a self-proclaimed scrapper, you need to be close to your enemy. To do that, you need a weapon that you can easily work with." He walks over to a cabinet at the back and pulls out the top four drawers.

I glance down and all I see is very shiny and sharp metal. "No practice or blunted weapons?" I ask, studying the different ones.

When I get no answer, I peer up at Astaroth and find him slowly shaking his head. "It's a good thing you heal fast."

I squint my eyes as he laughs and picks up two sets of weapons.

"Murmur likes to talk," he laughs as we head out of the room.

Damn Mischief Demon from hell. Let's add another reason why I want to poke his eyes out. That, and how he's running Knots into the ground as we walk past them.

Knots

I thought I had it rough when I was paired with Murmur, but I think Rez got the worst of it out of all of us. Astaroth just smiled when he called her name and said she's with him. I think Moni had a good pairing when she got Zissa. Although, Zissa's the one that's probably learning the most when it comes to patience. Every time Moni gets excited about a move she perfected, she faints and Zissa has to wake her up gently. From what I've caught, they are up to seven. JP's smooth and calming attitude was a good pairing when pitted against Knox and his anger issues. Lynx happily took on Ryker, and I wish I could sit back and see how both of their cocky attitudes battled each other. I couldn't help but notice how Chester appeared relieved to have Levi.

It's already been thirty minutes of intense blocking and flourishing attacks with Murmur, and I'm exhausted. I wipe away the sweat on my forehead as my breath saws in and out of my lungs, hoping I don't look as bad as I feel.

"Come on, Knots. Just fifteen more minutes and then we break for dinner," Murmur says, bouncing on the balls of his feet. "Then back to work! It's just like old times, even though you might not remember it."

He's right, just a few more minutes, and I can take a break. He pauses with his movement and really studies me.

"Or do you need to rest?" His concern is what kills me.

I can't remember the last time I've had to work this hard. Even when I had to defend against the Rebel attack, I wasn't this winded, and there was more than just one rival.

"No, I'm good," I say, before feigning an upper swing aimed for his head, and when he goes to block, I sweep low and crack him against his leg.

And it's on we go, back and forth, trading blows until he gets me right below the left ribs and I have to step back, raising my hand for a break. Wheezing, I lean over to help alleviate the pain, but when I do, black spots encroach on my vision.

'Knots!?' Is that Rez yelling for me? *Is she in trouble?*

I try to will my body to move, but I can't even feel it now. My knees slam into the floor, but strangely, no pain comes with it as the room tilts. I catch sight of feet running my way just as my vision goes black.

CHAPTER 22

The Devil Within

Knots

T he sun's rays warm my exposed skin as I lay against the cool ground. Tall green grass lightly sways in the breeze as I enjoy the scent of flowers in the meadow.

"Kanotiel! Where are you?" a feminine voice laughs.

"Maybe he's hiding?" a boy's voice speaks up.

"But he said he would train us," the girl whines.

"Maybe it's a test!" he blurts.

I chuckle, not able to hold in my laughter.

"Did you hear that?" the girl gasps.

The sound of them taking off reaches me, but I don't move until I hear them run in the opposite direction. I sigh and shake my head as I slowly get up and brush off my pants.

"Got ya!" they scream, tackling me from behind. I turn and take in Hannah and Gabriel, both with bright blue eyes and brown hair, just like their mother.

"How did you do that?" I ask in amazement.

"Momma said to keep it a secret," Gabriel teases.

"Fine, keep your secrets for now, but I'll find out," I say as I reach out and mess up his mop of hair.

"Momma sent us to find you. She said we're done with our chores and it's time for training," Hannah reminds me.

"So it is. Race you back!" I yell and start running, but the kids catch up soon enough and bypass me as we race through the waist-high grass back to the house.

"Knots! Please wake up." Rez's voice cracks, jarring me out of my dream. I think it was a dream. My head feels fuzzy, my tongue feels thick and heavy, and so do my eyes. To make things worse, my legs feel extremely warm.

"Rez," I croak.

"Oh! You're awake," she sighs, grabbing my hand. "Are you in pain?"

"Can't... open... eyes. Tongue... swollen," I manage to get out.

"Just relax, Knots," Lilith says, and Rez's soft hand squeezes mine. "I'm just going to apply some ointment to your eyes that should help relieve any soreness or pain. I also have some liquid that should soothe your tongue and throat."

"What are his stats, Lilith?" a familiar voice asks.

"Just one moment, Carl, and I'll get them for you," she snaps.

"I got it, Mom," Ryker says, and I hear him read off numbers that make no sense to me.

Lilith applies some ointment to my eyelids and pours a small amount of sweet liquid into my mouth, relieving my pain. A sigh escapes me from the immediate relief, yet my legs are still warm. I slowly open my eyes and the prettiest gray eyes stare down at me.

"Hey," Rez sighs.

"Hey yourself." I try to smile, but I can't find the energy. "What happened?"

"You fainted," Rez explains.

"Like a bitch," Lynx adds, and I swear it's on when he gets his memory back.

"Lynx," Rez growls. "Not the time."

'Help me sit up, please?' I ask Rez. I hate feeling this weak. I'm a Door Knight, a protector. But I know Rez won't make me feel lesser or judge me for this vulnerable moment.

Rez helps me sit up and JP soon joins her, both even propping pillows behind me. Glancing down at my legs, I now understand why they are so warm. Rez's little puppy is asleep on them. Lilith is standing next to a monitor where Dr. Steinbeck's image is displayed, and I can hear typing coming from it. I only have a few things hooked up to me, along with a bag of fluids that I've seen hooked up to Rez before, so I'm not too worried. There's a sink, counter, and some cabinets on the other side of the room, but besides Rez, her puppy, JP, Lynx, Ryker, and Lilith, the room is bare.

"You okay, man?" JP asks, looking worried as his eyes study me for any injuries.

"I don't know what happened. I just felt really weak," I admit.

"Well, Knots... If what Lilith told me is true and you were an Angel, that's probably the reason," Dr. Steinbeck says without glancing up.

"That doesn't make any sense. Lucifer, Astaroth, Murmur, and Bez aren't falling to their knees and feeling weak," Rez argues.

"Correct, Miss Taylor, and why is that?" Dr. Steinbeck stops what he's doing and studies us. As we stare back at him blankly, he nods, and I hear clicking on the other side as he continues. "Obviously, I've never had the chance to study an Angel, but L.A.M.B. are *fallen* angels. They chose to follow my love to Hell and make it their home. Given Knots condition, I don't believe he's a *fallen* angel, and being in Hell, he's suffering the consequences."

"Oh, shit," Rez says under her breath, but I hear her. She goes to pull away from me, but I grip her hand harder and turn her toward me.

"No. This is not your fault," I stress.

"Yes it is!" she says, dropping her eyes. "I pulled you here. I didn't mean to. I mean, I'm glad you're here, but I was being selfish. I wouldn't have brought you here if I'd have known you'd get sick or... ugh!" She throws her other hand in the air.

"Calm down, Nerezza. It doesn't help to stress out the patient, or have you been out of my presence so long you forgot that?" Dr. Steinbeck says in a patronizing tone. I'm surprised Rez hasn't figured out a way to slap him through the screen. As it is, she just stares at him, speechless.

"Rez, dear. We might have a temporary solution until you go home on Sunday, okay? There's a spell that could slow down the ill effects that he might have from being down here. It doesn't work as a shield, more like an IV drip to help sick patients with an infection. I think I just need a charm to hold his spell," Lilith explains.

I watch Rez as she bites her lower lip, and I already know what she's going to suggest.

'*No. You don't even know if you'll get new ones tomorrow,*' I try to sway her, but her set jaw tells me she's already made her decision.

"I'll be right back. I have something you can use," she says and runs out of the room.

"Fuck!"

"What is she getting?" Lilith asks, considering me.

"She's getting you a Demstone," I admit.

"Smart and resourceful. You guys have no idea what you have before you, do you?" Lilith smiles before walking over to the counter and opening a few cabinets. She pulls out a small caldron, adds the contents from a few vials and snaps her fingers, lighting the fire burner beneath.

"You're going to do the spell here?" Ryker asks, walking over to see what she's doing.

"Where else would I go? He's here, and the only thing I'm missing is the Demstone, which Rez is bringing," she says, and pinches Ryker's cheek.

"Dr. Steinbeck?" I ask, grabbing his attention.

"Yes, Knots?" Rez's puppy stirs and moves up into my lap, burying his head under his paw.

"I know your impression is limited due to lack of knowledge of Angels, but what is the worst-case scenario based on the facts that you have in front of you? With and without this spell?" I ask, concentrating on petting the puppy, not wanting to make eye contact.

Maybe if I don't see his expression, it won't hurt as much.

"Based on your stats and your condition... from what I was told of how you arrived there today? With the spell, you might feel weak, and a little groggy, as if you have a cold or fever, but you'll likely feel better once you get out of Hell," he reassures me.

"And without?" I push him.

"You'll slowly waste away in a few days, either dying or becoming a true fallen angel and possibly be trapped in Hell. So make sure you get back here before then," he advises me as the room gently rocks from his words.

"You won't tell Rez that part?" I ask Dr. Steinbeck.

"Doctor–patient privilege. My lips are sealed," he replies.

I nod and glance up to see Ryker, Lynx, JP, and Lilith studying me.

"No one tell Rez! We only show positivity, got it?" I demand.

Lynx and Ryker give me a reluctant thumbs up. JP nods

but doesn't make eye contact, and Lilith just smiles as she nods.

I lean back and close my eyes as I wonder what will happen next if this spell doesn't work.

I must have drifted off to sleep because Rez wakes me with feather light kisses.

"Hey, big guy. It's time to wake up and see if this works," Rez coaxes, and the smell of something delicious accompanies her.

I pull myself into a sitting position, looking around the room to notice we are now alone. "Where's the puppy?"

"Taking after his namesake right now, I'm sure." She giggles.

"What did you end up naming him? He was warm and comforting." I tell her and she laughs.

"I definitely didn't name him anything like that. While you've been asleep, he's been causing chaos. Chasing after Arte Demons, peeing everywhere, chewing on a few things he shouldn't be. So, he's been my little collector of chaos. He's a little reaper."

"So you named him Reaper?"

"Yep!"

"Fitting." I nod. Then I spot a covered tray behind her on the counter. "Whatcha got there?" I ask.

"Oh, that's our dinner," she answers. "But first..." She lifts up a rope chain necklace with the Demstone attached.

Mixed emotions hit me as I see the finished product of the spell in her hands. I know she needs it for Levi, and needs more for the others, yet she's giving me the only one she has.

"Rez—"

"Nope. I won't hear it. Besides, it's already done, and I

want you feeling better so you can see me get my ass kicked by Astaroth with these new weapons." She tries to wiggle her eyebrows, and it makes her look ridiculous but drags a chuckle out of me.

Sighing, I bow my head so she can slip the chain over it. Holding the stone in her hands, she whispers, "*Custodire.*"

"Protect?" I question, raising an eyebrow as she lays the charm against my chest.

Rez gives me a sheepish look and shrugs. "Lilith said it works mostly on intent from the user. So, do you feel anything?" she asks, biting her lower lip.

I shake my head. "No. I don—wait." The necklace starts to warm, but that's the only indication I feel that it's working. "The necklace feels warm." I smile at Rez, and she does a little dance and fist pump.

"Good. I didn't want to lose you either," she says, and pulls me in for a kiss, her lips soft against mine as I pull her close to me.

"Never," I promise, pushing her hair out of her face. My stomach growls, and she laughs.

"It seems like I can save you twice!" She pulls away and grabs the tray, bringing it over and climbing on the bed with me. "Dinner is served," she announces. Pulling off the lid, she reveals two bowls of soup and sandwiches. "Compliments of Lilith. Dr. Steinbeck advises you to take it easy for the rest of the day and tomorrow, and once you're back home, you should be fine."

"Thank you for taking care of me," I tell her, and sweetly she grabs my hand and squeezes it.

"Thank me by eating your food," she smirks.

"Yes ma'am."

CHAPTER 23

Baby Steps

Rez

I tried my damnedest to get out of the after dinner training with Astaroth, but the fucker came and found me with Knots. He didn't take my argument seriously when I told him Knots needed a nurse. Nope, the fucker gave me an ultimatum. He said for every minute I wasted of *his* time, he was going to cut into either Knots or my puppy.

Fucking sadistic asshole number two. He surpassed Bez when he said he was going to turn my pup into chop suey. Reaper's a sweetheart—he only got into the fridge and ate his weight in steaks... and pissed a small hole in the ground during dinner. I caught Fluffers playing with my little guy while I trained, and if I ever get a free moment, Knox might be able to help me out when it comes to training Reaper.

"Well, your limbs are attached and you're still alive," Astaroth says, giving me a once over. *If I could hold myself up, I would so flip him off.*

As it is, I can barely keep my legs under me as I'm bent

over, resting my hands on my knees and panting like my little puppers does. Shit, that was a work out.

"Is that a compliment?" I ask between heaving breaths.

Zissa laughs as she walks past. "Nope. He doesn't do compliments."

I peer up at him, and he just smirks as he turns to walk away. Thinking I'm done, I turn to put the weapons back when he speaks.

"Keep the weapons, you'll need them for tomorrow's practice."

I find myself chuckling as I turn to talk to his back. "Can't practice. We're leaving early to get Demstones," I inform him, mustering up enough energy to smile wide at him.

"Oh, really?" Astaroth turns to study me, and I give him a slight nod. "Well then, she's all yours," he says, peeking over my head. I turn and notice Murmur standing behind me, giving me a wide smile.

"Fuck me," I groan as I slump to the floor.

. . . . .

"We've been at this for hours," I sigh, glaring up at the Demon before me.

"And we'll be here all night too if I can't get you to advance in your training," he mocks me.

"I can't cover the damn bo-staff in a protective layer, Murmur. I told you this. I don't even know how my defensive shield works. Look at my bracelet." I raise my arm, showing him my magical bracelet we have to wear for school. It's supposed to track my power, and when it reaches a certain level, I can run the Gauntlet and then travel back to Earth. But it hasn't changed in the slightest. "I'm practically a dud according to this, I have no power." I growl out in a huff.

Murmur eyes my bracelet and huffs. "Of course you're a

dud, if you go by that," he says, pointing at my wrist as I let my arm drop. "Those are only attuned to Purgatory. It's not going to read down here."

I let my head fall back onto my shoulders as I let out a groan.

"Okay," he sighs. "I don't like to do this, because there are always side effects. But I think you need the boost," he says, approaching me.

"Do what? What kind of side effects?" I squint at him.

"I'll be poking inside your head at where your abilities lie, trying to find where your defensive shield is and hopefully give it a small boost so you can feel it and pull on it naturally. With that being said, there's usually the chance that I might brush up against the wrong thing and either boost or suppress some abilities." He shrugs like it's no big deal.

I step back from him as he advances. "So, you're saying you can take away my abilities?" I question.

"Nope, in your case, since none of them are really showing yet, except for your hit-or-miss defensive shield, I'd only be boosting them." He smiles and points at me. "You asked me what the side effects are in general... not what they are for you. But on a positive note, I might be able to see how thin the barrier is that's possibly holding back your abilities. Who knows, I might get lucky and be able to tell exactly what they are while I'm poking around and boosting them."

I chew on my bottom lip as I decide on if I want him to poke around in my head or not. The idea of us finding out what my powers might be is pretty tempting. Ugh.

"Or we can try this all night. I took a nap today, so I can go all night," he says, crossing his arms and leaning back on his *tail*!

Fuck it, I want to take a shower and go to bed. "Fine," I whine.

"Great," he exclaims as he approaches. "Now, try to relax,"

he instructs as he places his fingers along my temples. They immediately start to warm, radiating a comforting heat that causes my eyes to close as I relax.

My head starts to tingle as goosebumps rise along my skin. "I'm just searching right now, that's what you're feeling. Hopefully, you'll feel me going deeper once I find your magic," Murmur expresses.

The shift is noticeable, like when you wrap yourself inside a warm blanket when it's cold. My body completely relaxes and I feel my knees go weak, but instead of dropping, something wraps around my waist and holds me up.

"That's it... just a few more minutes," Murmur assures me as my head feels like it's being massaged. A deep tissue massage that I feel traveling down my spine, straight to my fingers and toes. I'm about to moan, but the sensation abruptly stops when Murmur's fingers leave my head.

"There! Let's see if that worked, but we'll start off small." His tail unravels from around my waist, and he sits down in front of me. "Well, come on, you didn't really want to waste all night, did you?"

Blinking a few times to chase away the dreamy state, I nod and sit down in front of him. "Wait! What did you find out in my head first?" *Now that I have a clear head.*

"Your barrier was almost completely gone, so I gently pulled it back so there's nothing blocking you from your magic now. You just need practice and knowledge." He winks at me.

"Okay, that's great. Did you get a hint of what my abilities might be, or what I will be able to do? Or hell, what species I am?" I almost plead with the Mischief Demon.

His jovial smile drops slightly before he leans forward. "I'm sorry, Rez, but even that information I couldn't pull from you. It was protected, but I could tell that you have immense potential that could even rival the strongest leaders put together."

Well fuck me with a rubber hose.

"Okay, let's try to pull from your shield to create a barrier," he says, placing a small knife in my palm like he didn't just drop a bomb in my lap. "Try to picture the silvery field as a layer of silk that's a part of you. It's able to manifest from wherever you want it to come from, and you can control it when it turns solid. I want you to concentrate and picture it surrounding the knife, sealing it," Murmur tells me.

I nod and stare at the knife. "It might be easier if you close your eyes at first," he guides me, and I guess that makes sense. Closing my eyes, I picture a big spool of silk deep inside of me, waiting to do my bidding. I imagine it traveling down my arm and out through my fingers. Wrapping a tight hold around the knife, I picture my silk becoming hard as rock.

"Open your eyes," Murmur whispers.

I slowly open my eyes, and my heart drops at the sight. Lying in my hand is just the knife, no defensive shield or anything. I sigh and try to hold back the stinging tears as Murmur observes me.

"I really thought I had it," I admit, trying to keep the disappointment out of my tone.

He starts chuckling and gently places his finger under the edge of the handle and slowly lifts.

"Who said you didn't?" he smiles as the knife lifts up without him physically touching it. I lean over and realize there's a solid silver shield around it, leaving the smallest gap between him and the blade. "You wrapped it so tight you couldn't even see it. It's as if it's wearing a second skin as protection. Congratulations."

CHAPTER 24

Unlocking Hell's Paradise

Rez

I'm absolutely ecstatic as I spend a few minutes practicing putting on the shield, trying to be a little faster with each effort. While I push myself physically, I also ask Murmur if he could tell what kind of supernatural I was while he was poking around in my head. Unfortunately, my signature wasn't something he was used to seeing, so that was a deadend. I continued to pull my shield until I mentally started to tire, then Murmur called it a night.

I waste no time heading back to my room and straight to the shower. Reaper follows me until he sees the closet and then curls up in front of the doors. *Poor soul got a work out in, chewing up the wooden bo-staffs.* I don't even bother to turn on the lights until I'm in the bathroom. The heat from the shower loosens my tight muscles as I slowly wash away the day's grime and sweat.

I would almost take today's treatment personally if my friends weren't getting rough treatment as well. I saw Moni working with Murmur earlier, and she was able to make a smaller boom bomb—her words, not mine—before she fainted from joy. Turns out Chester is a natural with Guandao, which—according to Astaroth—is a Chinese weapon. It has a massive blade at one end and a smaller spear at the other. His agility helps him when it comes to sparring. If it wasn't for his glasses slipping off of his face, he might have beat Zissa in their match.

Levi seemed confident with the bo-staff when he disarmed Ryker one-on-one. JP worked with throwing stars, and when he added his water to the mix, he was able to direct them into the dummies from across the room. *Talk about impressive.* Murmur tasked Lynx to practice shifting until it became second nature once again. Needless to say, he worked on it all evening. I just hope tomorrow's adventure is a success and we're able to get the Demstones and the bat flowers that we need.

Drying off, I don't even bother to go to the closet in search of clothes. There's no point. Moni is shacking up with Chester, and from her earlier conversation, learning a lot. I chuckle to myself, thinking of her kink slip-up as I get into bed. I moan as my body melts into the soft mattress. Leave it to Hell to at least have comfortable beds. I roll to my side and an arm slips around my waist.

"FUCK!" I shriek as the arm tightens around my midsection.

"Spitfire, it's okay. Calm down," Zeke says as he nuzzles into my neck.

"What are you doing?" I ask, flipping on the nightlight to the lowest setting and turning around to face him.

"I *was* sleeping." He cracks one eye open against the light to peer at me. It's not long before his hand shifts lower where my shorts would normally sit and he pauses. "Rez?"

"Hmm?" I bite my lip as I peek at him innocently.

"Are you wearing clothes?" he asks, sounding more awake.

"No," I confirm and smile.

"What were you planning on doing if I wasn't here?" he inquires, as his hand slowly glides over my hip and back up. Shivers run down my spine as I fight back the urge to shift my legs.

"Honestly?" I lean closer to him, and his eyes light up with excitement. That's not the only thing that's excited, if what's pressing against my belly is any indication; he's happy he's found me in this state.

"Yeah." His breath brushes against my lips as I glance down at them.

"Sleep," I say, pulling back and watching as his face falls at my abrupt tease.

"And here I thought I was getting a reward." He pouts, sticking out his bottom lip.

I can't help but lean forward and lightly bite it. Instead of the "ow" I was expecting, he melts against me and moans. Electricity runs through my body at the erotic sound, hardening my nipples, and I want to hear more. Shifting closer to him, I wrap my arm around his neck and pull him in for a kiss. It's slow and sensual as we explore and tease each other. His long, deep kisses and my light pecks have us giggling and moaning our frustrations out in the best of ways.

He gently pushes me back so I'm lying flat on the mattress where he can smile down at me. "Damn. You are so beautiful, Rez. Thank you for giving me this second chance."

"Well your second chance is gonna pass you by if you don't get on this," I tease, and he nips at my chin.

"No, it won't, or else I'll just have to chase you down," he points out.

It's like he doesn't know me at all.

One second he's gazing into my eyes, and the next I'm up and running for the door, as naked as the day I was born.

I look behind me to see if Zeke is following me, but my

hair slaps me in the face, blocking my view—"Gotcha!" Zeke calls out as he picks me up and swings me over his shoulder. "My dessert isn't getting away from me that easily."

"Your dessert, huh?" I giggle, throwing my hair out of my face.

"Yep!" He smacks my ass, and a thrill goes through me as I hold back a moan. "I have a sweet tooth, and you're the only thing that can satisfy it," he explains, and dumps me onto the bed.

I don't even bounce twice before he pins my legs, which automatically open for him. "See? You want to be devoured," he says, as his hands slowly caress up my calves. He flashes me a smile, popping a fang.

God, I love it when he does that.

A woosh sounds behind me, and the glow from the fireplace highlights Zeke's body. His lean muscles ripple as his arms slowly continue their pursuit along my legs, teasing me as he studies my body. His creamy skin is unblemished and smooth except for the soft smattering of his auburn-haired happy trail, leading to a wonder I have yet to unwrap.

I lean up on my elbows and reach for his boxers. "May I?" I ask, licking my lips. I would love to see what I'm about to have, and I'm dying to touch him.

His answer is a smirk as Zeke pulls his hips back and slowly brings his mouth to my inner thigh. I feel his feather light breath against my flesh before his tongue follows the same path. Fire ignites along my skin as I anticipate his next move. My fingertips start to caress my breasts, and I begin to swivel my hips. I need his mouth on me. This teasing is killing me.

"Zeke, if I was ice cream, I would have already melted," I hiss as my hands gently squeeze my breasts, making me wetter and sending pleasure radiating down my spine.

"It looks like you're already melting. Let me get that." He

chuckles as his fingers brush against my folds, collecting my wetness. I watch with a mixture of awe and frustration as Zeke licks my juice from his fingers, moaning at the taste. "Mmm. Just like I remembered. Peaches and fine wine. Hold on, spitfire, because I'm about to suck your soul out through your pussy." And with a wink, he dives between my legs.

His tongue greedily licks up my slit, swallowing the liquid pooled there before circling my clit, causing me to moan in pleasure. My hips follow with his slow torture, until he inserts one finger into my core and uses his thumb to apply light pressure along my clit. My breathing hitches as I try to enjoy the slow ministrations, but I want more. Reaching out, I grab his hair and push his face back into my pussy, where he chuckles, making me needy, before gently pulling my clit into his wet, waiting mouth. I use my other hand to pinch my nipple and moan as Zeke increases the speed of his tongue flicking against my clit.

Zeke removes his finger and wraps his hands around my upper thighs, pulling me tighter against him—which I didn't think was possible. Licking, sucking, and tongue fucking me as he continues to use my body to suffocate himself against my pussy, and it's pure, blissful torture. Lifting my ass up as if I am a platter, he gets creative and buries his entire face into me. I'm pretty sure his nose is even rubbing against my clit, but I'm not about to ask because I'm seeing stars.

"Fuuck," I moan and get a glimpse of Zeke's eyes staring back at me. He starts to vibrate his tongue against my clit, and I explode. I scream in ecstasy as he drinks and licks up my release as fast as he can, slowly lowering my ass to the mattress.

With a self-satisfied look upon his face, Zeke crawls up between my legs and moves a few strands of curls out of my face. "How's your soul?" he asks, lowering his body against mine.

"She packed her bags and left," I manage to get out between pants, and I'm rewarded with a chuckle.

"Good, let's see if we can bring her back," he says before leaning down and kissing me. I taste myself on his lips, and it arouses me even more while I run my hands through his hair, making him moan.

Zeke shifts his legs to remove his boxers, until I feel his cock lie against my thigh, thick, heavy, and rock hard. Reaching between us, I gently grab him, giving his dick a few strokes, and Zeke moans into my mouth.

"Damn, you feel so good stroking my cock," he murmurs against my lips.

"I know a place that will feel better." I smile and tuck my ankle around his leg to help roll us over so I'm on top. I start to slip down his legs to taste him, but his hand on my arm stops me.

"You put your Hoover of a mouth on me, and I promise I won't last," he says as I raise an eyebrow.

"Do you have a lot of experiences with Hoovers?" I ask, smirking.

"Hell NO!" He jerks back as if I struck him, and I chuckle as I give him a few more strokes. He quickly wets his lips and looks around as if checking to make sure it's only us in the room before explaining. "I can only guess though since it wasn't long for you and Levi... and..." He swallows thickly as a look of guilt crosses his face. "Ryker gossips like a girl." He shrugs as I pout.

He brings his other hand up to my face, and his thumb brushes against my bottom lip. "I promise I won't fight you any other time you want to have a lick, but I *need* to be inside of you," he pleads.

Dismissing but filing away the whole Ryker gossip girl information, I nip at his thumb and watch as his eyes go molten. I move back up to his hips and straddle him. Leaning down, I give him a passionate kiss, reaching between us for his cock and slowly rubbing it along my folds, teasing both of us. Unsatisfied, Zeke's hands grab hold of my hips and push me back so I'm at the right angle to take him. He's definitely the longest of my guys so I slowly sink down onto his long, hard cock, moaning as I take him inch by delicious inch.

Zeke groans as I bottom out and rest at the base of him. "Fuck, you're perfect and so wet," he moans.

Letting out a breath, I glance up and find Zeke's head thrown back, lips parted as he pants. Slowly, I rock myself back and forth while holding onto his chest, feeling his muscles contract below me. "Yeah, ride this cock." He grabs my thighs and thrusts up meeting my swiveling hips.

I continue my enjoyment as Zeke lifts one of his hands to my breast and rolls the tight peak between his fingers. My head falls back as my eyes close, and I enjoy the electric sensations he's sending through my body, every part of me lit up between the different stimulations, and I never want him to stop. His hips start bucking at a frenzied pace, causing immense friction against my clenching pussy, bringing me closer to my release.

"Rez," his husky voice pulls my attention back to him.

His lips part slightly, and I watch as his fangs elongate, and a different type of heat floods through me, instantly knowing he wants my blood. There's no hesitation in my eyes as I nod, my breath coming too fast to actually talk. Sitting up, he drags me with him as he slides up so he can lean against the headboard as I continue to rock on his lap. Zeke wraps his arms around my waist and moves my hair off my neck sensually before my head tilts to the side, his eyes on fire with lust for my every movement. Goosebumps pebble along my arms in anticipation of the high I'll receive as he leans in and licks along my neck.

There's a sting, and in response, I take in a sharp inhale as his fangs sink further into me. Heat blooms from my neck and explodes throughout my body, causing a euphoric feeling I've never experienced before. My nipples are so tight they are on the edge of pain, but I don't dare ask him to stop as he continues to drink while fucking me.

"Zeke, more," I cry out, needing him closer as I claw at his back. His hand slips between us, finding my clit, and applies pressure before I shatter. My pussy clamps down on Zeke's cock as I scream my release. He quickly removes his fangs, licking along my neck before he slams his mouth over mine as he roars. He spasms inside of me, filling me with his cum.

"Fuck," Zeke sighs and falls to the side, taking me with him. I try to smile up at him, but really, I just want to drift off to sleep. He moves the strands of hair out of my face and leans in to—

"AHHH," I scream as fire starts at the base of my neck and slowly rolls down my back to my tailbone where it barely starts to lessen. Reaper startles awake and starts barking as Zeke's wide eyes bore into mine.

"Rez? What's wrong?" he screams in panic. "Ugh," he groans in his own moment of pain. The fire in my back subsides briefly as right before my eyes I see a tattoo appear on his left pec of another horseman. The rider is wearing a dark cloak, holding a scythe and riding a pale green horse.

Scarlet eyes stare down at me, and I watch in fascination as yellow slowly swirls into their depths. I'm looking into the face of Death, and it's absolutely breathtaking. He runs his hands over my eyebrows, through my hair, and back to my jaw, cradling me. When he moves in close enough I can inhale his peppermint and earthy scent and feel his breath against my lips. "You will see me. You will see us, always. You will be our redemption."

A silent scream erupts from me as another wave of fire flares along my spine, stealing the air from my lungs.

"What is going on? Rez, talk to me. What hurts?" he asks, but I'm hopeless to answer. He glances at me and pushes me onto my back, and a sob is ripped from me as it only makes the pain worse. "Rez! What can I do?" Zeke asks as tears start to form in his own eyes. My entire back is burning and tears start to stream down my cheeks as I'm frozen in pain. Waves of heat roll through me as I suddenly start seeing black spots. *God, I'm dying. Just kill me now.*

"What the fuck?" Zeke yells as his attention is pulled away from me. My hearing wavers back and forth, and the next eyes I see staring into my own are bright green ones.

"I'm here, kitten," Knox whispers to me. "Zeke, go turn on the shower. It needs to be cold," he barks, and I feel him pick me up gently, trying not to touch my back, but it's impossible. "I'm sorry, baby."

Reaper growls and nips at Knox as he tries to move me from the bed, and I'm kinda impressed that he's trying to protect me. Knox growls in response, and I hear a whimper as my puppy quiets down a little bit, but I hear him follow us into the bathroom.

Knox steps into the shower fully clothed, and the sting of cold water is abrupt but welcome as I lean my head against his shoulder and let out a sob of thanks. We're only there for a few moments before the pain slowly subsides and I can tell them I'm okay.

"Thank you. I don't know what happened," I say as my teeth chatter.

"Holy shit," Zeke mutters, and I hear the swoosh of my fireplace. "You might want to bring her to the mirror," Zeke points with the towel instead of wrapping it around me.

Knox frowns but quickly follows Zeke and places me on the towel that's laid on the counter.

"Fuck." Knox sighs, and that's when I notice they aren't looking at me but at the mirror.

"What?" I ask, and turn my head far enough to see what's grabbed their attention.

"Fuuuuck," I agree. I thought the guys' tattoos were weird. I now have a full back tattoo along my spine. In the middle of my back is one big circle where it's evenly divided with three scenes. One is of Purgatory with a scene of a mash-up of the mountains, Ever Woods, and the Beach. Hell is represented by the red moon, the green and white grass along with a winding path leading to a pit of brimstone. The third holds an image of Earth, the planet of greens and blues, clouds and shadow. Around the edge of the whole image of the middle circle is a lock with a key hanging off of it. Four circles, which gradually get smaller, branch off and run up and down my spine. Each one of them has a symbol within the circle.

Instinctively, I somehow know what they stand for, except for the first one at the base of my neck. It looks like bright stars in the night sky.

The second one below that stands for Lynx. The dark purple, blue, and red storm clouds that roll in over the late sunset in an open field remind me of him.

The next one has a black background, but it's far from simple. The golden scale seems to float, and as I watch carefully, the plates move as if they are balancing something. This represented Levi.

Fuck. A living tattoo?

The last circle on the top half of my back has an immaculate crown hanging from the end of a notched bow and arrow. At the bottom of the picture looks to be people bowing down to it as it spins around in a slow circle. This is my Ryker.

What the hell is up with these living things on my back? I can't feel them, so why are they moving?

Continuing on below the big circle of the three worlds is a flaming white sword that cuts down cloaked figures. Squinting my eyes, I can actually make out that the figures look like *Rebels!* With each slice, the flame seems to scream and flash with anger, shooting out flames before taking another life. This is Knox.

Well shit! This is too surreal.

The next symbol is easy to decipher. It's Death's scythe. Although there is no Death to wield the instrument, it swings all on its own, and as it swoops down along the field, cutting through the decrepit bodies reaching up with lithe arms, I can see the black souls being released. This has to be Zeke.

The one below is something new to me but can only be one person. The multi-colored blue feathered wings spread across the circle in bright colors and seem to have an internal glow about them. That must be my Knots.

The last one has me a little confused, but it only leaves JP. In the small circle, at the tip of my spine is a ball of water with a bright flame of what I can easily tell is Hellfire since I've seen Bez playing with it so often lately.

But how does JP fit in with fire?

What the hell does this mean?

Something flashes and draws my attention away from my back. I shift more so I'm facing the mirror better and lean in. Have my eyes always looked this light? I twist my head trying to see if it's just the way the light is hitting me, but I could swear part of my pupil is changing. As if it's turning a lighter shade. Shaking my head, I peer up at Zeke and Knox in the mirror.

"I think it's time we ask L.A.M.B. and your mother what they might know about our tats," I say numbly.

"Agreed," Zeke and Knox mumble.

CHAPTER 25

Black is the new Black

Rez

The next morning, I wake up next to Knox and Zeke both spooning me and Reaper lying on my legs. After finding the tattoo along my spine, all thoughts of a round two vanished, but in its place came the reactions and theories. Zeke thought it was cool that he got a tattoo of one of the Horsemen on his chest. Knox explained that he had one too and swore Zeke to secrecy before showing off his tramp stamp.

Those guys were a bunch of loons, comparing their tattoos. It was like watching men compare their dick sizes. They are the same, by the way... the tattoos, not their cocks. If you wanted me to compare those... Let's see. Shit, I'm getting off track. We had no idea what any of this meant, and maybe since they were old as dirt, it was best to bring it up with L.A.M.B. or Lilith when we had a chance. So, with a change of clothes, we crawled into bed to sleep. Knox insisted on staying, and to keep my puppy from whining all night, Knox allowed him on the bed. The urge to pee has me fumbling with the covers and crawling over the guys.

"No. Stay," Zeke mutters and reaches for me.

"I gotta pee," I hiss as I stumble out of bed and head to the bathroom. A growl and a crash sounds behind me, and with a quick peek around the doorframe, I see Reaper's long tail smacking Knox in the face as he whimpers to get down from the bed.

Ugh. I forgot how much it sucks to have a puppy sometimes.

Rushing back in, I pick him up, carry him into the bathroom with me, and put him down on the bathroom floor before doing my business. I go to wash my hands and find my puppy pissing in the shower, and surprisingly, it's not eating through the floor. *Huh, well look at that!*

Hoping to get some more cuddles in with my guys, I walk back in and my hope plummets, finding them getting dressed.

Zeke walks over to me with an armload of clothes and nibbles on my neck before he heads to the bathroom.

"Aww. I wanted cuddles," I whine.

Knox snorts as he walks over and opens the closet, pulling out a black leather jacket. "Well, it's Saturday, so if you want those last ingredients, we need to leave here in a few."

Fuck. I forgot!

I didn't forget about the ingredients; I just forgot about the time limit. Zissa was going to go over everything during dinner, but I missed it to attend to Knots. *I wonder if he's okay to come today.*

Meeting Knox at the closet, I realize I have no idea how I should dress for this excursion. "Do we have any idea what to wear?" I ask, worrying my lip.

He shrugs. "Well, according to Zissa, the merchant said there are razor sharp plants and various monsters. So, my guess... protective wear."

I give him a pursed smile. "You're so helpful," I say sarcastically and roll my eyes.

"Anything for you, kitten." He laughs and kisses me hard on the lips.

A knock on my door pulls our attention away from each other.

"Come in," Knox calls out, and when you speak of devils, they always appear.

Zissa pops her head in and smiles when her eyes land on us by the closet. "Well, good morning. I'm glad to see you up and dressed," she says, walking in.

"To answer your question, Rez, something like that." Knox points over his shoulder, motioning to Zissa's attire.

It seems she has embraced Moni's assessment of her yesterday, dressed head-to-toe like Xena: Warrior Princess, but in a black leather dress and boots up to her mid thigh. What really completes the look is her battle armor over her tunic, with armbands, shoulder guards, knee guards, gauntlets, and a backpiece and breastplate.

"Are we going to war? I thought we were collecting ingredients?" I ask as I'm struck in awe at the vast difference of clothing choice between Knox and her. "Now, he's dressed like I would expect us to be while collecting shit."

She gives me a winning smile. "Yes, but his real weapon is shifting. What's yours?" she asks, raising her eyebrows and placing her hands on her hips.

My jaw clenches as I contemplate smacking her smug smile off her face. "Excuse me, missy. My weapon so happens to be a newly developed shield, which I can use at will now," I sass back with a little head roll.

"Oh really? So does that mean you've found your limits with it yet?" Zissa fires smoothly.

My eyes narrow as I take in my opponent across from me. *It's been a while since I've come across such a great foe.* I internally shake my head. Fuck, now I'm acting like Lynx. I'm giving her a chance here... She's not a complete foe... yet. *Hmm. We shall see how this plays out.*

I suck on my teeth as I decide how to approach this. "No, but it's still a skill, so it counts," I retort, taking it as a win. "But I do see your point," I say, and Knox chuckles before kissing me hard.

"I'll be down in the kitchen, packing some food," Knox says, walking towards the door. "Come on, Reaper."

I hear a yip from behind me as my pup takes off after Knox and trips over his tail. He's so cute. Turning back to the closet, I quickly think of something similar to Zissa's outfit and step inside to get dressed. I opt to wear black jeans, black knee-high boots and a lilac long sleeve top that extends over my knuckles. I make sure there's thicker material for my shoulders, elbows, knees, and wrist, and walk out, spreading my arms out for her inspection.

"Perfect badassery," she purrs, giving me a flirty wink, but I know it's harmless. I can't help but smile. *I have to admit it's nice having another female look at me as something other than garbage, like the Harpies. I might have to let her know I'm not into her that way, but she will do.*

"I agree." Ryker's voice comes out of nowhere. I peer over Zissa's shoulder and spot Ryker leaning against my closed door.

When our eyes meet, my throat suddenly goes dry at his haunted look. I haven't wanted to talk since I walked away from him in Lilith's spell room, and I'm not sure where to even start. He nibbles on the hoop in his bottom lip for a second as Zissa turns and smiles at him. Zeke walks out of the bathroom right as Ryker decides to say more.

"Can I talk to you for a second?" His voice cracks slightly before he clears his throat.

"Well, that's my cue. I'm going to run to my room real

quick. I'll meet you guys in the hall." Zeke waves on his way to the door.

"I think I'll join ya," Zissa calls out before joining him.

After Zeke and Zissa step out of the room, Ryker shuts the door and turns to face me once again.

His jaw clenches as I sit at the end of my bed and look down at my hands. I don't know who should apologize first. I was the one that overreacted in the first place, but then again he's the—

"Rez?" I glance up at his voice and visibly jerk back slightly at his presence in front of me. Kneeling down, he balances on the soles of his boots and grabs my hands. "I'm sorry."

"So am I," I confess.

"No, you're not allowed to say sorry," he chides, shaking his head and giving me a pursed smile. "You didn't do anything wrong." He squeezes my hands and closes his eyes for a brief moment, and my heart skips at his words. "I know it's no excuse for my earlier actions, Rez, but I've never had anyone I've cared enough to introduce, let alone a mate. So, it never occurred to me that what I did was even a mistake until Zissa laid into me."

I search for the truth of his words in his eyes, and I find it there as he stares back at me. He looks so lost, and his slightly widened eyes lead me to believe he's scared I won't believe him.

"Will you forgive me and be my feisty mate that tries to put me in my place?"

"Tries?" I scoff and stand up, placing my hands on my hips. Ryker falls back and lands on his ass, looking up at me with a cocky look.

"Yeah," he smirks as he gets up to face me.

"I'll have you know I do a damn good job putting you in your place," I say, poking him in his hard chest. "Of course, I forgive you, but if you don't watch it, I'll find another

Incubus, or even a Succubus, while I'm down here to replace you. I don't know if you noticed, but Zissa was just flirting with me," I say teasingly. Ryker gently lifts my chin with his finger and smiles down at me.

"Yeah, I heard about that, but I won't let that happen. You know why?" His warm breath feathers against my suddenly dry lips before I shake my head. My tongue darts out to wet my lips, drawing his heated gaze down to them before his green eyes flick back to mine. "Because I would tie you down and fuck you until your pussy starts speaking in tongues and you pass out from pleasure. Only to wake you back up with my mouth and fuck you back to oblivion."

Holy shit! I hear my fireplace erupt, but I don't dare take my eyes off of Ryker as he leans in and gently bites my lower lip, only to let it go. "Rez... my sweet temptress... You are mine, and I will never let you leave. Even when you're mad at me, I will fuck the forgiveness and love out of you," he says before claiming my lips in a fiery kiss.

A bolt of lust overwhelms me, and I pull him into me to deepen the kiss, but he breaks it off and leans his forehead against mine.

"I would love to show you how much you mean to me and how sorry I am, but we have to go, temptress."

"Since when did you become the responsible one?" I whine, and he chuckles as he steps back.

He walks backward toward the door with his arms out wide. "I have many hidden secrets. You have yet to unlock them all."

I'm horny as hell, and yet his eyes are still bright green, not the electric blue that normally shines with power. "What's up with your eyes? They aren't blue," I point out as I walk out into the hall and find Lynx, Zissa, and Zeke.

"Well, that's because someone already had a fulfilling night." Ryker chuckles as he slings his arm over my shoulder.

"Yes, I learned that one of my guys talks more than a girl. Imagine my surprise." I bat my eyelashes, and Lynx bursts out laughing. Ryker just clears his throat and shoots Zeke a glare.

Zeke shrugs, unfazed, and adjusts a few rings I didn't see on his hands earlier.

"What's with the rings? I didn't know you wore jewelry," I ask, feeling lost that I didn't notice this until now.

"Oh, they're my weapons," he tells me.

"Huh? Since when are rings weapons?" I ask, looking around at everyone's faces to gauge their reaction, and I see I'm not alone.

"Since this," he says before he flexes his hands and long blades shoot out like fucking Wolverine.

"Holy shit!" I murmur and the hall shakes slightly. "My bad."

"Since my main weapons are my fangs and speed, Astaroth thought fist weapons would work best for me. Apparently there are different types of them, but I'm trying these out today." He brings his hands up and rotates them so I can see all the blades, and I must admit they are impressive. With a flex of his hands, the blades disappear.

"Just be careful and don't stab me to death when you come in for a hug, okay?" I tease.

"Wouldn't dare." He laughs and addresses the group, "So, who all plans to go on this trip today?" Zeke asks, bouncing on his feet as he turns and walks backward toward the kitchen.

I swear, if he's not careful, he's gonna crash into something. Not long after he turns the corner, I hear a grunt, and Zeke crashes to the ground.

"Fuuuck," he groans. Ryker runs over to him and helps him up as I take in what he crashed into. Lynx, Zissa, and I chuckle at Bez's bewildered look, until he squints in our direction. Pursing my lips, I stare at the wall and act like I didn't see anything.

"Do you have everything?" Bez's deep timbre rings out as he takes in our group.

"Yep, just needed to get the stragglers," Zissa smiles up at him. He grunts in response and continues past us.

"If we're the stragglers, does that mean everyone is coming?" I ask since she didn't answer Zeke's question before he bounced off a Bez wall.

"Yep, everyone except Knots. Lilith is up and has advised him to save his energy," she fills me in. My poor Door Knight must be devastated. First, stuck as a door, then bound to the dorm, only to be pulled into Hell, and he can't explore? Sheesh. I wonder how he's going to take that?

I don't have to wait long because I can hear his voice from the hallway before we even get to the kitchen.

"NO! I don't care who you think you are; you're not keeping me here while they go out there and risk their lives without me," Knots growls out. We're too far away to hear the other side of the argument, but I start to speed walk anyway.

I walk into the kitchen and find Murmur's tail wrapped around Knots' body, but that doesn't seem to be stopping him from defending himself. Knots' sword is against Murmur's offending appendage.

"Try it, and let's see if you can grow back your tail," Knots hisses as he nicks the tail. His voice is deadly serious, and I find it so fucking hot that I shift slightly.

"Really?" Ryker whispers, but I ignore him.

Murmur's eyes flash in my direction, and if I'm not mistaken, there's relief when he catches my eyes. "Maybe you can talk some sense into him," he says, unraveling his tail.

"Can you grow back your tail?" Lynx asks, popping the top off a drink. Like the others, he's wearing dark jeans that hang off his hips and just a black t-shirt, and I'm jealous once again that someone else isn't required to wear the attire I am. I shake my head as I peek down and see that he's still barefoot.

I'm pretty sure he needs shoes at least.

"Can you grow back your tail in your animal form?" Murmur shoots back, giving Lynx a pointed glare.

"Don't know." He shrugs and chugs half his bottle. Wiping his mouth with the back of his hand, he smiles. "But I would rather not find out."

"Same." He turns back and eyes Knots before bringing his attention to me and the guys.

"I can!" Moni announces as she comes from the pantry in the back with her hands full of wrappers. I have no idea what she has, but they are piled up underneath her chin.

"Ho—how do you know that?" I'm lost for words.

She dumps her loot on the countertop, and Chester starts throwing it into a bag as she turns to face me. "Oh, that's easy. It was JP's fault."

We all turn to glare at him.

"Oh no! Don't be throwing me under the portal. Look, it wasn't my fault. Mom told me to catch the Gorat, so I set the traps," he points out and glares back at Moni.

"Yeah, but you didn't have to use *my* candy to do it. You know those ugly rat thingies love sweets, and El only gave me so many. She said they gave me hypertension," she argues, placing her hands on her tiny hips.

JP pinches the bridge of his nose. "Moni. She said they made you *hyper*, which made her *tense*. Not hypertension," he explains, shaking his head.

"Oh," her shoulders slump slightly. "Well, the point is, I went to get my candy back but I wasn't fast enough. One of the traps took my tail, but it grew back, better than ever." Proudly, she lifts her tail up, showing it off.

Murmur clears his throat. "Okay then. Like I was saying, before you guys go, make sure you stop by the training room and grab weapons. Then come see us before you take off. We'll be in the throne room. Lucifer is holding court for a few hours this morning. And you need to rest," he throws back at Knots before walking out of the kitchen.

Knots scoffs before he turns and starts throwing a few bottles of water into a satchel that's on the counter. I run my hand over his back before sitting on the counter to face him; the rest of the guys continue to pack around me.

"Are you okay?" I gently ask, staring at his expression as he shoves more items into his pack.

"I'm going," he growls out.

"I didn't say you weren't. I asked if you're okay, and don't lie to me. I deserve better than that." He pauses and sighs before slowly focusing on me.

"I'm frustrated. This is the first time that I can remember feeling such weakness, and I'm expected to sit on the sidelines." His voice waivers slightly, and I scoot over closer and pull him between my legs. Knowing he needs more, I wrap my arms around his waist and hug him.

He wraps his arms around my shoulders, and I speak into his chest. "Knots, you're not weak by any means. Your body is fighting the effects of Hell, and it's pretty fucking amazing that you're even standing here and fighting to come with us." I feel the small tremors in his body, but I keep quiet as he hugs me back.

"I'm a protector, Rez. It's what I've always known. To ask me to sit on the sidelines is essentially castrating me." He shudders in my arms, and something wet hits my neck. Slightly pulling back to glance up, I see tears in his eyes.

"Oh, Knots," I say, wiping them away. "I'm not going to make anyone stay behind, but I also want us to take precautions to make sure we don't hurt you either." He takes in a deep breath, his taut muscles relaxing under my fingertips as he blows it out.

"Thank you," he says, and presses his lips against mine. I melt against him as he deepens the kiss.

"Nope. None of that. We have places to be and asses to kick," Zeke says, plopping down a satchel next to me. Pulling away from Knots, I glare at my Vamp until he smiles at me and pops a fang. "What? It's true."

"Go ahead and get your weapons, while I make sure we pack enough food for our trip," Knots says as he helps me off the counter.

A fter grabbing the glaives I've been working with and sheathing them to my lower back, I meet everyone in the hallway. It seems I was the last one to get weapons, but I had to make sure I could safely pull them free without cutting off my own ass. To anyone else, we would resemble a group of warriors, even my puppy has a protective vest over his little body. All my guys are wearing dark pants and either long sleeves or a jacket. I think my favorite is Levi, who has chosen a long black coat that goes down to his boots and gives off a Nick Fury vibe.

Everyone else is dressed in dark clothes with thick guards along their arms and legs. Even Moni is sporting the Gabrielle outfit, including the sai attached to her hips from Xena: Warrior Princess, and I wonder if Zissa had anything to do with her choice of clothes.

How did I miss that in the kitchen?

She smiles up at Chester, and I practically see hearts in her eyes as she holds his hand. He's wearing a backpack and holding his weapon in his other hand, and it's Moni's tail that whips up to push his glasses back up his nose. It would be a total swoon moment if not for JP making the gagging noise. Moni's expression drops before locking her gaze on their feet as they walk. I walk over and pinch him hard on the arm. "Stop it," I hiss, "Or I'll deny you sex also. Knox, Levi, and

Ryker are already in hot water for making me drink armpit sweat." He does a horrible job of hiding his smirk, but I know better. "And that includes getting any from Zeke." I have to admit, I take great pleasure at seeing his smile drop. Hooking my arm through his, we follow Zissa down the hall to the throne room. "How would you feel if Moni didn't approve of us?" I ask, keeping my voice down. "I know you do it in teasing, but it must weigh on her at times. And you're her big brother. I know it would mean the world to her if you supported her when she's experiencing new things. Even if they are exciting or scary."

JP doesn't meet my eyes for a moment as we walk, but he does tilt his head in thought. "But that's my *baby* sister. It's hard to imagine her growing up," he counters.

"Yeah, and you're her *big* brother. Imagine how hard it is to have you hate her for what she's doing?" I reply.

JP visibly recoils. "I don't hate her," he says and peers over his shoulder. Moni catches his eye, and her bark turns a shade of pink before cycling to blue and seafoam green. She starts to drop Chester's hand. Not having any of that, he grabs her hand and leans down to say something in her ear, and JP focuses back on me.

"Doesn't seem that way." I shrug. "It's all about perception."

"Well fuck. I guess by keeping myself away and not listening to her body language, I was missing the signs," he admits.

"See, that's the first step," I say, smiling as we reach a silver door at the end of the hall.

"This doesn't mean I'm gonna stop picking on her. It's my right, as a brother," he says, pointing his finger in my face.

"Wouldn't dream of it."

I know better than to truly get in between those two.

CHAPTER 26

Follow the Blood Slick Road

Rez

W e walk into the room, and I stop dead in my tracks. I don't know what I was really expecting. When Murmur said throne room, I first pictured a big room containing a big elaborate chair at the end, with Lucifer sitting in it, bored out of his mind. But this is Hell, so I wasn't really anticipating that to be an actual thing. The night club feel was definitely a surprise for me, though.

Draped in front of us are sheer red, black, and silver curtains blocking the view, but a hypnotic tune plays on.

"Did we take a wrong turn?" JP asks, leaning into me, but Zissa walks past us and through the curtains.

"I guess follow the leader?" I say, stepping away from him and weaving through the fine material. As I walk through, I'm bumped from behind as I take in everything. To the right are booths set up like a nightclub; dark lights and heavy fog make it hard to tell what else is back there. I do catch sight of a bar and a few demons serving drinks. *What the fuck?*

Straight ahead is a glen out of a fairy tale. Talk about an

about-face, going from a club atmosphere to a forest. The back wall is a pale sandstone rock, where water trickles down into a small basin. A few Fae creatures with gossamer wings are gathered around the edge. Something splashes under the water, but I can't tell what it is. Trying to squint like that will help me see deeper into the water, a shadow moves above, distracting me. Glancing up, I see monkey-like creatures leaping from tree limbs, and I figure it's time to move.

Following the path that Zissa took, I head to the left. It's another drastic change from the green glen to a sparkling cave, where both stalactites and stalagmites are abundant. With a shiver, I notice there's a vague pile of stones in a corner that, from my point of view, look like a bunch of discarded skulls.

"Come on, slowpokes," Zissa calls as she slips through a crevice.

Following, I step out into a dark and dank dungeon. There are cracks in the cobblestone floor, where more lava flows down into multiple drains in the floor. The smell is atrocious, reminding me of rotten meat.

Stepping over the first crack, I warn the others. "Be careful of the brimstone, or is it lava? It's flowing pretty heavily."

"It's not brimstone," Zeke replies, and I glance over and see his bright eyes shining yellow and his fangs elongated.

"Are you okay?" I nervously ask, realizing what the river is now. *Shit, I'm a horrible girlfriend.* I didn't even think to ask him if he needed blood this morning.

He shakes his head and smiles at me, his eyes back to normal and his fangs retracted. "There's just a lot." Nodding, I give him a reassuring smile.

Walking a little further, I finally see a row of thrones with steps leading up to them as the room completely opens up. There's a large black one in the middle and two smaller ones on each side, both sets in gold. Smack dab in the middle is Lucifer, and he's shaking his head at something Bez is saying.

"Took you long enough," Murmur says, standing from his place at the end of the row of thrones.

"What the hell did we just walk through?" I ask.

"The throne room," he answers, rolling his eyes.

"But what's up with the different sections?" I continue, not taking that as the freaking answer. Lucifer chuckles, drawing my attention to him.

"It's as Murmur said, Rez. This is my throne room, and you walked through the waiting area. Those demons that you passed are waiting until they get called so I can listen to their grievances."

Lynx points to the drains in the floor behind me. "And what about the drains?"

A salacious smile slowly appears on his face as flames flash brightly in his eyes, scaring the shit out of me. "Those are for the ones I don't listen to."

Um...

Lynx purses his lips and throws up the O.K. sign before he slides behind Knots.

'*Now you want my help? Pussy,*' Knots teases, and Lynx just flips him off. There must be a story there. I need to make a mental note to find out.

"Aww, I see you picked the glaives. Nice choice."

"Is this why we had to come here?" I ask, getting a little frustrated. We're wasting time here, and he could have inspected us in the damn training room.

Laughter comes from behind the throne. "Of course not," Lilith says, walking out carrying a small cloth bag with pull strings. "I wanted to see you guys off." She comes up to me and pulls me into a tight hug. Feeling awkward, I look over at Levi, and he motions for me to hug her back. She's acting so weird that I'm not sure if this would be the right time to ask her if we can talk about my tattoo when we get back or not. I quickly comply, and before I get up the nerve to ask, she pulls away and then she goes to all of the guys, including Lynx, Knots, Chester, and even Moni. "I wanted to let you know I'm feeling better. I already have Demons out looking for Adam, and I plan on feeding him his own balls when I find him." She smiles gleefully at her promise. "Plus, I plan on working on the ingredients that I have already."

"And the bag?" Ryker asks, his brows pulled down as his eyes shift to Lilith and back to Lucifer.

"Oh yes! This is for you," she says, handing Levi the small bag. "It should help you get back here in time. From my calculations, you might have a way to go on foot, so I've created a small portal stone. You know how they work, Levi," she pinches his cheek. I stifle a giggle as he blushes slightly and shoots me a quick glare when she isn't looking. "I talked to Zissa, and the only place I know that's close to your destination is the Blood Rivers. So, I can open a portal to help with your limited time frame. I would go myself, but my jailers won't let me," she says with a tight smile.

"Lilith," Astaroth comes down from his seat. "You know you're healing and you're in a fragile state. We promised your mates that we would take care of you and make sure you stayed here," he says to her.

"Just be glad you can help them at all," Lucifer reminds her. She snaps her head to look at him over her shoulder and growls. "It was simply a reminder, Lilith, that you're healing and still weak. No offense needed to be taken," he calmly says. His eyes swing back to me before dipping down to see my puppy. "Do you think that's wise to take him? He's a menace."

I smile up at him. "Of course he is, that's why I'm taking him. Or... I could just leave him here with you," I suggest, giving him a wide smile. He visibly blanches. "Just be glad I didn't call him what I wanted to."

"Do I even want to ask," Lucifer drawls and raises an eyebrow.

"No, but I'm gonna share anyway. I wanted to call him Church but didn't think you would like yelling that in Hell," I say, and sure enough the floor shakes, and Lucifer clenches his jaw, flashing his eyes in warning.

"I said I didn't call him that. See, I'm playing fair." I smirk and turn my attention back to Lilith.

Lilith pushes Astaroth away from her and runs her hands down her black pantsuit before glancing over our group once more. "Is everyone ready?"

"Wait," Murmur states, coming over to me. "I thought we talked about this," he says, pulling me away from my group. "He should be resting," he emphasizes.

I pull my arm from his grasp and stand up straighter, staring him in the eyes. "First of all, it's his choice. Second, he's a Door Knight, and his purpose is to protect what is his. And third, he's my man, and I'm going to support him. So unless you have a suggestion on how I can help do that, then you have no say." I roll my neck and walk away.

"Okay. I have an idea," he admits, and I stop in my tracks, slowly turning to face him once again.

"I'm listening." *This shit better be good because time is short.* At least Lilith is helping cut down on time.

"It's not going to be easy for you, but it will work twofold. Your defensive shield?"

"Yeah?" I question. *Where is he going with this?*

"Place it around Knots like you did with the knife. I noticed some things when I was poking around inside that head of yours. If I'm correct, the signature I got off of it works not only as a defensive measure, but as a protective one as well. Think of it as a bubble. If you can place even a thin layer around him, it could help. Since the spell in the Demstone helps slow down the effects of being down here, maybe your shield can help by reflecting it off of him."

I can help Knots? What if I'm not strong enough?

My hands start to sweat, and I feel myself rocking.

Murmur must pick up on my worry as he grabs ahold of my shoulders, and suddenly the world steadies itself.

"Rez, look at me." I peer into his green eyes as he smiles at me. "I don't expect you to be able to hold the field the entire time, or even make it big enough to cover him completely. But every time you're able to do it, you will become stronger. Picture it like working your muscles. It will become easier, and next thing you know, you'll be doing it without thinking, okay?"

I let out a deep breath as what he says makes sense. It's the same thing I've been told over and over again in training or when I've struggled with learning something. The stupid saying "practice makes perfect." No it doesn't. Practice just makes it easier, but I see his point.

"Okay." I nod. "Thank you."

"All ready?" Lilith asks, and I give a thumbs up. "Fantastic." She turns, waving her hand in the air, and a portal opens up. On the other side of the portal, I can see trees, dirt, dark greenish grass, and lots of tiny rivers with varying degrees of red water.

She turns and motions for us to go. "I can't hold this forever." One by one, we walk through a portal to a worse place in Hell.

The Blood Rivers are adequately named, that's for sure. Stepping out of the portal, we find ourselves surrounded by three rivers all flowing the same way with trees all around us.

Some of the trees are burnt and rotten, while others are flourishing with various colors of burnt orange, reds, dark greens, yellows, and dark blues. The only smell I'm picking up is rot, soot, and soil.

"Um, does anyone have any idea where to go?" Lynx asks as he lifts up his bare foot and wipes it on some foliage.

"This is why you should have worn shoes," Knots says, shaking his head.

"Shows what you know," Lynx snarks back and points down to his feet. Where he's changed his feet into big tiger paws.

"How? I..."

"You should see what I'm packing in my pants now... It's grrrreat!" he says like Tony The Tiger.

"Lynx!" I groan.

"I've been practicing. Well, that's the only thing L.A.M.B. wants me to practice until I get my memory back," he says with a little disdain.

I don't blame him. Hopefully, I'll have my best friend back by tomorrow.

Laughter comes from behind me, and I see a few of the guys laughing at Lynx's paws. Levi's face has completely transformed. His stoic nature is gone as he laughs freely, saying something about the ultimate fuzzy slippers. I love seeing this side of him, and looking at his brothers, it's apparent they do as well. With the nagging thought of a timeline that's against us, the dread of Levi's up-and-coming ceremony hits a sour note for me. I'll be gaining my bestfriend back, but losing Levi.

"Hey, guys!" Zissa calls out, pulling me from my depressing thoughts. "It's this way. Once we are out of the woods, we make a left and follow the Blood Slick Road," Zissa instructs as she takes off, leading the group.

"Did she say Blood Slick Road?" Moni asks, shrinking down and catching a ride with Chester.

"Yep," he answers as he pushes his glasses up his nose. "I'm definitely not looking forward to learning why it's called that. But I also don't want to miss out on this trip either."

"My guess is thieves and robbers are known to hunt on this road, so there's always killings. Therefore blood," Ryker says, as he falls in line in front of me.

"I'm not taking that bet," I mumble as I step closer to Knots and lay a hand on his arm.

"You okay?" he asks, looking me over.

"Yeah, just going to practice on my shield while we're here, and hopefully help give you some extra protection while we're out and about. Is that okay?" I ask, not really looking for an answer.

"As long as it doesn't hurt you." He grabs my other hand and kisses the back of it in a swoon-worthy move. Who says chivalry is dead? Tell that to the tornado of butterflies in my stomach as I feel heat rush to my cheeks.

"Okay. I'm not great at doing this with my eyes open, so can you just make sure I don't run into a tree?" I chuckle.

"I got ya," he says, lifting me up bridal style. "Now you can concentrate." He winks and starts to follow the group.

I shake my head at the absurdity of it all. Here I am, supposed to be pushing myself to get stronger or better with my power, and he comes and takes away a hurdle for me. Knowing my luck, I would have tripped and broke something if I tried to apply my shield and walk at the same time. Oh well, beggars can't be choosers, right? I close my eyes, press my hand against his chest, and go searching for that silk spool inside myself. Surprisingly, I feel the threads already at my fingertips, willing to do my bidding, and I picture it wrapping around Knots' form as close as possible without hurting him. Protecting him.

"I can feel that," he whispers, and I smile as I continue to work. I feel some resistance, but knowing it's probably just my own power limit, I push against it and stretch out my reach. Once I picture it covering him, I slowly open my eyes and test how it holds with my concentration.

"How does it look?" Knots asks, stopping to set me down. I take a moment to look him over, and as he shifts, the light filtering through the tree hits him just right so that I see a shimmer. It seems to completely cover him.

"You look pretty hot." I smile up at him, and he gives me a kiss.

"Good, now let's catch up." He starts walking in front of me, giving me a great view of his ass, and apparently the only part I didn't cover with my shield. Well, I hope nothing happens to that! *I'll have to get that in a few. I'm wiped for now*. Thankfully, he has the Demstone and its protection.

We make it out of the woods fairly quickly, and it's become pretty obvious why it's called the Blood Slick Road.

"Oh shit. This is worse than I thought," Ryker gags, pulling his shirt up over his nose. Dead bodies in various states of decay litter the road.

I pull my hair down out of its ponytail and proceed to pull my hair under my nose and start braiding a relaxed fishtail mustache. Once I'm finished, JP and Knox take one look at me and start laughing.

"Shut up. It's the only thing I have," I manage to get out as I start coughing from the stench.

"You look like you could give Rip Van Winkle a run for his money," Zeke says.

"How do you even know who that is?" I demand.

"He's famous here," he admits.

"Yep. The only hybrid Supe to sleep through his twenty years on Earth." Ryker pipes up.

"Talk about time wasted. He got drunk, and his Sloth Demon slept so he easily got pulled back when his time was up," Zeke laughs.

"Here," Levi says, pulling out a black bandana from inside his leather jacket. "Does anyone else need one? I can conjure up more," he asks the group and hands one to Zissa and Ryker as well.

"Thank you " I say, and just pull my hair up and over, not caring how it looks. I'm going to be lucky if I can get the stench of death out of it as it is.

CHAPTER 27
Ravenous Ravine

Knox

Our progress is slow but steady as we pass a few scavenger Demons picking at some of the bodies. Zissa has us give them a wide berth while we pass, since we're not sure if they are friend or foe. I catch a few eyeing us hungrily, but they don't make a move. I believe we should err on the safe side and treat everything as a threat, but that's also how I was raised. Shifters are a different breed, more aggressive and tend to attack first and ask questions later.

'Yes, and that's why we tend to get a bad rep,' Baron says.

'No. It keeps us alive and teaches others not to fuck with us,' I correct my pompous Gryphon.

"Why didn't we stop?" Moni asks after we're out of sight range of the last of them.

"I'm sure they would have tried to kill us if we weren't as heavily armed," Zissa assures us. "No need to make ourselves an unnecessary target."

'See,' I point out to Baron.

'Whatever you need to say to make yourself feel better about

being an asshole. I'm going to preen. This atmosphere is doing nothing for my feathers.'

Moni turns pale white and tucks herself back into Chester's side. He leans down to whisper into her ear. She nods, standing up straight, and pulls back her shoulders to walk beside him. I have to admit, I wasn't sure how I felt about the lemur Shifter at first, but he seems to be a good fit for Moni. I'm glad she has a responsive and loving mate, but if he steps out of line, he'll answer to me. Zeke passes her and smiles down at her as he ruffles her hair. *Not to mention answering to her other brothers.*

We come up to a shady area with a small pond, where a couple of lizards are drinking, and Zissa calls for a break. "Let's take a quick break and hydrate."

I pull out a water bottle and a protein bar, worried that we should have grabbed more than this since we didn't eat breakfast. As I approach Rez, she leans against a small tree trunk and removes her bandana mask. My kitten looks more like a cougar prepared for war with all the gear she's wearing. Dressed in all black except for her top, she looks good enough to eat. It kinda turns me on. Yet, there's that tiny part of me that just wants to protect and keep her safe. I wouldn't be against keeping her pampered, barefoot, and heavy with my cub. One day... maybe.

"Thanks," she smiles up at me, taking my offer. I sit down and grab my own drink and bar, gulping down half the bottle as I feel eyes on me.

"How are you doing?" Rez asks, taking a bite of her protein bar.

"Good," I reply, before taking a bite of my own.

"Do you regret mating with me?" she asks, and I choke on my food.

I cough as my eyes start to water, and I quickly reach for

my drink, downing the rest of it in hopes to dislodge the burn in my throat and chest.

Finally able to catch my breath, I turn my gaze on her. "Why would you ask that? Of course I don't regret it."

She shrugs and looks down at her hands, where she starts to fidget with her water bottle. "I don't know. I just got the feeling that you might. I thought things were supposed to change or advance between us, and they haven't. I don't even know what to expect anymore. So it got me thinking that maybe you just regret it."

'She's right, you know. You've kinda left her to figure this out on her own,' Dusky agrees.

'How can I guide her when I don't know what to expect?' I argue. *'I just learned that you guys can communicate with me after all this time. I don't know how this whole mate thing works.'*

'Well, what do you normally do when you start dating someone? Go on... I'll wait.'

'Ugh. Just tell me. I don't have time for this round-the-bush shit,' I growl out.

'Try sharing your life with her. Opening yourself up and letting her get to know you. That's one way of strengthening your bond. And I don't appreciate your attitude, so until you learn to behave, you can get your advice from the others.'

Shit. *'Dusky, I'm sorry. Okay.'*

Nothing.

FUCK!

"See, you're twitching, and it makes me think I'm right and you just don't want to admit it," she confirms.

Turning to face her, I grab her hands. "Kitten, it's not like that. I was just getting frustrated with Dusky and—"

"Dusky?" Rez tilts her head, and I realize she doesn't know about his name or the fact I can talk to them.

"Yeah," I chuckle. "One of the things I guess that's

changed, besides us picking up on each other's emotions and thoughts, is I can talk to my animals now."

"Really?" A smile blooms on her face "You're not joking. What are they like?"

There's a commotion as Reaper takes off and chases a few of the lizards until most dip into the underbrush while one starts running over the water. He whines and runs over to Zeke before he plops down in front of him to be fed some snacks.

"Well, Fluffers is a jokester, and I swear, he has ADHD. Baron is a posh know-it-all." I feel him humph his displeasure at me. "Dusky is my Stardust kitten that you met. His voice is higher pitched like a kitten, but the way he speaks... He reminds me of a wise old man, and I'm still feeling him out," I sigh, shaking my head. "Of course, you still need to pick his name. That's the name he gave himself until you could find a new one."

Rez tilts her head to the side, and she thinks. "Well, I've already met him, and he was so adorable. The way he moved, his coloring. I think I want to keep the name Dusky. It suits him," she says with a smile. "That is, if he's okay with it?" she retracts before biting on her lower lip.

'You okay with that name?' I try to reach out, but apparently he's still upset with me. I, at least, get the impression of him giving me a firm nod and then turning his back on me.

"He agrees with the name," I tell her, and she rewards me with a bright smile. I let out a sigh before addressing her. "He's also the one that's telling me I need to share more of myself with you to strengthen our bond."

"Oh," she perks up and smirks at me. "So I get to learn all the secrets of my scary alpha?" she teases and finishes her drink.

Our group is starting to pack up, so I grab our trash and stash it in my pack before helping her up.

"I promise you, it's not all that pretty," I say so she knows I'm nothing special, but she steps into me and grabs my chin.

"Everything that you've gone through or have done has made you the man that you are today. So, that doesn't scare me." Her confession has pride rolling through me. My mate is clearly fierce, to stand here and say that. "What scares me, is the idea that you don't want me," she admits. "So, as long as that's not the case, I'm good." She smiles. "Now spill." She grabs my hand, and we follow everyone out of our rest area.

I help Rez fix her mask as we find more bloodied bodies, and the road starts a steep decline.

"Is this right?" I call up to Zissa.

She turns and nods, allowing Knots to pass her. "Yeah, we're almost there according to what the merchant said. This is the ravine, then there's a cave at the end where he normally goes to get the Demstones, and he said there's bat flowers there also." I nod in understanding, and she jogs to catch up with Knots.

"Knowing my luck, the bastard had the ingredients and he just said he didn't to get us to bring him more," Rez mumbles under her breath.

"You probably have a point," I agree. "I want you to know that I'm sorry about the way our relationship has been going. I truly didn't mean for you to feel like I regretted this. I couldn't dream of a better mate than you. I promise I'll do better to help our relationship grow, okay?"

"Thanks," she replies and lightly tugs on my arm. "Now stop stalling and get to the juicy stuff."

I can't help but smile at her eagerness.

"So all Shifters, including Shifters like Chester, have this rage, right? How do you deal with it? I know you mentioned something during the party at the beach, but what's the normal way?" Rez asks, and I shudder thinking she had to start there. The Blood Matches.

"Yeah, I'm sure Chester has some form of rage in him. But it's different for all Shifters. For as long as I can remember, there's been the Blood Matches. We have them once a month at least, more so if dad needs a release or we have visiting Shifters and we're celebrating."

"The name doesn't sound like a celebration," Rez points out.

"That's because it's really not," Zeke points out, cutting into our conversation.

"Do you mind?" I ask, giving him a pointed look.

"Not at all, I want to see what else I can ruin," he jokes, but JP grabs his hand and pulls him up with him.

"Sorry about that," JP calls back. I wave it off as we get closer to the bottom of the ravine.

"Blood Matches work on multiple levels. On the basic level, they are a way for Shifters to get out our aggression and test our abilities against our peers. Think of it as sparring with someone that's at your same weight and power level. On a different note, you can challenge another Shifter and fight them, and whoever wins is the more dominant Shifter. It can also be used as a punishment, or if someone is trying to prove a point; they can point you out and challenge you. Sometimes though..." I clear my throat and crack my neck. Fuck, why is this so hard to say to her? Rez squeezes my hand, and I feel her reassurance through our link. *I just have to trust her.*

"As you can imagine, sometimes as Shifters we tend to get carried away and..."

"Some of you don't come out alive," she guesses, and I nod.

We reach the bottom of the ravine, and suddenly, I understand why we were advised to wear protective clothing, or at least pants and guards. Large ferns with long needles sprout from the ground. The path we're on is still worn, so there's no problem staying on it, but the ground around it doesn't look pleasant. The grass is dry and seems to be sharp as a blade, and the few trees that are present are bare. From the glimpse of them, there's dried blood along the trunks. I continue to survey our surroundings as I explain more about the Blood Matches.

"They say the stronger your bloodline is, the more rage you have; therefore, you have more animals to shift through. The average is two, with a small and larger animal form. I'm obviously not average, given my parentage and what we've learned about Lilith's contribution to us. Baron says there's another inside me, but they don't know what, and I can't feel him," I admit, swallowing thickly. *Fuck. I can't believe I just admitted that. I haven't even told my brothers.* "If he's right though, that means I have four, which is almost unheard of."

We're quiet for a few minutes as we walk in comfortable silence. I don't feel any resentment or disgust through our link, so I continue to send her positive vibes while keeping my eyes open as we continue on.

"I think I see the cave," Moni points out, floating above all our heads. Focusing on the formation in front of us, I do see an outcrop that could be the entrance.

"Do the Blood Matches really bother you?" Rez asks once more, and I take a moment to really think about what's upsetting about them.

"What if I become lost to the rage?" I speak the words that have plagued me since I was a child. It's a weight rolling off my shoulders that I didn't know I was holding all this time.

"I won't let you," Rez says simply. I'm so moved by her I lean over and kiss her forehead and get a whiff of *something*.

'Fluffers? Could use your help,' I say, pausing.

"Knox?" Rez says picking up on my worry. "What is it?" The entire group stops and watches as I scan the area.

'Dude... We're about to be fucked. I smell about six

incoming meaties. Don't know what they are... but they're fast and.... hungry.'

Meaties is a term he uses for another predator that he's hoping he can chew on.

"Six incoming. Don't know what, but they are fast and hungry," I inform the group and fall back, allowing Fluffers to swing forward.

It's the first time that we've agreed to shifting since we mated Rez. The incident at dinner was all Fluffers just reacting, and I had to get his ass under control. This time though, we're ready.

I hear multiple weapons pull from their sheaths, and the smell of fear hits me. I know it's normal, but it's not helping the situation here. It's practically ringing the dinner bell.

"Guys, stay in pairs and let the advanced fighters to the front. It's okay, we got you," Zissa calls out as I track movement to the right.

'There!' Fluffers yells. *'Let's get them!'*

I take off, close to the ground and weave between the tall fern plants when I get my first glimpse of the creatures. Shit! I've seen Jurassic Park before and these creatures aren't far off the mark. They're Velociraptors, but with a skin flap that connects from their forearms to their legs. Open sores are along their tails, which I can only guess is a defense mechanism, and they all seem to be branching off.

"Pteroraptors," Zissa yells. "Stay away from the trees. They can glide and drop on you and cut you up with their claws."

'Great. Flying knives. Just what I need,' I hear Rez's voice in my head.

'You got this, kitten,' I say and send her some encouragement as the first raptor comes closer.

"Any weak points?" Ryker yells out.

"Yeah. Throats, belly, and eyes," Zissa supplies.

"Good to know," Ryker says. "Knox. One coming up," he

yells, and a knife flies through the air and into the closest one's eye.

It screams and stops in its tracks, shaking its head and bringing up its claw to try and dislodge the knife. Not wasting the distraction, I take off and leap for its neck. My teeth sink into the soft, vulnerable throat, and the beast doubles its efforts to dislodge me and the knife. My back paws come up and block his arm between his body and mine, and I push off, clamping my jaws tight as I flip into the air.

Landing on my feet, I let the monster's throat and foul blood fall from my mouth before searching around for my next target. Zeke runs toward another target, his blades catching the light as he bobs between the animal's claws, and he's doing a great job taking down his creature on his own.

"No!" I hear Rez yell, and I search behind me to see her and Zissa doing fine and taking on their own monster. So what was she yelling for? Red streaks catch my eye, and I internally groan. *Reaper is going to be the death of us.*

I take off after the pup that's heading for one of the Pteroraptors.

'Yay, playdate!' Fluffers yells.

'It's not a playdate. Do you not see the big killer turkeys running around?' I ask.

'But I've always wanted a little brother to play with. What are we playing? Tag?' Fluffers asks.

'We're playing, don't let the little guy DIE!'

'Oh! I like that game,' Fluffers jumps for joy, with his tongue lolling out of his mouth.

I'm flanking the Pteroraptor, and I put on a burst of extra speed. As it reaches down for the puppy, I jump and body slam into him, causing him to falter and my body to fall to the ground, where I become disorientated.

FUCK!

'I got this,' Fluffers says, and I get the sense that my tail is

wagging and my tongue is lolling out of my mouth as Fluffers barks at Reaper and they take off. All I see is gray and nothing makes sense.

'Did you just take over?' I ask Fluffers.

'Of course I did. You must have hit your head if you didn't hear me,' he tells me.

'At least let me fucking see!' I say, panicking.

My vision clears, and I immediately wish I couldn't see. We weave between the monsters legs and Fluffers is fucking prancing around on the battlefield.

'Are you kidding me? We're going to die,' I yell, trying to get through to him.

Reaper barks and chases after us, and that's when I see it. The Pteroraptor screeches as its legs get tangled up in Reaper's long tail and falls to the ground. Fluffers jumps over the raptor's back and rips the throat out of our second kill.

Mimicking us, Reaper grabs onto the dead predator and growls. Maybe there's some hope for him after all.

CHAPTER 28
Demstone or DemNuts

Rez

It's a mixture of pure chaos and beauty as I catch sight of everyone's fights. Zissa has just finished taking down the one that came toward us. JP shoots water arrows into the Pteroraptor that Zeke is slicing up pretty well. I quickly spot Reaper with Knots as he chews on the dead turkey, and that gives me some relief, but it's short-lived when I hear Moni scream.

Turning, I find blood gushing from her back as she rams her bo-staff into a Pteroraptor's eye and Chester jams his spear into its neck. It thrashes and yanks at Chester's Guandao. Lynx's black tiger comes out of nowhere and tackles the creature, ripping out its throat with a vicious roar.

A piercing shriek behind me has me turning and throwing up my arm with my glaive, but Levi is there with his bo-staff. He blocks the Pteroraptor before he can sink his claws into me. His sharp jaws snap at Levi's head, and I automatically reach for my barrier, feeling the heat traveling down my arm. Without much thought, I throw my hand out over Levi's shoulder and picture my shield. The raptor's head slams into my shield as Levi's eyes go wide at the proximity of those razor-sharp teeth.

Out of the corner of my eye, I see Knots run over to us with his glowing white sword. He swings it in an arc, disemboweling the raptor in one clean sweep. My heaving breath is so loud it blocks out all other noise for a moment while I look around for other enemies. What just happened? I reach out quickly while I know I still have my shield at my fingertips to check and reinforce Knots.

The noise slowly filters in as my shoulders drop, my heartbeat too rapid to count, and I reattach my glaives to the holsters. The slow dying calls of the Pteroraptors are the first sounds I hear before Moni's sobs. *Moni!*

Panicked, I stumble over to her laying in Chester's lap as Levi wraps a cloth around her tail. One-third of her tail is missing. Only the length of half of her forearm is left. It's not even enough for her to pull into her lap when she's her big-size self.

"I can't give you anything to help it grow faster, Moni, but I can help try to ease the pain," Levi offers.

Moni sniffles and nods her head while JP squats in front of her. "You know, since you've been hurt, it means you need a different weapon, right?" JP teases.

"No it doesn't, you liar, liar, pants on fire." I point to him, and he smiles up at me.

"His pants aren't on fire." Moni sniffles and looks at JP's pants.

"It's... nevermind. The point is, he's joking," I tell her.

"That is correct, Miss Moni. You are definitely a brave warrior," Knots says.

Chester swings off his pack and digs in until he finds a thermos. Knots reaches down and helps undo it, handing it back, and I get a whiff of what's inside. *Sparks coffee.*

"Here, drink this. It will help." Chester kisses the top of Moni's head as she smells the thermos and whispers thank you.

"The best part is now you can say you're a badass and you survived," Zissa adds. "You helped kill Pteroraptors. Not many can say that."

Moni brightens up and smiles up at all of us. "Thanks, I feel better now." She guzzles down her drink as Levi finishes dressing her tail in a bandage and stands up to address us.

"Does anyone else need me to check them out?" Levi asks.

"Well, I love being checked out, but I'd rather get mine from Rez or JP," Zeke says.

"Well, obviously you're okay." Levi chuckles.

Knox and Lynx switch back to their human forms, and I'm a little disappointed they are wearing clothes, but at least it doesn't slow us up.

"Can you clean the blood off of us?" I ask Levi, looking down at my outfit and my blood-splattered pup at my feet.

"Yeah, that might be a good idea. We don't need the reminder of our battle," Chester agrees as he looks down into Moni's eyes with a guilty expression.

"It's not your fault, Chestnut. Don't look like that." Moni tries to reassure him.

"I'm supposed to protect you, and I failed," Chester admits.

"You have protected me before. Remember the Fericrocs? You saved me then. But I'm a tiny warrior, and I have to earn my way too," she tells him, smiling up at Chester before leaning in to give him a kiss. I quickly turn my back to give them some privacy as Levi comes over to clean me up.

After we clean up, we quickly head into the cave we fought outside of, where Levi sends up orbs to light our way once the entrance light fades away. There are leftover torches placed at regular intervals, but we figure it's best to leave them and trust our own source of light. We follow the path until it branches off in three directions.

"So which way did he say to go?" Levi asks, and we're met with silence. We all turn to Zissa, and her mouth is flopping like a fish out of water. "He didn't tell you, did he?" he asks in a monotone voice.

"He just said the stones and the ingredients would be in here," she answers, sounding so unsure for the first time since I've met her.

"Well, ain't this great?" Lynx says, rolling his eyes and throwing his hands up into the air.

"Well, we could split up," Zeke suggests.

"No! Have you watched any horror movies that humans make? That's the first mistake before you die!" JP shrieks in disbelief. "Have I not taught you anything?"

"Oh, you've taught me plenty, but it wasn't about horror shows," Zeke purrs, and JP smirks.

"Well, if we split up, it would make this faster. Each group should have one warrior and make sure they have someone that knows what the bat flowers look like," Zissa says.

I don't like it, but we all agree to split up and meet back here in an hour. After Levi summons more lights and attaches them to our designated leaders, which are the ones who can find the herbs, we break off into our groups.

Group one consists of Moni, Chester, Zeke, and Ryker. They head off to the left, taking the first tunnel. Group two is Levi, Knots, and Knox, and each of them gives me a kiss on the forehead. Before Knots leaves, I try reinforcing his barrier before they head down the middle tunnel. I really hope that with the separation and distance between us, it will still work, but there's no actual way of knowing until we try. I don't know if I'm just tired from holding the barrier or if I'm just coming down from the adrenaline rush. Heck, for all I know, my barrier could just be weak and not really doing much in the first place.

Swallowing thickly, I turn to the right tunnel—which looks darker than the others to me—and start down it with Reaper at my feet. I decide to lead since I'm the one that knows what the bat flower looks like, and we can't do anything without those. Zissa, Lynx, and JP follow closely behind me as I make my way along the narrow tunnel. As expected, Levi's orb does a good job lighting our path, but it's the smell that's getting me. It's a mixture of blood, stale air, and an obnoxious perfume. *Why is that down here?*

"Does anyone else smell that?" I ask as I tighten my bandana.

"Yeah, it's too sweet to be down here," Lynx says, wrinkling his nose.

"You know who it reminds me of?" JP says as he sniffs the air before pulling his shirt up.

"Angel," JP and I say as it dawns on us.

"Who's that?" Zissa asks as we walk into a small cavern.

"She's a harpy from Hell," I mention as I catch sight of something purple between two stalagmites as JP explains.

"A harpy is a term Rez has given the mean girls at school. But she really is a part of Hell," he tells her.

"Really?" I ask as I reach for the purple flower. It actually resembles a bat in flight with its deep purple ruffled wings and long hanging filaments. I only know of these because my grandmother used to have a few of these in her shop I occasionally tended. They are a bitch to start from just the seed.

"Yep, remember in class when we were doing the DNA coding and percentages for our heritage? Angel got 50/50 with

Fae and Demon. Her and Emer's mothers are sisters. Her father is Asmodeus."

"Who is he anyway?" I ask, holding my hand out for a satchel. Lynx brings it over and hands me a plastic bag out of his satchel that I carefully lay the flower in before giving everyone my attention.

"Asmodeus?" Zissa confirms.

"Yeah. You mentioned him before with the medallion," I explain.

"And didn't Lilith or Lucifer mention his kids being delivered back to him on a pike?" Lynx reminds us.

"Oh, yeah," JP says.

Zissa pales slightly as she hears us ramble on. "Asmodeus is a prince of Hell. Don't get him confused with L.A.M.B.; they are the ultimate rulers and tighter than blood. They were the first to fall with Lilith. He fell years later; therefore, he's one of the princes. He's notorious for his temper, and it's a fact he's not happy with Lucifer's rules."

"So, he's a grumpy asshole," I conclude.

"That's putting it mildly." Zissa nods.

"Speaking of that medallion at the market, how did they know we would be there?" I ask, and everyone takes a minute to consider it.

"It means there's a spy in Lucifer's house," JP concludes, and everyone goes silent for a moment. That's definitely something we're going to need to discuss with L.A.M.B. when we get back.

"So what does the Bat flower smell like?" Lynx asks as I set it down in his bag.

"They say that no two people would smell the same thing from the flower, since it reflects what your soul is really feeling or what it's running away from. That's why it's a key ingredient to your potion," I explain.

Eyeing a few more, I pick those as well before we continue

on through the cavern and into another tunnel. As I approach another cavern, I spot something reflecting differently on the wall behind a stalagmite. The light hits a pinkish stone wedged in the stone. From my guess, it looks as big as an egg. A Demstone.

"Guys," I call back. "I see a Demstone."

I rush to it, but before I can reach out and pluck it from out of the wall, Reaper trips me. I'm sent sprawling onto the floor. Grunting, I silently thank Zissa that I wore these clothes with extra padding. I sit up to chastise him when a knife whizzes right by my nose. *Fuck!*

Three people are across the cavern by another tunnel. Well, two Demons, and one harpy from hell, Blonde Barbie herself. I pull up my shield and notice Angel running off as I keep my eyes on my would-be killers. Then I run back to our tunnel, crouching behind the stalagmites to not give away my ability yet.

"What's up?" Zissa quickly comes up to me and tries to peek around the corner.

"Angel's here alright, and she has two knife-throwing Demons with good aim," I spit out as my heart tries to beat out of my chest.

"Are you hurt?" JP asks, assessing me for wounds.

"No, thanks to my little Reaper here," I say, and give him kisses as he comes up and licks my face.

"Rez, how big can you make your shield?" Zissa asks.

"Ahh. I don't know. I haven't tried shielding anything larger than a personal shield. Why? What are you thinking?" I hesitate as she looks at me and then back at my weapons.

"I have an idea, but you might not like it."

Well, at least she's being honest.

"For the record, I don't like this idea. If I die, I'm haunting your ass and making Lucifer torture you," I say as I white knuckle my glaives. The rocks in this room range from mid-thigh to waist high, but that still leaves our party open to getting hit while we try to advance to the other side. And since I'm the only one with solid defensive capabilities, I'm playing bait.

The only thing I have going for me is JP and Lynx can read my thoughts easily and relay them to the group. But Lynx shifts into his tiger, so he's useless in conveying my thoughts now to the rest of the group as Zissa pulls her knives.

"When you're ready." She nods, squatting down next to the entrance.

Here goes nothing.

Pulling up my shield, I wrap it tightly around my body, noticing how much easier pulling it on gets, and take in a deep breath. *I'm gonna die!* I dash toward the first Demstone, and when I see the Demon, I dive, trying to dodge the knife. *Yes, I'm protected, but they don't need to know that. That's the whole point of playing bait.*

"What the fuck do you want?" I yell out to them.

"You," one of them yells back as I eye my next target to hide behind. It's a lower rock, so I won't be able to hide there long before moving on.

"Oh! Well, that's all you had to say." I wipe my sweaty palms on my pants before re-gripping my glaives and sprinting to my target.

"Dead," the other Demon says as a knife whizzes in front of me, causing me to jerk back and slip.

Fuck this.

JP! I'm just going to run. So send them out in a few seconds, but warn them, it's about to get bumpy.'

They want bait? Well, they are about to get it. Keeping my

eyes on the Demons, I run to the next stone but start singing in my head. My deal with Lucifer was only to stop deliberately trying to tear down his house. He said nothing about Hell in general.

"The B-I-B-L-E. Yes, that's the book for me. I stand alone on the Word of God. The B-I-B-L-E."

Unfortunately, that's the only verse I know from the random times a friend dragged me to church. My family didn't really attend church, so I sing it over and over again. As I planned, the ground starts shaking, and I continue to try to run and draw their attention.

"What's going on?" one of them yells, and I see a knife fly through the air into his neck. Zissa's aim is true even with the floor shaking. Lynx's tiger form has been slinking close enough that when the other Demon turns to see the knife in his partner's throat, he sees Lynx.

Instead of running away, like I thought he would, the Demon runs toward me. His arms come up to grab me, but I bring my hands up, and he crashes into my shield as his eyes go wide. I stop singing in my head while he just stands there for a moment until his eyes roll up and blood dribbles out of his mouth. Surprised, I glance down and I see my glaives stuck in his gut.

"Eww," I say and shake my arms, trying to dislodge him. "Um, help?" I say, looking over and finding JP hiding his chuckles.

"Congrats on your first kill!" Zissa says, grabbing a few Demstones as she makes her way to me.

"He won't get off," I say as his body goes slack and falls to the ground, rudely taking my glaives with him.

"Sounds like a personal problem," JP says as he runs by us and peeks around the corner.

"You know, I'm sure they have classes that teach you how

to get your man off. You might want to check into that," Lynx teases.

"Men," Zissa says as she comes over. "You okay?" she asks, giving me a sincere look.

"I—I didn't mean—" I'm so lost for words. I've never purposely killed someone before.

"On one hand, it gets easier," Zissa says as she pulls out my glaives from his gut and wipes off the blood on his shirt.

"On the other?" I ask, looking at her and feeling lost.

"It never really does; you just become numb to it," she says, handing back my weapons.

I don't know if I'm cut out for this badassery.

CHAPTER 29

Getting the Right Tune

Rez

After checking for Angel, or any other Demons hiding nearby, we gather what Demstones we can and head back to our check in. I take one look at the groups emerging from the other tunnels and I can tell they had their own scuffles. As soon as Levi sees Moni's group, he rushes over to check on them. Moni's covered in grime, and Zeke has blood around his mouth and hands. Ryker and Chester have blood on their weapons, but they look somewhat decent except that Chester's glasses are crooked.

"Did you cause that earthquake, or was that something else?" Ryker asks me.

"Yeah. We needed a distraction," I admit, and he gives me an appreciative nod before giving me a kiss and whispering that's my girl.

He gives Zissa a fist bump before turning to talk to JP.

Knox quickly makes his way over to me and pulls me into him for a hug, which I return, wrapping my arms tightly around him. I don't know why, but tears burn behind my lids as I close my eyes and just take in his embrace and strength.

"The first kill is never easy," Knox whispers. I give him a pitiful laugh.

"I don't know why I feel so stupid about crying over someone that was trying to kill me," I admit.

"It's because you have a heart and a good soul, kitten. Don't ever let someone take that away from you," he says into my hair. While I soak in his warmth, I reach out to Knots' shield and see that it's still in place and holding strong. Just to be on the safe side, I send out a little more of my magic and reinstate the hold. Knox rocks me back and forth until someone asks if we knew who attacked us.

"No clue," Moni answers.

"We saw Angel," I say, pulling away from Knox.

"Are you sure?" Levi asks, and I give him a deadpan look.

"No, now that I think about it. It was an elephant in a pink tutu. Yes, it was Angel, but she didn't stick around."

"Well, we got some Bat flowers and Demstones. You guys?" Knots points to his satchel, and Moni and I do as well.

"How many did you get?" I ask, checking to make sure we have enough. Once everyone counts out how many stones they collected, we're good to go. We have enough for the seller and for our potions.

"Okay then, let's get out of here."

Suddenly, the ground starts shaking and loose rocks start to fall. JP turns to me, "Rez?"

"It's not me," I insist.

Knox turns to Lynx. "Did you hear that?"

"Explosives?" Lynx nods and then jumps to the side when a large rock twice the size of a dumpster falls next to him. "Fuck!"

"Everyone get together so I can open this portal real quick!" Levi yells.

As dust and smaller rocks rain down on us, I check above us and notice cracks zigzagging along the ceiling. *It's not going to hold very long.* Focusing intently, I picture a shell over our heads, reinforced by layers and layers of tough, unbreakable magic. Rocks ping off the shield as Levi pulls out a small swirling stone. He holds it up at eye level while saying a few words, and a portal appears before him.

"Go. It should take us to Lucifer's throne room. I have to be the last one through," he coaches, and one by one, everyone slips through as I hold the shield. Eyeing the falling rocks as they hit my shield, I ease up close to the portal, and grab Levi's hand. And with a deep breath, we slip through at last.

W alking out of the portal, I find myself in another cave. "Since everyone is now here, let's say hi," Zissa says. It takes me a few slow minutes to recognize that this is the cave in Lucifer's throne room, noticing the stones that oddly look like skulls in the corner.

"I see our lovely host has been busy," Lynx comments as I hop and skip over the fresh, flowing blood.

We walk further into the room and find Lucifer staring with no emotion at a Demon stuttering at his feet. Leaning up against his throne, Trometh picks something out of his teeth with a bone, looking bored as well. I could almost mistake Lucifer for a statue until his eyes raise to take in our appearance. With a wave of his hand, the Demon at his feet vanishes.

"Um, we could have come back," Chester mumbles.

"Yeah, where did he go?" Zeke asks, looking around. Trometh jumps at our voice. His eyes go wide and the bone that was in his mouth clinks on the ground as his jaw drops slightly. He quickly schools his expression, but I know what I saw. *Shock.* I don't trust him, but I don't have any solid evidence against him, so I turn my attention back to the ruler of Hell.

Lucifer waves off the question. "I don't know. I wasn't paying attention to what level of Hell I sent him to. I'm sure he'll show back up if his complaint was important."

"You mean you weren't listening?" I ask, giving him a perplexed look.

"No. I was trying not to fall asleep, to be honest," he admits.

"How was your trip? I'm assuming it was good, since I see all of you came back in one piece," Murmur says, walking out from behind the seats.

"I'm not coming back in one piece. I lost part of my tail, see?" Moni flies up and presents her back to show her nub to him. "But like we mentioned before, it will grow back. I just wish Elayna could see how well I took it this time," she pouts.

"It's okay, Mo. Mom would have been proud of you. You helped kill that Pteroraptor!" JP says, pulling her into a hug before he immediately freezes.

"JP?" Moni squeaks.

He slowly raises his head and tilts it as he looks at Lucifer.

"What did you say?" he slowly asks the Devil sitting on his throne.

"You can read minds," Lucifer states, not moving an inch.

"And I read your thoughts. What do you know about our mother?" JP says.

Lucifer stands up and waves his hand, and I'm hit in the chest as air whooshes out of me. The room swirls around as I'm lifted off of my feet and slammed onto my back with a jolt. Opening my eyes, I find myself staring up at the training room's rafters that I've gotten used to seeing from this position. And from the groans around the room, he sent the others here as well. *I guess I can at least consider us lucky he sent us here and not somewhere else in Hell.*

"Ahh. I see Lucifer wanted privacy," Astaroth says, standing over me. "Well, come on. You don't have time to be lying down all day," he reminds me, holding out a hand to help me up.

He's right. I need to find Lilith and get these spells going.

As he helps me up, he looks me over and takes in my appearance. "You're in one piece?"

"That was a question?" I shriek, noticing everyone is here except Moni and JP. Even Trometh got banished here. I can't help the smug thought that he's not that special to hear what's going in the thorne room right now. But given everyone's state, we all look to have come out of that near-death experience unscathed. "You're telling me you had no confidence in me going out there with what you trained me on?" I point toward the entrance of the training room.

He shrugs, and my jaw drops as he just stares at me. I huff and turn to go when he catches my arm and pulls me back, which stops the others from leaving as well. "Hold on. Stand in a line, here."

"You know where I come from we're taught the word please," I mumble under my breath.

"I'm taught to start cutting and to listen for others to scream and beg instead of 'please,'" Astaroth comments back without looking at me, but I catch a smirk on his face as we line up without any more complaints.

"You have all seen battle today, have you not?" he says, and grabs Chester's Guandao.

He brings the spear end up to his ear and grimaces and then lays it down on the floor. Except for Zissa, he does the same thing with each of us. He releases her and steps before me. Grabbing my weapons, I suddenly have the urge to open my mouth. I was either hit in the head or have a death wish I'm looking to fulfill.

"So, what's up with you and getting up close and personal

with our weapons?" I ask as he shakes his head after repeating the process with my glaives.

"Your weapons are off," he says simply. "You're all free to go." He goes back to pick up the weapons he had deposited on the ground.

"Wait. What do you mean, they are off?" I ask, my curiosity getting the better of me. I check to see if anyone is staying behind, and a thrill runs through me to see Trometh sulking out behind the others.

"Once the weapons have had a taste of blood, they resonate," he says, looking at me. Given my wide eyes, he rolls his and cracks his neck before continuing. "Think of them as musical instruments. You strummed their strings and now they sound off. I need to tune them." He pauses and looks down at me. "Hmm, or better yet, I need to craft new ones to suit you all better," he says as a deep line creases between his eyes and turns. "Yes! New weapons would be better," he says to himself.

Well then. Who am I to argue?

"Wait. Astaroth!" I say, perking back up. He slows his pace but doesn't stop. "While we were out, yes, we were attacked, but it got me thinking. When we found the Demstones, I saw one of my classmates there. She's apparently Asmodeus' daughter."

That makes him stop and look at me. "And she was at the cave that you were at?"

"Yeah, I don't think it was a coincidence. With her showing up and the Goblins knowing we were going to the market, it smells like you have a rat," I say, giving him a smug look.

His eyes flash black for a moment, then he gives me his back. "I need to clean house, and if you want to have an appetite later, I suggest you finish what you need to with Lilith and take a nap before dinner," he says, then walks out of the back door.

Something tells me his idea of cleaning house isn't just doing a little dusting and asking around. I have a feeling he's talking about remodeling, and the new decor will be a gruesome red.

CHAPTER 30
New Heirs

JP

Wind whips around me but nothing happens as I glance around and notice everyone except Moni is gone as Lucifer descends the steps and takes in both of us. "Where did you send them?" I ask, worried about my friends.

"I sent them to the training room. They can find something to do from there. Come, we need to speak," he says, and goes to walk behind his throne.

JP... I'm nervous,' Moni says, directing the thought to me. Sure enough, she's sporting dark gray bark as she squeezes my hand with a death grip. I squeeze her hand back in three quick successions, letting her know I love her and I'm here. It's something we've done since we were little. We follow Lucifer through a door and down another hall until we walk into a small, cozy office.

"Try to relax. I won't let anything happen to you. Okay?" I whisper into her ear, and I watch as she takes in a deep breath and exhales slowly.

There's a desk in the back corner and a few bookcases. A

291

small bar lines a wall, but the sofas and coffee table take up most of the space. It's the first room that I've seen something other than marble or mats lining the rooms—well, besides the throne room. He's kept the black furniture, but the red carpet adds a different splash of color here, and I definitely approve of all the silver accents. It gives him more of a sophisticated touch and shows a more feminine side.

"Nice room," I say, looking around at his decor. Moni tugs on my arm, but I keep her by my side as we look around.

"Would you like a drink?" Lucifer offers. When we don't immediately answer, he pours himself one before downing it and slamming the glass down.

"It's that bad?" Moni asks, cycling through pale white and dark gray.

Lucifer looks over at us and picks up three fresh shot glasses and a bottle I don't recognize before sitting down on the sofa facing us.

"What do your colors mean, Moni? Is Moni short for anything?" he asks, pouring three drinks. Given what we've seen of him lately, he seems to be opening up more. His eyebrows are up, he's not scowling, and his shoulders seem more relaxed, but I feel like he's holding back something. *Why? Why this sudden change?*

Moni squeezes my hand once more before flying over to the sofa and taking a seat across from Lucifer. She grabs a glass and shoots it back. Tears gather in her eyes, and she clenches her jaw before coughing. She quickly pulls out a thermos, which I know has coffee in it, and scarfs down her drink before putting it away.

"Rez calls me a walking, talking mood ring! The way she says it, it makes me feel special instead of it being an embarrassment," Moni says, raising her chin.

I can't help smiling at the fact that she's standing up for herself, even if she really doesn't have to here.

"And my name is Monikaloy," she says as she reaches for her tail, only to find the shortened stub.

I walk over to the sofa and join her, grabbing her hand.

"Do you have a last name, Moni?" Lucifer asks, pouring himself another shot.

"What's this about, Lucifer?" I ask, getting frustrated that he has yet to tell us anything.

"Please, Moni, I promise to explain after I know." His eyes bore into Moni, and I feel her shudder against me. *That's it. I'm calling this off.* I go to stand up, but Moni stops me.

"It's okay, Bubba. My full name is Monikaloy Pastel, and I'm an abomination. My mother abandoned me and publicly disowned me, and JP's mother, Elayna, took me in and raised me," she admits. The only sign of pain is the small tremble of her lip that I catch before she clenches her jaw.

"That's what I thought," he says and turns to look at me. "And you're Elayna's biological son?"

"Yes," I growl out, not liking that he threw in biological there. Moni is as much Elayna's daughter as I am her son.

"Did your parents ever tell you the story about their younger years? Miss Teal or Elayna?" he asks as he gets up and starts pacing behind the sofa.

Moni and I share a confused look.

"Your silence is answer enough. Your parents were best friends from a young age. They were closer than most siblings. They even had a pact that they would try to marry brothers so they could officially become sisters. Did you know that?" He looks over his shoulder at us.

"Mother didn't mention much about her relationship with her best friend except that they at one time loved and dated the same Demon," I admit.

"Did your mother tell you who that Demon was?" he asks, turning to face us as he leans over the back of the sofa.

"No, and I didn't ask. Figured he didn't want me around, so why ask for the name of my sperm donor?"

Lucifer's eyebrows raise to his hairline, and it would almost be comical if it wasn't for my frustration.

"Why does any of this matter?" Moni asks, leaning into me, her shoulders rounded and hugging her knees into her chest.

"I'm sorry this is uncomfortable for you, Moni, but I promise there is a point," he states.

"Mind getting to it?" I urge, my frustration easily coming forward.

Lucifer smirks.

"Did you know that your mothers used to sit on that very sofa over twenty years ago? Used to drink tea, laugh, and tell me stories of their childhood?"

"Why would they do that?" Moni starts, but I gasp as I connect the dots and bolt upright from leaning into her.

"You?!" I spit out with a mixture of disgust and awe.

Lucifer holds his palms out, trying to placate me. "Will you let me finish?"

I reluctantly lean back and wait patiently for the answers I didn't know I was craving.

"I fell madly in love with your mothers, and we were together for a few years. We spent time in Purgatory and on Earth. But Marjoriekine started to change and pull away. She often accused me of loving Elayna more, which wasn't the case. I even pulled away from El to show Mar that it wasn't true, but nothing would change her mind."

Lucifer sits back on the sofa and runs his hand over his hair. "Shortly after that, Marjoriekine approached me and explained how they thought it was best to end our relationship instead of their friendship. I wasn't one to insist on breaking up what they had before me, so I let them go, with the caveat that if they wanted to come back, I would be here."

He lets out a heavy sigh and reaches for another drink. He quickly downs it and looks back at us. "It wasn't until I received a letter from Marjoriekine stating that the Sulks had claimed Elayna that I knew she was never coming back. I couldn't even attend her funeral because I wasn't notified until weeks after she was gone."

"I know I'm slow and all, but what does this have to do with us?" Moni asks. "I mean, besides making the bad choice to stick your wick in Miss Teal," she says with a sneer.

Lucifer chuckles and looks at Moni. "Your mother wasn't always like she is now."

"Pfft. Yeah, and I'm the Easter Bunny Shifter." Moni crosses her arms and stares at him. I swear, she's harnessing Rez. "The point is, she's evil now and runs with the Rebels."

"What?" Lucifer's eyes go round as he looks between both of us.

"Yep, what she said. She's a part of the Rebels," I parrot.

"When did this happen?" he asks.

Moni shrugs. "Don't know when it happened, but Rez and I found out a couple of weeks ago. Saw the tattoo and everything."

Lucifer's head drops and his shoulders round as he lays his head in his hands. It's the realest I think he's ever allowed himself to be in front of us.

Moni flies over and places her hand on his shoulder, and he jerks at her touch.

"I'm sorry. You just seemed sad." Moni's voice comes out unsure, worry etched on her face, until Lucifer reaches over and squeezes her hand.

"Thank you," he says, then clears his throat. "The reason I'm bringing all of this up is because of my vault."

"I knew it!" Moni screams and flies away to the far side of the room. "He brought us here to kill us. No witnesses, JP.

Run for it! We're going down. Code Red! Call in the enforcers," Moni yells as she zips around.

"Moni! Calm down," I yell, getting up and trying to follow her movements. It's like following a deflating balloon around the room.

"He's come to seek his vengeance. I didn't even get to try pegging yet. Chester is gonna be so disappointed." She stops right in front of me, grabs my shirt and yells, "JP, I can't die yet!" And faints into my arms.

I pause for a moment with my jaw dropped as her words finally register. *Pegging—umm, no. Just no!*

I walk back to the sofa and carefully lay her down. Looking over at Lucifer, I see he's walking back to us with a box.

He must have gotten up while I was running after Moni.

"She does that a lot?" he questions.

"She's actually way off mark since we've been down here. She would have been on number twenty by this time if we were home," I tell him. "Do you want me to wake her?" I ask, giving him a chance to decide.

"Do you think she will agree to a blood test?" Lucifer asks instead and sets a long black velvet box onto the coffee table.

This definitely took a turn that I wasn't expecting. Without answering him or taking my eyes off of him, I shake Moni awake.

"What did I miss?" she asks, popping up. "Oh, well, I see he hasn't killed us yet. Yay." She settles next to me and wraps her arm through mine as Lucifer opens the velvet box. Inside are needles and vials.

Does he just keep them hidden around places, or can he conjure them like Levi can?

"No, but he wants us to take a blood test."

"Why?" she asks.

"It got me thinking when you mentioned Elayna. I had

given them permission to travel to my residence and never revoked it, so they could pass through any wards or barriers."

Okay, but where is he going with this? I swear, being down here in Hell is making me feel slow.

"That still doesn't answer the question of how you portaled into my vault. Only those with highborn Demon blood can make portals into Hell and allow those with them to pass through without a protective device unharmed," Lucifer says, running his hands over the black fabric lining the box. "Neither one of you has ever been to Hell. Correct?" He glances up at us as our silence speaks volumes for us. "Yet you both ended up in my residence, and your friends joined you unharmed," he points out.

I glance down at Moni and see her turning magenta. Yep, she's about to go again; this time I might join her if he says—

"I think you're my children." He looks up at us, and I watch Moni roll off the sofa as all sound becomes muffled for me. My head falls back against the sofa, and the only word I can think of to express all of this is, "Fuck!"

CHAPTER 31
Knick Knack Paddy Whack, Give the Guys a Stone

Rez

After Astaroth's warning, I decide to hurry up and check on Lilith. I'm anxious to see what the timetable is for the potions, and if she can help me with the other spell I found in her book. Of course, I make a few wrong turns, and somehow end up in a massive room with monstrously high ceilings and a floor entirely made up of trampolines. Why L.A.M.B. has a trampoline room, I can't even begin to guess, but it sparks some pretty interesting ideas before I remind myself about my limited time. But soon enough, I find her study. I'm happy to find Lilith at her table with the Demstones—a stack of five set aside for the merchant—and the Bat flowers already laid off to the side. Maybe if she's in a good mood, I can ask her about my tattoo as well.

"Hello again," Benny says, climbing up to the tabletop. "Did you have any trouble finding the rest of the ingredients?"

"Nothing we couldn't handle." I smile down at the small helper.

"Benny, could you please start deseeding one of the Bat

flowers for me?" Lilith asks as she turns to smile at me. "Hello, Rez. So glad to see you. Levi said that you had an idea about another spell?" she asks, raising her eyebrows and waiting for me.

"Oh. I guess he beat me here."

"Yes. He just left a few minutes ago with some ingredients, saying he wanted to work on a spell in his room. He didn't say what, though," she says, waving his actions away, and goes back to smiling while waiting for my answer about the spell. "What was the other spell you had in mind?" she asks once more, prompting me to get back on task.

It's still a shock as she's asking me to lead for the first time. During the unbinding ritual, she was running the show and telling me things as if I didn't know anything. Granted, I didn't know anything about bindings, but I do know stuff about plants and some of their properties.

"Yeah, but don't we need to get the other spell going for unlocking memories first?" I ask, wanting to make that my priority.

"I've already got it started, over there." She points to two small caldrons. "I was told Levi has to be at the Hub in Nova at ten o'clock tomorrow, but the spells should be ready shortly after that if you want to stay back to perform them and help with the grounding."

"Yeah, I would like to get their memories to them as soon as possible. Besides, I don't think I'll be invited to Levi's ceremony." I give her a pursed smile and reach for the book I read last time. "But here you go. This book here has this spell that I thought could resist memory spells if they are used against the guys."

"Who? Who would do that to my boys?" Her tone waivers, and I feel as though I'm sitting on the edge of a knife. I don't want to lie to her, but I also don't want to send her spiraling when I need to make sure these potions are done right.

"I'm just taking precautions. They mean the world to me, and I don't want someone to take them away, so they agreed to take precautions to make sure that doesn't happen." I fudge the truth.

"Oh." She forcefully exhales, grabbing her pearls. The Stepford Wife getup is the outfit choice for today's spell casting for some reason, but I'm not about to complain if she's sane enough to work. "Yes, they need all the protection they can get. I'm so happy they have you looking out for them," she says, reaching over and pinching my cheek.

I fucking take it back; she's definitely not sane enough to handle this. Where's Bez to carry her off?

"Well, let's get started." Lilith grabs the book and the ingredients, and we get to work.

Working beside this unpossessed Lilith isn't as bad as I thought, though. As Benny deseeds the Bat flowers for Knots' and Lynx's spells, Lilith and I work together to make the protection potion for memory loss.

· · · · ·

"Good job, Rez. You're a natural," Lilith praises me as I smile down at the nine sparkling white vials lined up on the table.

"Thank you for helping. I wouldn't have been able to do it without you." I grin at her.

"Well, the fun part comes next," she says, and turns to the Demstones. She grabs nine random stones and sets them before us.

"So, how does this work?" I ask, rocking back and forth to dispel the anxiety clawing at my skin.

"Demstones have a long history, but let me give you the

Cliff Notes. They are a rare combination of brimstone and star rubies. They are the best for holding powerful spells and are extremely hard to acquire, as you probably saw by the Blood Slick Road. Most mines have either been claimed, sold, or are known to be quite dangerous to get to."

A shudder runs down my spine as I stare down at the pretty pink and yellow swirl stones, remembering all the death and the life I took. It wasn't pretty.

"We are lucky to have such unrefined stones," she says almost giddily.

"Why's that?"

"Because you'll be able to shape them as you apply each spell," she tells me. I quirk an eyebrow, and she laughs as she lightly pats my shoulder.

"Sorry, I tend to forget how new all of this is to you. When applying spells to unrefined stones, you're able to shape them with your mind and fingers to what you want. For example, if you wanted a ring, it would mold it into it. What attributes you want it to do, you would just think of and it will do it. Like if you want it to shrink with the wearer, it will." She gently pulls me in front of her so I'm directly across from the stones.

"When it comes to Demstones, it works best for the person applying the potion to be shaping the stone all at once. Since this is your project, I think it's appropriate that you do it. Besides, you know what suits each of them better than me. I would just be guessing," she admits with a hint of sadness. "Anyway, to do this, think of the person you want the spell to work on, pour the spell onto the Demstone, then pick it up and mold it into something for them to wear. Don't worry. I'll be right here to make sure you get it right on the first one," she says, and I feel her step back from me.

Sure. Simple as that.

I let out my breath and think of Levi first, since he's the

first person up for me to lose. Tomorrow afternoon, he takes his vows and I'll lose him. If Emer has her way, he'll lose all memory of me as well, but I won't let that happen. He needs to be protected, but not with something obvious that sticks out.

Grabbing one of the vials, I pop the cork and pick up a stone, holding it in my hand. I slowly pour the white liquid onto the stone and watch it absorb all of it. Trusting Lilith that it's as simple as she says, I grab the stone with both hands before I close my eyes and picture what I want. Pinching the middle, I make two separate stones. Amazingly, the stone's hard surface turns soft as putty.

I crack open an eye to peek, making sure I'm not imagining anything, and close my eyes again when I see the stones. I picture the shape that I want and rub my thumbs over the stones, sucking in a breath as I feel the material move on its own. Once the weight becomes heavier, I open my eyes. A giggle escapes me as I look down at what I created.

"Yes, that is definitely Leviathan, and it's stylish too," Lilith says, peeking over my shoulder.

I set down the cufflinks that I shaped as scales, like the tattoo he has on his hip, which reminds me that Lilith or L.A.M.B. might know more about that than we do. Turning to face Lilith, I decide to just tackle it head on.

"Okay, I'm just going to say this, and I know it's awkward since you're my... harem's mother? I'm not sure what to call you." I cock my head to the side and Lilith breaks out into a huge smile.

"Call me Mom!" she says, and wraps me into a tight hug. "I always wanted children, and now I have a daughter-in-law. My little black heart is so full right now." She sighs as she rocks us back and forth in her embrace. "I could skin a thousand Demons and still not be this happy."

"Oh... okay." I pull out of her embrace and look up at her

smiling face. *Don't piss off the crazy lady... my... holy shit. Lilith, the original Demon, is my mother-in-law.*

The room starts shaking and Benny yells "I got it" as shields go over the valuables, securing them in place.

Lilith just gives me a knowing smile. "So what was it you wanted to say?" she asks, bringing me back to my point.

"Oh, yeah. Well, I know this sounds weird, but I don't know who else to ask. But after solidifying my"—I clear my throat and swallow the lump forming there—"relationship with your sons, they, umm, received... kinda–well... a magical tattoo," I stammer, and hold my breath as her eyebrows slowly raise toward her hairline until I can't see them anymore.

"A tattoo?"

I nod.

"What kind of tattoo?"

"Well, you see, they are similar but all different," I manage to get out as she stares at me with a new intensity I've never seen before.

"Go on."

Shit. Maybe I shouldn't have brought this up with the unstable and fragile Demon that loves to torture creatures here... in Hell... where I stand.

Gathering my courage, I state hesitantly, "Each of them has one of the Four Horsemen on them." I scoot back, hitting the table as her eyes flash black for a moment.

She shakes her head and grabs her pearls as she starts mumbling to herself for a few moments. When I realize she's repeating words, I try to pay attention.

"*Four protectors bound in one soul,
Torn asunder through a hole.
Four souls split a part,
Tearing through a bleeding heart.*

Climbing through the ranks of Hell,
The rebels you shall not repel.

. . .

Four young souls will embody thee.
To save us all, she will be the key.
Thy body will encompass true evil's hate,
When gone for long without thy mates.

Win them back for true love's power,
To tackle thy battle of the twelfth hour.
These tasks you must complete,
Or else all will be obsolete."

S he's more or less in a trance as I stand here listening to her rhyme. I have no idea what it means, but I'm getting the creepy vibe until I see a streak of blue walk by.

"Murmur!" I yell.

"You rang?" he leans back and peers in.

"Help."

He raises his eyebrows but walks in. "What's going on, Lilly, pa—"

He quickly turns his accusing eyes to me, and I throw my palms up. "Hey, I was just asking her about a weird Horsemen tattoo and she started doing that," I quickly deflect.

Lilith grabs Murmur's biceps with a death grip. "The prophecy. Murmur, it's happening. I need to talk to you all. Where are all the guys? I—I need to find them. I need—"

"I got you, Lilith," he says gently as he turns her to head

out, glancing over his shoulder at me. "If you saw Horsemen tattoos, we'll talk later tonight, after dinner. Right now, finish what you must and get to your hall. We're cleaning house, and it's best if you're out of the way." He reinforces what Astaroth mentioned and rubs Lilith's back as they walk out of the room, leaving me confused.

Why would the mention of tattoos send her over the edge? And why would she start mumbling a rhyme or a prophecy?

I groan as I pinch the bridge of my nose. *Okay, Rez, get your shit together.* There's nothing I can do about that now, but I should finish these Demstones and pass them out before I take a shower and hopefully a nap.

The hardest part in making the Demstones was deciding what each person would like. As I head down to my hall, I hear guttural screams and Bez's mocking voice. "You can run, but you can't hide. We'll find you." He laughs maniacally.

"Go ahead and run, little bunny. We love the chase," Murmur's voice rings out, and a chill runs down my spine, making my stomach churn. I'm glad I'm not leaving my hallway for a while.

My first stop is Moni and Chester's room, where I knock and hope I'm not interrupting anything.

The door opens up, and I find Moni's bright pink face while she hides her body behind the door. Chester is under the covers.

"I promise to make this quick," I say, biting my lower lip while trying not to laugh at my own joke. I swear, I'm an adolescent boy at heart. Moni makes eye contact with me and snickers too, so I don't feel so bad. "I just need Chester's glasses and your hair for a moment. I'll wait out here while

305

you get his glasses and put on a robe," I say, closing the door.

A few moments later, Moni comes outside with Chester's glasses. I pop out his lenses and pull out the last Demstone. I realized I needed his glasses to finish his stone, so without cere-mony I quickly open his glasses and put the stone on his nose piece before pouring his vial on the stone. Thinking of a stronger nose piece for him, yet flexible enough for him that it's comfortable, I watch in awe as the stone transforms and molds to his glasses.

"Wow! It's magic," Moni whispers. My mouth drops open as I stare at my best friend and just shake my head.

"You're a PIMP, and you're shocked by magic? You *are* magic, Moni." I laugh as I pop back in his lenses, handing them over to Moni, and she gives them a quick clean with the edge of her robe.

She's unusually quiet, and I see her cycling through dark gray, white, and light teal.

"Okay, little mood ring, spill," I say, placing my hands on my hips.

She sighs before reaching for her tail. It's already grown longer, but it's still not back to its normal length. "So, you remember when Lucifer pushed you guys out?"

"Yeah, what happened?" I ask. She seems unharmed, but that doesn't mean anything. It's been proven that emotional pain can be worse than physical.

"Well, it turns out that Lucifer knew JP's mother and my egg donor. They actually dated, and one thing led to another... And we didn't get used to heal a sore throat. So—"

"Wait, did you just make a swallowing cum joke?"

She giggles. "Yeah."

"Oh my word, I don't want to be around when or if JP hears that," I say, leaning up against the wall.

She snorts. "I already did! I screamed it over and over in

my head until we made it back to our rooms." She laughs so hard that she falls over, but I catch her and the glasses.

"Woah there, I worked hard on those potions." I help her up and look her over. "Here, this is yours. I hope you like it." I hold up the FairyTail. "It's a wrapped hair cuff, or in this case, it's for one of your vines."

Tears suddenly gather in her eyes and she starts sniffling.

Shit, did I do something wrong? Break a custom? Ugh, why is this so frustrating?

"I'm sorry, Moni, I didn't mean to offend yo—oopmh."

Moni grows to her normal height and tackles me, knocking the air from my lungs. "I love it so much. No one has ever given me beauty products before. Thank you. You're the bestest friend I could have ever asked for. You're like the opposite of a cursing in disguise."

"Don't you mean blessing?" I groan as the floor rumbles, and I hear Lucifer scream my name.

"No, I mean curse, so my father won't yell at me," Moni says, smirking at me as she lifts a vine for me.

"So, wait. You mean that cum joke was your way of telling me Lucifer might be your father? When? Shit! Wow," I sputter, flabbergasted.

"Oh yeah. We did a blood test, and we'll find out after dinner if he's our dad. He said it would explain how we all teleported into his vault," she explains as I wrap her Demstone around her vine. Once it's secure, I step back and look at her smiling face.

"Well, I can't wait to find out if I have immunity to the big bad or not," I say.

Moni tilts her head in question. "What do you mean?"

"Well, I doubt you would let your dear ol' dad kill your bestie, right?" I smile at her, and she laughs.

"Of course not... Wreak all the havoc in the underworld; I won't let him hurt a hair on your head," she promises.

"I'll hold you to it. Okay, shrink and see if it shrinks with you. I tried to add in that caveat," I instruct. She zips down, making me smile when I see the stone resize appropriately. "Awesome. As long as Chester keeps his glasses with him, he should be protected, but um... I'm gonna let you get back to having your fun while I pass the rest of these out."

CHAPTER 32

Roasted and Toasted

Rez

After hitting up Moni and Chester, I figure I might as well go down the hall and hand out everyone's Demstones. I start in JP's room, and I'm pleasantly surprised to see Zeke there. I made Zeke two thumb rings that have scythes on them. When he's in battle, he'll hopefully be able to activate them to elongate and it will help protect him along with the other rings Astaroth gave him. When JP tries to give me a heads up about Lucifer, I inform him that Moni already told me, but I can't wait to find out the official word. Before I leave, I hand him his Demstones and tell him to get Zeke to help him put them on. He takes one look at the dick piercings and laughs.

Finding something for Knots was harder than I thought. The only thing that seemed to be a constant with him was his sword, so I made a jeweled pummel that would fit at the end of the hilt of his sword. When I show him, he pulls me in and gives me a fiery kiss that ignites my greedy pussy, but I have to remind myself I stink and still need to finish my work.

Next, I knock on Levi's door and hear a muffled "Come in." I walk in and find Levi standing in front of a desk and Ryker walking out of the bathroom in just lounge pants.

"Hey, temptress. Coming for a quickie?" Ryker makes a beeline toward me, pulls me into him, and gives me a searing kiss.

"Mmm. Tempting as you are, I'm here to give you guys a present." I step back, smile up at him, and pull out some jewelry. The first thing I made for him was a new lip ring shaped like a bow. The Prince Albert ring has a crown engraved into it, and arrows for the Jacob's Ladder. I show him each piece and explain what they are before I drop them into his palm.

"Does this mean you get to help me replace these?" Ryker winks.

"Um no. You can switch those out in the bathroom." As I side step him, I pat him on the chest. "I promise to check them out later, though." I blow him a kiss as I walk over to Levi.

"Hey," I say as I gently run my hand up Levi's back and peer around his shoulder. "What are you doing?"

"I'm about to find out who wrote this note that Knox found," Levi explains as he puts down the mortar and pestle and grabs said note.

"Really? You've already made the potion?" A thrill races through me as he lays down the note and sprinkles what he just ground up over it.

"Yes." Levi gives me a warm smile before he grabs a vial of yellow liquid. "If this spell works properly, we'll see an image of the person that wrote this note."

"Oh, can't wait to get that answer," Ryker chips in on the other side of Levi.

Levi pours the liquid over the paper and mumbles words in another language. I fixate on the paper as red and silver smoke billows up from it. Instead of showing the person's face like I was imagining, a small scene plays out above the bowl.

A man stands up fast enough to send his chair flying into the wall behind him and reaches for a pen. He bends over and furiously jots down the words on the note. From his hunched form, I can't make him out, but his size is enough to give me pause.

When he stands up to his full height, I finally get a look at the man that's been keeping track of me. Dark shuffled hair hangs down over his forehead and into his dark blue eyes. They would be gorgeous if it wasn't for the scowl and darkness I can see in them. His uniform shirt flexes and stretches over his wide chest and shoulders as he puts away the pen and picks up the paper.

"Who was that?" I ask when the scene fades and I'm left looking at the blank wall.

"Brooks," Ryker answers. "Fucking Capt. Brooks."

"Second in command to Chief Cloak," Levi explains and turns to me with a worried expression.

"Well, that is until Knox steps up and takes his place," Ryker says. "So, the question is... Why is Brooks keeping tabs on you?"

A chill runs down my spine at the thought of who might be behind everything.

Levi starts to clean up, and it shakes me out of my musings. "Oh Levi, here," I say, holding out my hand with his cufflinks. "This was the reason I came by. I hope you're okay with them."

"These are wonderful. Thank you," Levi says and gives me a brief kiss.

"I'm glad you like them. I need to pass out the others. Want me to tell them what we found out?"

"Who else do you need to visit?" Ryker asks.

"Just Knox and Lynx." I shrug once I get to the door.

"Yeah, you can tell them, and I'll go tell the others before we lock down for this house cleaning." Ryker joins me at the door. As I head toward my Shifters' room, Ryker heads down toward JP and Zeke's room.

I find my Shifters in their shared room and my little hero of a pup with them. My guys with piercings were easy to come up with something for them to wear. As soon as I walk in, I'm engulfed by Knox's big arms.

"What's the wonderful occasion, kitten?" He kisses me lightly on the forehead before letting me go.

"Well, I brought you new studs." I place the jewelry in his hand.

"Ahh. Are these from the Demstones?" Knox asks as he looks over the nipple studs in the shape of swords.

"Yep. I hope you like them." I smile up at him.

"I already love them. Thank you, kitten. I'll put them on after my shower." I look around the room and finally notice the bathroom door is closed.

"Is Lynx in the shower?" I ask, wondering if that's why Knox was out here just waiting.

"Yeah." He cocks his head, "But it sounds like he's almost done, so it's about to be my turn."

"Correction, it *is* your turn," Lynx says, smiling at us from the now open doorway.

"Well, that's me, kitten." Knox leans down and gives me a sweet kiss.

"Wait, before you hop in the shower, I need to tell you both what Levi found out."

"What do you mean?" Lynx walks over and leans against the bed.

"Levi performed the magical Imprint, and it was Capt. Brooks who wrote that note."

"Fuck!" Knox says under his breath, but of course we still hear him. "I knew he was up to something." He shakes his head. "Well, there's nothing we can do about it now. I'm going to take a shower. Thank you for telling me." He kisses me on the head before walking into the bathroom and leaving me with Lynx.

Lynx was the easiest yet strangely the most frustrating to make something for because he doesn't know me. Yet, I know him and how he doesn't have piercings or tattoos. He doesn't like to wear anything too binding, so how do I make him something that he doesn't know he likes?

"Here," I say nervously as I turn to face my best friend. I hand Lynx the Demstone weaved through some twine I found in Lilith's shop. "I've made it so you can shift into whatever you want and it will adjust to you."

He sits down on the floor and Reaper runs over and starts licking his face, so I pull my puppers onto my lap as Lynx ties the bracelet around his ankle.

"Thank you, Rez. I appreciate it." He gives me a smile. "I'm sure there's a reason behind it I don't know, though."

I chuckle as I dig my fingers into Reaper's flame, warming my fingertips. "Yeah, you don't like clothes, and when we were around twelve, we made each other friendship bracelets," I tell him. "But we grew out of them, and then, well, you've just been stuck in your lynx form." It almost feels like talking to a complete stranger. I look up and find him with a small wrinkle of concern on his face for a brief moment before he smiles at me.

"Well, hopefully in a few days, I'll have my memory back," he tells me as he rests his hands on his propped up knee.

"Oh, that reminds me! We should be able to do your memory spell tomorrow. I'm not invited to Levi's ceremony, so we can stay behind and do it—that is—if you want," I say hesitantly, letting Reaper up.

"Can't wait to remember what I've forgotten," he says and helps me up. "You did a great job today. Wanna take a nap and cuddle?" My heart stops as the words leave his mouth. I've missed cuddling with my Lynx, and I want to more than anything, but not like this. Not without his memory, and besides, I still reek.

"Raincheck? I need to shower." I sigh and he smirks.

"Sure. Besides, I owe you that massage, so it's not like you're going to let me get away with it," he tells me, and I laugh while heading to my own room across the hall with Reaper following me.

Happily I find my room empty, so I grab a fresh pair of clothes from the closet and go into the bathroom, where I strip and start my shower.

"Want to take a shower too, you reaper of chaos?" I ask Reaper, and he just yips and wags his long-ass tail. I swear, it's like a bullwhip. He follows me into the shower, where it quickly turns into a steam room once the water hits his fiery mane. I briskly wash my body and hair, and Reaper plays and tries to eat the water. He gets washed down with the body wash I have since that's the only thing I have left, and I rinse him off before I turn off the shower and attempt to dry us.

He barks and runs off into the bedroom, probably to roll around, so I try to rush through my hair routine but give up when I hear him barking. Putting down the brush, I tuck my towel tightly around me as I walk out after him. "Reaper! Chill. The room's not on fire, so there's no n—"

"Ma chérie, there you are. Come see my new piercings you made for me," JP offers. He's sprawled out on top of my bed in nothing but his shorts, which are pulled down, and he's slowly stroking his cock.

Damn.

"There's no fire, but it's about to get hot." Zeke's voice filters from the closet. He walks out and quickly shuts the door behind him. He's also just wearing shorts, and there's an impressive tent in the front.

"Um, not to say that I don't appreciate the drop in, but what did you do with Reaper?" I ask.

A yip and the sound of scratching comes from the closet, and Zeke does an about face, standing in front of it for a second before quickly opening and closing the door.

"Please tell me you didn't just magic him away," I squeal and run for the door.

Zeke laughs and picks me up over his shoulder to walk us to the bed. "Relax, I just gave him some toys so JP and I can play with ours."

Well, I like where this is going.

Before Zeke can put me back down, I feel JP's hands run up my legs and over my ass, pushing my towel up. "You are wearing way too much. But I do love this view," he purrs, and my breath hitches as his tongue licks along my slit before he pushes my legs apart to suck lightly on my clit. "Mmm. Delicious," he says before smacking my ass. A thrill passes through me as heat blooms at my backside.

Zeke gives me to JP but rips off my towel during the shuffle. "No clothes in the bed, sorry." He smiles but doesn't look apologetic at all.

"Well—in that case—the same can be said for you," I say smugly at Zeke. I plop back on the bed, my wet hair smacks me in the face.

Yes, very sexy, Rez. This is what the guys want.

"Sorry, ma chérie, but you can't." JP's timbre causes my lower abdomen to clench with desire. Desperate to see what's waiting for me, I claw at my hair to get it out of my face, and I'm rewarded when I see JP's smirk. Following the movement that draws my eye, I see him stroking his hard, inked cock with his new jewelry while he's straddling me. *And he's right. I can't make the same statement about him needing to take his clothes off. He's a fucking masterpiece.*

Taking the moment to appreciate all of him, my eyes

slowly travel up his strong, tan thighs and up to the tattoo of vines and water droplets that wrap around his cock and up his hips. The muscles in his arm and stomach flex as he slowly pleasures himself. I continue my perusal over his taught chest and wide shoulders, right up to his slightly open mouth and heated gaze. His hair falls into one of his eyes, but he doesn't break contact with me when the bed dips and Zeke climbs up next to him.

I've never noticed how different their skin tones are against each other, but I love the contrast. Zeke's pale skin pops against JP's when he leans into him and licks up his neck, causing JP's eyes to become heavy as he moans. They haven't even touched me and just that lick has my hands moving. I grab one breast, kneading it, then lightly teasing my nipple as my other hand travels down my body. Zeke's eyes zero in on me as my hand finds my clit and I rub my finger around my tight bundle of nerves. Pleasure rolls through me, and I let out a moan. I lightly pull on my taut nipple as I slide my finger along my slick slit, and another moan escapes me as I push it inside me and curl it up.

He gives me a slow and sensual smile as his hand caresses JP's chest and pinches his nipples before following the same path mine did until his hand meets with JP's. Zeke grabs JP's cock and slowly starts stroking him, and my breath hitches as I watch my own version of porn right in front of me. JP turns Zeke's head and roughly slams his mouth to his, angling it for a deeper kiss.

"Fuck me," I moan.

JP pulls back suddenly, nipping at Zeke's bottom lip. "We plan to," he says with a wicked glint. He kisses Zeke passionately while he reaches down and strokes his long cock a few times, moaning as pre-cum leaks from both of their heads.

As if they timed it, they both pull away and Zeke leans down and runs his tongue over JP's slit, collecting the pre-cum there. A moan is ripped from JP's throat as he throws his head back and rocks his hips, slipping into Zeke's mouth. My jaw drops, imagining taking JP's cock into my own, and my hips slightly lift as my body silently begs to join in.

Fuck it. I'm joining.

I shift to sit up and JP's hand grabs my ankle, stilling me. Glancing up, his chocolate brown eyes are staring into mine as he slowly shakes his head and tsks. Zeke slowly licks up JP's shaft before backing away as JP moves so my legs straddle his thighs, and he fits snugly between mine.

"Get your finger out of my dessert," JP demands, and I slowly pull my finger out of my pussy, making sure to rub it against my clit. Grabbing my hand, he holds it up so the light shines off of my wet digits and smiles at Zeke. "Want a taste?" he asks as he presents my finger as if it's the next dish he's serving.

Zeke leans in at the same time as JP, and they both begin licking my juices off, ending the clean-up with a kiss.

"Hmm, definitely one of the favorite dishes you've ever given me." Zeke's husky voice drops as he licks his lips.

"Just wait." JP winks as he leans down and wraps his arms around my thighs, locking me in place. He looks up at me with a smile before he makes a point of licking his lips, closing his eyes, and leaning in to inhale my scent. "Perfecto." I feel his hot breath right before his wet tongue runs up my slit and circles my clit. Electricity surges through my body, like flipping a switch as he continues devouring my pussy.

Goosebumps run over my skin as Zeke kisses up my throat and along my jaw before he works his way to capturing the breathy pants JP is drawing from my lips. His tongue easily sweeps into my mouth, allowing the flavourful mixture of my and JP's tastes to explode in my mouth. My fingers dig into his hair, pulling him into me as I hang on for dear life, desperately wanting everything.

"More," I plead when Zeke pulls away and kisses along my jaw once again.

"What do you want, spitfire?"

"You. I want to taste you," I beg, needing him in my mouth. Watching him take JP earlier, savoring his taste, has left me wanting to do the same, but to him.

His eyes close briefly as he bites his lower lip. "Damn, I just can't say no to you," he groans and shuffles closer to me, so his erect cock bobs in front of me like an offering.

Licking my lips, I reach out and stroke his shaft a few times. I'm rewarded as pre-cum glistens on his tip. I guide him into my mouth and swirl my tongue around his head, enjoying his salty taste.

"Fuck, your mouth is heaven," he moans, and fire shoots up in the fireplace behind him, but no one pays it any attention. I moan around his shaft as JP inserts one finger into my cunt and begins finger fucking me.

JP's finger curls inside of me and strokes me just right as I bob up and down Zeke's dick. His hips begin rocking along with my motion as his fingers dig into my damp hair, lightly holding my head. I glance up at him and smile around his cock as I find his eyes closed, a blissful smile on his face as he pants. Knowing I'm giving him this pleasure makes me feel powerful, beautiful, in ways that only they will know.

A gentle bite on my inner thigh brings my eyes back to JP, and I see him smirk as he inserts another finger, slowly pumping in and out while flicking my clit with his tongue.

"Why don't you make use of this wonderful dessert, Zeke, and make our baby come," JP suggests before going back and sucking on my clit.

Zeke pulls his dick out of my mouth with a pop, and I groan in frustration. "Don't worry; I'm about to help you see stars." He leans down and takes my mouth once again, but it's too brief before he moves down my throat to my chest, taking a nipple into his mouth. My back arches as pleasure rolls down low into my abdomen. His tongue teases the nipple as his other hand lightly pinches and rolls the other sensitive peak.

JP's hands caress up my legs and above my mound as he continues to lavish me with his tongue. My body is on fire between all the sensations I'm feeling. Looking down my body, I see two sets of heated gazes staring back at me. Brown and green, and when Zeke pulls away and blows on my breast, making them harder, I about cry.

"What do you want, Rez?" Zeke asks, blowing along the trail that he just licked down between my breasts.

"I want to come," I manage to get out between pants. Zeke looks to JP before I see his fangs descend. The idea of him biting into me again gets me wetter, and I silently can't wait to find out where.

"She likes that idea," JP says before using his tongue to dive deeper into my folds.

"Fuck," I moan and thrust my hips up. "I'm so close," I tell them. Zeke's mouth latches onto my nipple once again as he licks and sucks before I feel it. The sharp sting of his teeth sinking into my flesh. The harsh hiss of breath is the only sound I make before heat rushes through my body. Sparks fly when JP latches on to my cunt as my legs start twitching and I feel myself fall off the ledge with a scream.

Before I'm completely overwhelmed, Zeke licks his bite marks with his healing saliva and JP moves off the bed as I lay there in paradise. I feel the bed dip as Zeke and JP both move. My heavy lids close on their own, and I feel my body wanting to drift off into sleep.

"Here, let me have a taste," Zeke says. I pry my heavy lids open at his words and find an erotic sight before me. My men are in a heated lip lock with their bodies pressed up against each other. Both of them are stroking each other's cocks, and the visual stirs my body back to life. Forget taking a nap! I'm

319

stirring for round two as I watch them nip at each other and moan against the other.

JP reaches back for the bottle of lube on the nightstand that they must have brought in and squeezes out a generous amount. He ends the kiss and smirks before squatting down and taking Zeke into his mouth.

A moan leaves Zeke's mouth as JP takes him down to the base and bobs up and down his shaft a few times while his hand with the lube reaches between his thighs to play with his ass before standing back up. "There, now you're ready for our girl," he says as he turns and winks at me. Zeke climbs back onto the bed, and I quickly decide to turn around and get on my hands and knees.

"Changing it up on us?" JP chuckles.

"I want to *feel* what you guys can give me," I tease. "How much power have you got?" I ask, looking over my shoulder.

"We have enough to make you go cross-eyed," he assures me. "But I'm glad you picked this, because now I can reveal this," he says, and reaches for the wall behind the bed and slides his hand down it.

A sheet I hadn't noticed drops along the wall to reveal a mirror that's attached behind my bed, giving a perfect view of what's going on behind me.

"How in the fuck did I not know that was there?" I ask in awe.

"While you were in the bathroom, we prepped the room," Zeke says proudly as he reaches out with a finger and runs it through my wet folds, pebbling my nipples and causing my skin to tingle once more. I rock back, wanting more, as he rubs my clit and strokes his own cock.

"Bend over," JP demands as he crawls up the bed with the tube of lube and gently leans Zeke over, running his hands over his muscular backside. Zeke's abs flex as JP slowly works his ass with his fingers, his biceps flexing as he does.

JP leans over Zeke's shoulder and nips his ear. "Why don't you show our girl what we can do?"

I'm practically drooling in anticipation. "Yes please. I'm dying over here. Look, I'm basically leaking all my fluids," I whine and pull a few pillows to prop myself up just in case my arms give out.

"Well, we'll just have to fill you up with some more," JP says with a smile, then bites into Zeke's shoulder.

Zeke grabs my hip as he slowly rubs his mushroom head along my slick folds, teasing himself and me. I push my ass against him, trying to impale myself, and he chuckles as he gets the hint. He guides himself into me, and I whimper, allowing my walls to adjust as he slides inch-by-inch into me. Once he's fully seated, he pulls out and slams back into me, causing me to almost drop to my elbows.

My breasts sway and graze the pillows, giving me the friction I'm craving as he sets a punishing pace. It takes everything in me to keep myself on my hands and knees. I peek up and catch JP's hungry gaze as he strokes his cock and slowly arranges Zeke behind me.

I can feel the exact moment JP eases himself into Zeke, because his thrust pauses before he surges forward once again. "Damn, this ass is so tight. I might not last long," JP warns.

"You say that like I'll be lasting. I'm on the verge of exploding now," Zeke pants.

"Well, I'm not seeing stars, so I'm expecting someone to do something. Or else I'm kicking you all out," I tease.

"You heard the lady." Zeke chuckles, and then groans when JP slides out and slams back into him, causing a daisy chain effect to rock into me. Moans take over our conversation, and I get the pleasure of watching JP fuck Zeke's ass as he takes me. Desperate and ready, I drop down to my elbows and pull out the pillows before reaching between my legs to play with my clit.

As Zeke smoothly slides through my wet heat, I line my fingers around his cock and squeeze, making him jerk slightly, and his pace falters. "Fuck, Rez. What are you doing to me?" he hisses.

"Playing," I admit, but go back to focusing on my clit. A low groan tumbles out of JP, and he white knuckles Zeke's hips, pumping into him at a frenzied rate.

Zeke pulls one of JP's wrists to his mouth, and I watch as his incisors elongate and cut into his skin, spilling blood when he latches on. JP groans as his release hits, but he continues his thrusting pumps into Zeke. The thought of his cum filling up my boyfriend's ass brings me closer to the edge of my own orgasm.

Zeke licks JP's wrist, sealing his bite, and smacks my ass before slamming into me with abandonment. "I'm so close, Rez. I'm going to cum," he says as he closes his eyes and leans his head back.

JP slides out of his ass quickly, and without missing a beat slides below me, batting my hand away. He gently pulls my clit into his mouth and starts alternating between sucking and flicking my bundle of nerves. My legs start shaking, and my eyes roll back as JP gently grabs my nipples and rolls them between his fingers. If there was such a thing as being over-stimulated by sex, I think this would be it. My vision blanks out for a moment as all I feel is pleasure and lightning coursing through my body.

Heat engulfs my body and floods my system as my pussy spasms around Zeke's cock. Little shockwaves ripple through me as my legs spasm, and Zeke roars his release. As he pumps into me a few more times, my body goes slack. JP somehow manages to wrap me up in his arms and pull me against him as Zeke collapses beside us. My eyes close as I drift off to sleep between my men, inside my warm cocoon.

"No, ma chérie. No napping yet; let's take a quick shower

to clean off and then you can have your blessful sleep." JP chuckles as the fireplace whooshes with brimstone.

"No, it will take forever," I protest and snuggle against his chest, yet a loud thump and a squeak has my eyes cracking open. I glance over at Zeke, and he gives me a questioning look as well. Something yanks hard on our covers, and I shoot up in shock.

"Are their ghosts in Hell?"

"There's all sorts of shit in Hell," Zeke says as he, too, sits up. I notice the covers start to get pulled off the bed on JP's side, and I hold my breath as I peer over the side, only to find Reaper tugging at the sheets.

"Reaper, what are you doing? How did you get out of the closet?" I ask, and figure since I'm already out of the blissful euphoria, I might as well get my shower and clean up.

"Did he open the door?" JP asks, gazing at the closet.

"Great, now we need to magic up a damn lock to keep him out, else I'm gonna have a wet nose on my ass," Zeke mumbles.

I swear, I don't know what to do with all of my guys.

CHAPTER 33
Off with Their Heads

Rez

The knock at the door has me rolling over and shoving my head under the pillow. "Go away." My voice comes out muffled. JP chuckles before I feel him shift and leave the bed. A few moments later, I hear Knox on the other side, whispering. I slip over and try to curl up against Zeke, but instead, my hand just pats an empty spot.

"No," I groan.

"Come on, sleepy head; aren't you hungry?" Zeke asks as he rips the sheets off of me. Without thinking, I grab my pillow and launch it toward the end of the bed and smile when I hear an "oopmh." But my stomach growls at that moment and I give in, rolling out of bed. I quickly change into leggings, a tank top, and slip on some ballet flats. Zeke and JP change into pants, t-shirts, and tennis shoes, and we step out with Reaper zipping between our feet.

We stop and wait for everyone to come out of their rooms, but Reaper takes off. He half runs, half trips down the hall and turns toward the parlor room. I'm sure he's smelling something yummy and is about to drive Lucifer up the wall. *That's why I love the little guy.*

"Does anyone even know what time it is?" Chester asks, grabbing Moni's hand.

"Well, the screams of death stopped, and my stomach is growling, so I believe it's dinnertime," Knox growls.

"Yep, the screams of ecstasy only stopped about a half an hour ago," Lynx chimes in, smirking my way. I smile and shoot him the bird. I almost feel bad about it until his eyes heat and he raises an eyebrow.

"Well, according to my watch," Levi says, pushing back his sleeve that his new cufflinks are on. "It's almost eight."

"Definitely time for some food," Knots says, rubbing his belly. He starts walking, and I quickly slip in beside him.

I haven't had much time with him lately, and I'm a little worried about him. I check on his shield and realize that some areas are thinner than I originally had it. *Fuck!* I've been slacking, and honestly, I wasn't thinking about it when I was with JP and Zeke. To make things worse, it's not like I was concentrating while I was napping. I bite back my frustration and quickly reinforce his shield. He seems okay, but my brave Door Knight isn't the type of person to bitch and complain about stuff. Nope, he's the type that would hold it in and suffer in silence.

Right as I go to open my mouth to ask Knots how he's feeling, I hear Reaper coming. His little paws scramble on the marble floors, and he tumbles across the entrance to our hall with something in his mouth. As he rolls to a stop, the object falls from his mouth, so he growls at it before picking it back up and running toward me.

I can't make out what he has. From here, it just looks like a dark red or black ball. I wonder if Murmur gave it to him. His tail whips around in excitement and ends up tripping him as he reaches me. Plopping into me, his "ball" falls onto the floor with a wet plunk, and he looks up at me with the biggest eyes while his tongue lolls out of his mouth.

"Aww, you're just so cute," I coo, before looking over at the ball and immediately gagging.

"What's the matter, Rez? He just wants to play fetch," Lynx teases and swings his barefoot back to kick it.

"No!" I shoot my arm out, but it's too late. My bestie kicks it and sends it rolling down the hallway. Reaper barks and chases after it.

"What the fuck!?" Lynx says, looking down at the blood and eyeball stuck to his big toe. "What was that?"

"Again, this is why you should wear shoes," Knots reprimands, giving Lynx a deadpan look.

"Was that a head?" Moni asks as her bark turns a yellowish-green. She looks exactly how I feel right now.

"Yeah, but who did it belong to?" JP asks.

Levi steps in front of us and peeks down the hallway that Reaper had come from. He stands up straighter, messes with the lapels on his jacket, and slowly looks back at us with a clenched jaw.

"Lynx, you might want to get shoes."

"Fuck, I hate foot prisons," Lynx grumbles as he goes into the closest room for a pair of shoes.

I decide to put on my big girl panties and join Levi, and when I do, I wonder if I can conjure up a clean hall.

"What the hell? Is this what they meant by cleaning house?" I ask as I watch a different type of Demon—a pink crab-like creature with a pig nose and tail—dragging a headless body down the hall. Another Demon, this one with a feline head and tail but with daddy long-legs, skitters along the wall cleaning the blood off the walls and ceiling.

"Wow. They really did do some housecleaning. It's almost spotless," Moni says before taking a sip of her coffee.

Pools of blood line the halls as far as I can see, and I *think* dead Arte Demons are scattered everywhere. *If this is cleaning house, I would hate to see what Moni would think of a dirty one.* I feel something on my legs, and I look down to see that Reaper has returned. Now his front paws are up on my leggings—his *bloody* paws. This time, instead of a head in his mouth, he has someone's dick.

"Eww. No. Reaper. Drop the dick!" I scream. I quickly pick him up and jostle him to make him drop it, but all it does is make him bite down harder and growl. Fluid, which I refuse to diagnose, flies out of the end of it and sails into Moni's hair.

"Ahh!!" Moni screams as she turns magenta. She turns to look at Chester wide-eyed as her hands flap in the air. "It's in my hair! It's in my hair! Chester, get it. It's in my hair. Save me!" She cries as her bark starts to cycle through her colors.

"Ahh, fuck no," JP says as he notices it too. "Hit the deck," he yells as he drops to the ground. But right when he says that, Reaper drops the severed dick onto my arm. The yellowish-blue liquid is still dribbling out of it, and I fling my arm out, accidentally hitting Moni as she turns, knocking her out cold. Luckily Knots catches Moni's cup of coffee before it spills to the floor.

"What did you do?" Chester accuses me as he kneels down to check on her.

I hug Reaper against me until he starts licking my face, and knowing what he just had in his mouth, I drop him. *He's a big boy, he can handle the fall.*

"I saved you," I said confidently. "Now Levi can clean her cum-stained hair and you can take the credit. Simple. You can thank me now."

I look at Levi, and nod toward my bestie that's knocked out on the floor, and he slowly shakes his head as he tries not to smile but fails. He quickly magics her clean and comes over to me and does the same to my arm before stepping in close and grabbing my chin. "You're lucky you mean the world to me," he says, and kisses me briefly.

"Wh-what happened?" Moni says as Levi steps back.

Before anyone else can say anything, Chester leans over and kisses her gently. "I saved you, darling. You're safe, and the liquid is off of you." He looks up at me.

"Oh, did I faint?" she asks.

Oh, of course she had to ask. I'll take the bullet.

"You went down like a rock," I comment, completely fudging the truth.

"My hero," Moni yells, and wraps her arms around her mate.

. . . . .

Walking into the dining room, Reaper runs over to the bowls, yes, bowls of food sitting out for him. I don't recognize the meat that's overflowing in his bowls, but it looks to be a combination of cooked and raw meat. Um, could that be parts of the demons they just cleaned the house of? *It's probably best that I don't guess at that when I'm about to eat my own meal.*

There's covered plates set out on the table and a notecard sitting in front of Levi's seat. Picking up the card, Levi proceeds to read it.

"Well, it looks like it's just us for dinner, but we'll meet with the others in the parlor afterward," he says before taking his seat. Tormeth walks out from the kitchen and sets down a few pitchers of drinks and turns to leave without saying a word as we all sit.

"So they didn't completely clean house?" Moni questions, giving the Demon a curious look.

He turns and sneers in her direction. "What makes you think they didn't?" His tone comes off challenging.

"I—I didn't..." Moni stumbles over her words as her barks turns pink.

"Hey!" JP calls out. "She didn't mean anything by it. She was just shocked that after the bloodbath we walked through that anyone made it through alive."

"Pfft. I'm too important. I am L.A.M.B.'s right-hand Demon. Their assistant. Things don't get done without me," he says, before turning sharply and shuffling back to the kitchen. I take a moment to take in the others around the room and notice they have the same bewildered look on their faces. Lynx breaks the tension in the room by reaching for the pitcher that Trometh left.

After walking through the halls of death, I'm a little hesitant to look under my lid, but taking the chance, I find fried chicken, mashed potatoes, green beans, and a dinner roll.

"Oh, chicken!" Moni says and digs in.

I turn to look at Knox, who's sitting next to me, and whisper, "This isn't fried Arte Demon is it?" I ask, and Moni yaks across from me.

She spits her food out into her napkin.

"It's okay, Moni; it's not Arte Demon," Levi announces.

"Yeah, they have a more rubbery substance to them. At least, that's what I've been told. It's another reason they are used as 'chew toys,'" Ryker elaborates.

Glancing back at Moni, I catch her trying to stare daggers at me, but all she's really doing is pouting.

"What? It was a valid question after walking through what we did," I point out.

She tilts her head in thought before nodding and smiles before going back to her chicken. Dinner is quiet as we eat and make quick work of our food. It's kinda odd to not have Arte Demons milling around. I wonder if they will get around to replacing them, or get different ones to help with the odd work I've seen around the house. Soon enough, we head into the parlor where L.A.M.B. and Lilith are waiting. Their five chairs are placed in front of the fireplace, facing toward the other sitting area.

I walk in and immediately feel eyes on me. Glancing over at the fireplace, I find Lilith glaring at me. I violently flinch and Knots squeezes my hand as he guides me to the end of the sofa, where he pulls me down onto his lap. JP and Zeke sit on an extra large chair, where they cuddle up, and Lucifer gives them an approving look. Moni and Chester sit down in the other armchair, mimicking JP and Zeke. Levi slides in at the end of the sofa while Knox and Ryker push each other to try to sit next to me while Lynx jumps over the back of the sofa, taking their spot and the decision out of their hand.

"Ass," Ryker hisses before he sits on one of the footstools.

"Yes, it is *purrfect*. Don't be ashamed to check it out from time to time." He blows Ryker a kiss and winks at me.

Knox simply sits on the arm of the sofa, taking my hand before he rubs his thumb over my knuckles. A throat clears, and I reluctantly turn my attention to the front of the room.

"How was dinner?" Lucifer asks before he sips on a drink. He always seems so laid back and unruffled. Well, until I tried to take down his house. But tonight he's decked out in a red pin-striped suit, which looks wicked against his white wings.

"It was great once I was convinced it wasn't Arte Demon," Moni says innocently enough.

Lucifer chokes and clears his throat. "Excuse me?"

Chester speaks up, "Rez thought the chicken was left over Arte Demon, see—"

"Let's just say we ran into some... pieces... on our way to dinner." I smile awkwardly, and Astaroth huffs.

"Told you guys that you wouldn't have time for clean-up before dinner," he addresses Bez and Murmur, but they just shrug his comment off.

"It was fun either way," Murmur comments.

"Needed to be done," Bez says as he twirls something in his hand.

"Yes, well. We will have a new crew of Demons tomorrow morning," Lucifer states, but my attention is torn away, back to Bez's hand.

Focusing on it once again, I find it's a weapon of some sort. He catches me taking an interest and holds it up so I can get a better look. Then it melts into his hand and he reforms it into a different design. "Plastic works just as well as metal," he says with a cruel smile.

Okay then. Leave the scary gentle *killer alone.*

He's a gentle killer, Rez. He gently ripped off the guy's dick and painted the walls red. I forcefully swallow and everyone turns toward me.

"Oh, you heard that?" I ask and immediately look down at my lap. *Someone say something,* I scream in my head.

"So, did our test come back?" JP asks, and I mentally thank him for taking the bullet.

Lucifer's gaze swings to JP and then Moni. "Yes, but we can talk later if you prefer. I have not told anyone about that," he admits, and judging by the confused glances of the rest of L.A.M.B. and Lilith, he's telling the truth.

JP turns his attention to Moni, no doubt hearing what she's saying. She nods and Zeke squeezes his hand as JP considers L.A.M.B. "I don't know about them," he starts and surveys our group. "But they are my family, and what you tell me and Moni can be said in front of them."

"Very well. The same can be said about L.A.M.B. We were considered a family even before we fell and followed Lilith to a less restricted life." He smiles at us before addressing everyone.

"In the throne room, it had come to my attention that JP and Moni knew Elayna. And yes, gentlemen," he says, addressing Murmur, Bez and Astaroth. "The same Elayna. JP is her biological son, and Moni is Marjoriekine's daughter, whom she disowned."

Peeking at Moni, I see her bark start fading to blue, and if I had a harder shoe than a ballet slipper, I would throw it at Lucifer for upsetting my PIMP.

"Why would she disown you?" Bez speaks up. "You are quite a powerful lil' one. Does she not know how wonderful you are? You knocked me—The first Vengeance Demon—on his ass." He points his makeshift weapon in her direction. "That is not an easy feat."

A smile slowly grows on her face as she cycles from her glitter bomb, shock color, to her pastel yellow bark, expressing her happiness.

"Really?" she asks.

"Yes," he replies.

Murmur gives a long whistle. "Damn, birdie; Bez never gives compliments."

"That is true," Lucifer agrees. "The point is, knowing that information and my history, I ran a blood test. Moni and JP, I am your father, and I'm sorry that I didn't know."

The room goes silent as everyone takes in the information that was just dropped. Wow. JP and Moni are the next rulers of Hell? Is that how this works?

I hear a snicker and look around, but I can't see where it's coming from. It gets louder and turns into a chuckle, and that's when I see Moni's shoulders bouncing. She throws her head back and lets out an obnoxious laugh, falling off of the chair. She continues to laugh as she picks herself up, floating in the air, and slaps her knee.

"Did you break my Moni?" I ask Lucifer as I glance back at Moni.

"I—I—What's going on?" Lucifer asks, as completely lost as we are.

"She's gonna kick her own ass, treating me like shit! Call

me Karma, Queen of the Damned!" Moni shouts at the top of her lungs. She laughs and falls from the air, trusting Chester to catch her, which he does, barely.

"Who—"

"Miss Teal," I giggle as it dawns on me. She was treated like shit all of these years, and she's a princess—for lack of words or official titles—of Hell.

Feeling overjoyed, I get up and rush over to Moni to hug her. Wrapping my arms around her, I squeeze tight. "Congratulations, badass."

"As interesting as this is—and congratulations—I have a matter to bring up," Lilith interrupts, grabbing her pearls. She quickly drops them and brings her hands to her lap. "You guys will need time to bond and talk about your responsibilities now and such... but," she shifts in her seat, and I give Moni a worried glance before going back to my seat in Knots lap. "We have more pressing matters to discuss." Lilith lets out a visibly shaky breath as she straightens out her skirt.

"Like what?" I ask hesitantly.

"LIKE YOU DRAGGING MY BOYS TO THEIR DEATH!" she screams, and jumps for me.

CHAPTER 34

Prophecies of Old

Rez

Every male moves at once. All of L.A.M.B. stands and reaches for Lilith. Knots throws me onto the sofa as he switches places with me, while pulling his sword. Fluffers bursts forth, baring his teeth at his mother. Levi jumps up along with Zeke, JP, and Ryker. Lynx even stands before me, which actually surprises me. I look over with wide eyes at Moni to see that Chester's on his feet as well. Moni shrugs and shakes her head at the chaos before us.

Everyone is talking over each other, and the commotion is too much. L.A.M.B. is trying to get Lilith under control while my guys are yelling at her and defending me. I catch Trometh poking his head in before running up to L.A.M.B. to see if he can help. To be completely honest, they are all acting like fools, and that's saying something coming from me. I motion for Moni to come over before crawling up on the back of the sofa and speaking into her ear.

"Want to help stop this shit? I'm getting a headache," I ask and tell her what I have planned to break this up.

Moni stands in front of me and holds her hands out to the side with her palms facing out. She's been practicing controlling her booms, so this will hopefully work. Her shoulders raise up before she flexes her hands and pushes her shoulders back down while small sonic booms flow out of her hands one after the other. It's not enough force to knock anyone on their ass, but enough to get their attention. Like standing next to a big speaker when the bass drops. *I bet she will be a hit at all the parties now.*

"Hey!" I yell as the room quiets. "We're not solving anything like this. Obviously there's a hot topic we need to discuss, so let's act like adults and talk this out. I can't be the only one lost here," I say as all eyes focus on me. Knox slowly transforms back to my brooding, yet loveable alpha, and Moni flies back to Chester.

Lilith pulls away from Lucifer and tucks some of her hair that came undone behind her ear. "Fine, but I take back what I said about you, Nerezza. You can't be trusted. Don't think about calling me mother," she spits out as she sits down. Trometh smirks, and he backs up between Lilith and Lucifer's chairs.

My jaw drops as my eyebrows raise. "Excuse me? What have I done to deserve this?" I scoff, pulling Knox down and crawling onto his lap this time as I feel his need to be near me. He wraps his arms around me tightly and nuzzles into my neck.

My Door Knight moves beside the sofa but doesn't sit back down. Hell, he still has his sword out, but it's on a belt he somehow conjured up.

"You're the Devil," Lilith seethes.

"Pot, meet kettle. Did you really call me the Devil? When you're sitting next to him?" I argue.

I catch Lucifer's subtle motion to Murmur before the

Mischief Demon walks behind Lilith. His hands wrap around the chair and onto her shoulders.

"Relax, Lilith. We're just talking here," he coos, and Lilith sinks into her chair. Murmur catches sight of the purple Demon and frowns slightly. "Trometh, could you retrieve Mammon? I'm not sure what level he's on." The tiny demon bows and turns to run out, but I don't miss the scowl on his face.

"What she means," Lucifer begins, pulling my attention back to him. "Is she thinks the prophecy she was told by Anwen is about you and her boys."

"Wait! There's a prophecy about us?" Ryker asks, leaning forward as he practically drools at the news. "Why haven't I read about this in any books?"

Zeke rolls his eyes and whispers something to JP, causing him to snicker until Lucifer's gaze turns his way.

"Wanna share with the class?" Lucifer quips.

"That's such a dad thing to say," Lynx says, and my group chuckles slightly.

"Just said that only Ryker would find a prophecy of us dying fascinating." Zeke smiles as Ryker flips him off.

Astaroth sighs and leans back in his chair. "The thing about prophecies is they are never black and white. They are true and they come to pass, but sometimes not even the Fates themselves know what to make of them. Most creatures find them terrifying, not fascinating."

Ryker's response is to shrug, not caring at the slight dig. "I like what I like. I'm not ashamed of that."

"That is true about prophecies," Knots speaks up. He's put his sword away, but he's standing with a wide stance and his arms crossed. His eyes haven't left the five Demons sitting across from us. "I might not remember everything about my past, but I do know that prophecies are something we do not mess around with."

"So is that what you were mumbling or chanting about in your room, the prophecy?" I ask, and Lilith's right eye starts twitching.

"Lilith, why don't you lie down? You've worked hard today and should probably rest," Murmur says softly.

"NO! I want answers," she demands, slamming her hand down onto the arm of the chair.

Lucifer pinches the bridge of his nose, and his gaze travels over us once more. "Lilith mentioned Horsemen tattoos?"

"Yeah." Ryker says, rocking on the edge of the footstools. "I have one behind my ear," he supplies.

"May I see?" Lucifer asks.

Ryker gets up and walks over, showing the five Demons the tattoo behind his ear before he takes a seat.

"Does everyone have one?" Murmur asks as his blue tail whips back and forth around the chair legs.

"Yeah." Zeke gets up and walks over and does the one-arm shirt removal thing, making me bite my lower lip and shift my weight. Knox takes a deep breath and softly chuckles into my neck.

"Shut up," I whisper as he squeezes me.

Zeke shows off his tattoo on his pec, and afterward, everyone looks at Levi and Knox.

"I have one. A black horse with a rider engulfed in flames carrying a golden scale," Levi says, not moving from his seat.

When eyes swing toward Knox, he simply says he has one and goes back to hiding against my neck.

Lilith growls under her breath now that it's confirmed that her four sons all have magical Horsemen tattoos, sending me death glares as she twirls her pearls around her fingers. If she's this upset about their tattoos, I'm not volunteering anything about the one that covers my back, because I deeply suspect she'll try to skin it off of me, judging by the look in her eyes.

"Well, it looks like there's some good news and possibly bad news," Lucifer says, getting up and going to the bar. "Anyone want a drink?"

Murmur raises his hand but ends up going behind the bar to make them.

"How can getting a mysterious tattoo be a good thing?" Moni asks, playing with her hair.

"Well, Lilith says you have a ceremony tomorrow, correct?" Lucifer arches a brow as he turns back to our group.

"Yes," Levi clears his throat. "I have to make my mage vows tomorrow at noon to Emer Elverson."

Murmur shudders. "Isn't she the awful daughter of..." he starts snapping his fingers while he tries to remember. "What's his face... King Elverson? Alrin? Or something?" He points with his index finger once he spits out the name.

"Yeah," Ryker chimes in as he shifts.

"She's also Angel's cousin, who was spotted in the cave trying to kill us while we were getting the Demstones," I add.

"The same Angel that's related to Asmodeus. Yeah, that doesn't sound suspicious at all," JP says, rubbing his chin as he leans into Zeke's embrace.

"Ohh. The plot thickens." Lynx chuckles as he waggles his eyes.

Skittering feet and tiny yips precede Reaper as he chases a small rat-looking Demon down the hall. As soon as he sees us, he gives up the pursuit and runs in, looking for some lovin'.

JP leans down and picks him up so he's getting double attention from him and Zeke.

Lucifer rolls his eyes. "At least he's good for running out rodents," he says as he does a finger gun motion at the rat, and it disintegrates into dust before our eyes.

"That still doesn't answer my question," Moni insists.

"Ah, yes. Sorry, sweetie. Well, if I remember correctly. There are two ways to claim a so-called mate. Your magic can pick one, or you can take an oath in front of your partner that binds you. Is that still true?" he asks, turning to face Levi completely.

"From how it's been explained to me, yes. Although I don't know the logistics of how my magic would pick a partner," Levi confesses, and Lucifer smirks.

"I see. Well, there's the good news. You don't have to make your oath tomorrow because it won't work." Lucifer chuckles as he takes his drink and walks back to his seat. "Yes, you can go through the motions and appease the petty little princess, but it won't actually bind you." Lucifer swirls his drink for a moment before continuing. "You are already bound."

A gasp leaves me as my stomach plummets. He's already taken? NO!

"Huh?" Levi says as he looks between me and Lucifer. He's sounding the most undignified I've ever heard him. His eyebrows rise as his jaw drops before sending me a panicked glance.

"Part of the prophecy states: 'Four young souls will embody thee. To save us all, she will be the key.' Rez, do you, by chance, have your own tattoo?" Lucifer smiles over the rim of his drink before sipping the brown liquid, and my entire body freezes.

Right now, dear old Lucifer is reminding me of a mobster that knows he just caught an underling doing something wrong.

How in Hell does he know?

"I got one after being with Zeke," I admit in monotone, only willing to move my eyes to meet his.

"The last of the four?" Lucifer pushes, and I nod tightly. "Does it have something on it that would resemble anything like the phrase I just quoted?"

Fuck. I don't know how to explain it. Whatever, it would just be easier to show them. Unlocking my limbs, I pat Knox's arms so he releases me, and I stand to face him. I pull my tank top up to expose my back tattoo.

"Wow! Love the artwork!" Lynx purrs, and someone runs their fingers down my spine, tickling me.

"See, I told you!" Lilith shouts, and I quickly cover up and turn around, determined to keep my skin. "She's the one in the prophecy. She's going to lead them to their deaths."

Lucifer sighs and turns to Lilith. "Lily," he gently starts. "You know I love you, right?"

"No. Don't you dare start that shit with me, Lucy!" She narrows her eyes at him.

Glancing around my group, I notice they have the same unsure look on their faces as I do.

"Fine, if he can't start it, I will." Astaroth leans over to get her attention. "This all started with you and Adam. It's how you lost your men in the first place. If you want to blame someone and get it off of you, then send it back to the person who deserves it."

"Your boys and Rez are innocent, and unfortunately, have been given a heavy load," Murmur adds and hands Lilith a drink. "Here, drink this. It will help calm you so you can see reason."

"But—"

"No buts, Lilith. Look at them," Lucifer pleads.

"They are my babies," Lilith cries out as a few tears fall from her blue eyes. Lucifer hands her a handkerchief from his jacket as I feel sadness filter through my link with Knox. Squeezing his bicep, I send him encouragement and love.

"They are *not* your *babies* anymore. They are grown." Lucifer waves his hand before the group of us. "Yes, you missed out on their younger years, but that doesn't mean you've lost them. They are right here, and Rez isn't taking them away. It just means they have bigger responsibilities now, and you've gained a bigger family to love. I've gained children I didn't know I had, and that includes you gaining a nephew and niece. So, don't hold on to anger at the ones who aren't responsible. If you need to, we'll go hunting later so you can lash out and feed that side of you, okay?" he promises. Lilith takes a moment to examine all of us and then looks back at Lucifer before nodding her agreement.

"When you say feed that side later, does that mean another..." Lynx points to the hallway that we had to travel down to get here. "You know... bloodbath?"

Bez's deep chuckle draws my attention, and flames ignite in his hand, forming a ball of flames that starts weaving around his fingers, as if it's a coin he's moving over his knuckles. "That was just cleaning house. Getting rid of any possible spies."

"Nah, feeding the craving is finding the depraved souls and having fun with them," Astaroth smirks.

"If we really want a workout, we go hunting and go on a chase for them. That's my favorite," Murmur admits, and I shrink back into Knox's embrace.

Yeah, I almost forgot they were Demons, but that did it. Thanks for the reminder, but I'm still lost about this prophecy.

"Question!" Moni shoots her hand up in the air like we're in class. Lucifer smiles and nods her way.

"So does this mean Rez helped Levi cheat on his mate?"

"Damn, way to put it out there. I mean, we were all thinking it, but she just comes out wham, bam, thank you, ma'am," Lynx exclaims.

Heat crawls up my neck from the eyes that swing my way. I can't bring myself to look at anyone, just in case Lucifer confirms what Moni says.

Please don't agree.

"Not at all. See, when Rez and Levi got together—"

'Did the nasty, the horizontal tango, the boot scootin boogie. BSB... Wait, isn't that a boy band? Why do I remember that?'

'Are you trying to kill me, Lynx?' I emphasize with wide eyes in his direction.

'Is that a possibly with embarrassment?' he asks.

'Ugh. I can't with you,' I say, and glance up to see my guys looking at me and Levi wearing a big smile.

"Wait, what? I'm sorry. I was distracted," I admit sheepishly.

"My tattoo is evidence that my magic has picked you, and it won't allow me to bond with anyone else," Levi repeats for my benefit.

"Eek!" I squeal, jumping out of Knox's arms and plopping down into Levi's lap as I wrap my arms around him.

"So does this mean you don't have to go to the ceremony tomorrow?" I ask, squeezing him to me and nuzzling against his neck.

"No! I d—"

"Actually, Levi, that might not be smart on your part. Your father mentioned it was King Elverson's idea for your betrothal before they left Lilith in our care. If you slight him and stand Emer up at the altar, you or your loved ones, might be who pays. And I'm not taking that chance with my children."

Moni turns a seafoam green, clearly showing her confusion, and JP's eyebrows slightly raise at Lucifer's choice of words. I might have to ask them what they think of Lucifer stepping in and talking on their behalf. They have had Matthew for the longest time, so what are they thinking? Man, I wish I had JP's abilities right now.

'Are you okay?' I send to JP. He glances my way and gives me a smile and a thumbs up, but that's all. I can't really tell what he's thinking or feeling with that. Fuck.

"Well, what do you suggest since my magic won't let me

bond with her and standing her up is out of the question?" Levi questions.

"Why don't we leave early in the morning, and we'll go with you and speak with the Council before you're needed at your ceremony? We might even have to give him proof that you've been taken, and with us as witnesses, he'll be less likely to retaliate as he's been known to do," Lucifer directs.

A weight is lifted off of me for once, and I couldn't be happier that Levi doesn't have to give his soul to the Queen Harpy. "So what does the prophecy say about our tattoos?" I finally get around to asking Lucifer.

"Well, I don't have the actual answer for that," he admits. "No one will truly know your purpose, Rez. But as for the guys, it seems they are going to be the new Horsemen," he says, dropping a damn bomb on us.

I hear a squeak, and from the corner of my eye, I see Moni turn magenta before she hits the floor with a plunk.

"Wait. What?" Ryker asks as his face drains of color.

"Ha. How do you like prophecies now?" Lynx laughs at the slacked expression on Ryker's face.

CHAPTER 35

Sparkle Buns

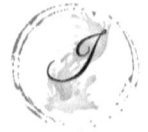

JP

The Four Horsemen? Fuck. And I thought learning about Lucifer being my father was a shitshow. I squeeze Zeke as Lynx laughs at Ryker's expression, but I can't help agreeing with him. Ryker has always been a secret freak when it comes to old histories and stuff of that nature. Well, maybe it's not that secret since he takes his conquests to his office full of his possessions, or at least used to. I know that's changed since Rez has come into the picture as his mate.

Asatroth leans forward and clears his throat. "We've always assumed that the four would somehow resurrect one way or another since they now protect our world. They would need someone to embody what they need to accomplish in the physical world. They were so much more than just their personas."

"Yeah, I have no idea how they got such a bad reputation from the humans." Murmur shakes his head. "They were great up until the end. It was like something switched in them, and they became off balance and just snapped."

"Boys, if there's anything I can do to help. You know you can come see me, right?" Lilith pleads, and they all give her their assurance.

"I think we've shattered enough barriers this evening. I say we call it a night so we can have an early morning to work out a plan of attack on Elverson," Lucifer says, helping Lilith to her feet. Murmur starts to walk out with Lilith when Lucifer calls back for me and Moni.

"JP? Moni? May I speak with you for a moment?"

"I'll keep the bed warm for ya. Go speak with your old man," Zeke says with a smirk. I hand him Reaper, and they both give me a kiss before joining the others. Knots takes a little longer to move but is quick to hide his struggle behind a smile when Rez reaches for him. I'm sure he's still hiding the fact that without that Demstone, he wouldn't be upright but bedridden. I hate the fact I can't tell her what's going on, but I have to respect his wishes. I just wish he wouldn't keep this from her, especially something this big. As they walk out, they leave me and Moni with our old man.

Lucifer moves two of the five chairs that were at the front of the fireplace so they are more of a circle and sits down, beckoning us to join him.

We sit down and proceed to just look at each other for a moment. I easily pick up Moni's thoughts of us actually being blood related, and I try to repress my smile. Her thoughts mirror mine; we can officially say we are related and not just say we were just raised together. It's one of the best feelings in the world. Lucifer's penetrating gaze seems to scan over me and Moni as if he's trying to pick up what traits we have of him. Or that just might be me projecting, since I'm doing the same to him.

"Is this awkward? Or is it just me finding this weird? It's awkward, right? I feel like we should be on that Tom n' Jerry show. Is that the name of the show Rez has quoted in the past?" Moni says as she twirls a vine between her fingers while her bark flashes to a dark gray, exposing her nerves.

"It's somewhat, I suppose. I would like to think it's more refreshing to sit here and know I have a true family," Lucifer reveals.

"About that," I jump in. "How does that work since... Well, we're mutts and live in Purgatory and you're..." I wave my hand at him, not knowing what to say.

"Lucifer? The Devil? Lord of Darkness? Satan? Unholy Royalty? Something like that?" He quirks his lip and wiggles his eyebrows, reminding me of myself and the shit I pull at times.

"Yeah." I lean forward and rest my arms on my legs. "I mean, here's the deal. Obviously, just like you pointed out to Lilith, we're grown, and when we lost Mom, we had a father figure step in to raise us and make us feel wanted," I explain, and out of my peripheral, I see Moni nodding along.

"Matthew has been like a dad to us," she agrees.

Lucifer's face falls slightly, and it would be almost unnoticeable if I wasn't watching him so closely.

"But that just means we don't *need* you, we *want* you," Moni says and flies over to stand before him with her fingers wiggling and shaking her arms wildly.

"Moni, what are you doing?" I ask, stifling a laugh. She turns and glares at me.

"What do you think I'm doing? Get up here and join me," she insists.

"Doing jazz hands?" I ask, confused, but I stand anyway and slowly approach.

"No, silly. I'm doing the jazzy hand butt grab thingy," she says, hopping up and down. "Come on, come on. Altogether now like one big happy family," she motions, and amazingly Lucifer gets up and moves so we're all within reach, and we both look at Moni. "Okay, now grab each other's butts!"

Before I can ask her any questions, like where in the hell did she hear that, or why she even thinks it's appropriate, she leans in and slaps my ass. By the surprised gasp from Lucifer, Moni got him too.

"What the hell, Moni?" I yell, jerking back.

"What?" She looks up at me all innocent like. I swear, her eyes got twice as big as normal. "I thought that's what we did as a family," she says as her bark changes to seafoam green. "I see them do it all the time on the TV. They get in a huddle, give inspiring words, talk about being one big family and being there for each other, then slap each other on the butt. Should we change into tight pants first? Is that what I did wrong?"

"No, darling. That was just fine, but to save my back, why don't you fly up here and we can do a jazzy hand back slap?" Lucifer suggests, and Moni smiles as her bark shines a bright yellow. She moves higher, and we all come together for a hug as Moni slaps us on the back.

Yep, we're gonna have to work on the family dynamic.

"Still awkward now?" Lucifer asks, stepping back and looking at Moni, and she just shakes her head. "Good."

We take our seats once again, and he turns his attention to me for a moment. "To answer your question, I would make an announcement that I have heirs. As far as Hell is concerned, I am royalty and I run it. But as you have seen, I don't do it alone," he says leaning back. "I am just one member of L.A.M.B., and we enjoy being known as such. We have been in a choir even before we fell, so it's only natural for us to stay as such. You are the only people, besides Lilith, to know of our past."

Damn. Talk about laying some heavy shit on us.

"A choir? So you sing?" Moni asks, and I stifle a chuckle. Lucifer's eyes warm as he bites his bottom lip to hold in his laughter.

"No, sweetie. A choir is a group of Angels that are born or work together as a group. Think of your friends; if you were all Angels, you would be considered a choir," he explains, grimacing when the room shakes from his curse words.

"Now, with that being said, I can hold off with the announcement if you would like."

"Why would we want that?" Moni asks.

"I'm Lucifer, sweetie. I have enemies everywhere, and if I announce that I have heirs, that would not only give you power and prestige in the underworld, but—"

"It would also paint a huge target on us," I finish for him.

"Oh," Moni says as she sinks into her seat, blue starts rising onto her bark.

"Hey," I say, reaching over. "Let's take tonight and think about it, and maybe talk to the others, okay?" I suggest. I know how much it means to her to have this validation finally. "Because no matter what, it involves Chester and everyone else, not just us."

"Okay. We can do that." From the cycling color she's sporting, she's nervous about the idea, but still hopeful.

"Like I said, we can wait on the announcements, but I would like to spend more time with you and get to know you both, if that's okay. Since I now know you have my blood running through your veins, you might have some tricks up your sleeves that you have yet to tap into, and I would like the chance to train with you."

"Really? You mean I could become a badass?" Moni asks, imitating a Kung Fu kick.

"You're already one. Like Bez said, it's not easy to knock us down. We've been in battles since the beginning of time. But I would like to see if you have any traits that I might be able to jump start. But we can work out a time on the weekends so it doesn't affect your school," he says, smiling at both of us. "I just wanted to see how you both felt, as this has all come as a shock, but a pleasant one, I hope."

I glance over and find Moni smiling, and I try to assess my own feelings, but I don't really know how to process them. So, I tell the truth.

"To be honest, I don't know. I always believed my father wanted nothing to do with me, so I never thought much of it. When Matthew took us in, he filled the hole that was missing. But I would like to learn from you, and share experiences. I just can't tell the future and tell you how that's going to turn out." I shrug, and he nods.

"Understandable, and I respect that answer. I'm here if and when you do want me. Or when you need my help. All you have to do is ask, since I'm not as versed at mind reading. That was always your mother El's trait." He smiles as if he is recollecting a memory. A small pang hits me as I think of my mother. Her memory haunts me sometimes. It's normally happy memories that pop into my head when Moni or Matthew says something, but as Lucifer brings up mom's ability, it hits hard. I miss her so much.

"Will you tell us more about her?" Moni whispers, pulling me out of my musings. It's as if she doesn't want to break his serene expression.

"What?" he startles. "Like a bedtime story?"

"Oh! Yes! Bedtime stories are the best. Tell me a bedtime story!" Moni cheers as she bounces on her seat.

Lucifer chuckles. "I don't think your mate would appreciate me telling you a bedtime story and tucking you into bed."

"Oh, Sparkle Buns! I forgot about Chester." Moni squishes her cheeks together as her bark turns to glitter bomb. "I need to go!" She darts up and starts out of the door.

"I guess it's time for me to head off to bed too," I say, getting up as Moni comes flying back in.

"Good night!" She slams into Lucifer and gives him a quick kiss on the cheek, flying out of the room once again.

"Is she always so affectionate toward others she barely knows?" he asks as he watches her green trail.

Unshed tears burn behind my lids as I look at my biological father. I wonder what kind of life Moni would have had if she grew up down here instead of with her mother and then abandoned. Hell, would I have even been in her life?

Lucifer turns, and something on my face is answer enough for him as he purses his lips and nods. "I can tell it hasn't been an easy road for her."

"She's a lot stronger than she looks, but yes, if she considers you family... She will treat you as such," I tell him with a smile, then follow my sister back to our hall.

CHAPTER 36

Prey or Predator

Rez

We walk back to our rooms without JP and Moni. Since tomorrow Levi is leaving to deal with the Elversons, I'm hoping to spend some time with him tonight. Before I can slip into my room and change to surprise Levi, Knox comes up behind me, engulfing me in his arms. "Do you mind if I stay with you tonight?" After our discussion on our adventure this morning, I couldn't help but agree to his request. Maybe I can spare some time with Levi in the morning? I turn my head to smile up at my alpha and grab his hand, leading him into my room. Reaper easily follows and kicks the door shut behind us.

"Did he just shut the door?" Knox asks, and we both stare down at my little man.

Reaper glances up at us and then sneezes before running over to the closet and wiggling his tail.

"I think he did." I look back at Knox. "I don't know what to make of him. Can you pick up anything?" I ask, wondering if his ability allows him to talk to Reaper.

"I can't talk with him like my animals, but I know he loves you and he is aware of what his prior owner was going to do. He knows something bad was going to happen and you saved him, so he's loyal to you," Knox informs me, and my heart breaks for my little guy.

Walking over to the closet, I squat down to hug him to me. "I won't let anything happen to you, Reaper. I just want you safe and happy, okay?" I squeeze him, and he licks my face before trying to climb up into my lap. "Nah. We're not climbing up now. We're getting ready for bed," I say.

After getting Reaper settled in his dog bed with a few chew toys, I get dressed and crawl into bed, waiting for Knox. He doesn't disappoint as he comes out of the bathroom shirtless.

His chest is well defined, and the perfection travels down to his abs, which are silently begging for me to lick them. My gaze travels down to his narrow waist and to the happy trail that I would love to follow down to his prize possession. His shorts, which are barely hanging on his hips—get your mind out of the gutter. A sigh escapes me as I frown. Yes, if I had sex right now, I'm sure my pussy would just fall out and run for the hills, but this is my alpha. I kinda want to play a little... Okay, a lot.

Knox stops by the side of the bed and cocks his head to the side, reminding me of a wolf, and sniffs.

"Aww, kitten. Do you want to play?" he asks as his hands come to his waist. I turn to my side to get a better view of him as he slowly pulls down his shorts until I see his cock head, which is glistening with pre-cum, but he covers it back up when I lick my lips.

"Aww. Tease." I pout.

"Beg." His voice comes out growly, and a thrill goes through me.

Now how to play this? Be a bad girl and deny him what he

wants, or be a good girl and get what I want. *Fuck me.* I roll my eyes and move onto my back to shimmy off my shorts. Next, I take off my top and throw both of them past Knox and continue to keep my mouth shut. Instead, I make a point of sliding my hand down my body underneath the covers and bringing my legs up, parting them.

Before I can reach my pelvic region, Knox growls, and I pause, biting the shit out of my cheek to keep from smiling.

"Kitten," he warns, and the sound of his voice goes straight to my nipples and clit.

"Hmm?" I say, trying to control my breathing already.

"What did I tell you about coming when you're with me?" His tone speaks of danger, and all I want to do is push until he snaps. How long before I can get him to lose control?

I feel the bed dip, and take a chance after biting my lower lip, peeking in his direction without moving my head. My hand leisurely continues its track down to my clit, and I slowly make circles with my finger.

All I see are his forearms leaning on the bed and his bare thigh. My heart starts beating faster now that I know he's taken off his shorts and is leaning on the bed, so close. It's as if this flirting foreplay is actually prey vs predator, and in this situation, I'm definitely the prey.

"Kitten," he growls, and my pussy becomes soaked. Shit. I take it back. I want to be a good girl and be praised, but I'm too far gone.

"That if I want to get off, I have to rely on myself," I say, shocking the shit out of myself that I got it out in one breath, and without laughing. Knowing very well that's *not* what he said. In fact, he said I was not to come unless he allowed it. Pfft.

Knox rips the covers back and grabs my leg, pulling me toward him, and I go with a yelp. Before I can protest, he turns me over and spanks each ass cheek.

Smack. Smack.

"Fuck," I moan as the pain quickly turns to pleasure.

"You really wanted to be a bad girl, didn't you?" he growls into my ear.

"Who said I was a good girl to begin with?" I argue as my face is pushed into the covers. I look over my shoulder and smirk when I meet his glowing green eyes.

"You're really trying to push me, aren't you, kitten? You have no idea how rough I can get; you'll run for the hills and then I'll have to chase you." The way he says it makes me think it's a good thing.

"Let's see what you've got, Alpha," I tease.

His eyes narrow for a moment, and arousal courses through me when I see a slow smirk appear. I inhale sharply and take my chance, rolling to the other side of the bed and sliding off.

"Oh, that's the game you want to play, is it? It just means I'll get to punish you when I catch you," his voice rumbles.

"Who said I was an easy catch?" I quirk an eyebrow as I spread my legs wider and get ready to take off.

Knox hits the bed, and I take off, not realizing that it was a feint. I slip as I catch him coming around the foot of the bed for me. Squealing as I pivot out of his reach, I jump back onto the bed. Laughter bursts out of me when he trips over a squeaky ball that suddenly found its way to the bed. I glance over at Reaper and find him licking his paw and pulling his long tail back to him. He peeks up at me for a quick moment before his eyes dart back down.

My little man. He's getting extra loving tomorrow!

Knox picks himself up off the ground and shoots Reaper a dirty look before growling at him. Reaper, not caring at all, just huffs and goes back to minding his own business.

"I would have had you, kitten, if your little accomplice would have stayed out of it."

"Would of, could of, should of. All the same as did NOT." I smile back, standing in the middle of the bed. Knox glares up at me from the foot of the bed, and I'm ready for him, no matter which way he goes.

Apparently, my Shifter has the ability to defy gravity and clears the end of the bed like Wolverine on steroids.

"Eek!" I scream and dive off the bed, but before I can hit the ground or massively hurt myself, Knox tackles me midair, pinning my bottom half to the bed.

"Aww, kitten. You were so close. Now it's time for my reward, and you're going to take it like the good girl you are," he says, running his hands up the back of my thighs.

I'm so turned on that I will agree to anything he wants to do to me.

"Good girl." He nibbles on my ear. "Spread your legs for me."

I adjust myself, trusting he will keep me from slipping off the bed, and he pulls me back so only my top half from my breasts up hangs off the bed.

He guides his cock into my pussy, groaning in the process as he stretches me open to accommodate his size. I let out a moan as he grabs my hips and pulls me further onto the bed, then onto his shaft. *I've just become his sex doll,* I realize. *And I'm loving it.*

He reaches with his free hand and grips my hair, pulling my head to the side, giving him access to my mouth. He slams his lips to mine. Desperate for his familiar taste, I slide my tongue against the seam of his mouth, looking for entrance, when his hips start to move. It's a fight for dominance as we kiss and nibble, while our tongues struggle to take control.

"Play with yourself," he orders, pulling away breathlessly and lifting my hips up. Not needing to be told twice, my hands slide between my legs. I start rubbing my clit and brush against his shaft as he continues to slam into my drenched pussy.

"I need to see you, kitten," he says, pulling out and slapping my ass, making me yelp. "You love it, don't you? It makes you cream so well on this cock."

"Yes," I admit feverishly.

He easily flips me over and moves me onto my pillows like I weigh no more than fifty pounds.

"Let's see if we can wake everyone up," he says and grabs both of my wrists, pinning them above my head to the mattress.

"No—"

"Why not, kitten? I've laid in bed every night pleasuring myself to your moans and the feelings of pure pleasure that I feel from you through our link," he admits and slams his cock into me, making me cry out. "And yet it was *me* that had to seek you out, and when I did, you had the audacity to worry that I didn't want to be mated to you. So why not make everyone else experience what I had to?"

A whimper escapes me as multiple feelings pour down our connection. Excitement, anger, pleasure, and something darker, like possessiveness, hits me. Fuck, my greedy pussy gets wetter when it should be trying to pack a bag and run. But I'm in this for the long haul. *I have mates now.* My original worries melt away when he closes his lips over mine again. My pussy clamps down on him, forcing a moan into my mouth, and I arch my back as my nipples graze against his chest.

A whimper escapes me as I flex my hips, trying to get him to go deeper, needing more. "Knox," I gasp his name and he chuckles.

"Yes, kitten. Did you want more of my cock?"

His dirty talk alone almost brings me to the precipice of ecstasy, and I just want to meet that blissful end.

"Yes," I admit.

"Did my brothers make you beg? Do they make you come on their cocks like mine does?" he questions, getting in my face and staring into my eyes.

"I only beg for you," I manage to get out between pants.

He nibbles on my swollen bottom lip. "That's what I thought, kitten." I feel the swelling of his knot as he slowly stretches me until I feel as if I'm going to be ripped in two. The pressure is immense, and all it does is add to my pleasure. The sounds of our bodies slapping fills the room as his free hand reaches down to play with my clit. My legs go weak as heat blooms throughout my body.

"That's it, kitten," he whispers into my ear. "Come for me," he says, biting on his mate mark, and it's just what I needed to be sent over the edge. I spiral off that cliff as I explode on a scream while my pussy clamps down on Knox, triggering his release.

CHAPTER 37
Delving Deep

Knox

I can't help just staring at my kitten as she sleeps. Her serene facial features look like an angel's as her curly hair frames her face. I brush back a curl as I feel my knot deflating, and I slowly slide my cock out, trying not to disturb her, but it's useless.

She smiles while keeping her eyes closed. "So no round four? And here I was hoping," she mutters, and I can't help but chuckle.

"I think he would fall off if I tried to use him again, to be honest."

"Oh, really? Well, it's a good thing you dragged my pussy out with you because she just boycotted. Or is that now girl-cotted? You ruined her," she jokes, and I'm greeted by her gray eyes.

'You know, if you want to strengthen your bond the correct way and get a deeper connection, try sharing a memory.' Baron yawns.

'I've already done the sharing part, Baron. I told her about

the blood matches when she asked about them,' I growl at my featherbrained animal.

'Nooo. You told *her about the blood matches, you didn't* share *a memory. Connect with her, like they teach people with Familiars, and think of a memory that you want to share,'* Dusky answers, surprisingly.

'I thought you weren't talking to me anymore?' I question him.

'What makes you think I'm not getting something out of you making a deeper connection?' Dusky retorts.

'What are you getting out of a deeper connection?'

Crickets.

What's up with my animals not talking to me when they actually have a chance?

"Were you talking to them again?"

I glance over to find Rez propped up on her elbow, smiling at me.

"Yeah," I admit, embarrassed. "That easy to tell?"

"Kinda. You always have this far off look, and you send this annoyed feeling down the link."

"Sorry about that." I wave off her concern. "Baron and Dusky think there's a way to strengthen our bond, if you're up for it."

'Strengthen our mate bond? Hell yes!' I hear Rez, but wait to see if she says anything else.

"I would love to strengthen our bond. Do you think we'll gain anything special with a stronger bond?"

"I don't know, but I assume so since Dusky clammed up when he hinted he was going to get something out of the deeper connection."

"Oh, this is exciting. How do we do it?" She claps and sits up. I'm not ashamed to say that my eyes drift down to her breasts. "Knox?"

"Huh?" I say, still staring at my wonderful delicious pillows I want to bury my face in.

"How about we clean up and get some clothes on so I can have a normal conversation with you?"

"Uh huh!" I say as I watch her throw the covers off and climb out of bed.

"Hey, where are you going?" I ask in a daze.

. . . . .

I take some time to check over Rez's new spine tattoo while we shower. It brings on a whole new meaning to me as I wash her back, knowing the symbols of the Horsemen are meant to be my brothers and me. Hell, I even figure the other symbols out after looking at the Angel's wings and the water and fire symbol. That weird yet hypnotic storm cloud has to be Lynx. The only one I'm not sure about is the one at the base of her skull, the one with all the stars.

Dressed and cuddled up on the bed, I'm slightly hesitant about how to begin this conversation.

"So how do we do this?" she asks as she flings her wet braid off her shoulder. I internally snort, thinking I shouldn't have been worried. Knowing Rez, she just jumps in with both feet.

"Dusky mentioned trying to connect to me like you did in Familiars class while I think of a memory. I just don't know what type of memory to pull."

"Well, obviously you don't want a bad one, right? What about a happy one with your father? Or one with Zeke, or your other brothers?" she offers, but I draw a blank. She bites the bottom of her lip. "I'm not even sure it's going to work because when I connected to Lynx, that was different. He obviously wasn't my Familiar, but my best friend."

"True," I say. "But you were still able to connect with him," I remind her.

She lets out a sigh as unease flitters through our link. "That's because he's also my mate."

I freeze as her words penetrate through my thick skull. *Mate? Isn't he a Shifter?* The skinny, short-haired blond Thor wannabe is her—No. *Normally Shifters don't share the same mate? How does that affect us?*

"Knox?"

I immediately think back to my conversation with my father about mates, and I feel a pinch in my brain as the scene plays out before me.

Zeke leaned against my bed, looking at a dirty magazine as I heard footsteps that could only be Dad's.

"Incoming," I warned Zeke as Dad walked down the hall toward my bedroom.

Zeke quickly shoved the mag underneath my bed and grabbed the book beside him, looking up as Dad stepped into my room. He'd always been an imposing figure, standing at six feet and as broad-chested as a bear, but seeing him from the floor up was something altogether different. He ran his hand over his shaved head before glancing around my room.

"Boys, I'm going to have to head out tonight for a mission. I ordered food, and it should be here in about thirty minutes." Dad stepped in and reached for Zeke's book, turning it right side up. "This might be more convincing if you had it the right way. So what were you really looking at?" he said, not really asking.

Zeke reluctantly pulled out the magazine from under my bed and handed it to my father.

He chuckled as he peeked inside it, but handed it back to Zeke. "I was wondering when you guys would get interested in girls." He grabbed my desk chair and turned it to straddle the back of it.

"I'm not going to sit here and give you guys the talk. I don't

have the time for it, unfortunately, but I will tell you this," he said as he ran his hand down his beard. "Our world is brutal. It's not like the human world, where you hear about people falling in love in this magical whirlwind romance, where they get married, have babies, and live happily ever after. We don't get that chance, as a Shifter and for those who are unique." He glanced at Zeke and then back to me. "We have to take what's given to us and make the best of it. Sometimes, though, you have to watch out because not everyone is honest. Some will stake a claim on your mate, but always trust your animals, Knox. That's where you might have to challenge someone for your right to claim your mate."

He got up, put my chair back, and walked out of the room. "Good night, guys. If you need to hide a body, the tools are in the shed." His voice filtered down the hall.

"Do you think he really means that?"

I turned to look at Zeke. "Yeah. I've seen them." A shudder ran through him as he opened up his magazine again.

"What would you do"—he put the mag back down in his lap—"If your mate was taken by someone else?"

"That wouldn't happen," I said with confidence. I'm an alpha's son.

"Yeah, I know, you have girls dying to be with you, but let's play 'what if.' What would you do?" Zeke pushed, and I decided to play along.

"Depends on who it is. If I knew them and knew I could take them without a doubt, I would just tell them to back away from my mate or else I would challenge them in the next Blood Match."

Zeke sighed. "Of course, you would leave the fun shit out. And what if you didn't?"

"I would be using Dad's shed and asking for your help."

Zeke threw his head back and laughed. "Yeah, that's more like you."

A gasp for air has me blinking rapidly as the memory recedes, and I suddenly start coughing as if I'm trying to expel something. My eyes start to water, but I desperately search around and find Rez wheezing next to me.

"Fuck," she hisses and wipes her eyes. "That's never easy," she moans and peers up at me. "Shit! Knox, breathe," she says as she straddles my lap and gets in my face.

"Slow down your breathing and concentrate on me. I know it's a trip, but you're fine. You're here," she coaxes me, and I grab her thighs and follow her instructions.

"What the fuck just happened?" I cough out, and she smiles at me.

"Well, I sort of slipped into your memory," she admits with a smile.

"The memory I just thought of?" I ask in awe, and then my face falls as I realize she heard a private conversation between me and Zeke about mates. *Shit. Does that mean she saw that dark side of me, where there's a part of me that isn't bothered by killing someone?* I start to slide her down my thighs, but she grabs my hands, stopping me.

"No. I know you're upset. I feel it, but we need to talk," she urges.

"No, we don't." I easily push her to the side and slide out of the bed. I don't need to be here, and I can slip back into my room across the hall.

"You know your father is wrong, right?" she calls out, and I pause to look back at her.

She's kneeling on the bed, with her hands crossed in her lap and the saddest-looking eyes in the world.

"Humans don't have magical whirlwind romances where they get married, have babies, and live happily ever after. They work their asses off to make it look easy. There are mistakes, arguments, crying, and laughter. But every relationship that works has one thing in common." She shuffles to the edge of the bed and continues to give me her version of puppy dog eyes. "They both want it to work, and they both give 100% to that relationship."

I can't seem to look at her as shame engulfs me, and I turn toward the door to keep her from seeing my face as I fight my own demons. I'm not one to run from a fight, but I don't want to hurt her emotionally either.

"Please don't walk away because you're scared," she pleads.

"I'm not scared."

"Yes, you are," she says, and I hear the bedsheets move. Her hand touches my shoulder before she appears in front of me. She wraps her arms around my waist and gazes into my eyes. "And that's okay, because I am, too. This is something new for both of us."

I sigh as I wrap my arms around her, and she rests her cheek against my chest. "I didn't even know dating more than one person or mates was a thing a month ago. Will you please come back to bed and hold me while I explain about Lynx and set everything straight?" She leans back and looks up at me. "To the best of my ability? I kinda want to cuddle." She smiles, and it draws a chuckle from me.

She makes a good point. Even with Father pointing out that we need to trust our animals, we do live in a world where we do have to date multiple people. The only question I need to worry about is, are my animals happy with Rez?

'Of course we are happy with our mate! What kind of question is that?' Baron huffs.

'Then why the animosity toward her?' I ask my animals.

'She has another mate! What if she wants him more than us? We did come second. She will leave me,' Fluffers howls.

"Is—is that Fluffers howling?" Kitten asks, shaking me out of my mental conversation.

"You can hear him?" I ask, completely shocked.

"I hear howling. Is he okay?" she asks, searching my eyes.

'Is this what you meant, you little starbrat?' I hiss at Dusky, but all he does is laugh.

"Yeah, he's okay. Just upset that he's not your *first mate,* and he's afraid you're going to leave him." I run my hands up and down her back as I walk us back to the bed.

I climb in, and she lays her head on my chest before shocking me once again. "I want to try something." She closes her eyes, and it takes a moment, but I feel something tickling my brain before I stifle a laugh.

'Check check check. Check one, two.'

'It's not a mic check, kitten.' I chuckle and she pinches the shit out of my nipple. *'Fuck!'*

'Fluffers?'

'MATE!' Fluffers yells, and I see him plop down on the ground, rolling onto his back as his tongue sticks out.

'What's he doing? I can hear him doing something, but all I see is black.'

'He's being a goofball, and he's showing his tummy. A true alpha right there.'

Rez giggles. *'It's okay, Fluffers. There's no need to worry about me leaving you. I'm in this with Knox and all of you until death, and who knows what will happen after, okay? So there shouldn't be any doubts. Only happiness.'*

'Okay! Yup. I like that idea,' Fluffers says, and starts running and playing. I'm kinda glad she can't see the goofball as he runs around in circles.

'Now where's my resident sour puss?' she asks, and I groan as Baron pushes forward.

'Hello, my lovely mate. It's good to finally speak to you one-on-one. This lazy sack of bones has been taking his time in connecting to you properly,' Baron greets Rez and disses me at once.

Rez laughs and agrees with him, but she suddenly cries out and breaks the connection.

"Are you okay?" I lean down and look for any injuries.

"Ugh, yeah, just a sharp pain in my head. Sorry."

'It's a power she will have to use to become stronger, just like her own magic. I'm assuming she over taxed herself on her first time. But she did an amazing job connecting with the small amount of thread that was there,' Dusky explains.

'What do you mean, the small amount of thread?' I ask, starting to get really frustrated with these little advancements or fucking tasks my animals are giving me.

'Think of it as a rope bridge that's crossing a chasm. She's crossed from one side of her cliff to your brain, the other cliff. The rope bridge only had one thread on it. Each time that she crosses, that bridge gains another rope and becomes stronger and therefore easier for her to cross and stay for longer,' Dusky says slowly.

'You're a bigger asshole than Baron, aren't you?' I ask Dusky, and he scoffs.

"You really should be nicer to him." Rez raises an eyebrow at me.

"Aww fuck, you heard that?" I ask, feeling like shit that I was caught red-handed.

"Yep. No cuddling for you," she says and turns away from me.

"Oh, come on, kitten," I plead.

I think this deep connection bullshit is gonna get me into more trouble than it's worth.

CHAPTER 38

Our Last Night

Rez

I jerk upright in a blind panic and grab my chest. My breath rushes out of my lungs as I try to push away the remnants of my nightmare.

Knox's hand squeezes my thigh gently. "You okay, kitten?" he mumbles.

"Y—yeah." I glance over and tap my phone to see that it's 2 o'clock in the morning and I've only been asleep for a few hours. "Just a bad nightmare."

Knox shifts and rubs my back. "Do you need to talk about it?" His voice comes across thick with sleep, but he's more awake now.

"It was just about Emer and how she took Levi away from me—from all of us, and I couldn't get him back," I admit, my voice going soft at the end.

Knox sits up and pulls me against him, kissing the top of my head. "Kitten, I think you need to go to him and spend some time together before he leaves in the morning."

My jaw drops as I look at Knox in shock, and he chuckles

lazily before laying back down. "Baby, you haven't spent any time with him recently, and you'll feel better once you do. I got my time in with you, so it won't bother me, honestly. I promise, I'm going to roll over and get my beauty sleep, but you need Levi to feel better." I'm flabbergasted for a moment. Did he somehow read my mind from earlier? I was planning to spend tonight with Levi, but I didn't want to deny Knox his time with me either. I open my mouth to dispute his claim when he pulls the rug out from beneath me in one smooth reply. "I can feel it through our bond. Now, go so I can sleep. I'll see you in the morning, kitten." He leans back up and gives me a quick kiss before rolling over and burrowing underneath my covers.

Huh! Okay then.

I quickly slide out of bed and give Reaper a kiss as he stirs. Slipping out of my door to find Levi down the hall, I send thanks down my connection with Knox. I don't even make it to his door before I'm startled though.

"Rez!" Levi whisper shouts when he sees me. "What are you doing?" he asks as he quickly walks toward me. It looks like he just came from the kitchen, since he's holding a water bottle in his hand. His night clothes still look fresh, like he hasn't slept in them, but other than that, he looks a mess. There're bags under his eyes, and his hair is all spiked up like he's been running his fingers through it.

"I—I was coming to find you, actually." I confess, walking up to him. "Are you okay? Have you even slept?" I caress his cheek, and he just melts into my touch.

His shoulders slump as he sighs and looks at me with heavy eyes, shaking his head. "I can't. There's too much on my mind. That's why I went to the kitchen for water." Well, at least my guess was correct. "What about you? Why are you up?" He surveys my attire, for what I can only guess is to see if I'm hurt.

"I can understand the not sleeping," I give him a sad smile. "I had a nightmare about your ex taking you away from me and I couldn't get you back," I confess, emotion slightly choking me, and Levi quickly pulls me into him.

"I won't let that happen," he says, squeezing me tight, and I wrap my arms around him, lying my head on his shoulder.

"That's the thing, Levi. You didn't have a choice. It was taken away from you, away from everyone," I whisper into his body.

"Well, you've already thought ahead and took a step forward in the right direction, so I have no doubt we'll figure something out," he says with confidence, and I pull back to peer up at him.

"You know what, maybe we should change your name to Foundation instead of Robot," I tease.

"Oh really." He raises his eyes. "Why?"

"Because you're really the foundation or the solid force that holds this family together. You've been the rock; it's as if there's no other option for you." He blushes under my scrutiny, but he doesn't pull away from me like I expect.

"Robot has kinda grown on me," he whispers, and my jaw drops.

"Ahh!" My eyes get big at his confession.

"Don't you dare squeal, though." His eyes narrow down at me. "I'll have to come up with a horrible punishment if you do." He chuckles as I mimic his last expression but can't hold it long and giggle.

"So were you really coming to see me?" he asks, doubt obvious in his face as he tilts his head down at me.

"Yeah," I say, pulling away a little and chewing on my bottom lip. "I guess I wasn't really thinking it through because you're staying with Ryker, right?" I ask.

"Yeah. Sorry for the disappointment. I wouldn't be able to sleep much tonight anyway," he admits, frowning.

I can't have his time with me be full of bad juju. I refuse to let that evil bitch ruin my time with my man. An idea pops into my head, and I smile up at Levi before taking his hand. "That's fine. I have a better idea anyway," I say as I drag him down the hall and on an adventure.

. . . . .

L evi balances on the edge of the high beam, and just when I think he's going to make it across to the other side to safety, he falls. He tumbles in the air and lands hard on his feet, before immediately propelling himself back into the air and doing a flip as he laughs. Shaking my head, I jump off of one of the large blocks we found and hit the trampoline, joining him in doing flips.

I figured if we couldn't sleep, we might as well have fun. So we stopped at the kitchen first for more water and snacks before spending some time trying to find the massive trampoline room. Who knows what L.A.M.B. uses this room for, but Levi and I decided to use it to let off some steam. So instead of turning on the lights in the room, we let the hallway lights guide us around until we became familiar with the room and then let ourselves loose to go crazy.

"I'm coming for you, Rez!" Levi yells, and I spin around to see him slowly jumping and spinning in my direction.

"Eek!" I scream and jump to the next trampoline. I think I'm getting somewhere until I glance back and it looks like I'm not making any progress at all. I'm not as agile as him. Don't let the nickname Robot fool you. Levi looks like he would be a natural at tumbling or acrobatics in general. He took one look at the room, kissed me hard on the lips, took off his shirt, and jumped into action, and he hasn't really stopped.

"Gotcha!" Levi yells as his arms wrap around me in midair. He flips us a couple of times as I scream out in excitement.

Finally, he slows us down, and we end up lying down on the trampolines, laughing as we catch our breath. "How did you find this place?" he asks as he magics the two water bottles over to us through the air.

I untwist the cap and gulp down half of my bottle before I tell him how I accidentally came across the room, and I thought it might raise his spirits.

"It definitely has," he chuckles. "It felt like flying."

"I guess it does a little bit," I admit.

"You don't like it?" he asks, assessing my mood.

"No, it's not that; I enjoyed it. I just freak out if I'm too high because I'm scared of heights," I admit, and understanding shines in his eyes.

"Ahh. Now I understand. So those were screams of fear when I was flipping us." He nods his head.

"No." I lightly shove his bicep. "Those were definitely screams of joy. I feel safe in your arms," I tell him. "Always."

He leans over me and cups my jaw, adoration shining in his eyes. "Thank you, for being you. I've never had anyone take the time to check on me like you do, or find ways to just alleviate the pressure I sometimes put on myself... I didn't know there was another way."

His eyes search mine for something, though I have no idea what, but my heart breaks for him. That he's had so little fun in his life that just jumping around gave him so much happiness even on the eve of doom is reward enough for me, and I lean in and claim his lips.

He doesn't hesitate in kissing me back as I straddle his lap. His hands lightly run down my sides and cup my ass as I rock against his rapidly forming length. I moan against his lips as I run my fingers through his short, soft hair and tilt his head so I can deepen our kiss.

"Rez, I want you so bad," he moans into my mouth as I nip along his jaw.

371

"Good, we can skip the foreplay then," I agree as I get excited at the prospect of us fucking in the middle of a room without doors. I lean to one side and try to grab my shorts to slide them down, before toppling over and ending up bouncing around on the trampoline like a buffoon.

"Ugh. Why is everything conspiring against me right now," I growl out, and I hear Levi's chuckle. I throw a glare his way, but the insult I was about to send his way dies in my throat. There, lying in the middle of the trampoline, is Levi laying on his back, still shirtless but with a glistening sheen of sweat, and now his pants are lowered past his hips while he strokes his cock.

Hot damn. Fuck trying to take off my clothes. As I crawl back to Levi, I become very aware of how wet I am as my juices start to pool between my thighs. Once I make it back to Levi, I take in my shirtless prize. He's all laid out for me, one arm behind his head and the other slowly stroking himself as if he's saying he's keeping my seat warm.

Why thank you! Don't mind if I do.

I bat his hand away from what's mine and swing my leg over him. Reaching between us, I slide my shorts over to expose my dripping pussy. Grabbing his thick cock with the other, I slowly guide his head into my sore core and pause to let my walls relax around him.

Fuck! I don't know how these women with multiple men do this without needing to switch out their pussies every other week.

"Fuck, you feel so good." Levi moans, and I'm too lost in the feel of him to even reprimand him for talking without permission. I raise up, allowing his head to slide out, and slowly guide him back in, inch-by-inch, as Levi rests his hands on my waist.

Look at him being trained right. I moan as he finally sheaths himself fully into me, and I slowly rotate my hips. The motion grinds my clit against his pelvis, and I let my head fall back with the pleasure. I slowly start bouncing, and I realize my mistake when Levi and I become slightly airborne.

FUCK!

Instead of me falling off of him like a girl on a bull in a western bar, Levi pulls me against him and wraps his arms around me tight. He rolls me so I'm on my back and he smirks down at me.

"I know you normally lead, Mistress, but do you mind if I do this time, since you're going to make us fly in more than one way?"

I smile back up at him. "What are you waiting for? Make me come."

"As you wish," he says before kissing me. He rocks into me slowly while he lifts my shirt. He takes one of my taut nipples and sucks it gently into his mouth as his other hand lightly plays with my other breast. Moans fill the air as he plays me like a well-tuned instrument. He swivels his hips just right so that with every rock of his pelvis he makes me see stars, bringing me one step closer to that cliff.

I gently grab his face and bring it in for a heated kiss, where I capture his moans. He hikes up one of my legs over his hip and angles me just right for him to go deeper than ever before.

"Fuck!" I moan into his waiting lips. He stares down at me with those hazel eyes that say so much, and in that moment, I know, without a doubt, I'm it for him. Yes, he's said it before, but the eyes never lie.

"I love you, Rez... But I don't think I'm going to last much longer," he pants out. I would laugh if I could catch my breath, so I do the only rational thing to do.

"I love you too," I say, and then pull him in for a kiss, reach down inside of my clothes, and start rubbing my clit like a mad woman on a mission. I swivel my hips and grind against my man like there's no tomorrow. Ecstasy explodes through me as my pussy spasms around Levi's cock, squeezing out his release.

"Fuck!" he cries out and empties himself into me with one last pump. Spent, he sweetly rolls us so I slump against his chest, and I raise up to kiss him.

"How's that for getting your mind off of things?" I ask, resting my head on his chest. He chuckles and lazily plays with my hair.

"I'm definitely more relaxed than I've been since being here," he admits. "Here, let me clean us up before we get too comfortable," he mumbles, already drifting off to slumber. I shift, allowing his spent cock to slip out of me. With a whisper of his magical words to clean us up, we're clean once again, and I snuggle into his body. He squeezes me once before his breaths deepen, and I kiss his pec before following shortly behind him.

CHAPTER 39

Portal to my Doom

Levi

The grumblings of Demons getting breakfast ready as they walk past wake me up. Finding Rez passed out on my chest brings a smile to my face as I think of the memories of our night. I don't want to move or disturb her, but Lucifer did say we needed to get up early to figure stuff out.

"Hey, sweetie, we need to get up," I say as I gently rouse her awake, picking up only calm emotions coming from her.

"Ugh. No," she moans, and it's the best sound in the world. I can picture myself waking up to her every morning. Even if her hair is wild and she might be drooling a bit. It's because she does things like that, perfectly imperfect examples of real life that confirm she's the one for me. She can be herself and I can be me, and we have no expectations of each other beyond that.

And we're bonded, I remind myself in wonder. *She bonded with me first.* Not that it's a competition between us as brothers, but I'm still honored and equally baffled that I could be so lucky to have her. I just know it's the greatest thing that could have ever happened to me, to all of us. But would reminding her of our bond scare her right now? As special as it is to me, she didn't ask for any of this, least of all ask to be bonded to me.

She came to me last night, though. She's with me right now, so I push the intrusive thoughts aside and pull her a little closer.

"Come on. The servants just went by to make breakfast, so you know L.A.M.B. will be up and moving. Do you really want to answer why we are in here?" I tease. I'm sure they really wouldn't mind, but Rez doesn't know that, and the slight threat works.

She pops up with wide eyes and spins around to look at me. "Well, what are you waiting for?"

We quickly head back to our hallway when we see Trometh standing outside my doorway. For a split second, I suspect he may be listening at the door, but he's already in the process of stepping away as my eyes drop to him, so I let it go. Besides, he's supposed to be loyal to L.A.M.B. They wouldn't have let him survive the house cleaning if he wasn't. And L.A.M.B. wouldn't spy on us, even if they are Demons. Not with the fact that we are the sons of Lilith, plus the revelation of JP and Moni's paternity.

"Trometh," I nod politely.

"Lord Lucifer wants to see you," he says in greeting.

I give Rez a quick kiss before she steps into her room, and I walk down to my door.

"I'll be right out," I say before slipping into my room.

Ryker turns and glares in my direction as he grabs clothes out of the closet.

"I don't like that asshole," he comments.

"Me neither, but is there a particular reason why you don't?" I ask, walking over to him and taking his place as he moves to the bathroom entrance.

"Yeah, the fucker woke me up in the middle of a great dream," he grumbles.

"Yep, that's reason enough," I point out.

"Look, you would agree if you were dreaming about Rez and the purple monster woke you up. Instead, you were fortunate enough to be living it." He cocks an eyebrow at me. "See ya at breakfast," he says as he slips into the bathroom.

I think of a new suit, step in, and get dressed, making sure to put on the cufflinks Rez made, only to meet a pacing Trometh in the hallway.

"Took you long enough," he grumbles before he scuffles down the hallway.

He leads me down a few passages I haven't been down previously, before we come to a door and he stops.

"Lucifer's office," Trometh sneers, and turns to leave to do more of his boss' bidding. I can't help but smile as I think of what Rez would do. *Kill them with kindness.*

I knock on the door before calling out to thank Trometh, to which he grunts in response from down the hall and walks away. Picking up on his grumbles, he's cussing me out.

"Come in."

I enter Lucifer's study and find it smaller than I thought it would be. Dark wood paired with red carpet, while matching red sofas take up most of the room with a small bar off to the side.

"You asked for me?" I say, taking a moment to straighten my jacket.

"Yes, come on in, Levi; have a seat." He motions to the sofa across from him and I turn to sit, wondering why I've been summoned so early. Of course, I was already stirring, but I figured we would talk after breakfast.

"I just got done talking to your father and the rest of the Council leaders," he says, and the news shocks me enough that my well placed stoic face slips. "Yes. I know, I know. I said we would do it once in Purgatory, but I started to think that if we're up against Elverson, then he probably has eyes everywhere."

That is a good point. "He has alluded as such with his blackmail," I supply, and Lucifer nods.

"As relieved as he was, we've agreed that it's probably best to act like you're carrying out your end of the deal and show up with only your immediate family in tow. Well, of course, Astaroth and myself will come as well, but being leaders of Hell, I doubt he would see a big problem with that." Lucifer smirks.

"So, does this mean the Council has a plan?" I ask, feeling hopeful that I can put this behind us.

"They are more than likely working on a fall out plan as we speak. Knowing Elverson, he's not going to be happy with this turn of events. Depending on what his reasoning is for wanting this merger in the first place, he won't just let this go without retribution," Lucifer tells me.

"That's what I'm worried about. He said he had access to Rez's mother, and he knew my family's routines. I don't know what to do," I admit.

Lucifer gets up and buttons his jacket, and I do the same. "Don't worry about it. We will take care of everything; it's our job. I just wanted to give you a heads up before we take off." He places his hand on my shoulder and leads me to the door. "Go enjoy breakfast with your actual bonded. I'll be there in a few minutes, and once we're done, we'll leave."

As I head back to our hall, I meet up with the others on the way to breakfast, and I find myself lost in thought. There are too many variables, and it's making me anxious. Elverson is a big player, and having Lucifer validate my concerns doesn't make me feel any better. What is he going to do when he finds out he can't get what he wants? Is he going to follow through with his threats? Attack Knox or Ryker?

His threat to do something to Rez's mother is a moot point, it seems. Maybe he was misinformed that she's dead. I wouldn't put it past him to go directly after Rez, though, since he can't use her family against her. My mind feels scrambled, and I can't think straight, since I didn't get much sleep last night. I almost pass the dining room when I hear my name called.

I shoot Knox a small embarrassed smile and pull myself out of my musings to find the dining room already set up and everyone but Lucifer at the table.

"Aww, look at my family. Looking fresh eyed and bushy tailed," Lilith squeals as I walk into the dining room.

"Ugh!" Rez says as she lays her head on the table. I take my usual seat and lean forward with a smirk.

"Long night?" I tease, keeping my voice down.

"My pussy has clocked out. She's on vacay, and she's not coming back," she mumbles, and I chuckle, not expecting that answer. She raises her head and looks directly at me. "No one told me the downside of having multiple partners. Is there a cream or a store where I can switch out my body parts when they start to become raw? This is a delicious torture."

"Sweetie, the trick is having gangbangs so you please all of them at the same time and then you can rest in between," Lilith chimes in.

"Yes!" Lynx does a fist pump. "Gangbangs, baby!" He cheers and does a little shuffle in his chair.

I blink in shock at what my mother just said and then force myself to forget it as I try to hide the grimace of picturing it.

"Thanks, Lilith," Rez says with pursed lips.

"Nonsense. Call me Mom! We're family... And I'm sorry about my little outburst from before. I shouldn't have told you to call me differently. Though it's not an excuse, I wasn't myself. Hopefully, you'll forgive me. Now eat so we can start our day." She doesn't even wait for my forgiveness or reply before sending the plates around the table.

"Did Lilith just give you permission to have gangbangs with all of her children and then some?" Knots asks on the other side of Rez.

"Yep." Rez deadpans as she grabs some biscuits off a flying plate. Her response doesn't give enough away to indicate what she thinks about the practical execution of that act, but I definitely can't say I'm against the idea. As my mistress, she can have anything her heart desires.

We make quick work of breakfast after that wonderful advice mother so wisely gave us, and we all head to the parlor. Lucifer clears his throat to get our attention. "Okay everyone," he starts. "This is how today will go." Everyone turns to face him as he continues. "Astaroth and myself, along with Lilith, will leave and head to Purgatory, accompanying Levi, Zeke, Knox, and Ryker."

"Aww," Moni whines and leans into Chester for comfort.

"I know it sucks, honey, but the council and I have decided it will be best to play as if everything is going to Elverson's plan, up until the very end."

"Still don't like it," Moni mumbles but relents.

Lucifer nods and looks over our group and focuses on Rez. "During this time, Rez, you can work on your potions and bring Knots and Lynx's memories back. Hopefully, by that time, you guys will be able to join all of us at the Hub and we will have sorted all of this out."

"What about us?" Moni asks as she takes a sip of her coffee and cuts up some food.

Murmur smiles as he steps forward. "Ahh, my little niece. You guys get to play with me in the training room."

"Ugh," Moni whines again, and I stifle a laugh.

"Okay, let's get ready to go," Lucifer announces, moving past me to head down a hall toward the front door.

Rez says her goodbyes to Knox, Ryker, and Zeke, before pulling me off to the side. She tucks herself into my side as we find a small nook to talk in, and despite our night together, it feels great that she includes me in her goodbyes, given all the crap we've been through in the past. I wasn't sure how she felt about being claimed by my magic without having a say, and we didn't go over any of that early this morning.

"I feel guilty," she admits.

"Why?" I question as she wraps her arms around my waist.

"Well, because one: I'm glad I'm not going with you because I might not be able to handle myself around Emer. And two: I can stay here and work on getting Knots and Lynx their memories back. Then again, I'm missing out on seeing Emer's face when you tell her you're already mine." She smiles coyly.

"So, you're okay with my magic claiming you?" I ask, a little shocked that she's this open about it. I would think being raised as a human and not knowing how things work, she would be more upset about all of this. Time escaped us after learning about the prophecy and what my magic did for us. We needed that stress relief from the trampoline room more than just sitting down and talking.

"Yeah, why wouldn't I be?" she asks, tilting her head and peering up at me with a worried line between her brows.

"Well, you didn't have a choice in the matter," I point out. "And I know how big it is in the human world to have a choice." *Was I worrying about all of this for nothing?*

She giggles and squeezes me. "Levi, just a few days ago we were worried that you were about to sign over your life to the Queen Harpy, and it turns out you already chose who you wanted to be with, and it's me. Do you know how amazing that is?" she asks, her eyes sparkling with mirth, and I feel her excitement.

"We chose each other," I correct, realizing it wasn't all one sided. "And I guess I just never looked at it that way. I was afraid you would feel like you were trapped and stuck with me," I admit.

"Never. I will admit that it's been one hell of a learning curve, and being mated to you all, one after another, is mind blowing. But I'm happy with you and the others, and most of all, I'm relieved that you're free from Emer and you can be with me."

I sense a thread of worry, and I pull back to gaze into her beautiful gray eyes. "What's wrong?"

"You do want to be with me, right? You're okay with your magic going AWOL and choosing me?"

My cheeks hurt from how big my smile spreads. "Of course I am. The Fates brought you to me before I even knew I needed you in my life. You are the best thing to ever happen to me," I say as I cup her face and gently kiss her. "I'll see you soon, and we'll all celebrate my freedom from the Elverson debacle and Lynx and Knots' memories being restored. This will all be just a bad memory," I promise as I hear the moody Door Knight himself down the hall.

"Keep it up, fur ball, and I *will* make you into a pair of boots as soon as you get your memory back," Knots threatens.

Rez laughs as she leans against me. "Or a funny memory to bring up down the road."

"Or that too." I chuckle as I grab her hand and guide her back to the group, where Lucifer stands with the rest of my family.

It's amazing to look at everyone here and consider them all family. At the beginning of the school year, I kept to myself and only thought of what I could do to receive Lilith's approval. Now though, Rez has crashed into me with the force of the Fates and has freed me from the road of loneliness and self destruction I was heading down. If I had continued upon it, I'm pretty sure I would have ostracized myself from my entire family and not have even seen it coming.

"All ready?" Lucifer asks, glancing over our small group. I nod and give Rez another kiss before stepping away.

"Hopefully, we'll meet up with you in a few hours," Lucifer calls out and walks out the door with our small entourage following.

The red sun is barely grazing the horizon as we walk down the path from L.A.M.B.'s. mansion to the black iron gate surrounding the premises. We follow the path down to the crossroads where instead of going right—toward the market—we go left.

"Where are we going?" Zeke questions as he spins the ring Rez gave him.

"To the Crucible," Astaroth says as he smiles over his shoulder.

"Why is it that every time you smile, it's never a good thing?" Ryker states, coming up behind me.

"Because you're learning," Astaroth calls back.

"Isn't a crucible a vessel that's used to melt extremely hot metals and such?" I ask, wondering how they settled on the name. "Why didn't you just open a portal like you've done in the past?" I ask.

"We tried, sweetie. For some reason, we aren't able to. So we're going to the Crucible," Lilith explains.

"Is that—is that normal?" Knox asks, shooting me a concerned look.

"No," Lucifer says.

"Should we be worried?" I press.

"Murmur and Bez are looking into it," Asatroth supplies without any indication if we should worry or not.

I can't even pick up on any emotions from them, but Knox, Ryker, and Zeke are pumping out enough annoyance and frustration to easily mask any other emotion.

"That's why we are going to the Crucible. It's the main melting pot where we can take a portal back to Purgatory," Lucifer says as we continue to walk down the path. This pathway is different from the last one we went down. Along the road are cliffs and large skeletons of long-dead monsters. I can see barren trees line the edges of the cliffs and a few outcroppings of homes in the distance. They don't look as luxurious as L.A.M.B.'s but they still look to be a decent size.

At the end of the path, a large building finally comes into view. It's made out of wood and leather skins with some massive wooden beams exposed in some areas. As we approach, there's yelling and a large crowd is gathered just inside the entrance. They are all standing in what looks like a foyer of the building.

"What's going on?" Zeke asks, peeking over a few Demons.

Lucifer slides over to the side and taps a Demon on the shoulder. He turns around with a growl, but when he sees who's in front of him, the color drains from his face as he stutters out an apology and bows.

"What's going on?" Lucifer demands.

"Sorry, Lord. The guards won't let any of us into the inner sanctum to use the portal. They will not tell us why," he says shakily, and slowly rises.

Asatroth turns toward the crowd and his tail begins whipping back and forth in irritation, making small booming sounds. They start off small, but they have a ripple effect, and soon I feel a vibration against my legs as thunder rolls inside of the building. Lucifer stands before us and motions for us to stand back while Demons continue to scream and push each other in front of us.

Lucifer's hands start to glow, and I see a shield go up between him and Asatroth, cutting off the vibrations from his tail. Although we are protected, the Demons and other creatures in the room before us are not. I watch in fascination as some turn and finally notice the Wrath Demon right as they get knocked off their feet.

"I would hate to be them," Ryker leans in to whisper.

"I agree."

Asatroth doesn't wait for them to get up, he starts walking as they scramble to not get stepped on, and we follow behind Lucifer's shield. The noise in the room starts to die down and turns into a different type of buzz as we get further into the building. As the crowd parts, I'm finally able to see a large stone structure that runs the height of the building, and standing at the massive doors are four Demons dressed in black and red heavy armor.

"My Lords, my Queen." The biggest one dressed in all red bows his head before Astaroth.

Lucifer drops his shield and steps forward to address the guard. "What's going on? Why are you barring the portals?"

"We were about to send a servant to give word," the guard explains, stepping inside with Lucifer. Astaroth follows along with Lilith, but when I start to follow, one of the guards throws out his arm, stopping me.

"Can't go in," he growls out. I glance up at him and point at my family.

"Excuse us, we're with them," I say, and point just in case this dimwit doesn't understand who "them" are.

He peers back to see Lucifer continuing walking without us and gives us a cocky smile. "Doesn't appear so."

"Look, fucker," Knox growls, stepping up in between us and getting into the Demon's face. "That's our—"

"Let. My. Children. Through," Lilith says through clenched teeth. She stands behind the guard in front of the structure, only her arm and hands visible, and they are currently choking the guard. Her claws pierce through the armor around his neck as he wheezes, trying to breathe.

"Did you see her move?" Ryker whispers behind me.

"Nah," Zeke answers, unfazed by the display of power.

"Yes, my Queen," the guard manages to get out as he slumps to the ground and we walk past.

"I'm glad we're on her good side," Zeke whispers.

"You could never be on my bad side. You boys are perfect in my eyes," Lilith professes.

The concrete area is empty except for a dozen or so portal shells lined up against the walls, and a massive one on the top of a platform. It's the only way to describe them because they look like portals, but without the swirling magic emitting from their surface. Right now they look like dead and cloudy white mirrors.

"Shit. Are the portals closed?" Ryker asks, stepping up to the big one and walking around it.

"Lucifer? What is going on?" Lilith asks as she catches up to him next to the guard.

"It started early this morning. First, the portal to Nova was acting up, then we noticed the smaller ones started to... uh... shut off," the guard standing next to the stairs says, not making eye contact with any of us.

"What do you mean, acting up?" Asatroth asks, his tail whipping out and sending thunder rolling through the room.

"Guys?" Ryker calls from behind the portal.

We quickly walk around to meet him as the guard hastily tries to answer.

"Well, simply put, our patrons weren't getting to their destinations safely."

I walk around the stairs and stop dead in my tracks at the sight. Piles of body parts lay before us. Arms, tails, horns, a few torsos, and some heads.

"How are we not smelling all of this?" Knox asks, glancing at the Demon guard.

He clears his throat before pulling at his neck guard. "I

have an affinity for shields. I tried to shield the smell of the body parts themselves."

Lucifer turns back to look at the guard and the leader in red. "Are all the portals like this?"

"No sir," the leader states. "That was just the beginning. Now we can't even enter." He opens a leather satchel on his belt and tosses a coin at the gate on the stairs where it bounces off of it and rolls back down the stairs to his feet.

A light flashes at the gate and a faint image of chains crosses the portals.

"Did anyone else see that?" I ask, making sure I'm not seeing things.

I turn and find the guards shaking their heads, but Lucifer gives me a slight nod. He turns to the guards. "Leave the shield up until Bez comes. He'll dispose of the bodies."

"I think it's best that we go home to discuss this," Astaroth says, turning to start walking out.

Lucifer passes by me and slows down. "It looks like we might not be seeing the king after all."

He walks to the entrance of the Crucible and his wings unfurl with a flourish, propelling him into the air. Watching him take flight, I almost trip, but Asatroth catches me and urges us to keep moving.

"He's going to make an announcement while we walk out, so it's best to keep moving."

It's easier to make our way out of the building now that everyone knows Asatroth, Lilith, and Lucifer are here. There's a few that Asatroth pushes out of his path, but we make our way as Lucifer addresses the crowd.

"Dear subjects, I am sorry for the inconvenience, but until further notice the portals to Purgatory will be closed off. Anyone willing to go against these orders or attacking my guards will find themselves answering to L.A.M.B. personally if they haven't been killed first. Now, leave the Crucible and go about your day."

There's a pouring of frustrated grumblings, but Demons start to scatter and Lucifer joins us as we begin walking back to his mansion.

"Well, that went well," Zeke nervously chuckles, as we watch a few Demons leave and shoot our group scathing looks.

"Maybe too well," Knox says, and I have to agree because that's not what I'm picking up from the group. Boiling anger is the only thing that's potent in this group of Demons, and it's starting to choke me. Hopefully Rez is having better luck than we are.

CHAPTER 40
The Fall

Rez

I bite my lip as butterflies take off in my stomach while we walk back down to Lilith's room. Before she left, she said she arranged everything for me and the potions were ready. I just have to follow the directions and be their anchor while the spell does its job. *Simple enough.* So, why am I scared shitless?

"So, who's going first?" Lynx asks, pulling me from my musing.

"I don't know what I'm doing, and I'm a little nervous," I admit.

"Well, that solves that question—I'll go second." Lynx chuckles and slips behind me as we turn into Lilith's room. Most of it looks the same, but instead of it being empty in the middle, there's now a small altar covered with a silver sheet draped over it and a pillow.

"An altar. Why is there always an altar for these things?" I mumble as I walk over to the table and find the spells and directions.

"For purity," Knots answers, as he strips down to his

underwear. "It's a way to keep the body pure if going through a transformation, or a way to bring honor to those that you are worshipping," he adds as he folds up the last of his clothes and lays them down on the bench that Lilith had placed in the room.

He winks at me once he's standing in his tight boxer briefs and shoots me a smirk. "I mean, if you feel like worshipping me later, I won't say no."

I roll my eyes and scoff. "Get your sexy ass on the altar and behave." Determined to make this happen, I skim over the instructions, and it seems simple enough. He just has to drink it while I say the words and be his anchor. *Great. How the fuck do you become an anchor?* I glance around the room not seeing what I'm looking for, so I call out, "Benny." I peer under the table. "Benny, are you here?"

"Here I am." I hear a chirp and see Benny scurry out from behind a bookshelf.

"How did you even fit back there?" I ask as she climbs up the table. Her long dragon body stretches out once she reaches the top.

"Magic!" Her whiskers bristle, and I smile at her before pointing at the spell.

"This seems simple enough, but do you know how I become an anchor?" Hopefully, she has a clue because the only other person in this room no longer has his memory and is browsing books over by the door while giggling at the titles. I don't even think I want to know what's over there.

"Yes, it's simple. Just maintain contact with them throughout the process," she nods.

"That's it?" I ask. *Surely there's more?*

"Yep! Anything else you needed?" she asks, but I shake my head, and she crawls down the table leg and runs back behind the bookcase.

"You okay over there?" Knots asks, looking over at me. I give him a small smile and nod as I grab his vial.

"Yep, just wanted to verify something so I don't fuck this up."

He grabs my free hand and squeezes. "You've got this, and I trust you. Lynx would trust you implicitly if he just remembered," he whispers, but I peer over toward Lynx and notice how he's paused in his perusal of the books.

"Thanks." I lean down and give him a gentle kiss before pulling away. "Okay, let's restore the memories we didn't know you lost, huh?" I move to the end of the altar where his head is and hand him the vial before placing both hands on his shoulders, and he makes quick work of downing the contents. Saying the words for the spell, I hold my breath as I watch for any little sign of it working.

Knots closes his eyes before he seems to go immediately into a deep sleep. His eyes start bouncing back and forth under his eyelids before his body warms. My instincts kick in, and I go to pull away, but Lynx's hand shoots out to still my own.

"Don't. You have to hold on. Here, I'll help."

He comes up behind me, lending me his support and pushing me closer to Knots when all I want to do is step back from the heat that encompasses me. My eyes close as his hands gently wrap around my wrists and hold me there as he whispers into my ear.

"You can do this, Rez. Just concentrate." His words slowly fade away as I feel my body gradually drift forward. A gasp leaves me as I feel myself fall.

When I open my eyes, I find myself in a meadow. The sun is high in the sky and warming my body, while the grass is up to my hips, swaying in the gentle breeze. Tall, green trees surround me, and as I turn around, I notice I'm all alone.

"Knots!" I call out, but I get no answer besides hearing birds

in the far-off distance. Taking a chance, I turn toward the woods, keeping the meadow in my sight, and look around for any sign of life. Laughter comes back from the meadow, and keeping to the shadows, I creep closer to see what's going on. There's a little girl wearing a faded dress, holding a little boy's hand, who's wearing only pants.

The two children slowly look around the meadow. From where I'm standing, I can tell they are talking, but I can't make out their words. The girl is slightly taller than the boy, but they both have brown hair and bright blue eyes. They slowly smile and turn to run the other way, only to teleport in a blink of an eye and pop up behind the spot they were just at.

Knots suddenly stands up from out of the tall grass and wipes off his leather pants, and the kids quickly tackle him, making him chuckle. They exchange words and a thrill runs through me as I step out of the woods and approach. Knots hasn't changed much, except he's wearing his hair tied back and he's shirtless.

"Knots!" I shout, but he doesn't respond. As I get closer, his words come across crystal clear.

"So it is. Race you back!" he yells, taking off in a run with the kids chasing after him.

Fuck! I didn't know I would have to exercise during this spell.

I take off after all of them as we dart through the grass and into the woods. There's a clear path, so I don't have to worry too much about tripping, and soon enough, we come to a small log cabin.

"Momma, we're home," the little girl calls.

"We found him," the boy calls as he grabs Knots' hand and pulls him into the cabin behind him.

I slowly walk in, and since no one can sense me, I finally realize this must be a memory of sorts. Glancing around the cabin, I notice it's all one room. An open fire pit has a funnel at the top to allow the smoke to rise out, and skins and pelts lay on the other side of the room, probably making up a sleeping area. There's a table that someone must have made by hand that's next to the fire pit, and there are hand-crafted utensils laid out.

What era did we end up in? It's a mixture of the stone age and home on the prairie.

"Let's eat while the food is warm," Knots says. The familiarity stabs a hole in my heart as I watch him pour water over the kids' hands, then his own, before sitting down at the wooden table.

"Thank you, Kanotiel, for the food," the kids both say before helping themselves to the meat sitting in the middle of the table. As the kids busy themselves with the food and drinking out of small leather pouches, another person walks into the cabin, and jealousy really does rear her ugly head.

A gorgeous woman with brown eyes and long blonde hair walks in wearing a long pale green dress. "What are you silly willys doing? You're supposed to be training your skills, not filling your stomachs." Her voice is musical, and when she smiles at the table, I have the undeniable urge to push her out of the cabin.

"Can't let the food go to waste. I did work hard to kill it," Knots says as he takes a bite.

The woman sits down across from him and smiles, but this time it doesn't meet her eyes. "About that. You know you don't have to do that," she starts, and clenches her fist in her lap. Knots frowns but continues chewing. "In fact, each time you reveal yourself to us, you're making yourself a target. I knew what I was doing when I chose this life."

"Angelette," he sighs. "You know I cannot turn my back on my flesh and blood," he stresses, looking over at the children eating, and tears gather in my eyes. Oh, God. Did Knots have a family and children?

"Kanotiel, how many times do I have to tell you that you

didn't turn your back? I did. I walked away from Heaven. I decided to fall to Earth and give up my wings and live this life."

Knots bows his head for a moment. "But you are the only true family I have. We were born of the same flame. Siblings. You are my world." His eyes start to water as he stares at his sister, and I feel awful that I even had a glimmer of jealousy toward her. I watch as she reaches across the table and grabs Knots' hand.

"Yes, and we will always have that connection, brother. But you still serve a higher purpose while I fell for love." She smiles and looks at her children.

"Yes, and where is he now?" Knots asks, and she pulls her hand away as if he burned her. Her jaw clenches, and she takes in a deep breath before looking back at Knots.

"I can only hope that he comes back to us, but I do not regret my choice. The point is, as a Guardian Angel, you know you shouldn't be revealing yourself to us." She smiles. "You shouldn't even have us as wards. Who did you bribe?"

"I'm still not going to tell you." Knots laughs as he winks at the kids next to him.

I see a flash of light, and the sensation of falling comes again before I land on my ass with an oomph. Glaring up quickly, a gasp leaves me as I see Angels standing around the room before me. Males and females with different colored robes and wings mill about, but their attention is not on me, it's on Knots.

He's in the middle of the room, but he has the most beautiful wings along his back, every shade of blue covering their beautiful surface. He's kneeling before a panel of Angels in white robes, who are sitting in chairs. I can't make out their faces since they seem to glow from within, but their voices give away their sex.

"Kanotiel of the Acetylene flame," the Angel in the middle lords over him. "You are hereby accused of disobeying orders and protecting mortals we had marked to die. How do you plead?"

What? I run to the front and bring my attention to Knots as

his face raises to address the man in front of him. Even though he can't see me, I take a step back at the fire burning in his eyes and the blood on his face and clothes.

Oh, God. What happened? *I cover my mouth to hold in the sob as Knots' voice comes out in a feral growl.*

"Guardian Angels protect their wards. Your orders were wrong."

"That is not your place to decide," another voice speaks up.

"How can you condemn one of your own to die?" *Knots yells back, pulling on the restraints I now see holding him to the ground. They are almost invisible except when he moves them, but I can see them ripple, like a glamour.*

"You broke the rules, Kanotiel. As a Guardian, you should not reveal yourself. They had to be taken care of."

"As God's right hands, we protect his cherished creatures, do we not?" *Knots counters.*

"Your job is to follow orders and obey. Look into the Seraph and be judged."

The Angels in the room start to sing as a light shines before Knots. I turn my gaze up but have to shield my eyes as it's too bright to look at. It's only a few moments before the Angels stop singing and the light dims. I bring my attention back to the front and shriek.

"Fuck! Oh my god, you're uglier than the Arte Demons," *I cry out and jump back. If this is an Angel, the Bibles have it wrong. What's before me is a massive eyeball with eight wings and smaller eyes on each wing.*

It starts spinning upright before us, and an image forms like watching a TV. I watch as I see Knots running out of the woods like an avenging Angel, his sword pulled and easily slicing into the man that had grabbed his sister by surprise. The kids scream and run toward Knots, and he spins to swipe upwards into one of the bandits, cleaving him in two. There's a total of ten men that Knots kills to protect his family. The scene cuts off shortly after as Angelette goes to Knots with wide eyes and yells at him that they know and he needs to go.

Knots' head drops to his chest as he takes in ragged breaths. "You are hereby granted your deepest desire," another Angel says.

Knots' head jerks up as the Seraph's wings fold in front of itself.

"Since all you've ever wanted is to protect and take care of your loved ones, so be it." The Seraph's wings blasts open, breaking Knots' restraints and sending him flying backward with a flash of light.

Once again, I wake to find us in the meadow with the long grass and the trees that lead us to his sister's cabin. I nibble on my lower lips as I wait to see what happens next. The Angel said he would get his deepest desire, so is that being with his family? The anticipation is killing me as I turn to look for Knots. He finally gets his deepest desire. I watch as he picks himself up from the ground and brushes himself off. He peers up at the sky and squints before eyeballing the glen. He pauses when he sees someone in the trees.

Angelette walks out cautiously. "Kanotiel? Are you alright?"

"I'm sorry. Who are you looking for?" he asks, rubbing the back of his head with a confused look.

She gasps and covers her mouth for a moment, wrapping her arms around her waist as her eyes turn glassy. My heart shatters at her reaction because I know that feeling. Her loved one is so close to her, yet so far away.

"I'm sorry, ma'am. I don't mean to bother you, but do you know where the closest town is?" he asks, and she nods with tears in her eyes.

"Yes. It's that way, about a day's walk." She points. "If you go to the inn, just tell them that Angelette vouches for you."

"Thank you." He starts to turn and walk away, but stops. "Ma'am. I'm sorry if this seems very forward, but are you okay? For some reason, I feel like I should ask if you need anything *from me before I take off." He gives her a small smile, and she smiles back through the unshed tears.*

"Thank you for asking, but I'm good and happy. It's very considerate to think of others before yourself, though. It's an amazing quality to have in this world. Don't let anyone take it from you."

"Thanks. Oh. Who was the name you said earlier?"

"Oh... It was nothing." She waves it away with a watering smile.

"Really? It sounded like a very unusual name. I was going to adopt it," he says as he starts walking backwards and away from his sister.

"Well, in that case, I would just shorten it to Knot or Knots." She shrugs. "The other one really doesn't fit the times."

"Thank you..."

"You're welcome, Knots. Take care of yourself."

"You too." He gives her a warm smile before turning and walking away from the cabin and his family.

I fall back against Lynx as I sharply inhale and cough. Tears stream down my cheeks as my eyes focus back on Lilith's room.

"Shit. Rez, are you okay?" Lynx asks, but I'm so emotionally torn that I can't answer, just shaking my head.

A gut-wrenching scream comes from Knots as he shoots up into a sitting position. The glorious multi-colored blue wings I saw in his memories shoot out of his back, and I hear the faint sound of something breaking, but my mind fixates on Knots. A new onslaught of tears starts up because I know that type of scream, I lived it when my mother died. I've experienced it recently when I thought Lynx died. I dodge under Knot's wings and quickly climb onto his lap.

His shoulders hunch as he pulls at his hair and lets out another scream of anguish. Tears stream down his face like a living river, wetting his face and chest. All I can do is wrap my arms around him and squeeze him as his body starts to shake.

"I left them! Why would I leave them after everything I gave up, Rez? Why?" His voice breaks, and I pull his head into my shoulder, rocking him as his arms lay limp at my sides.

"It was the Seraph, Knots. It wasn't your choice. They took your memories from you and dropped you to Earth. You didn't fall, you were pushed. All because you have a heart and love your family."

"Then why did I leave them? I left them unprotected," he cries, and my heart shatters because I don't know how to heal him. I don't know how to make his pain go away. I wish there was an easy button or spell to cast to wash away the pain from this torture. I peer over to Lynx where he's giving Knots a worried look, and it's the first time I wonder if I should give up and not give Lynx his spell. Will he be able to handle getting his memories back and deal with the fallout?

'Remind him of all the good that he's experienced,' Lynx says, and I give him a small, grateful nod.

'Thank you,' I tell Lynx.

"Knots, first of all. Remember before you left, you talked to your sister," I say between sniffles. "Look at me," I order, gently pulling his head up so I can look into his eyes. "She had a chance to tell you. She had a chance to bring you home and reunite you with the rest of your family. That moment wasn't only on you. You have to see that. Even before then, she was trying to separate you and her, because of your duty." He pulls away from me as fresh tears burst from him while he shakes his head.

"No. It was becau—"

"Knots!" I yell. "I will not let you lie to yourself. I was there in your memory, and I have a clear understanding, even though I can feel your pain as well. She. Let. You. Go. For whatever reason she had for that moment, she let you go live your life where you could experience the world, love, hate, and find your own family to protect," I say as I force him to look at me once again. "She loved you enough to let you go. Now you need to love her enough to honor her wish and stop blaming yourself."

I watch as he battles with his emotions as I continue to try to soothe him the best that I can.

'I'll be back,' Lynx says, and I hear him leave the room as I run my hands up Knots' arms and dry his tears while he silently cries. A few minutes later, his eyes start to dry up and he's left with just sniffles. Lynx returns and hands us a cloth so I can use it to dry Knots' face, leaving his eyes bloodshot and tear stained, but he looks gorgeous to me. This is a man that's gone through literal Hell to find out who he is, only to learn an awful truth, and it hasn't been pretty.

Knots' hands slowly move from my waist up to my face, and he just gazes at me for a moment. His breath slows down before he sniffles, and a faint smile appears on his face. "I don't know what I would do without you," he says breathlessly, and then presses his lips to mine.

Unfortunately, we can't kiss for long because neither one of us can breathe out of our noses, but it does the trick. "You okay now?" I ask, and he nods, so I shimmy off of him, but he frowns.

"What?" I ask nervously.

"Missed opportunity. I should have said no while you were still in my lap." He smirks and hops off the altar, heading over to his clothes. I walk around the altar and see Knots' sword on the ground.

"Hey, Knots, how did your sword get over here?" I ask, picking it up with two hands. *Shit, it's fucking heavy.*

"When my memories resurfaced, my powers kind of got a rolling jump start so my sword did too."

"Does that mean you have angelic powers now?" I grit my

teeth as the room slightly shakes while I try to hold on to the sword.

"I'm sure I'll have the powers that I did before I fell—well, was shoved from heaven. The fact that these wings are now a hazard is proof of that," Knots says as he turns and promptly hits a potted plant with his wings.

"Yeah, you might want to get a crash course from Murmur before we leave," I suggest. "Does this mean you're considered *fallen* now?" Hopefully, this means he's not feeling the effects of being here.

"To be a *fallen,* you have to *choose* to fall to Earth. All I received was just my memories back." I catch a hint of dejection.

I wish I knew what to say to make him feel better.

I never got a close look at Knot's sword before, but it's gorgeous. All the swirls and runes along it. I really should study what they mean. I turn the handle to see the Demstone I've made for him, and my stomach drops. The cracking noise I heard was the Demstone breaking.

Thank fuck we're leaving in a few hours. With Knots' power increased and not having all of the ingredients more readily available I would hate to think of what would happen if we had to stay here any longer, so this is perfect timing.

For once the Fates are finally using lube when fucking me in the ass.

CHAPTER 41
The Upside Down

Rez

I check on Knots to make sure he feels okay, giving his shield an extra layer of my protection, before he decides to head to his room for a shower then get something to eat. As he leaves, he promises he will come back and check on us afterward if we don't track him down first. Comfortable with the steadiness he has on his legs as he exits the room, I turn to give my full attention to Lynx. He's leaning against the altar and staring down at his bare feet.

"You sure you want to go through with this?" I ask, biting my sore bottom lip as I wait for his answer.

"I really don't think I have a choice," he states before focusing his turquoise eyes back on me.

My lip jerks up into an awkward smile. "You always have a choice. I would never force you to go through what Knots just did," I say. Anxiety takes over about what choice he'll make, and I grab the hem of my shirt, twisting it to give my hands something to do.

I'm a bundle of nerves. On one hand, I do want my old

Lynx back, but what kind of person would I be to ask him to relive his torture and death? If I had known what awaited Knots, I would have warned him beforehand. Either way, it's their choice, but I can at least help them by playing devil's advocate.

"I don't like feeling like a part of me is missing. I mean, you and the guys do a great job of making me feel included, but... I don't feel whole. I want to do it, Rez. If anything, I want to have a deeper connection to you. I feel as if we should, but something is blocking it," he says and starts undoing his pants before pushing them down.

"Fuck, Lynx." I turn quickly and give him my back. "What is up with you and Ryker not liking underwear?"

He chuckles as I slowly maneuver to the altar and grab the drape and hold it up. "Oh, come on, you know you want to peek. It's magnificent!"

I raise the cloth between my hands and hold it out to him. "Somehow it seems wrong since you don't have your memory. So, do me a favor and wrap your shit up, will you?" I tease.

"You're such a cocktease, you know that?" Lynx pouts but takes the drape from me. "Okay, I'm decent... somewhat."

I turn and give Lynx a teasing smile. "I'm not a cocktease. I use them properly. Never had a complaint yet. Now get on the altar," I instruct and bat my eyelashes.

His hand morphs into claws and he playfully swipes his paw in my direction. "Rawr!"

"Changing your mind?" I ask, holding up the vial that he has to drink.

"No," he says, hopping up on the altar. He quickly takes the vial and swallows down the contents as he lays down.

Retaking my position at the head of the table, I once again say the words for the spell, but this time I'm ready for the side effects. I don't pull away when Lynx's body begins heating; instead, I lean into his body and move my hands onto his chest to brace myself while closing my eyes. This time, instead of a falling sensation, I feel myself getting pulled into darkness.

Opening my eyes, all I see is emptiness. My own breathing is the only sound I can hear. I flex my toes, and I feel some type of liquid at my feet, but since I can't see, I can only hope it's water. Before my mother's murder, I had been in a sensory deprivation tank once. It was Dr. Fisk's idea when I started having problems with sleeping and headaches. She finally talked Mom into letting me try it since it was a more "natural" solution.

That's what this reminds me of; although I'm standing instead of lying down in a coffin of sweaty tears left by prior patients. I highly doubted they cleaned those that often.

"Lynx?"

I cautiously take a step and listen to my own breathing as I try to remain calm. "Okay, Rez, you're here for Lynx. Find, Restore, and Save. Find, Restore, and Save," I repeat the mantra over and over as I slowly take another step.

"Lynx? Where are you?" I ask. My heartbeat starts pounding as my mind races with other thoughts. Will I be able to leave this place? What if I can't find Lynx?

I hear someone sniffle, and I pause mid step as I slowly turn around. A faint light shines down, highlighting a young Lynx sitting down with his knees drawn up to his chest.

"Lynx?"

He rocks back and forth and occasionally wipes the tears from his eyes. He's probably no more than ten-years-old, and he's wearing our old friendship bracelet, tattered pants, no shirt or shoes.

I start walking his way, and a large cage slams down over Lynx, jarring the floor. I barely keep myself from falling when I gaze up and see the bars of the cages fill in with solid blocks.

"NO!" I scream and run over to the cage. "Lynx! Can you hear me?" Pressing my ear against one of the cool stones, I can barely make out his crying.

"Ugh, now how do I get you out of there?" I ponder as I lean my head back and look up at the monstrosity before me. I close my eyes and let out a frustrated sigh, slapping the cage before me. "FUCK!"

Determined, I wipe my eyes aggressively and turn my attention back to the bricked cage before me. Running my eyes briefly over it, I notice one brick looks lighter than the others, so I step back to get a better look. All the bricks are a dark gray, but there are different symbols on them in black. There's one block with black writing that looks like a lightning bolt, and it has turned white. Out of curiosity, I run my hand over the shape and notice a warm sensation.

Hmm.

The block next to it looks like a chain with interlocking circles, so I touch it and feel the block warm while the black outline turns white as well. The block starts vibrating under my palm, so I quickly step back as I hold my breath and watch the two stones glow brighter and then they suddenly flash red.

"What the f—"

Lynx's scream penetrates through the blocks, and I run back to the wall.

"I'm sorry. God, I'm so sorry, Lynx!" I cry out. "I don't know what to do."

The blocks slowly fade back to their original black, and Lynx's cries die down to sniffles. Feeling defeated, I sit down in the liquid, not caring what I'm sitting in anymore, and drop my head in between my legs.

"I don't know what to do, Lynx," I sigh. I glance up at a block by my foot, noticing a chain symbol, and drop my head once again. "You're trapped in a fucking box behind probably the worst man-made memory matching game ever."

I dig my fingers into my hair and scalp and try to think of what I can do. Memory Game? I jump to my feet and begin studying the different blocks. There are different symbols alright, but some of them repeat, and most of them I recognize from our past together. The question is, how complicated is this and how much pain will I cause Lynx if I fuck up?

Please forgive me if I mess up, Lynx.

I press on the block with the chain symbol and then the corresponding one. It flashes green quickly, but then turns black, causing Lynx to let out a yelp.

"Shit, sorry." I start pacing as I think out loud. "Okay, so obviously I have to find matches, but something about that was wrong. What could have been wrong? The..." My eyes travel over the blocks again and I see one that makes me think of the first time I met Lynx. "Could it be in the wrong order?"

I reach for the block I just saw, but something else catches my eye. It's not a memory that I would have of him, but it would probably be his first memory. There's a block with two Lynxes and a kitten sleeping on the ground, and this time I don't hesitate to press it. It lights up and I walk around the cage looking for the matching block and press that once I see it.

The block glows green and then disappears, revealing a hole that allows me to see Lynx. A sob leaves me as tears of joy gather in my eyes. "Okay, Lynx. I'm coming for you. I know what to do now."

The first five blocks are tricky because they are from a time before Lynx came to me. There are blocks where both of his parents are reading to him; his father in the forest with him; his mom healing a boo-boo; and all of them crying while holding hands. The only consolation about picking the wrong ones is that at least I had them matching and Lynx didn't cry out.

Once I get to the point he showed up on my doorstep, it becomes easier to match up the blocks. Knowing what my mother did to him turns out to be a blessing because they're on some blocks too. The spells she cast, the helicopter penis block from when he first turned into a boy, our first kiss, their talk the night she died, and even when I saw him in Purgatory. It's as if I'm *walking down memory lane with him. Each touch to a stone, the heat seeps into my palms and I feel more alive, more aware of all the stuff Lynx and I have been through. It's amazing what we've gone through, and we haven't fallen apart completely.*

There's only a few blocks left when I reach for the matching one that has a woman that resembles my mother standing at bars and Lynx in a cage. Was this in the dreamscape? When did this take place? How? *My breath hitches as I press my hand against the block.* Does this mean that Ryker really did see my mother... my dead mother? The only person to answer this question is Lynx.

My hand starts trembling as I reach for the block that shows me holding his hand as he died. Pressing it in, it glows and disappears, leaving two more matches. The fall to Hell is next. As I quickly press both blocks that are at eye level, they light up and disappear, and in their place are two turquoise eyes staring back at me.

Standing in front of me isn't the ten-year-old that was crying on the floor, but my... "Lynx!" *I say breathlessly.*

"Hey, Rezzi-bear!" *He smiles.* "We're almost there."

I have the biggest smile on my face when I slam my hands on the tiles showing Lynx on the altar. They flash green and disappear, along with the black bars of the cage.

I don't hesitate as I throw myself at Lynx and completely miss.

My head hits something hard, making my eyes tear up.

"Oww," Lynx says. "You sure know how to make a guy see stars, Rezzi-bear."

Hearing my nickname has me forgetting all about my achy head and watery eyes. I look up and find Lynx still lying down on the altar. Leaning over, I grab his cheeks and give him an upside down spiderman kiss. There's no way I'm passing up this chance to kiss him and tell him how much I love him.

He moans into my mouth as he kisses me back.

'*Ugh. I don't know how in the hell they made this look sexy. It's uncomfortable,*' I complain.

'*I agree, so move your sexy ass over here so I can defile you properly,*' Lynx teases.

I shuffle around the altar, not daring to break our kisses, but in the process, I almost trip and we end up laughing with our lips still touching.

"You are such a klutz," Lynx points out as his fingers cup my jaw.

"Yes, but you love me anyway," I retort, and Lynx pulls back sharply.

His smile melts off his face as he looks deeply into my eyes. "Yes, Rez, I do. I love you with all of my heart and soul. And no matter what obstacles are in front of me, I will always fight to come back to you."

He sits up and moves so I'm wedged between his legs and I grab the sheet to hold it in place while he's still holding my face. "You are my world, my moon, my mate, and I love you. And if we weren't about to be interrupted, I would bend you over this altar and show you." He waggles his eyebrows and laughter bubbles out of me.

"Oh, my God, Lynx," I say, smacking him in the shoulder as the room starts shaking.

"Hey, everything okay in here?" Murmur asks, poking his head in. "Besides trying to renege on your promise?" He raises his eyebrows and gives me a pointed look.

I roll my eyes and step away from the altar to face Murmur. "Yeah, we just finished, so we're all good." I throw him a thumbs up.

"Good, because we have a problem. Everyone's in the parlor," he announces and leaves.

"What kind of problem do we have now? Can't we get a break?" I moan.

I turn to look at Lynx, only to find him hopping off the

altar and looking for his pants. I quickly give him my back as I blurt out my question, ripping the bandaid off as fast as I can.

'Lynx, do you remember seeing Mom during your time in captivity?' I ask, biting into my lip.

'Jillian? No... wait, why?' He asks as I hear him fumbling with his pants. *"What happened?"*

'It's probably nothing, but while I was unlocking your memories, there was one with a woman on it that looked like Mom on one side of the cage you were in. The setting looked like the dreamscape I visited you in.' I ramble on as I play with the hem of my shirt.

'Shit, I'm sorry, Rezzi, but that time is still fuzzy for me."

I exhale the breath I was holding and let my shoulders drop as my last hope dissipates into the air. *Just shake it off. It's just a coincidence.*

'Who dressed me this morning? These are horrible pants,' Lynx whines.

I turn to find him pulling at the crotch of his pants, and it brightens my mood. *Is he kidding?* "You did. You've been dressing yourself since we got here."

"I picked this? How did you let me out of the damn room?" he winks as we start down the hall to the parlor.

"Simple, you're a grown-ass adult and I didn't feel comfortable telling you what to wear when you didn't remember me. Hell, I don't even think you believed me half the time."

"Hmm. You might have a point," he relents, and I give him a smug smile. "But you could have solved that easily."

"Oh really? How?" I inquire.

"Simple. All you had to do was rub a little lower and maybe bathe me with your tongue and I would have purred all night and believed anything you said."

"Ugh, but you wouldn't have appreciated it without your memory."

"Who's telling lies? Let me at them. Any male with a dick appreciates a blow job. Wait. Were you going to use teeth? Claws? Vibrators?" he asks excitedly. "Oh, what about those little vibes that you can wear and your partner controls it? Butt plugs. I heard they have vibrating ones! Awe man, why didn't you try that on me?" He pouts as his mind takes off with more ideas.

Welcome back, Lynx... I missed you.

CHAPTER 42
Gates of Hell

Rez

We walk into the parlor, and I stumble when I see Levi standing by the fireplace.

"What happened? I thought you were leaving?"

"So did we," Ryker says, propping his feet up on the coffee table.

"Got your memory back?" Knox asks Lynx as he comes around the sofa to sit down.

"Yeah. I remember that I don't much like you. The last interaction I had with you before all this, you were playing a mean trick on my Rezzi-bear," Lynx tosses out as he steps past and sits down in one of the love seats. JP walks out of the kitchen and pauses with his eyebrows up and his jaw slackens, and I see I'm not the only one caught off guard.

"Why are you still here?" he asks as he wipes his hands on a dish towel. He tosses it on top of the bar as he sits down next to Zeke.

"That's an excellent question," Lucifer says, walking in from the other hallway with the rest of L.A.M.B. following behind. He locks eyes with everyone around the room before stopping in front of the fireplace and facing the room. "Where's Knots?" he asks the group, but then turns to me. "Did the spell work?"

Before I can answer him, Knots' voice comes from the kitchen door. "Yes, it worked. I just needed to refuel my body." His voice strains as he tries to walk out of the door. His wings get stuck, and he struggles to free himself as something crashes on the other side of the doorway. "And it looks like I might need help in relearning how to handle these things." His shoulders droop for a moment until his wings drag on the floor, and he sighs before standing back up straight, pulling his shoulders back. "What's going on?" he asks as Reaper runs in through his feet with a bone in his mouth, bumping into Knots' legs.

"Fuck all is going on. The portals are closed in the Crucible," Murmur says, going to the bar. I swear, he might as well live behind the damn thing.

"What he means is, as of right now, we can't leave Hell," Lucifer mentions and sits down on his seat.

"Wait. Did you just say we're stuck here?" I ask, walking toward him. My breath gets caught in my throat as my heart slams into my chest. *I'm hearing things, right?*

"Not stuck, just unable to leave at this time," Lucifer drawls, watching as Reaper runs over to the fireplace, lying down with the bone.

"Well, that solves everything. Levi is unable to make his appearance to the King of Berry Pickers, which is probably going to start a war, and Nova will be hit hard, which means we should start calling it SuperNova," Lynx grumbles and looks at JP and Zeke. "You know, because of all the explosions." He looks back at the group as a whole. "But everything will be peachy because our asses are down here roasting in a comfortable temperature of *ball sweat,* all because We. Can't.

Leave. At. This. Time. Fucking. Peachy." The room goes silent for a moment. "Did I miss something?" he asks, and Lucifer's jaw clenches.

"I think you were better with your memory gone," Astaroth comments.

"You only say that because you can't handle the full awesome power that is my intellect, but that's okay. I'll grow on ya. It's a power of mine." Lynx winks.

"I'm sure I will... like a fungus." Astaroth grumbles.

"Can we get back to the fact you guys are still here?" I ask, as I wipe my clammy hands on my pants. Knots doesn't have any protection from this place except my shield, and these oafs are just sitting here like there's no worry in the world.

"Don't get your panties in a twist, Rez." Murmur chuckles. "Want a drink?"

"I'll take a Java Chip Frappuccino with four extra espresso shots, please. I'm coffeeing real bad," Moni insists, rubbing her arms.

"You mean jonesing, Moni," I say with a heavy sigh.

"No, why would I be jonesing?" Her head tilts to the side as a line forms between her eyebrows. "I don't even know a Jones. I know coffee, though."

"Ugh, I give up!" I throw up my hands. "And I'm not wearing panties, Murmur. They went up in flames along with your damn brain cells. Don't you see the fucking issue here? We're on a timetable. Knots' protective charm blew when he got his memories back, and King Elverson is as petty and vindictive as his spawn of Satan." I look over at JP and Moni and grimace. "No offense, guys."

"None taken," they both say.

"We're gonna miss class, which is the whole point of wearing these damn bracelets," I say, waving my arm about. "I don't even know why we're still wearing them since they can't even measure our progress while we're down here," I yell, and try to take off my bracelet. "Fuck! I can't even take the damn thing off now. Is everything malfunctioning around here? Is there no other way home? Are you just gonna sit there and— and watch me like a bump on the log?"

"We are doing something," Lucifer calmly states, and I see red. With a burst of anger, I fling my arms out with a frustrated scream and feel something shoot out of them, directed toward my friends. Suddenly, Bez throws multiple balls of Hellfire out in an arch, and before I can scream as the fireballs head my way, they start to hiss and pop, stopping mid-flight. As the fires die out, multiple pings sound as a few things hit the floor. Levi reaches down and picks up a long silver weapon. As he turns it, I notice it's sharp and pointed on both ends, and it's about four inches long. It looks like a deadly knitting needle on steroids.

He slowly touches the tip, jerking his hand back and hissing in pain where it cuts him. He flinches again when the item pulls from his grip, levitating for a moment. A movement catches my eye as all the other ones in the room rise and start spinning.

"Ahh. Does anyone else get the urge to run out of here screaming?" Moni asks as she grabs Chester's hand and slowly gets up. Her bark turns pale white as the little death needles begin to shake.

In a blink of an eye, they zip across the room but in the wrong direction—mine! In the split second, I have to defeat the oncoming cross-stitch needles from Hell. I throw my hands up and summon all the powers of all my mighty crossing guards around the world. If they can't make these damn things stop, then there's no hope for me.

My palms spasm and twitch as the needles slide into my skin without pain. Once it ends and I realize I haven't been un-alived, I pull myself up straight. With the steady hands of someone going through withdrawals, I turn them over to assess the damage. Nothing. There's no blood, holes, scabs, blemishes, or anything. *Am I seeing things?*

"How did you do that?" Bez demands, standing up and approaching me.

Great, now the gentle mass murderer wants to get up close and personal. I bet it's to stab me.

"I—I didn't do anything," I insist, backing up until I hit the bar.

"Yes, you did. I saw them fly from your palms. It was the Hellfire that made them visible," his voice turns menacing.

Wait. He's saying I did that? I made those things fly out of me? How is that even possible? I just do defensive shit.

"Hey," Lynx says, getting up and heading over with Ryker and Knox on his tail.

"I swear, I don't even know what they are," I yell, shoving my palms out.

"Back off!" JP says, coming around the other way too... I don't know what these guys plan on doing against Bez. I haven't personally trained with him, and I think that fact is scary enough.

"Well, that's our cue to train and find out," Murmur says, as his tail wraps around my waist and he pulls me out of reach of everyone.

"What are you doing?" I yell, yet hold onto his tail for dear life.

"Saving yours and their lives. It's not smart to get in between Bez and what he wants to understand," he says as he flies us down the hall and into the training room, where he drops me on the first mat.

"Then what does that say about you? I mean really, Murmur? This is *not* the time to train. Did you hear anything I said in there?" I argue as I pull myself off the mat with a huff. I push my hair out of the way and glare up to see Murmur smirking at me.

"What?!"

"I heard everything, but I'm more concerned with what flew out of your hands, so let's see how we can control that," he says, placing his hands on his hips. "It looks like it's time to get you angry."

"Pfft. I'm like Bruce Banner—I'm already angry," I growl.

"Well then. This training exercise shouldn't last long." He raises an eyebrow right as I feel his tail wrap around my ankle and pull a foot out from underneath me.

I land with an oomph, and the air whooshes out of me.

"Hmm. I might be wrong," he says, rubbing his chin and leaning over my body. "You're gonna take all night, aren't you?"

"I hate you," I mutter.

"Good. Use that anger."

Grumbling, I roll over, pulling myself up to glare at Murmur.

"What makes you think I can even make whatever happened back there magically happen again?" I ask, pulling my hair up and putting it in a ponytail without a tie. *If you haven't done it before, you're missing out. Or your hair is too short. Believe me, it's possible.* Hopefully it stays, but I have a feeling he's gonna be knocking the thing loose all day.

"Well, Bez was right. Whatever those were, they came from you. The question is, why and how?" he says, circling me. I turn, keeping him in my sights. "You still don't know what you are, right?"

"Yeah. I'm an unknown who can pull up a defensive shield and apparently has invisible anger daggers," I mumble.

"Your disdain is an art form itself. You know that?"

"Is that really necessary for this?" I ask.

"No, just poking the bear to see how angry you really are," he states, and his tail whips out, but I see it in time to jump over it. "Well, at least you're paying attention. So, let's focus

415

on what we do know. You're mated to the Four Horsemen at least... Did anything happen? Did you get a vision? Did the guys? Something?"

I glance over to the door, wondering if I can make a break for it, but Murmur pops up in my way.

"Ah ha! You do know something!" he yells in excitement.

"Of course, I know something, but it's personal," I remark.

"Oh, Rez. There's nothing that is considered personal between you and your trainer," he sighs and shakes his head at me.

"Oh, come on, Murmur. I haven't even told the guys this or even Lynx, and he knows everything," I point out.

"Oh, this is gonna be good then," Murmur says, rubbing his hands together. "Tell me, tell me. I need more."

I laugh and shake my head at the Demon before me, who looks like he's about to get up to no good. "You are worse than Ryker. You know that?" I tell him.

Murmur throws his head back and laughs. "Ha. Of course, I am. Ryker and I have spent years together. Who do you think taught him the *art* of sharing information?" he challenges.

"Sharing information?" I ask, rubbing my head. "I don't think that's considered sharing information. Don't you mean gossiping?"

Murmur's tail slams into his chest along with his hand as his jaw drops with a gasp. "Oh, no no no no. Rez, there are differences between gossiping and sharing information." Murmur scoffs as he stops circling me.

I stop in my tracks and place my hands on my hips. "Oh, I can't wait to hear this," I say sarcastically.

Murmur clears his throat. "There are two types of gossiping. The first one is when you find enjoyment in passing on high-quality knowledge that you've gathered to those less deserving." My jaw drops as I stare at him.

What?

"No. How in the wor—"

"The second type of gossiping is when you pass on low-quality information, such as rumors or lies, to ruin someone's reputation. Never deal with those types, they darken the soul and you end up down in level five, hating your afterlife," he says, wagging his finger in my face. "But sharing information? Mwauh"—he does a chef's kiss—"It's the art of perfection," he says breathlessly and places his hands on my shoulder before looking off into the distance. His eyes go glassy, as if he's actually seeing what he's talking about.

"It's when you're on that tightrope and you have to find that perfect balance before falling to your death." He looks back at me, his eyes shining with excitement. "Sharing info, Rez, is when you seek to increase your knowledge," he says passionately. "It's when that dire need hits you to find answers and solve that puzzle, and you can only do it with someone else's information."

I gently grab his hands and remove them from my shoulders, taking a step back. "You're really crazy, aren't you?"

His eyes flash black before they return green, and he gives me a salacious smile. "And they say I'm the sane one. So, come on... Share with teacher."

"Fine, but you do know if you tell the rest of L.A.M.B., I'll consider it gossiping, so it stays between us," I counter, and Murmur sucks on his teeth as he raises a finger up.

"You are learning!" He holds out his hand. "Deal."

I shake his hand and finally tell someone else about the two visions I had when I first went through the portal for school and when Lilith's unbinding spell went to hell, so to speak. It still gives me goosebumps to think about as I explain how I saw the Four Horsemen, and how, before they could run me over, I heard them whispering. They said I had come and I was Redemption, and then I came to in Zeke's lap. I don't leave out anything, remembering from before I woke up from my small coma after the session with Lilith, and again when Zeke got his tattoo. I tell him about Death's words, *"You will see me. You will see us, always. You will be our redemption."*

Levi's tattoo came with the words, *"You will balance all with heart and soul."*

Murmur nods and says "Famine" before motioning me to continue.

So I explain about Ryker's tattoo and how the words *"The veil of deceit of thy enemies shall be revealed"* came to me when he got his. I mention how that power worked when I stepped out of the glen and there was an ambush.

It's almost humorous to see his eyes go wide as I tell the story. Then I reveal Knox's tattoo but refuse to tell him its location when he pushes for information. "He will kill me," I emphasize.

"No, he won't; you're his mate," Murmur counters, waving away my concern.

"You're right. He will kill *you* for knowing," I tease. "Anyway, those words were, '*Rage shall be thy weapon as your hands wield it so,*'" I say and shrug.

"Eureka!" Murmur says, unexpectedly standing up and doing a little dance. He reaches down and grabs my hand, pulling me up.

"What?" I say, trying to catch my balance.

"It's War that you're channeling," Murmur says. "You said it right in the words. Rage. What you created back there was rage, and it manifested into..."

"Invisible icicles?" I guess.

"Well, that's what we're about to find out. You're in for a long night," Murmur says with a smile and walks over to where the dummies are.

"Hey, but what about the gate? And Knots? And finding a way out of here?" I ask, trailing behind him.

"That's what the others are for. You... my protégé, I get to train, so train you I shall," he says, moving a dummy off to the side. "Now, get angry and hit that with your raging fingers of fury," he smirks.

"Did I tell you that I hate you yet?" I glance at him with an annoyed look.

"Oh, chickadee, you haven't started to hate me yet." He gives me the cheesiest smile ever.

I wish I had this power down pat because I would love to punch him in his pretty mouth.

CHAPTER 43

I Spy With my Little Eye...

Lynx

Murmur flies off with my Rezzi-bear down the hall as Bez spins around and heads back to his seat with his fists clenched. "She's a danger to everyone," Bez growls. My chest rattles out a warning, as does Knox, as we both take his words for what they are: a threat. We might have stopped our approach, but that doesn't mean the Vengeance Demon isn't a threat to my mate. Knox's eyes shift in my direction, and I find myself warming to the asshole.

Yes, he played a trick on my Rezzi, but the fact he's as protective over her as I am earns him some points in my book. I nod in solidarity, and we both focus back on Bez.

"She only lacks training, which is where we come in," Lucifer says. He turns his attention to us. "No need to get upset, gentlemen." Moni bristles at the wording, and Lucifer smiles as Knox and I share another glance before taking our seats. "And, princess. Murmur is great at working through problems; he'll get to the bottom of this."

Even though everyone is seated, the tension in the room remains palpable, and I have the urge to just to run out and check on Rez to make sure she's okay. Or just to escape this horrid group right now. I feel like I've been out of the loop for decades. Rez has made up with everyone that I last knew did her wrong, and she has other mates? How am I supposed to take that? I hear the faint click clack of heels down the hall and immediately know that Lilith is on her way in, and I swing my gaze in her direction.

"Get to the bottom of what?" Lilith asks, as she walks into the room with Trometh and another Demon by her side. Trometh carries a box about half his size. She rolls her pearls in between her fingers, but I notice her smile doesn't reach her eyes.

"Rez apparently has a new power that Murmur is going to help her work out," Astaroth says with a bored tone.

"Hmm," she says, taking her seat.

Trometh and the other Demon move to the back of the room and start to polish and clean the bookshelves. Trometh moves items around to make room for the items from the box. *Looks like busy work to me. Hardly work for a glorified assistant for a few centuries.*

"What did you find out?" Lucifer asks Lilith, bringing my attention back to the Demons before me.

Lilith sighs and purses her lips before glancing around the room, settling on Lucifer. "That the portals are down. I talked to Matthew and explained that we can't make it to the ceremony. He's going to try to smooth over what he can with Elverson."

"Well, at least there's some good news with the portal being down," Ryker says.

"That is?" JP asks, looking unconvinced.

"Having the portal closed can be the excuse for Levi not being at the ceremony. It's a temporary solution, but it buys us time until the portals open. When will that happen?" Ryker asks, threading his fingers behind his head.

"That was another reason I reached out to your fathers. Carl, or Dr. Steinbeck, for some of you, is as old as dirt and loves to read as you might imagine. I asked him if he's ever come across anything in his studies as to why the portals might be closed. I, for one, can't remember a time, but I admit, I don't always pay attention to the happenings around here." Lilith shrugs, not looking at all apologetic.

"With us bouncing between Earth and Hell, we haven't been as vigilant, and that's on us," Lucifer admits.

"The point is, he doesn't remember coming across anything explaining why the portals might be closed," she admits, and I see JP and Zeke slump against the sofa. "He did recount reading something about a master switch to unlock the portals."

"Did he say where he read it?" Chester asks, completely intrigued if the way his eyes perk up is any indication.

"No, only that he read it in one of my books," she tells us.

"Typical," Ryker sighs with an eye roll.

"Wait, didn't we move your books here?" Astaroth says, turning toward Lilith. "When you decided to spend more time in Purgatory, we brought your books here. Yes!"

"Oh! I'll help look then!" Moni says, and flies over to the bookcase by the bar and starts browsing the shelves.

Lilith's laughter rings through the room eerily until Moni turns and frowns at her. "What?"

"Oh, sweetie. They would be in the library. Not here. Come, I'll show you." We all get up and follow her out of the room. Reaper darts in front of the group and takes off, spotting another rodent... nope. That's a servant darting into another room. Well, he might become a chew toy, depending on how Reaper feels. I kinda wish he would use Trometh as a squeaky toy. Speaking of the little Demon; before I step out of the room, I look over my shoulder and only see the random Demon still working, but no... one-eyed, one-horned flying purple people eater. That definitely stinks to me. *And if you're old enough to know what that is, did you sing it?*

"Does it feel like the Fates are bending us over and jamming toys up our asses?" I ask no one in particular when I catch up.

"You're getting toys? Shit, I think I'm getting probed by a sword with no lube," Knots says.

"Oh! Chester!" Moni squeals.

Chester's face turns a bright red as he clinches his butt cheeks and covers his ass, "NO!" He turns so he's walking backward and looking at Moni.

I burst into laughter, and a few of the guys join me.

"Aww, what's the matter? Not into adventures?" Knox teases.

"You try to take a tail up the ass and then come talk to me," Chester fires back.

Hmm. My curiosity is peaked.

"How was it?" I ask with a straight face.

"Are you serious?" Chester's eyes widen, and I'm kinda scared they're going to fall out of his head.

"Deadly. It's not like Rez has one, so you're the only one for me to ask about getting a tail up the ass. Come on, spill. I need the deets," I say, snapping my fingers. *The crazy loon is just staring at me like I'm the crazy one.* "Should I get a potion for Rez to drink to grow one?" I turn my attention to Lilith ahead of us and raise my voice. "Is that possible? Can she get a temporary tail?"

"Lynx, you are such a delight. Anything can be whipped up, but what makes you think she would use it on you?" Lilith cackles with mirth when I hiss at her.

The she-devil.

I like Chester; he seems like a cool guy. Wish I would have been around to know how he came about, but I have to trust that he's treating Moni right. What am I saying? I'm sure Rez would put him in his place if he didn't. I'm really going to have to get him alone and get the tail story out of him, one way or another.

I observe the people around me, and I wonder what else I missed while my memories took a hiatus. Besides Rez adding to her harem, did I miss anything else? My time with the Rebels seems fuzzy at best. A chill runs down my spine as a few moments flash in my mind of some of the torture I went through. The knife, rope, the burns. I shake my head to dislodge the memory and find us in front of engraved double doors.

We walk into a room that I've never been into before, and all hope fades from my existence. "Are you kidding me? You have more books than the Beast that had hair everywhere movie. With the rose, singing utensils, and bookshelves," I state, looking up and up along the wall to my right. There's a bookshelf immediately to my left that's blocking the rest of the room, but I'm sure it's huge as the rest of the group filters around it.

"Oh! Are you talking about that one movie where she attacks people with a round metal bubble blower thing? She's marvelous! I was trying to find that weapon in the training room, but they didn't have it," Moni asks as she spins around and looks around the room.

"Moni, do you mean *Tangled*?" JP asks. His hands are on his hips as he cocks his head to the side and stares at her.

"No! She had really long beautiful blonde hair until the end when it was cut and it turned brown, but it was never tangled, JP," she scoffs and then giggles. "Get your cartoons right, sheesh."

As everyone continues to follow Lilith, I linger behind.

"Are you sure they are yours? I'm surprised they've lasted this long," Bez growls to Lucifer, and the latter smiles.

"They are definitely mine, and one thing's for sure, Bez, I missed out on a wonderful childhood. Could you imagine all the Hell they would have raised down here?" he chuckles.

"That's what I'm afraid of," Bez mumbles.

"Aww. Here we are. This is the Lilith section," Astaroth says, stopping in front of an alcove that's eight bookcases wide and two tall. *Well, that ain't too bad.*

Astaroth reaches for a book and pulls on it, releasing an audible click. He smirks before pushing the bookcase in and slipping through the doorway.

I take it back; this is Rez's wet dream and my worst nightmare.

The floor is set up with little nooks and places to lie down and read. Soft pillows decorate every surface except for the one table in the middle with a couple of plush chairs. Looking up, the book stacks continue up to the same height as the ones in the normal library outside of this hideaway. Fairy lights twinkle, giving off a soft magical glow. If it wasn't for all the books ruining the atmosphere, this would be a great place to get hot and sweaty with my woman.

If I brought her here, she would be more interested in the books than me, though. Don't judge me; it's happened before. It wasn't even her girl porn books that I was shut down by, some kind of magical world that she got lost in, and I got nothing. *Now that I think about it, I think Jillian would have skinned me alive if I would have done anything with Rez then.*

My jaw drops as the thought of Jillian hits me. When Jillian was murdered, we went to live with her grandparents, but now that I think about it, we never brought up how she died. Why didn't we ever talk about her to Rezzi's grandmother? Isn't that odd? Not once did we mention it to them, or ask her to look into Jillian's death.

'*Rezzi, I need to ask you something!*" I yell, and I hear her yelp in surprise.

'*Can it wait? I almost just got skewered by Murmur. I promise you'll have all my attention tonight,*' she calls back.

'*Ugh. Yeah. I was just wondering why we didn't ask Grams or Pops about your mother's murder. Isn't that weird?*' I ask, not at all waiting as she wanted.

'*Huh. Yeah, it is. I guess that's something we'll have to ask them when we get back to Earth. Dammit. I gotta go. This blue-balled Demon is yelling at me to get my head in the game,*' she tells me.

'*His balls? Now, why does he get to show you his balls and you always yelled at me when I tried?*' I whine.

'*It's not his ballsack, Lynx... He's throwing balls at me. Think of dodgeball, but with blue balls that fucking hurt! Fuck! I gotta go!*' I feel her push against the link with urgency, and I finally get the point.

Tuning back into my surroundings, I listen to the last part of Lilith explaining where she believes the book might be, and I try not to die of boredom.

"So let me guess, we're all supposed to spend all our waking moments reading through these books, trying to find something about portals and not fall asleep," I ask with a yawn.

Lucifer smiles in my direction. "Not exactly. So you don't die of boredom, we'll be dividing your time between reading and training."

"I think I got my shifting down, Hoss. No need for training," I wink at the big scary Pride Demon.

Bez throws back his head and lets out a hefty laugh, making me and everyone besides Lucifer and Lilith jump. *I think I just peed a little.* Forget his scary posture, glare, or his constant playing with fire. Have the fucker laugh, and you too will immediately want to run out the door.

"Not that type of training. Now, you'll be training with me and Lucifer." Bez smiles, and my asshole puckers as I try to shift away.

"Bez and I will join in with training while all of us rotate through and search the books. Since you are here for an extended stay, it's best to be trained up. Hell isn't the most hospitable place, as I'm sure you've noticed. If you're trained properly, we won't have to watch out for you. We might as well start searching while lunch is being prepared," Lucifer says before walking down an aisle and grabbing a book off the shelf. Everyone follows his lead, but I grab Levi's attention.

"Hey, Levi. Can I have a minute?" I ask, trying to taper down my nerves. I'm a little embarrassed to ask, but he's the only one I know that can help me.

"Sure. What can I help you with, Lynx?"

"Um. I was wondering if you happen to have any BC potion I could use? You know," I fumble and run my fingers through my hair. *Fuck, why is this so hard for me?* I've dreamed about this chance for years and never thought it would happen. I admit, I'm nervous, and a part of me is scared that Rez won't want to cement our bond since we are such good friends. *Ugh!*

Levi smiles and saves me from further embarrassment. "Say no more. I have a fresh batch, and I have a few extra vials in my room. Feel free to take one. It's in the right night stand," he says and heads back toward the Parlor where everyone else is going, but I have a better idea.

Now that I have my memory back and feel as if the bindings that were once holding my magic are gone, I want to do what I'm good at. Question is, what's the best version to get around here as. Just as I think it, Reaper comes running down the hallway chasing a rodent.

Perfect! But first, I need to take my birth control meds.

. . . . .

I don't know how in the world this hellhound functions with this weapon of mass destruction. I swear, it has a mind of its own. As a Storm Shifter, I'm blessed with not only being able to shift into whatever animal I want, but I'm also able to take on their abilities. Unfortunately, that means taking on Reaper's damn uncooperative tail. You know those old books that were written back in the late 1990s, the *Animorphs*? I swear, Katherine and her hubby had met a damn Storm Shifter and decided to write about them. They just made them aliens, painted them blue, and *voilà*—animorphs. Granted, we're rare, but it doesn't mean we are extinct.

I was going to snoop around the mansion and maybe delve into Lucifer's secrets, but another scent drew my attention. Trometh. My gut hasn't failed me yet, and it's telling me he's a rat. I decide to follow his scent and see what he's really up to. Imagine my surprise that it leads outside. It's pretty easy to slip out of Lucifer's mansion, but it's a different story to leave without tripping his ward. After rounding around the premises, I do find a weakened point in the barrier to slip through and head down the road, picking up Trometh's scent once again and finding the path that leads to this mysterious Crucible. *I need to tell L.A.M.B. about that spot I squeezed through. It looks like someone has been picking at it for some time. With Trometh's stench being strong there, I can only guess who's been doing it, but I'll wait until I come back.*

As I approach the Crucible, I lose Trometh's scent, noticing a crowd of Demons, and I figure there's no way I won't be spotted, so I shift into my ferret form and weave my way into the building between their feet, listening to their chatter.

"I heard Asmodeus has more power than L.A.M.B."

"Did you see it? L.A.M.B. delivered his children's heads on pikes."

"Ugh. How am I supposed to get to Nova now?"

"What kind of explanation is *go home*?"

It seems not everyone is happy with their fearless leaders. Inside the building is dead, besides the guards doing their sweeps, and to keep from being spotted, I stay to the shadowy edges. There's a larger area in the middle with guards surrounding the entrance, and I bet that's where the portals actually are.

Damn!

Maybe there's an area in the back I might be able to squeeze through to look around. As I hop around the outside of the room, I see a guard walking by, doing a sweep, so I enter one of the empty stalls as quickly and quietly as possible.

"Shh. He's coming," a voice whispers, but I don't see anyone.

Am I hearing shit now?

There's a heavy tarp separating the back from the front, and I catch the slightest movement, indicating someone is back there. Slipping through on the farthest side, I let my eyes adjust as I restrain myself from attacking the fuckers in front of me.

Crouching down in the darkened corner between a few boxes are Angel and Trometh. Or too much meth if you ask me. The harpy seems to tower over L.A.M.B.'s cowering errand Demon.

"Well?" she hisses. "Did you find it? Is there any other way out of here we need to block L.A.M.B. from?"

"No. But things have become a little more dangerous for me. They've already 'cleaned house' once, and I'm lucky to still be alive. They're in the library searching for another way, and you're asking me to risk my life once again, so I think we need to reassess my contract. You know, sweeten the deal?" he states, looking smug.

"What do you mean by 'sweeten the deal?'" she hisses. "What more could you possibly want?"

"Nut butter," Trometh says, smiling shyly. *Uh... Does he mean what I think he means?*

"Nut butter?" Angel spits out in disgusted shock.

"Not just any kind. I want that fancy type. The chocolate nut butter type," he says, his eyes light up with excitement.

"You've got to be kidding me."

"Do you know how hard that is to find on the black market? I would have sold off my niece if the guy would have taken her for the half jar he had last time." Trometh starts drooling.

I thought I had it bad for spying at times, but this guy... He takes it to a new level!

"Ugh," Angel flips her hair over her shoulder, and I internally laugh, knowing Rez would find it funny. Angel's hair gets tangled up in the boxes and the material behind her, and it takes her a few moments to pull her hair free. Trometh does a good job pursing his lips together as he watches her struggle. Once she's free, she throws a glare at the small Demon.

"Fine. But it will take me some time; it's not like I have free range to get to Earth and get your stuff personally. Nutella, of all things. Pfft." Angel shakes her head as Trometh nods his head. "And just so you know," she smiles wickedly. "Father *won't* be happy," she spits out and leaves out of the side of the stand after making sure it's clear.

"Ungrateful brat," Trometh utters under his breath before he straightens his shirt and pulls back his shoulders. He turns and starts walking toward me as I slide out from the shadows.

"Eek!" Trometh shrieks like a girl before he sighs and rolls his eyes. With a chuckle, he lifts his foot as if he's going to try to squish me. "Just another ugly rat species, too dumb to know when to die out," he says with disgust.

I quickly shift back to my human form, where I tower over the Demon and glare down at him. "I'm not the rat, but you are," I say with a smirk before I shift once more and lunge.

I hope he runs. I do love a chase.

CHAPTER 44
Archimedes, the Stuffed Chicken

Rez

I drag myself down the hall to the busy dining room. Everyone is sitting around the table and already busy talking and grabbing food. I throw myself into my normal chair as Knots sets a plate full of food before me.

"Here you go. It looks like you need it." He smiles and gives me a kiss on the forehead, regardless of my sweat.

"You might have to feed me," I mumble. Murmur seriously ran me through the wringer, but I was able to reproduce my sharp needles once, but that was because he belittled a few of my men. I couldn't direct them to any of the dummies that he wanted, though. My entire body aches, and I just want a shower and a nap.

"I'll feed you." Ryker winks across the table from me.

"I don't have the energy, but I could feed you. Do you have a face-sitting fetish? Because this would be the time to do it. There would be no problem with this woman hovering over your face. You would suffocate while I slept."

Zeke spits out his drink all over the table while JP perks up and looks over at me. "Really?"

"Which part?" I ask as my head rolls across the back of the chair, cracking my neck.

"Suffocating me?" JP asks.

"With the way I'm feeling? Yes," I groan.

"Ah, I see we've gotten to the porno portion of the evening. You kids keep us quite entertained," Lucifer speaks up at the end of the table.

I roll my eyes, which takes a great amount of effort, and mumble, "That's just because you're not getting laid."

"I heard that," he says.

"You were supposed to," I sing-song, and notice one person is missing. "Has anyone seen Lynx?" I ask no one in particular.

"No, now that you mention it, I haven't seen him since we checked out the library," Moni informs me.

"Library?" I ask, perking up in my seat. *There's a library here?*

"Yeah! While you were being tortured, we were too!" Moni says cheerfully. I raise an eyebrow in question, and it's Chester who answers.

"We're looking to see if there's another way out of Hell, or anything about the portals."

A growl rings out from the hall as Lynx comes trotting in with Trometh, who's crying and hanging from his mouth. By the looks of the blood dripping onto the floor, I'm sure Lynx isn't holding him by just his clothes.

"What the fuck?" Astaroth yells, jumping up from his chair.

"I knew he was crazy, but to piss off the Wrath Demon? Fuuuuck!" Ryker hisses. "Lynx must have bigger balls than any creature I know"

"Don't tell him that. It will all go to his head," I hiss out.

"Nope, it's gonna go to his balls, where it should... apparently," Ryker states.

"Astaroth, no need to murder anyone," Lilith purrs and motions for him to sit down. "Lynx, why don't you release Trometh so we can get to the bottom of this."

'The fuck I will,' Lynx replies with a scoff. Unfortunately, I'm the only one that can hear him, and I realize it too late as everyone stares at him, waiting.

"Oh, um... He doesn't feel comfortable letting him loose, yet," I relay and quickly glance between Lynx and Lucifer, when the latter's brow quirks and the rest of L.A.M.B. shifts. "I'll find out why."

"That would be best," Lucifer says in a dead voice as fire dances in his eyes.

I clear my throat as I bring my attention to Lynx. *'Want to tell me why we aren't releasing the Archimedes of Arthur and Merlin's group? I'd rather leave Hell in one piece.'*

'Pfft. Archimedes is nothing but a stuffed chicken, or in this case, a big rat. I found him talking to Angel in the Crucible about their contract, and they were negotiating when I came upon them,' he says smugly, and all color drains from my face.

I do what any sane person does in this situation. I slowly start laughing as I stand from my chair and start backing up from the table and subtly shoo Lynx back from the room. *Yep, we're all gonna die. I saw what happened when L.A.M.B. thought they had a rat in their service and had to clean their house. What would they do when we presented the big cheese right here at the dinner table?*

I sure as Hell don't want to know. The sound of a chair scraping on the floor brings my attention to JP's shocked look as he looks at Lynx and back to me.

Fuck! He read my mind!

"Um. Just out of curiosity. How are... um... traitors... handled in Hell?"

Bez seems to sit straighter in his chair at my words.

Astaroth's tail whips out in irritation, releasing a thunderous boom. Murmur just squints in our direction, and Lucifer, he becomes as still as a statue. He doesn't move, except for the fire flaming in his eyes.

"You can't kill the messenger, and Lynx is very good at his job," I go on, standing before Lynx, protecting him from L.A.M.B. I trust Lynx with my life, but it doesn't mean that they will. They've known Trometh longer, so why would they have any reason to believe my friend and mate?

"Release him, Lynx," Lucifer orders.

'Rez! I can't. He will run. I had to chase him; he has a device on him, and if I let go, I'm sure he'll disappear! Here, come see. It's why he's bleeding. It's embedded in his shoulder. I tackled him when he tried to use it, and biting down and dragging him here like this was the only way to stop him."

I look back at the scary murderers at the end of the table before I squat down and look up into Lynx's mouth. When he tilts his head, it makes Trometh cry out. He tilts enough for me to see an edge of silver metal poking out of the skin where the blood is slowly dribbling down Trometh's arm.

'I see it, Lynx.'

"Murmur, I need your help," I plead. The blue Demon arches a brow while he cocks his head in my direction. "Trometh has a device implanted in his shoulder that he was trying to use to escape." Murmur heads over once he hears that. "But if Lynx lets go, he'll be able to use it."

Murmur crouches down, and Lynx repeats the process, showing him Trometh's shoulder. Before Lynx can blink, Murmur's tail whips out faster than my eyes can keep up with, and Trometh is screaming bloody murder while Murmur's tail is holding a silver dollar-sized coin covered in blood.

"An Aeroportal?" he says, inspecting the coin. He throws the coin through the air for Bez to catch it as his tail wraps around Trometh's neck and lifts him from Lynx's mouth to his eye level. "Where was this to take you?" Murmur calmly asks the sputtering Demon.

"My guess is Asmodeous," Lynx says, popping up in his human form. He decided just to shift into low-riding jeans and no shirt. His tanned abs stretch as he uses me as a wall and leans on me. "But I think he had a split-second scare after Angel said her father would be pissed that he was trying to 'sweeten the deal,' so who knows." He shrugs his shoulders and looks around the table. "Damn, I'm starving. Whatcha got to eat?" he says as he plops down in the empty seat across from me and starts serving up food.

"Did he just bring a traitor into our midst and then sit down to eat like it was nothing?" Chester asks Moni. She just looks at Lynx with wide eyes, like she's never seen him before. In her defense, she hasn't seen this side of him before.

"Oh, yeah, I forgot. I'll be right back. I gotta wash my hands. BRB," Lynx says, getting up. "And before I forget, I think he snuck out through your ward. There's an area that's weakened, and it looks like someone has been picking at it over some time," he calls back before running off to the kitchen.

Lucifer slowly walks to the sniveling Demon curled up on the floor, clicking his tongue before speaking. "Trometh. You, out of all people, should understand how I loathe wasting my time. So, let's get started. I have training in thirty minutes. Let's see what we can get done in that time," he says, and smiles as he snaps his fingers, sending the Demon, Lilith, himself, and the rest of L.A.M.B. away. Probably to his torture room.

. . . . .

Lunch is pretty short, and soon enough, I'm grumbling just like everyone else when I head to the training room. Although this time, the sight is something to behold. Bez and

Lucifer are wearing shorts while they spar in the middle, and they look like yin and yang on a dessert platter for dear old me.

Bez's darker skin pops against his black wings and white shorts as his muscles flex while he sends fireballs flying toward Lucifer. The Devil himself dodges and rolls closer to Bez, springing up to throw jabs at him. His black shorts hang dangerously low on his hips, and I bite my lip as I stifle a moan.

"You really need to get that under control," Ryker teases me as he walks by and smacks my ass.

"I can't help it if they look yummy," I state.

"Ugh," Moni says in disgust. "I can handle my brother, but that's my *dad.*" Her eyes go wide as she shakes her head and moves off with Chester.

"I just like to window shop, Moni," I yell. "I have enough dicks. I have a carousel I can ride already. I don't need any more rides," I say, throwing my arms up. Rolling my eyes, I turn to find my guys in different states of amusement. JP and Zeke laugh together, holding each other up. Knots smirks at me while Levi's eyes are smiling at me. Lynx, the little ass, rolls on the mat, holding his belly. Ryker's eyebrows raise as if to ask "really?" and that's when I hear a throat clear.

"If you're done drooling over your so-called *pony rides*, we might be able to begin some training," Lucifer states with a wickedly evil smile.

"Fuck me," I groan.

"Which ride are you calling for?" Lynx asks between his laughter as he sits up on a mat. Ignoring him, we all start stretching as we watch Murmur, Bez, and surprisingly, Lilith stroll in wearing workout clothes.

"Your mom is training?" I lean over and ask Levi.

"Apparently so." He nods.

"Okay, that's enough stretching; let's get started," Astaroth yells and starts to pair us up. He goes down the list and gives us partners for this session, telling us we will be rotating through our five trainers. Moni and Chester are an obvious pair since they are mates. She practically glows brighter than the sun when she flies over to Lilith for their first training session with her.

Ryker is paired with Levi, and Murmur only gives the pair a haughty smile as Ryker gives him a head nod in greeting. I really wish I was a spectator instead of the one getting my ass handed to me. JP and Zeke get sent over to Astaroth, and a part of me mourns not getting picked to work with the growly Demon first. The Wrath Demon has kinda grown on me, plus even though he's firm in his training, his temperament meshes will with mine. Lucifer beckons Knots and Knox over, which leaves me and Lynx. I can't help but assess how Knots looks without his Demstone. He still looks healthy, but that doesn't mean he will stay that way for long. We turn to look and see Bez leaning against the wall, smiling our way.

'Aww, fuck. Rez, promise me you'll take good care of my hide when I'm dead and skinned?' Lynx groans as we slowly walk over to the gentle mass murderer.

'What makes you think I'll be alive long enough to wear you?' I ask as we walk up to Bez.

Bez's dark eyes scan over us before he closes them and takes in a deep breath, sighing with a slight smile. "I love the smell of fresh meat." His deep baritone rings out. Lynx swallows audibly and looks over at me.

"Let's work on your fire ability," Bez says, and pushes off the wall.

"We don't have any," I squeak, backing up.

"You will when I get done with you," Bez promises with a sinful smile.

438

CHAPTER 45
Full of Gadgets

Lynx

Bez was right. By the time he's done with Rezzi-bear and me, we have some kick-ass fire abilities. The fucking ability to shield ourselves or manipulate its direction, that shit. By the way, if you're not concentrating, it's the fastest way of getting rid of your hair. *I wouldn't recommend it.* I don't think I'll ever get hair to grow back on my left calf. We might not be able to conjure Hellfire, but with Bez's help, we are able to now redirect the fire to work for us and not against us.

Astaroth presented all of us with new weapons when it was our turn to work with him. Since I spent all my time learning how to shift, I was presented with two black Demon Push Daggers that pop out of wrist guards that I can wear. *Talk about fancy.* They're spelled so if I'm wearing them when I shift, I'll be able to still use them. Can you imagine it? *A deadly fishy popping up out of the water. Ka-cha! Who's the sushi now!?*

Astaroth handed Rez two silver handles a little longer than her palms, and she about threw them back at him when the blades popped out and almost cut her. Apparently, he made her glaives that could retract, and depending on her mood, they present certain colors and have abilities. *What abilities? Fuck all we know so far.* He didn't elaborate, and I guess we'll just have to find out at our next training session. All we did during our time was learn how to mentally connect to our weapons—*yeah, I know how weird that sounds*—and how to activate them to open and close.

Murmur did a round of making sure we each had some kind of defense, and if we couldn't make our own defense like my Rezzi-bear, he equipped us with it. He ran me through a few shifts to prove that I could protect myself from ice, wind, heat, rocks, and his fucking Hokey Pokey brain thing. To be honest, I thought I was going to fail that one, but ever since I got my memory back, things seem to be coming easier to me. My shifts are seamless, I am faster and more agile, and to top it off, I'm with Rez once again. My mental shield is flawless when I actually want it to work, but mostly, I want it down so I feel the connection to Rez.

Our time with Lucifer was a trip! I mean an acid trip. Ever play two truths and a lie with the Devil? Well, I have. Learning how to spot half-truths and lies was like Lucifer giving us a green light to see into his *soul*. How many people can say they learned how to spot that shit from The Deceiver himself? I think if I died today, I would be a happy man. Not because I would be separated from Rez, just the opposite. I'm confident enough that I could spot half-truths and finagle my way back to her side with this kind of knowledge.

Here's a tip, watch the direction of their eyes. Yes, it's true people can maintain eye contact with you while they lie; Lucifer is a pro at it. But subconsciously, most of them will try to cover up a lie. Like covering their eyes or mouth while lying or their eyes will dart. My favorite was watching how he either embellished or kept things too short.

As we walk over to Lilith, she holds up two small black backpacks. She has a table set up behind her with all sorts of vials and herbs and even a few binders. *What are we about to do? Go to class?*

"Look what I have for you, just in case you can't access your pocket dimensions," she says with a smile.

"What is it?" I ask.

"I'm so glad you asked, Lynx. It's a mini pack I've created that magically attaches to you and will shrink or change along with your forms. Plus, it's nearly indestructible. Pretty stylish, huh?" she asks, and hands the packs over to me and Rez.

It's soft leather, and I open it up and see how small it is. "No offense, but how in the Hell am I supposed to fit anything in it?" I ask, peering into the side pocket.

"Are you sure you're a Supe?" Lilith asks, cocking her head to the side as she regards me. "The bag is spelled to hold all sorts of things. Have you ever seen Mary Poppins? Think of her bag... It's endless. Her bag was crafted to mimic a pocket dimension."

"This is beautiful, but what's a pocket dimension?" Rez asks, closing up her pack and setting it on the floor.

"Oh! I'm sorry. I thought you knew what that was. A pocket dimension is a small space where you can access and store items, like weapons, and survival items—"

"Like coffee!" Moni yells and pulls out a coffee just to demonstrate. She's standing next to Chester, where she should be training but obviously is listening in on us.

"Exactly. That's what Knots and Moni use all the time," Lilith explains.

Rez shoots Moni a glare across the room and holds up a finger to Lilith before she takes off running. She tackles Moni at Murmur's station and runs her fingers up and down the sides of Moni, tickling her.

"Magic? Really? You really couldn't tell me that you had a

S.I.N. box that you kept coffee in? Ugh, you're the worst," she says with laughter, getting up when Moni yells "uncle."

"I didn't know what it was called. So don't get mad at me, bestie. You know I would tell you everything! You're my bosom bumpkin buddy. What's a S.I.N. box, anyway? Is that what it's really called? Lilith didn't go over that part with us. Instead, I got a sack that I'm gonna use to collect herbs and a bunch of smelly spells," she says as fast as possible.

'I swear, we need our own class to learn Moni. Do you think we could get credit for that?' I ask, catching Rez's lip twitch before she answers Moni.

"Lilith said it was a pocket dimension, but I'd rather call it a S.I.N. box. Survival Items Needed. Like your coffee," Rez explains.

"Or extra underwear for you when you're not home!" Moni fires back, and I immediately choke on my tongue.

No, she didn't.

"Moni!" Rez shrieks as red coats her cheeks and she stares at her best girlfriend. No one can replace me as the best friend. The room goes silent as everyone turns toward the girls.

"What? Don't you need extra underwear? You're always running out," she points out. "I thought humans did that wash and rewear thing, or turn them inside out if you can't wash and don't have a closet available, but that sounds gross to me."

Rez leans in and tries to keep her voice down, but it's no use. We all have superior hearing. "I only run out because the guys keep ripping them off of me."

"Ooh!" Moni says with understanding. "Well, that's easy to solve. Just go without."

Rez lets out a groan as her head falls back and her shoulder slump. I let out a whistle, and Ryker and Zeke join me in my cat calling. Knox lets out a few growls, and Rez's cheeks turn pink. "I just can't with you," she says as she walks back to

Lilith and me. Knots and Levi chuckle as they turn back to their instructors, who seem to be entertained as well.

"She does have a good point," Lilith says once Rez rejoins us. "You can keep extra clothes in the sacks or in your S.I.N box." Rez sends a pointed look at Lilith, but she either doesn't mind or doesn't see it as she starts our training. "Let's see if you can reach yours."

⁘ ⁘ ⁘ ⁘

After thirty minutes of Rez and me straining and not reaching our S.I.N. box, Lilith calls for a break. She goes over vials and spells that aren't on the curriculum at school, but she insists they are vital here in Hell. Honestly, I kinda zone out and watch Rez's ass wiggle as she gets excited.

Someone clearing his throat pulls my attention away from her shapely ass, and I see multiple eyes trying to peek at what I've been feasting on. Ryker makes eye contact and waves for me to move so he can appreciate the view. Smirking, I move, blocking his view. I snicker as I hear the grumbles behind me, but they're short-lived as Lucifer calls for a break.

"Okay, let's take a break and eat. After dinner, we can spend some time in the library looking for information about the portals. We'll start back up tomorrow morning." With a clap to finalize his point, he heads out for the dining room.

Rez leans into me and I wrap my arm around her, pulling her into my side.

"What's wrong?" I ask as we follow everyone out of the room.

"I'm a little disappointed that I don't have a S.I.N. box," she pouts, and I chuckle at her words.

"Oh believe me, Rezzi-bear, you definitely have a box that's full of sin. I bet it's hot, wet, and tight. Fuuuck," I hiss and adjust myself.

Rez glances down at my crotch before her heated gaze returns to me. Instead of giggling at me, like I expected, she bites her bottom lip and blushes.

'*Cat got your tongue?*' I ask, smirking down at her.

'*Don't you wish?*' Her eyes smile back with mirth.

'*Well, this cat wants something other than your tongue,*' I admit as we walk into the dining room.

'*Later,*' she promises as she sits down.

My eyes roll back in my head as I moan internally. '*Really? You're gonna leave me hanging?*' I pout, and she giggles next to me before Levi grabs her attention.

We quickly devour our food. Training will do that to you. Soon Lilith leads us back to the library. Rez skips to the front of the group and starts asking Lilith all sorts of questions about the library, and to my shock, Ryker joins in the conversation.

"Since when did he know how to read?" I grumble, and Knots chuckles next to me. "What?" I question, giving him the stink eye. I haven't forgotten the time he locked me up after the whole Familiars class incident. He wouldn't let me out to find my Rezzi. I really should have peed on him when I had a chance. *I could always do it tonight when he's passed out. Yep, that sounds like a good plan. Hmm.* Then again, we did work pretty well together the night I was taken. *Double hmm. You're lucky... Door Knob!*

"It's just funny. That's all," The Door Knight... or Angel says.

I'm not sure how I feel about that knowledge. I think I liked him better when he was an inanimate object that could talk. At least that way I could get away from him just by walking away. I guess it doesn't really surprise me that the untouchable Door Knight would fall for my Rezzi-bear. She's delicious, and no one can resist her wiles if she turns her sights onto you. He's at least proven his worth, unlike the guys she's dated in the past. As much as I hate it, it's her life and her choice to pick the men she wants to shack up with... and the "real boy" isn't too bad. But there's no way in Hell I'm telling him that to his face.

"Okay, Pinocchio, wanna share with the class?"

Zeke snorts and Knox lets out a boisterous laugh while Knots just glares back at me.

"Ryker reads more than anyone here—well, besides me," Levi says. He reaches up for his tie and bristles when he notices he's still in workout clothes.

"Aww, does poor stick up the butt feel uncomfortable without his suit?" I tease. The only sign of discomfort I get from the Mage is his jaw clenching and hand flexing.

Suddenly pressure surrounds my feet, making me trip. Even with my fast reflexes, I'm not able to catch myself before I land face-first onto the marble floor.

The air is knocked from my lungs with an oomph.

"Lynx!" Rez yells out. She reaches down for me as I roll and notice the shoes on my feet.

"Really? You magicked shoes on me?" I accuse Levi.

The prissy Mage just smirks as he raises an eyebrow and continues into the room.

"Dammit. I hate these things," I groan as I try to figure out how to undo the contraptions.

Rez reaches down and starts to swiftly undo the laces. "You really need to get used to wearing shoes again, Lynx."

"Nope," I say, popping the P. "Foot prisons are my worst enemy, besides old woody there," I declare as Knots blows me a kiss before walking into the library. I gently rub my toes after Rez releases one foot from the death trap.

"Pfft. I promise there are more comfortable footwear than pointe shoes," she admits as she releases the ribbons and shows me the offending pink monstrosity, a barely contained smile hinting at her lips. "You could wear sandals or Crocs, you would probably like those. Ballerina shoes probably aren't your type." She helps me up, and I knock the man-made killer shoes out of her hand before pulling her into the library.

"I'll take your word for it," I mumble, leading her around the corner.

"Oh my... Wow! Lynx, look at this place," Rez exclaims, dropping my hand and spinning around to take it all in.

"Yeah, it's peachy," I deadpan.

Rez stops in her tracks and turns her attention back to me. "What's wrong? Doesn't this excite you? I mean, look at all the books."

I don't even waste my breath in answering and just purse my lips, giving her an annoyed look.

She sighs before leaning in and wrapping her arms around me. "I'm sorry. I just get carried away sometimes when I see libraries. You know they're an escape for me."

Sighing, I peer down into her gray eyes and open myself up, feeling grateful that I'm able to at least hold her. "I know, but there was a time when I was your escape. I'm just afraid I'm losing you," I admit.

"Oh, Lynx," she says, looking at me with pity. "You'll never lose me; you're mine just as much as I'm yours. Nothing has changed."

She presses her mouth against mine, and I swear, I see fireworks. Her soft lips melt as I kiss her back. I cup her jaw in my hands, tilting her head so I can deepen the kiss as a connection I've never felt with Rez starts burning within me. Heat starts swirling within my gut and spreads like wildfire, urging me to let go of my restraints.

Rez moans against my feverish embrace as I pull her closer and dig my fingers into her curls to hold her against me. Her hands claw at my back as she breaks away from my kiss teasingly and starts to nip at my bottom lip.

"If we don't go help, I'm sure they will come and find us," she whispers against my lips between her playful bites.

"I don't care," I confess, reaching down to grab her thighs and wrap them around me. She giggles, and it does something to me, knowing that I'm the one making her happy. I'm the one who's bringing her pleasure, even if it's as simple as this.

The fire in her eyes promises a good time all around, and I start to walk us to the back of the room when the Devil decides to fuck with me.

"Ahem. I don't want you to get lost." Lucifer's voice rings out behind me. Turning, I throw the asshole a glare, and he has the gall to give me the biggest smile ever.

"Last time I checked, you were the Devil. Aren't you supposed to be advocating debauchery and fornication?" I growl out as Rez nibbles on my earlobe, whispering dirty, dirty suggestions. *Fuck. If Lucifer here wants to watch... He's about to get his wish.*

'Rez, I love all those ideas, but you're going to make me blow before you get to see my magnificent cock in person.'

"Not when we need help in searching for information on the portals. Come on, before I have Lilith spell you so you can't find *relief* until we find answers."

Rez bites down on my earlobe, and I yelp. "Oh shit. Sorry, Lynx," she says, sliding down my body. Her eyes are wide as she stares at Lucifer in shock. "She can do that?"

"Do you want to find out? Besides, it's imparative to someone in our group that we find that information." He raises an eyebrow and turns to leave. Rez and I follow him into Lilith's lair of knowledge.

This is Karma biting me in the ass. As I adjust my hard-on, I now understand how much it sucks being cockblocked.

CHAPTER 46
Between the Stacks

Rez

We follow Lucifer behind an open bookcase while I try to figure out what he meant about our search being 'imperative,' but I get distracted and I'm immediately thrown into nirvana. Bookshelves line the walls, and there's at least five stacks of shelves on each side of the room. It's more like a book oasis for me as I take in the massive area. Pillows line the sunken square seating area in the center, allowing room to walk around to the bookcases. There are little nooks and crannies everywhere, promising a cozy getaway. Glancing up, I notice fairy lights hovering over the room, giving the impression that this place is magical.

What am I talking about? Everything about books is magical. Though I'm sure some could bore me to death, but as I take in the scent of the room, all I smell is the hint of vanilla, paper, and ink. I wish I could bottle it up and carry it with me always.

There's a table in the middle where Levi and Bez are

already seated and looming over books. Moni is perched on Chester's shoulder as both of them are looking over a book in the corner. Ryker is already in deep with a book, and Knox is reading spines overhead on one of the ladders. Lilith and Murmur are reclining against some pillows with a big black book between them. Something scurries across the back of the room. Squinting, I notice Benny climbing up a bookcase and working to get a book out. I quickly walk around the sunken pillow area and get there in time to help her.

"Need help?" I ask, grabbing the heavy tome for her.

"Ah! Thank you, Rez. Yes. I've been searching, and I think this might be a book of interest. I was going to give it to Lucifer," she explains. "Would you mind helping? It's quite heavy, and I wasn't expecting that." Her whiskers bristle as her tail wraps around her body.

"No problem." I smile and take the tome over to Lucifer, who is making himself comfortable on a pillow and leaning against the table leg. It's surreal to see the Ruler of Hell in workout clothes and bedding down on the floor to dig into a book. I bet people would literally die to see that.

The last of my guys, Zeke, JP, and Knots are lined up against one of the bookcases with their noses in books. Knots doesn't stay standing for long and slides down the bookcase to get comfortable on the floor. I hope he's just getting comfortable and doesn't *need* to sit down. I can't help but wonder how he's holding up. I don't see Lynx at all as I take in the room as a whole.

'*Where are you?*'

'*Slowly contemplating my death. Never thought I would die by reading,*' Lynx grumbles.

I laugh internally and begin looking between the bookshelves until I spot Lynx leaning against the wall, his eyes fixated on a shelf.

'*Find something good?*' I ask, walking up to him. He turns to face me, putting his back to the wall and eyes me up and down.

'*I have now!*'

'*Very funny, Lynx,*' I joke.

'*Do I look like I'm joking?*' he asks, and I take a moment to study his form. He's trying to project a relaxed stance, but I know my bestie. The muscles in his chest and arms are tight, and as my eyes travel down his torso, I notice a slight bluge in his pants.

At least I'm not the only one that was affected by our kiss. It definitely wasn't a kiss like we had when we were little. It was more feral, addictive, and I want more.

'*No. You look like you can't concentrate and you're frustrated. Both of those we can't have if we're supposed to be looking for something about the portals. So, I think I know how to help,*' I say. I walk up to him and give him my signature smirk.

'*What did you have in mind?*' Lynx asks, his breath picking up.

'*Let's get your mind off of what you're thinking about,*' I say, licking my dry lips. His heated eyes drop to my lips as his slightly open in response.

'*I highly doubt that's going to work.*' He chuckles through our link.

'*It's actually really simple,*' I explain, dropping to my knees. I glance up, and Lynx's eyes go wide. I would laugh out loud if I wasn't trying to be quiet.

'*What are you doing?*'

'*Getting your mind off of it,*' I say as I grab hold of the waistband of his shorts to pull them down.

'*Woah, Rez!*' Lynx grabs my hands, stopping me before helping me stand back up. Disappointment and shame fill me from his rejection, but he pulls me close to him as he looks deeply into my eyes.

'*You have no idea how much I would love to have you choking on my cock right now. Because you definitely would be tapping out first,*' he says jokingly. I barely crack a smile and roll my eyes before he continues. '*But I want our first time to be special, and I want no chance of being interrupted again.*'

'*Oh, you don't mind cockblocking as long as it can't be turned around on you?*' I tease. I do kinda see his point, though.

Lynx snarls, and a laugh is ripped out of me. My heart warms, though, to his words and his thoughts. It makes me love him even more for waiting to wait. I lean up and give him a kiss on the nose before I turn and study the books before me.

'*What are we supposed to be looking for again?*' I ask since I wasn't here the first time they discussed this.

'*Dr. Steinbeck read something about a master switch to the portals in one of these books eons ago. You know, before dinosaurs roamed the earth, and now it's our job to look for it,*' Lynx snarks.

I sigh and lean against one of the bookcases, letting my eyes glance over all the books before us.

'*So, what you're saying is we're going to be searching forever, huh?*'

'*Yep!*' he quips, leaning next to me and reaching down to hold my hand.

There has to be a better way than just picking out books at random to see if they mention the portals. As my mind drifts for a solution, my eyes are unfocused until everything becomes a blur. A slight blue glow grabs my attention to my left. Turning to inspect it, a dark maroon color also shines on the other side of the room.

What the fuck is going on?

'*Rez?*'

'*I don't know what's going on, but I think I see two glowing books?*' I explain as I let go of Lynx while slowly moving toward the glow. Lynx follows close behind me. Without reading the spine, I grab the glowing blue book and hand it to Lynx before crossing the room to a nook by the door. I pull out the red book and turn to look for Lynx, but I find him and everyone else staring in my direction.

"What?" I ask, feeling a little self-conscious.

"Bestie, your eyes were glowing. Not to freak you out or anything," Moni says, staring at me as she pulls some coffee out nervously.

I look to Lynx, and he slowly nods. It's Murmur who comes over, looking like he's found another prize, though. I pull the book against my chest and throw out my hand to stop his advancement.

"Oh no!" I say, shaking my head. "I'm not doing any more training."

My eyes start to feel really heavy, and I follow the urge to close them for a few moments and rub them with my palm. When I open them, Murmur's looking like a dog that's lost his bone. Speaking of dogs, Reaper comes running into the room and takes a running leap, landing in the pile of pillows where he begins rubbing against them. If I'm being honest, I'm a little jealous of him right now.

"You are right, at least for tonight," Murmur tells me. "Tomorrow is a whole other deal. For now, tell me what happened before you came walking out of the stacks with glowing eyes," he demands.

"Nothing really," I insist. "Lynx told me that we had to go through all of these books to find the answer about the portals, and I thought we would be searching forever. So I leaned back and thought about how there must be a better way of finding the answer. My eyes unfocused, and then I saw these two books glowing. This one is a deep maroon color, and the other is blue." I indicate the book in my arms as Murmur leads me over to the table and lays the book down on it.

There's no wording on the dark gray spine whatsoever, and if you ask me, I probably would have never picked it up. Lynx brings over the book I gave him, and it's a smaller white book with leather bindings that are tied to each other to keep the pages together. Once again, there's no words or markings indicating what they are.

"So you have no idea what these are about?" Murmur asks me.

I scoff. "Do you? They don't belong to me," I point out and look around the room. Everyone has stepped away from their own books and has gathered around the table.

Murmur tips his head in my direction. "Good point."

Lucifer grabs the gray book and flips it open. The front page has an inked illustration of some kind of map, but he flips the page before I can read any more of it.

I feel as if my skin is being poked by pins and needles as his eyes fly over the pages faster than I can track. Suddenly, he lays down the book and slams his hand down.

"There!" he says, pointing to a passage. I can't make out the words whatsoever, but the longer I stare, the more ink swirls on the page, suddenly becoming legible, and I can read it. "It looks like there's another portal we can use. According to this, by using that portal and this incantation"—he points to another passage—"it will open the portals back up."

"How did the portals even close?" Moni asks.

Thunder crashes in the room, making most of us jump until I realize it came from Astaroth's tail.

"Asmodeus," he growls out. Chills run up and down my spine as I take in the Wrath Demon. I can feel the power rolling off of him as his jaw cracks with the force of his clenched teeth.

"As it turns out, he's behind the closing of the portals. Although, I don't know how he did it, yet. It takes a substantial amount of energy to block or even disrupt them," Murmur says, and I give him a perplexed look.

"Trometh squealed like a stuffed pig," Bez answers my unspoken question. "Too bad he didn't last as long as one. I'll have a new purple hide for my machete in a week's time." A cruel smile graces his smile, and goose bumps erupt along my skin.

Eww.

"Yes. We've never blocked or closed the portals before, but we've had to divert some energy off the portals a few... How long ago was it, Lilith?" Lucifer asks, but Lilith waves his question away, though the worry line between her eyes deepens. "The point is, it took all of us to do it, and it left us weakened for a few days before we were back to normal."

"Shit," Chester and Moni whisper.

"So, either Asmodeus is stronger than all of you, he has allies, or he has some special device to help close them. Does that sum it up?" Knots asks, leaning on the table.

I watch him for a moment and notice how the muscles in his arms are slightly shaking and he looks a little sweaty. Did he work too hard during training, or is his time here starting to affect him again? Shit! Was the shield I put on him not strong enough? *I'm a horrible girlfriend.* I quickly pull up my shield and apply a thicker coating, thanking the Fates that I don't have to physically touch him now.

'Hey, Knotty! How are you feeling? You doing okay?' I ask, and his eyes swing to mine. He gives me a slight smile.

'I'm doing fine. Just a little tired from the training and ready for sleep. Nothing to worry about,' he assures me.

'Promise?'

'Absolutely.'

I blow him a kiss and catch Levi staring at Knots as well, concern plastered on his face. Hopefully, he's just checking up on him as well and not picking up something worrisome through his emotions. I worry my bottom lip as I debate going behind Knots' back on this. I just want to make sure he's okay.

JP, is Knots okay? Is he projecting? Can you hear him? Is he in pain? Can you check?' I send my thoughts to JP, and his head jerks up with shock. He clenches his jaw and backs away from the table before slowly making his way to me as Lucifer explains where this Master Portal is.

I'm surprised as JP grabs my arm and gently pulls me away from the table. Once we are away, I take a look at him and know I've fucked up. JP runs a jerky hand through his hair. His muscles tense before he lets out a shaky breath. Leaning down, he looks me in the eyes.

"Rez, I know you mean well and you want to check up on Knots, but it's not fair to ask me," he says with a clipped tone.

Immediately, tears start to sting my eyes at his words.

"I'm sorry. I don't mean to come off like an ass, ma chérie. But you have to see it from my point of view. I've had an easier life than Moni, but not by much. I've been accused of dipping into people's private thoughts, and it's a trigger of mine. Having you ask me to do that with one of your mates and my friend..." He sighs and looks down at his feet.

"I'm sorry," I tell him as I grab a hold of his arm. "Please forgive me," I whisper. "I didn't mean to upset you, and I didn't know. But you're right." I try to keep the emotion out of my voice, but some slips out as JP looks up at me, his face softening.

"It's okay," he says and pulls me into an embrace. "I know you didn't mean to and your heart is in the right place, but you also have to trust us, Rez."

He leans back and looks down at me. I feel better that he didn't flat out yell at me and then leave me here standing alone. If anything, I feel more love pouring out of him now that he's taken the time to explain while still holding me.

"If I ever pick up something troublesome and I need to

call in the cavalry, I will, but until then, if you're worried about one of us, come ask us." He lets go of me and cups my cheeks. "Coming to us one-on-one when you're worried about us makes us feel special too," he says with a smile and kisses me briefly. "Now, let's go see what we missed." He grabs my hand and pulls me back to the group around the table.

CHAPTER 47
The Labyrinth

Knox

I can feel Kitten's worry as she looks at Knots, and it doesn't take a genius to know she's talking to him. What does stump me is JP suddenly walking around and grabbing Rez, pulling her away from the table.

'How dare he grab her like that. Attack! Protect mate!' Fluffers yells in my mind.

'Settle down; she's his mate too, so he won't hurt her,' I reason with him, that is until I feel her shock and sadness. Focusing on JP, it's easy to see the anger he's carrying. If his clenched jaw and fists weren't an indication, his agitated state and jerky movements would tip off anyone if they are paying attention.

The fuck?

Yeah, that's not going to fly when I'm around. I push away from the table and try to squeeze around Bez when Fluffers starts laughing.

'That didn't take long to switch sides,' Baron taunts me, but

I know better than to comment back. It will just be something else he can possibly hold against me.

Before I can make headway to my kitten's rescue and JP's ass whopping, JP pulls her in for a hug and I feel her relax against him, but I need my own reassurance as Fluffers pushes for me to shift. I send my worry down the link to Rez, and as she walks back to the table with JP, I feel her assurance; she's okay.

It's not complete happiness from her like I'm used to, though. It's putting me on edge, but at least it's enough to keep me from ripping into JP. I feel something else shift inside of me, though that brings me pause.

'Did that come from any of you?' I ask, but it's silent for a moment. *'GUYS!'*

It's my turn to feel Rez's worry come down the link, and I give her a smile I know doesn't reach my eyes, but I have bigger problems going on.

'No. It wasn't,' a strong voice slithers in my head. I immediately go on the offensive. Who's in me that doesn't belong? Anger surges inside of me as I assess my body and realize I still have control of it as I bare my teeth.

'Who are you? Are you like Cain, a parasite catching a ride?' I accuse.

'Pfft. You should be grateful I chose you to bind my soul with. We will talk later. Pay attention so we don't look like fools.'

I don't know what or who this thing is, but he does have a point. I need to pay attention and think of this as any ops. So I let go of the fact that *something* is inside of me and pull my attention back to the table before me. I can deal with myself in a moment.

"So it's located in the seventh level of Hell. What's the big deal?" Zeke asks, looking at Lucifer.

Lucifer sighs and pinches the bridge of his nose, so Astaroth answers the question.

"If it was that easily placed, then we wouldn't need the Crucible. Anyone would be able to pass through, even the souls that were damned to stay here."

"Oh. That's a good point," Moni nods. "So how do we get to it?"

It's almost comical as L.A.M.B. shares looks back and forth and Lilith fidgets against the table.

It still blows my mind how much she's changed since we came to Hell. Before, she wouldn't have been caught fidgeting or showing any emotion, but here, within a few days, I've seen her flying off the handle to having emotional breakdowns. It almost makes you wonder which side is real. Is she just healing from being possessed, or is this how she is normally?

"Here, can I see that?" Rez motions for the book that Lynx is holding and flips it open. A sheet of paper comes flying out of the book and lands on the table.

"What is it?" Knots asks as Lucifer turns it around at different angles.

"How old are your books that they are falling apart before we even open them?" Lynx asks Lilith. She arches an eyebrow in his direction.

"Most of my books were around before many civilizations fell and you were just a tingle in your great great great grandfather's ancestor's ballsack." She smiles sweetly and Lynx gulps, holding his prize possessions in his hand.

"Good to know," he replies.

"I think it's a map," Rez says as she looks down at the book. "Is this the same illustration that was in the gray book?" she asks, and Lucifer shakes his head but doesn't open the cover to show all of us. Hmm. I wonder what that's about. Rez taps the map, bringing my attention back to her.

"According to this—if I'm reading it correctly—there's a pathway that leads to that portal." She peers up before looking back at the paper.

Yeah, there are pathways on it, but I can't make heads or tails of the landmarks on the paper.

"See this door right here in the corner?" She points to a door that has *Hgmnb ez Eghr* scrolled above it. "It says Trail of Worth, and that's here in the book, but I don't know what all of this stuff is to get there."

Levi strains his neck to look at it from his position. "May I?"

"Of course," Lucifer says and allows Levi to look at it. Ryker slides up next to him and they both study the map.

"Doesn't that figure right there look familiar to you?" Levi asks Ry as he points at a figure right off to the left-hand side.

"Oh shit! Yeah. That's the booby lady," Ryker calls out and slaps the table.

"Booby lady?" Lynx asks, raising an intrigued brow.

Ryker laughs. "Yeah. When Levi and I were kids and we came down here, sometimes we had spare time on our hands, so we would explore the grounds at... Mom's," he says, smiling at Lilith. "There's this statue at the corner by the fence that Levi and I said looked like a naked lady."

"Matilda," Lilith sneers. "She *is* a naked lady."

"What?" Ryker snaps his head in her direction as he's taken aback.

"She was a personal assistant of mine until I found her trying to... persuade... my men."

"She was coming onto them," Lucifer explains.

"Oh," Levi and Ryker both exclaim and clear their throats.

"Well, the point is. If that's... Matilda?" Levi questions, and Lilith smiles sweetly. "Then this tunnel, I'm assuming, is somewhere attached to your house, Mom. That's the tunnel that leads to the Trail of Worth."

"And if that tunnel is at Mom's, that means you guys have a tunnel here somewhere that leads to Mom's. It's like an underground roadway. But of course, we can just go over to Mom's tomorrow and search for it," Ryker says with a fist pump.

"Yes! We don't have to be here forever!" Lynx does a little shuffle, and Rez laughs.

"Shit, I had forgot about our safety tunnel. Lucy, when did we have those built?" Lilith asks.

"I believe within a few years of falling here. I have no idea what state they are in," Lucifer answers and then shrugs off his thought.

Lucifer steps away from the table to address us all. "I'm glad there was a quick turnaround in here, thanks to Rez and her newest power that we *will* be exploring tomorrow. You guys might as well get some sleep. We'll start early in the morning after breakfast and head over to Lilith's to find that tunnel. That's our biggest priority next to your training."

"I think I'll stay up and see if I can find that tunnel here in the house, if anyone wants to join me. I don't plan on staying up too late," Murmur says.

"I'm up for exploring," Zeke says, not surprising me at all. What does surprise me is Chester and Moni volunteering too. It's nice to see her stepping up, though, and branching out, trying new things. Reaper's growl pulls my attention as he viciously disembowels the pillow, sending feathers flying around the room. Zeke quickly scoopes up the little Hellhound and makes his way out the door, following Murmur.

I watch Lynx grab Rez around her hips, swinging her over his shoulder as he leaves the library in a hurry. I don't blame him; he finally has his human body back, along with his memories. I'm sure he'll take care of our girl.

The question I have is for the man that's sliding out of the room before me.

'Hey, JP. Wait up!'

JP slows his steps as he turns and smiles. "Hey, Knox, wh —" The smile falls from his face as he takes in my stern look.

'We need to talk.'

"Okay. What do you want to talk about?" he asks, not giving away that he can probably hear me cussing him out.

"You and kitten. It looked like—"

"None of your business, Knox." JP turns and looks at me straight on. I'm taken aback for a moment as I wasn't expecting that answer at all.

"None of my business?" I growl out.

"Yes." He lowers his eyes and sighs. "Look, she triggered me, okay?" he says and glances back at me. I know he's uncomfortable having this conversation with me since he's shifting on his feet, but I want to make sure kitten is safe around all of her mates, even my friends.

"How did she trigger you?" I ask, my voice coming out gruff even though I try to keep the accusation out of my tone.

He peeks around us to make sure we're not being over-heard before he responds. "She asked me to look inside of Knots' mind," he admits.

Aww shit! JP used to get picked on in PP when he was younger. Most parents don't think to teach their children how to shield themselves from mind readers, so it was easy for JP to hear their thoughts. He was accused of it a lot until Matthew stepped in and we took him under our wing. I can understand how her innocently asking him to do that would send him spiraling.

"Yes. I lost my cool for a split second, but I explained what her asking did to me. I also told her she needed to trust Knots. If she needs to talk to us, then she should come to each of us. That's how a relationship should work. We made up and we're good. So when I say it's none of your business, Knox, it's just that... not your concern. None of us would hurt her." Stopping, he clenches his jaw with a sad smile and rests his hand on my shoulder. "It seems like you need a lesson in trust also." He squeezes my shoulder before walking down the hall.

Fuck!

'He's wise beyond his years,' Dusky says.

Reluctantly agreeing, I start to walk back to my room and a thought hits me.

'Do you know what's moving around in there with you?' I ask Dusky.

'Yes. It's your other form,' he admits, and I feel him pull away and go silent.

Ugh. Out of all of my animals, he's the most stubborn. I would have thought Baron was. Baron doesn't speak, but he bristles at the insult. I quickly get to my room and see Reaper, covered with feathers still, running down the hallway. He must have gotten away from Zeke. I whistle for him, and he skids as he tries to stop before running into me. Picking him up, I bring him to my room as he gives me kisses. I quickly set him up with a bowl of water and some toys from the closet, then head into the bathroom. I need a damn shower. First to clean off, and second just to calm down. My emotions are starting to get to me. I wouldn't call it aggression, but I'm on the edge of being anxious. It's as if I feel like I need to shift, but no one is calling to me, not even my mystery animal.

I think I'm still in shock that I have four animals. Even my father only has his three, which is the most I've ever heard of a Shifter having. Alphas are the ones that normally have the highest number of animals, but even among them, I would be unique. Four? What does that say about me? I would be the first Shifter recorded to ever have this many animals. Maybe it's because of what L.A.M.B. said. My brothers and I *have* taken over the Horsemen, so that's another possibility.

Shit, that's a whole other can that I'm not ready to open up yet. Turning on the shower, I quickly strip and step underneath the hot spray. I briskly wash, then allow the water to pelt against my back and drip down onto my face as I relish the feel of the heat surrounding me and soothing the turmoil within me.

It happens gradually, my muscles start to relax, but I have an urge to shake out my limbs. First my arms, my back, and my legs, and then when I try to stop, tremors wrack my body. The shift comes over me in an instant, like a spontaneous flash of heat. My eyes go wide as I try to understand what's going on. This isn't anything like shifting into my other forms. I've never experienced this feeling before, and I'm not sure how to handle it. Instead of the familiar shift of my Gryphon or Wolf, I drop to my knees as my bottom ribs burst outward, knocking what little air I had out of my lungs. Two limbs slide free, and dark hair sprouts across the strong appendages where the paws stretch, flexing the sharp claws at the end. My arms and legs twist and pop as they rearrange, and black fur covers me from head to toe.

The claws on my back feet slide across the shower tiles, leaving gouges, as my body elongates twice as long as Fluffers. Muscles lengthen as my shoulders separate, and bizarrely, two whip-like appendages pop out of my shoulders with a crack. They appear to be long as they flop around in the air, while my nose and mouth widen and stretch to accommodate the sharp teeth and fangs. My ears and tailbone stretch like they normally do when I shift, so it doesn't surprise me when I feel my tail whip back and forth in irritation. What does surprise me is the sensation of needles poking out of my long whip-like appendages at my shoulders. I was assuming this form was some type of jungle cat until those appeared.

Most shifts are quick and easy, but the first shift into an animal is the slowest. From there, it almost becomes instant. With Fluffers, he was almost an instant shift for me; we were that connected. Baron, though, my first shift with him took five minutes. This one, I would guess, has taken me a few minutes. Yet, I still have no idea what I am or what I have merged with.

Getting the feel for my new body, I walk to the mirror and hop onto the counter. I turn to look at myself.

'*Boo!*' the voice yells at me, scaring the shit out of me and making me fall.

'*What the fuck?*'

Laughter echoes inside of my head. Fluffers is rolling around laughing while a new voice joins him.

Rolling my eyes, I hop back up onto the counter, prepared this time, and take in my form. First of all, it's not black fur that's covering me, it's blue-black fur, and it seems to ripple as my muscles move. I am about nine feet in length, and my guess is I weigh about five hundred pounds. I have six legs, a tail, and two long five-foot tentacles that sprout out of my shoulders and are moving along my back. At the ends of the free-roaming whips are pads with sharp thorny barbs. My green eyes seem to glow, and I wonder how good my night vision is. My best comparison of what I'm looking at is a six-legged panther with tentacles and the face of a bat. It's so foreign, I can't help but wonder if Rez will like the new form or even find it attractive. He's not really looking all that cuddly. A growl rumbles in my chest as my thoughts hit a sour note with my new beast.

'*What are we?*' I ask. I have no clue what I am bonded to. This is nothing like what I've learned in class or even in mythical creatures books. A thrill runs through me at the prospect that this might be an extinct or extremely rare beast.

'*You won't find us in any book, buddy. I'm pretty sure there are less than ten of us alive, if the Elves haven't killed us all off,*' the voice replies.

'*Elves? What do they have to do with this?*' I ask.

'*Well, here's the short version. Once upon a time, there was*

465

an evil king that used to employ us to do his dirty deeds and clean up his messes. Then he decided to send his Elves to eradicate us so we couldn't squeal on him. Over the years, we hid in the elven realm and only ventured out to hopefully merge our dying soul with another to once again live on. The end.'

'So you died?' I ask in utter shock.

'Damn, he's really not that bright, is he?' he asks, and it's Baron that answers.

'Not even close.'

'I take offense to that,' I huff.

'How? I didn't think you were even intelligent enough to understand what I just said,' my new animal says.

'I'm just going to act like you didn't say that. So, again, what are we? And what should I call you?' I ask, trying to move past this awkward moment.

'Fair enough. I'm a Netherwraith, and you can call me God."

The room shakes, and my claws try to dig into the marble countertop to no avail. I slip off and growl.

'Yea, no. I'm not calling you God. If you want those letters though, I'll be happy enough to call you Dog!' I say while another explosion from the blasphemy happens in my fireplace.

'You already have one of those, I believe, so just call me Slayer. It's what my mother called me,' Slayer concedes.

'Okay. That I'll agree to.'

'Good, now let's go bond. I need to stretch my legs,' he says, and I feel the urge to run.

Jumping off the counter, I use the tentacles to turn off the water before stepping into my bedroom and finding Reaper passed out. *Well, I guess he's not going to run with me.*

I open the bedroom doors with my whips and very carefully close them, turning to find the hallway empty.

'Let's see what you can do,' I challenge.

'*Aww, this is gonna be fun.*' Slayer laughs as we take off running. One of the pads whips out ahead of us, attaching to the wall and lifts us into the air, propelling us further.

'*Oh shit, what am I getting myself into?*'

Slayer just laughs as we whip around the corner.

CHAPTER 48
A Whole New World

Rez

"Lynx!" I yell as he almost drops me. All I manage to see is his feet and firm ass as he carries me away from the library. He slides going around the corner so fast that he almost loses his balance and takes me down with him.

"Hold on." He laughs as I squirm right before he smacks my ass.

"Ouch!"

"You love it."

He's right; I do. He opens the door to my room and kicks it shut before plopping me onto my bed.

"Wanna get dirty?" he says, wiggling his eyebrows.

I laugh at his antics. "Actually, I'd rather get clean. I feel dirty and my muscles ache."

"Well, I do owe you a back massage. I guess I can relent and let you take a shower first." He smiles and helps me off the bed. I don't let go of his hand, though. Instead, I bring him to the bathroom with me.

"I'm pretty sure you need a shower too!"

"Holy shit! Will my first time be in the shower? Is this something I can write to Penthouse about? Do they still have a magazine?"

I grab his cheeks and push them together, making duck lips and kiss him quickly. "You're just too cute, but shut up and get naked!" I giggle.

"Yes, Mommy!" Lynx chuckles.

"Eww. Don't do the whole mommy thing," I state, switching the shower on then undressing. "I think that's the quickest way to end things in the bedroom with me," I tell him, wrinkling my nose. I'm left in my underwear and sports bra.

"Aww, so we can't play Mommy and Daddy?" Lynx whines before swirling his hips. His shorts slide lower on his hips, accenting the already large bulge there.

"Oh, we can play; just don't use those words," I offer as I pull my sports bra over my head and look at Lynx over my shoulder.

His eyes track my body as I slowly step out of my underwear and into the shower, and he quickly steps out of his shorts to follow me. As his eyes feast on my body, mine do the same to his. I track his movements as his body moves like a panther on the prowl. His muscles ripple as he follows me, and I gaze at his smooth skin down to the small path of blond hair that leads to his...

'Holy shit, Lynx, you weren't kidding.'

He reaches me in time as the room shakes and I hear the whoosh of the fireplace. Dammit. Me and my cursing.

'What? Didn't you believe me about beating the record for girth and width?' He chuckles as he manhandles the trunk between his legs.

'Of course not. I'm not even sure you're going to fit,' I admit.

'Don't tell me you're scared. You weren't scared to be with the others.'

'True. I'm not scared, but I can't go around comparing them to each other. I'm different with all of them.'

This piques his interest slightly. He pulls me against his hard body, and I feel his cock pressed against my thigh. *'How so?'* he asks as he kisses my throat. My breath catches as I try to think of what he just asked me.

'Well, with Levi, I'm his mistress.'

'Figures.' He chuckles, and then lets out a hiss when I pinch him.

'Hey, no shaming. You asked, so I'm explaining,' I scold, but promptly swoon as he backs me up into the hot stream of water. Sweetly, he turns me around and starts to wash my hair. His fingers gently dig into my scalp, and I swear, I have an erogenous zone where my noggin is concerned as a moan escapes me.

'Knox is my dominant alpha.'

'Of course.'

'With Zeke, it's more of a cat-and-mouse game, and, of course, I'm the mouse. He likes to chase me.'

Lynx chuckles and starts rinsing the shampoo out of my hair.

'Knots is my protector in every way and is very dedicated to taking care of me. JP is the same, but with more teasing and a flirty flare.'

Lynx nibbles on my ear, and my knees go weak. He chuckles again and wraps his strong arm around my waist to hold me up against him before grabbing the conditioner.

'You were saying?' he probes, and that's not the only thing that's poking me. I feel his erection digging against the crack of my ass, and I smile to myself when I hear a groan from him.

'And Ryker is my sparring partner. It's a back-and-forth relationship with him. Neither one of us wants to give in,' I tell him.

'So what does that leave for me? It seems like you have every

aspect covered,' Lynx slyly asks as he works the conditioner through my hair like he's seen me do a million times.

I know he's playing it off as it doesn't bother him, but I *know* him.

'I do have every aspect covered except for the most important one... YOU!' I say, turning around and throwing my arms around his neck. *'You're my Lynx. You're too big to fill just any hole,'* I say, and he smirks down at me, his eyes sparkling with mirth.

'You sure about that?'

'Yes! Look how big you are,' I scoff, before looking down between us, and my jaw drops. *'Um. Is there something wrong with my eyes?'* Lynx's massive erection has changed, and instead of the smooth skin, there're ridges up and down his shaft.

Lynx's head falls back as laughter tumbles out of him. He grabs the body wash and squirts some onto the cloth and hands it to me before grabbing some for himself.

'So you remember when I told you about being a Storm Shifter and how we could shift into anything to help the Horsemen?' he begins, and I nod as I start absently cleaning myself, eyes locked on his intimidating appendage.

'Well, it turns out, I can also change a part of my body to... fit my needs.'

'No way,' I gasp, even though I can see it with my own eyes. My mind starts running with all sorts of possibilities. "Fuck getting clean. We need to get dirty, NOW!" I say out loud and grab Lynx's arm, thrusting him under the shower head to rinse off.

Lynx just laughs and grabs my neck, pulling me to him as he slams his mouth to mine. We're a tangle of limbs, teeth, and water as we try to rinse off and stop laughing at our own antics. I finally reach around and turn off the water, and we make our way over to the bench for the towels while we're still lip-locked.

'Why use towels?' Lynx asks, and I know there's a reason, but my mind goes blank when his hands slide up my body and brush the sides of my breasts.

'Good point, fuck it,' I say and reach down to stroke his shaft. Our hands and tongues have minds of their own as we explore each other's bodies and make our way around the divider in the bathroom. I slip and grab hold of Lynx's bicep, but he loses his balance, too. We both plummet to the ground, laughing.

'I think that's why I was going for the towels.' I giggle as I try to push back my wet hair.

'I guess you have a point.' We both laugh as he helps. As soon as he frees my face from the monster that is my wet locks, he's back to kissing me again as I lay on the wet, cold floor.

'As much as I love feeling you against me, this cold floor isn't doing it for me,' I admit, but Lynx slides between my legs and presses himself against my aching core.

'It's not? I'm sure it's doing something for me.'

I reach up for his hair and grab hold of it tightly with a yank, making him yelp. *'I'm not letting you lose your V-card on the bathroom floor.'*

'Aww, come on, Rez. It would bring a whole new meaning to Shaggy's song, "It wasn't me." You know, banging on the bathroom floor.' Lynx pouts.

'That's the point,' I say, and roll us until I'm straddling his lap. *'Come on. Last one to the room has to perform oral,'* I challenge, and start to crawl up and over his body.

'Why wait?' he says and grabs my thighs, halting my progress. *'I've been dying to taste you. Instead, I had to watch everyone else get to experience this.'* He guides my hips until my center is pressed against his face and my legs spasm as his hot,

wet tongue swirls around my clit before he takes it into his mouth.

'*Fuuuuck!*' I moan. My upper body is supported by my elbows and I'm stretched out, straddling Lynx's face as he eats me like a starving man. '*There's no way... This is your first time,*' I pant out.

I hear him chuckle as he starts flicking his tongue against my bundle of nerves before he licks up my slit. '*I've had years of dreaming about how you would taste and what we would do. This is beyond anything I could have imagined, Rezzi-bear.*'

'*At least let me up so I can have some fun,*' I whine.

'*Nah, I'm good,*' he teases me.

Fine. I can play that game. He's not the only one that's going to have fun here. I've been waiting for him too. I bring my legs together and lean back so there's more pressure on him.

'*Yeah, baby. Sit on Daddy's face. Suffocate me!*'

I roll my eyes. '*Why is that a thing? It's like a kink that all men love... for us women to sit on their faces and smother them to death.*'

'*Think of warriors, Rez,*' he says as he starts to tongue fuck me. '*It's like a rite of passage. It's the best way to go out of this life. Death by pussy suffocation. I would be branded a fucking HERO!*'

'*Yep, that would only be a man thing. No woman would want that shit on her tombstone. Here lies Rez, died by a dong down her throat,*' I say, and Lynx laughs, and then chokes. I try to get off his face to make sure he can breathe, but his arms are like clamps around my thighs. '*Don't die, Lynx! You need to pop your V-card first.*'

I reach back and lightly run my left hand up the side of his stomach, and just like magic, he bucks and squirms. He's still ticklish, and I love it. I reach back with my other hand and attack, and soon enough, he lets go of my legs to try to grab my arms, but I make a break for it. I roll off of him and start crawling away as fast as I can until I reach the bed, but Lynx is right behind me.

'*That's cheating!*' He glares at me, but it holds no heat.

'*All's fair in love and war, baby!*' I say saucily.

He just smirks before he picks me up and throws me onto the bed, but I'm ready for him this time. As he lands on the bed next to me, I swing around so I'm facing his cock and I don't waste any time. I grab it, and I feel the skin rippling.

'*What is my Rezzi-bear's wish? What kind of dick do you want to die on?*' he jokes, but I look over my shoulder and see what he's hiding. He's nervous, but there's no reason to be.

'*Lynx. I just want you. No ridges, cords, or extra anatomy. Give me my Lynx,*' I say, and I'm blessed with his smile. The hard ridges of his dick smooth out, and I learn that the "real" Lynx is really his massive, intimidating size. '*Promise me, if I die, you won't put that I died with your cock down my throat?*'

Lynx shifts his hips up so he almost pokes out my eye before he winks and leans up, running his tongue up my slit and making me moan.

'*I promise. I'll just say I poked out your eye instead.*'

'*Asshole,*' I grumble as I lick up his shaft, tasting his salty sweetness.

'*I can be one, but yours looks so pretty. I want to lick it,*' he says, and he does just that. He goes on licking, sucking, and worshipping me as I try to focus on him, but it's hard. As his tongue slides between my folds, my arousal starts to drip, and it's not long before I find myself gasping in pleasure.

He's waited his whole life to be with me, and I want to make it good. I lick up his shaft and collect the pre-cum at his slit before I take his head into my mouth. It's a tight fit, but I don't complain as my lips go taut around him.

'*Aww fuck, Rez,*' he moans, and it's like electricity going straight to my clit.

'I apologize if I can't do this properly, Lynx. You are seriously too big for my fucking mouth. I take back everything I said about it being small.'

'I'll forgive you if you let me lick you awake in the mornings,' he says, and I moan at the idea.

'Deal.'

I ease him back out, licking and sucking as I go. I feel his legs start to shake as I lick him from base to tip before bobbing my head up and down as far as I can go. I find a good rhythm with my hand until I work him into a frenzy.

'Rez, I'm close to coming!'

'Good, let me taste you,' I say as I roll his balls gently in my hand. They draw up, and I watch as his toes curl before Lynx vocalizes his release with a roar. Hot spurts of cum shoot to the back of my throat, and I quickly swallow everything he gives me. I lick him clean, and before I can do anything else, Lynx flips us so I'm on my back, and moves to another position.

'That was the best feeling in the world, but I couldn't concentrate properly,' he says, smirking up at me between my legs. *'Now it's my turn to make you scream in pleasure.'*

He closes his eyes and devours me whole, licking, sucking, and tongue fucking me as I grind my pussy on his face. I reach down and dig my hand into his wet hair while using my other to play with my breast. My breath increases as he continues to lavish my pussy and lick me like a cat going for its cream. I'm already close from all the teasing and back and forth, so it doesn't take long to bring me to the edge.

'Shit, Lynx. I'm so close. Don't stop,' I tell him, and he doubles his effort. His tongue flicks against my clit before he sucks it between his teeth. He lightly bites down, causing me to see stars as I explode. He moans as he licks up my release as fast as he can, making me dissolve into a puddle of goo on the sheets.

'*Good to know you weren't faking with me,*' Lynx says as he kisses his way up my body.

'*Oh, you're that confident about it?*' I tease.

'*Hell yeah, I am. Remember, I've seen you faking before. You really want to go down memory lane?*' He chuckles.

'*I'd rather not.*' I purse my lips. '*Or try it, and I'll finish my night out with a vibrator,*' I counter.

'*Oh, like this?*' Lynx kneels and starts shaking his hips back and forth as his dick changes once again. The bumps and ridges lining his shaft come back into view as he starts to twerk and his dick starts bobbing up and down.

Laughter bubbles out of me as he bites his bottom lip and starts grunting. I laugh so hard a cramp in my side has me buckling over.

'*You dare laugh at the great Lynx? I'm my own vibrator, you won't need Hoppy or Wiggly ever again.*' He reaches down to start tickling me, but I know how to stop him in his tracks.

I quickly pull him against me and kiss him deeply, tasting myself on his lips. He moans into my mouth and melts against me. Ready for more, I wrap my legs around his waist and reach between us for his cock, finding it smooth once again and stroke it a few times as his hips rock with my movements.

I start to guide him into me. '*Rez, do you think I'll fit? Do I need to change? I don't want to hurt you.*'

'*Yeah, just wait,*' I manage to pant out. '*You're just a little... big, so we have to go slow or else you'll rip me in two and you'll never get to do this again.*'

Lynx freezes, and his wide eyes fly to mine in panic.

'*Kidding!*' I say. '*Kinda. 'Here. I can get on top and do it that way if you want,*' I offer. We try to move at the same time as he looks down between us, and we head butt.

"FUCK!"

"SHIT!"

"Sorry!" we both say simultaneously and then laugh. Lynx

leans down and kisses my forehead before peppering kisses down my face to my jaw as he starts to rock his hips. His cock teases me with each pelvic flex as his head pushes into my folds.

'If you don't stop teasing me, we're gonna have problems, Lynx,' I growl out, and all he does is chuckle as he continues. He nips along my neck and down my chest, taking one of my pebbled nipples into his mouth and sucking hard.

'I've been studying, so I know what you like. So shut up and take it,' Lynx tells me as his hand starts playing with my other breast.

'Well, if you know what I like so well—' I moan as he runs his tongue around my nipple before flicking it. *'Then fucking give it to me. I want the D, Lynx,'* I demand and scratch him down his back.

He groans and flexes his hips as he pushes—

'Woah, woah, woah!' I tighten up my hole and shift away from him.

'Rezzi-Bear, I'm trying to find the hole,' he grunts as he pushes against me.

I squeal. *'Lynx! That's my asshole, you fiend!'* I point out to him, pushing him back. *'That's it. Let me be on top. That way we can both have fun,'* I tell him, and he pulls back and shifts onto his hip.

I realize too late that we're on the edge of the bed, and when he goes to move back, he tumbles off, taking me with him.

I squeak as I land on top of Lynx.

'We are a fucking mess.' He laughs as he moves my hair out of his face.

'True, but I have you where I want you.' I easily reach between us and guide him to the right hole and start to rock myself along his shaft.

'Damn, Rez. You feel so good,' he moans as I slowly allow

my walls to adjust around him. He's so big that he's on the brink of painful, but he finally sheaths himself fully before I cautiously start to rock as Lynx reaches up toward the bed. He starts pulling on the sheets, and I give him a bewildered look until the pillows and bedspread fall over us. He grabs a pillow and shoves it behind his head and gives me a wink.

'*Now I'm ready to watch you ride. Giddy up!*' He bucks his hips, and I lean forward, slapping my hands on his pecs to keep my balance. '*Want a bull ride?*' he teases.

'*Do you want to enjoy this or come super quick?*' I ask as I lightly run my hands over his chest, hovering my fingers at his nipples. His eyes go wide, and he quickly covers them up.

'*My nips! They are tender.*'

'*Well, mine aren't, get to playing,*' I smirk and circle my hips. As I grind against him, his massive cock hits my magic spot, causing ripples of pleasure to flow through me. I barely have to do any work since he takes up so much room. Not only is he wide, but he's long, and I find myself sliding down him like a stripper pole. I smile as his eyes roll back in his head.

'*Damn.*' He moans louder than I've ever heard him as his hands come up to play with my breasts. I continue to rock my hips and alternate sliding up and down his cock as Lynx sings praises about my pussy.

'*She's a goddess that needs daily prayers. Fuck, she's so tight. Can I hug her all night?*'

'*I love you, Lynx, but you're going to make me lose my concentration. Dammit.*' I reach behind me for his balls and start rolling them in my palm. Lynx grabs my hips in a punishing grip and moans.

'*Rub my clit. It will help me come with you,*' I manage to get out between pants. Lynx reaches down between us and rubs my clit with his thumb before he brings up his legs, shifting my weight forward.

My breasts swing before him and he opens his mouth for a

nipple to slip in as he starts to pump into me at a frenzied rate. I'm so close to the edge and any extra little stimulus will send me over. Lynx smirks around my tit like he knows what I'm thinking, and he lightly bites down on my nipple, sending me crashing over the edge.

I cry out my release as Lynx grabs my hips and forces me down on him. Exquisitely, I feel his cock spill into me as my pussy spasms around him.

"FUUUCK," he cries out as he pumps into me one last time. Exhausted, I collapse onto his chest and giggle. Before I can catch my breath, a burst of color catches my eye and I lean up to get a better look.

'*Woah!*'

'*What?*' Lynx asks as he tries to look down at his chest.

He has a living tattoo of an infinity symbol that stretches across his sternum in a rainbow of colors. They shift and move along his skin, mesmerizing me for a moment until I notice a new color forming below it.

"Does that hurt?" I whisper as I watch a watercolor turquoise and purple colored heart appear slowly from under his skin, attaching to the symbol.

"No. It's just warm," he says in awe. Our eyes meet for a moment before we look back down and see a lock appear around both of the tattoos.

"Is that the same lock that's on my back?" I ask, and I turn to allow him to see.

"Yeah."

The hitch in his voice makes me pause. '*What is it?*'

"Your tattoo... is moving. As in, all the circles look like they are alive."

"Oh! Well, the good news is, I can't feel it and it doesn't hurt! So yay!" I chuckle because what else is there to do? '*Are you freaked out?*' I ask Lynx as I look into his eyes. I'm a little nervous as to how he's going to take the mark on his chest.

A big, goofy smile splits his face as he laughs. "Are you kidding me? This is fucking awesome. You marked me and apparently I'm the best because your tattoo came to life with my dick!" He wiggles his eyebrows. I giggle at his craziness, but it does the job at releasing the tension. I lay my head back on his and start to trace his tattoo.

'So, on a scale from one to ten... How would you rate your experience?' he asks as I try to catch my breath.

'Did you just pull a Jeremy Baker?' I ask incredulously.

'Yep, wasn't he the one that always wanted you to rate his performances?' he recalls.

'Yeah, and there's a reason I didn't stay with him.' I chuckle.

'It's because you were waiting for a ten, right?' he jokes.

'I'm not even going to answer you, but just for that, I'm gonna make you give me that back rub tonight.'

'I knew it was so good you want my hands on you, too.'

And this is why I love him.

CHAPTER 49
Marks of a Warrior

Rez

A knocking on my door stirs me, but all I do is pull the pillow over my head and roll over. I feel Lynx shift and crawl out of the bed.

'No, it's too early. Don't answer it. They will go away,' I grumble.

"Come on, lazy bones. I'm not going away until you get out of bed. Come on." It's Ryker's voice on the other side of the door.

The sound of the door opening makes me groan. I don't know what time it is, but I swear we just went to bed. Lynx made up for lost time by going so many rounds, I think he even fucked me while I was sleeping.

The pillow is ripped from my head, and Ryker's brilliant blue eyes shine down at me. As a matter of fact, he's practically glowing.

"Why are you glowing?" I mumble.

"Apparently I was hooked up to the energizer bunny last

night while someone kept on coming and coming and coming." He smirks and rubs his jaw. "It was as if I was being fed pure lust and sex... hmm. Any idea where that came from?"

"I'm in no mood," I whine, before Ryker leans down and gives me a savory good morning kiss.

"Oh come on, princess. You should be in the best mood with how much sex you got last night," he teases, poking me in the shoulder.

"I know I am," Lynx chimes in.

I groan as Ryker goes to the closet. "It's okay, I'll pick you out something to wear."

"NO!" I yell.

I tumble out of the bed and run over to him, naked as the day I was born. Ryker raises his eyebrows as he takes in my appearance. Lust hits me, hardening my nipples and making my pussy sing like the insatiable hussy that she is, and I smack Ryker on the arm. That's when I notice he's dressed for combat. Hmm, I guess we have more training today, along with searching for that tunnel at Lilith's place.

"Knock it off. I'm lucky I can even move," I growl out. Grabbing hold of the closet, I think about my outfit for today and what would be appropriate.

"Yeah, I did get miles out of her last night." Lynx laughs.

"That's what I'm talking about," Ryker says and gives Lynx a high-five.

"What the fuck? You know I'm right here and I can still close up this shop, you assholes," I reply.

"Ahh!" Lynx points to me. "Half lie; your tone in your voice raised and your eyes shifted."

Fucking Lucifer and his knowledge.

"Fine. I won't close up shop because I like you guys too much—but I could. That's the point," I huff, opening up the closet doors and grabbing my clothes. "Now, if you'll excuse me while you guys bond over your sexual escapades, I'm getting dressed." I sashay my way back to the bathroom, adding a little more wiggle to my hips than necessary.

I clean up and get dressed in all black. Most of the items I conjured up come with built-in areas to hold my glaives, and I smartly came up with a black halter top with straps higher up across my chest to help support the girls. Who knows what L.A.M.B. will be having me do in training today. I quickly braid my hair back, finally getting sick of it being wild, and walk into my room to find a fucking miracle.

My jaw hits the floor as I take in Lynx's outfit. He's decked out in dark leathers, but what's most shocking are the boots he's wearing. I glance at Ryker and back at Lynx. "Okay, who is that?" I point to the imposter. "And what have you done with my Lynx?"

They both laugh at me, and Lynx comes over, his boots clomping as he does. He gives me a quick kiss. "Ry showed me how I can customize these puppies," he raises a foot. "The trick is to make them big enough so I can't feel them on my feet but tight enough on my ankle," he grimaces. "It's a learning curve."

I stifle a laugh and simply nod. "I'm proud of you for making this great sacrifice."

"You best believe it. Now, bow to the king!" he says, throwing his fists onto his hips.

"I like him. Where have you been hiding him all this time?" Ryker laughs.

"He was right in front of you, just as a huge-ass cat!" I say, passing them to pull open the door.

We find Knots and Levi outside, waiting, and it seems the entire hallway got the same memo to dress in leathers. Knots looks as if he was born to wear them, and Levi looks as good in them as he does in a suit. Maybe even better. I quickly say good morning and give them each hugs and kisses as everyone slowly appears out of their rooms. Moni once again looks like a tiny warrior as she clings to Chester while he yawns and straightens out his glasses.

"It's too early for this shit," Knox grumbles as he comes lumbering out of his room with Reaper on his heels. His hair is rocking the bedhead and there are bags underneath his eyes.

"Hey, Alpha, what time did you go to bed?" I ask, giving him a hug and looking up into his mesmerizing eyes. They seem to be glowing a brighter green despite his tired appearance.

"Not early enough," he gripes.

Don't let him fool you, mate. He was off bonding with Stalker,' Fluffers grumbles.

'*It's Slayer. You fleabag,*' a deep voice growls. I flinch at the unexpected voice and look up at Knox with a wide expression. He purses his lips and rolls his eyes.

'At least I'm not a mutant,' Fluffers replies back.

Aww, it seems someone is hiding something... or someone from me. I press my head against Knox's chest as I close my eyes and concentrate on the new voice.

'*Um, hello, Slayer. It's nice to meet you. I'm—*"

'*My delicious mate... I can't wait to get you beneath me,*' he purrs.

"Okay then." I pull away from Knox's animals and his chest, peeking back up at my man. "So, you had fun last night?" I ask with raised brows as I try to hold in my laughter. This new Slayer guy must have ridden my man hard. That definitely explains the dead look on his face.

"Let's just say I'm ready for this day to be over or at least ready for a nap," he grumbles, giving me a kiss on the forehead.

JP and Zeke are the last to join us as we head off for breakfast. On the way, Zeke, Moni, and Chester fill us in on their mini adventure last night. Apparently, they did locate the tunnel, or at least a tunnel leading out of the mansion. Murmur decided it would be best to find the tunnel from Lilith's house first and trace it back to here to see if it is the same one. But since he promised they weren't going to stay out too late, he called it a night.

L.A.M.B. and Lilith are already seated and talking amongst themselves when we enter. Reaper runs into the kitchen, probably to terrorize the cooks and beg for some goodies.

"Ahh. Here's are our lovely pupils," Lucifer greets us as we take our seats. I pull Knots down next to me because I feel the need to check on him while we eat, and I tell him so. He just smiles and gives me a sweet kiss before making me a plate of food. As he does so, I make sure to check and reinforce his shield around him. He looks a little paler and there're bags under his eyes, but maybe that's the light since he normally doesn't sit in this seat. I'm trying to take JP's words to heart and trust that if there's a problem, someone would let me know.

"So, what's on the agenda today?" Levi asks as he cuts up the meat on his plate.

"Training," Astaroth grunts as his tail whips back in agitation. I'm surprised it's not making booming sounds like it normally does. *I wonder if he can control that.*

"I thought we were going to look for Lilith's tunnel first?" Moni asks, frowning. She pulls out her thermos of coffee and sniffs it before sighing.

'*I'm sure her tunnel is all dust by now. I'm surprised the council can even plow her, since she's been around since before time.*' Lynx chuckles.

I choke and cough as juice comes bubbling out of my nose, making my eyes water.

"Fuck!" I reach for a napkin, and Levi quickly helps me clean up.

"Oh. Dear, Rez, are you okay?" Lilith asks. I try to catch my breath and attempt to conjure up lasers shooting from my eyes to fry Lynx.

"Yeah. I'm good. Sorry," I finally manage to say.

"You will all be training first this morning. Astaroth needs to show you how to care for the weapons that he made for each of you, and then we'll spend the rest of the day looking for the entrance to Lilith's tunnel," Lucifer explains over the clatter of silverware and drinks being poured.

"She could shave it, that would be easier," Chester replies softly, right as everyone in the room quiets down. His eyes go wide as he realizes what he said, besides the fact we all heard him. He cautiously peeks up at Lilith, and to our surprise, she laughs. It's as if she gives us a green light and the tension breaks as the rest of the table joins in.

"My man!" Lynx cheers and gives Chester a high-five. Who knew there was a little perv behind those glasses?

After breakfast, we all follow Astaroth back to the training room, where he hands out our weapons.

"These will stay with you at all times," he instructs. "You never know when you might need them."

"But what do we do with them when we sleep?" Moni asks, looking at her sai before attaching them to the belt around her waist.

"Sleep with them," he answers.

"You've got to be kidding, right?" Chester asks, looking uncomfortable. "I mean, we're here, safe in your place. You don't really expect us to have them in the bed with us. Not really?"

"They belong there, or within arm's reach," he fires back. His tail hits the mat and thunder rolls throughout the room.

What pissed in his cheerios this morning? "What did you think we were training you for?"

"Exercise?" Lynx throws out with a shrug. I smack myself in the head and hide my face from the crowd. *I do not know this guy. Nope. Nada.*

I hear Murmur's voice behind me before I see him. "Nice try, Lynx. But no." He comes to stand next to Astaroth and looks over our group. "The fact is, we're preparing you for war."

"War?" I squeak. "I thought we just needed to learn skills to level up and get to the ritual to go to Earth." I throw up my hands. "Or to protect ourselves while we're in Hell. Wasn't that a reason also?"

Murmur laughs and shares a look of disbelief with Astaroth. "Yes, that's still what you are doing, but things are changing. Look around you. The Withering Sulks are back, Adam has escaped, Cain is gone, the Portal to connect us to Purgatory is closed, and our most trusted are actually traitors; it all points to something unsavory occurring."

"Yeah, but war?" I ask.

"War isn't just about the kill or a fight. It's also a way to protect yourself so others can fight in your stead," Knox remarks.

"Jessup has taught you well." Astaroth nods his approval.

Murmur starts to pace before us, "Yes, our training started out as just teaching you skills, but as things are becoming more clear—"

"We're preparing you to defend yourselves if there's a time when the Gates come crashing down and all the creatures of Hell show up on your front porch," Astaroth finishes.

Aww. Fuck me with a pitchfork. Could Hell get any worse?

MONI

JP holds my hand as he knocks on the door to Lucif—I mean Dad's study. I'm gonna have to get used to calling him that. It's still so unreal that I have flesh and blood besides JP that wants me. My egg donor never did.

"Come in." We hear from the cracked door. We walk in and find Dad sitting on his sofa.

After the revelation from Murmur and Astaroth, they pulled JP and me off to the side first, showing us how to clean and take care of our weapons before sending us here. They said Lucifer wanted to see us separately.

"You asked for us?" I ask, breaking free of JP and giving Dad a quick hug. He tightens his arms around me and beams down at me as I take a seat beside JP, while they do that weird head nod greeting.

I swear, men are weird. It's like they think they can get cooties from each other. *Wait. Are cooties real?*

"Yes, Moni. I know I haven't been able to spend a lot of time with you like I would prefer, but I wanted to offer you guys something. Hopefully, you'll take it, but I'll understand if you decide not to." JP shifts in his seat as Lucifer reaches for a box that's under the coffee table and sets it on top. I pull out my essence of life and take a sip of my Sparks coffee as we take in the small silver box with the initials L.M. on it.

"What do the initials mean?" I ask.

"Lucifer Morningstar. I was named after the first star, my dear." He opens the lid and inside, there's a big ass futuristic gun and a bottle of black and silver ink glowing in a small glass bottle.

JP pats my arm to get my attention, and I realize I've been squeezing his hand so hard that his knuckles are white.

"Sorry," I whisper.

'What is that?' I ask JP.

"You want to give us a tattoo?" JP asks curiously.

My bark turns to glitter bomb mode with swirls of pale white as I repeat JP's words.

"Yes, but not just any type of tattoo. It will work as a branding, marking you as my children or *mine,* and it will allow you to communicate with me, like a calling beacon or pager," he states.

"What's a pager?" I ask. I know I have bark, but I don't want to be turned into paper for a book.

He laughs and shakes his head. "I'm sorry. I forgot how young you are. It's a device that humans used to use back in the day. They went off to alert them someone wanted to get ahold of them. It was before cell phones. The ink would work the same way, just in case you were in a tight spot and your phones wouldn't work," he explains. His words have honesty in them, but they sound off. Not quite a lie, his speech pattern changed slightly and his tone dropped as he talked about a tight spot and our phones, but before I can say anything JP speaks up.

"Okay, that's a half-lie. What else does it do?"

Lucifer's grin spreads into a full-on smile as he gets called out. "I see you've been practicing. It's also a tracker. All three of us will be able to feel each other. Rub your hand over the ink, and you'll be able to know, or at least have the sense of where the others are. I have the same with the rest of L.A.M.B. I would like to have the same reassurance with you."

This time his words ring clear like a crystal bell, and I smile. "Yes! But you have to finish it even if I pass out, especially when I pass out," I admit, cuddling into JP's arm. "That gun looks scary."

"Oh, it's not a gun. It's a needle," Lucifer corrects me.

"Ahh! That's even worse!" I scream.

"Moni, calm down. We got this," JP says, patting my leg. "Is that something I might be able to learn?" he asks.

"What? Tattooing?" Dad asks, leaning back in shock.

"No. Well—Yeah. I guess. Weaving the tracer or tracking spell into the ink for others. Is that something I can learn?" he asks.

"Yes, that is something you should be able to learn. Let's practice on Moni!" he says with a smile. JP turns to me with a smile, and that's the last thing I see before the lights go out.

CHAPTER 50

Storming the Gates

Rez

W hy did I have the more complicated weapon to clean? Mine takes longer than all the others, but when I finally finish, we're released and told to meet in the parlor. I sidle up next to Knots as we walk back.

"Do you really think there's going to be a war?" I ask as I slip my arm in his. He's wearing a dark blue long sleeve shirt, and I notice it somewhat feels a little damp.

"In my long existence, I can say there's always war, Rez. There are only small bouts of peace between them," he points out and takes a deep breath.

"Damn. I never thought of it that way," I admit. I bite my lip before I bring up his condition. "You're feeling a little sweaty. Are you okay? How are you handling the effects?" I ask.

"I'm fin—"

"Nope. Don't want to hear that bullshit." I stop, and he turns toward me. "I want to know what the effects are. I already know you're fine. I can see that myself, Knots. That is if you consider 'fine' being able to stand up and nothing else. I want to know what's happening to you. How are you feeling? What's becoming difficult for you? If anything you should be training us, not sparring with the rest of L.A.M.B.," I state as I move his hair out of his face. He's left it down today, and I can see where it's starting to stick to his forehead where he's sweating.

"I'm just finding myself more lethargic, that's all. That's the only side effect I'm feeling right now." He smiles at me, though it doesn't reach his eyes. "But we'll be out of here soon enough, and everything will be fine. You'll see." He pulls me against him and kisses me.

The way he kisses me leaves no doubt that he's still capable and strong enough to do other things. I go to deepen the kiss when Lynx calls down the hall.

"Come on, slowpokes; we're waiting on you."

"I really am going to skin him," Knots mumbles against my lips.

"I'm sure he would like to see you try." I laugh and pull him along with me.

We walk into the parlor, and it looks like everyone is ready to go. They are only waiting on us. *Oops.*

"Sorry," I apologize.

"Now that everyone is here," Lucifer begins, and pulls out the map that I found yesterday.

"Wait, Zissa isn't here yet," Astaroth says.

"Oh, she's coming with?" I ask, perking up. I haven't seen our Succubus friend since our adventure out looking for ingredients.

"Yes, she will be helping us in our search. Once we find it, she'll stay here with you all while we go to the Trail of Worth. It's best that we do that since we have no idea what it contains."

"Did the other book, the white one, mention anything else

besides just having the map in it?" I ask. After we were dismissed yesterday, Lynx carried me off and I never thought twice about it.

"Yes. It stated there's a Gatekeeper who has a beast unlike any other guarding the door to the Trail of Worth. They either find you worthy to pass and go to the trails, or you have to defeat the beast. We'll be able to take the beast. We're the oldest and strongest," Murmurs says, not boasting, just stating facts.

I guess that makes sense.

Lucifer clears his throat, grabbing our attention once again. "If we can get back to the map. Our best guess is that this tunnel is on the east side of her mansion and probably the access is either on the first floor or in the basement."

"I sent Benny over there this morning to sniff around, so by the time we get over there, she should—"

"LILITH! My Lady!" Benny yells. *Holy Hell. Speak and ye shall come.* The fireplace flares slightly at my thought and I feel eyes on me, but I refuse to look. Nope, not falling for that trick. Benny runs out from behind a bookcase. *Is there another hidden door back there?*

"Benny!?" Lilith says with raised eyebrows. "I wasn't expecting to see you until we got to the house. What's wrong?" she asks, bending down so Benny can hop onto her palm.

"My lady," Benny bows quickly. "There're... Demons. They have breached your home and are desecrating it. It's as if they are looking for something."

Lilith's face goes blank for half a second until her whole body starts to shake. I quickly reach out and grab Benny, bringing her to my chest as Lilith blows up like a volcano.

Her back bows like Moni does when she has her sonic boom, and a scream is ripped out of her.

"Ahhh! How dare they!" she yells and throws her arms out

in a wide arc. Books fly off the bookcase behind us. Zeke and I dive for the bar as everyone else takes cover behind the sofas, looking for shelter from the flying objects. Reaper has the worst timing because he runs into the room at that point. Since my hands are full with Benny, Zeke dives and grabs him before he can run out into the fray.

"Dude, I think your mom is a little unstable," I admit to Zeke.

"Nah, you think?" he hisses back as a book whips around the edge, almost knocking us out.

Murmur jumps in front of Lilith and places his hands on her temples. "Calm, Lilith. We will go over there and teach them what happens when they disturb what is not theirs. But first you need to calm down so you don't hurt the children," he yells to be heard over the noise, and then promptly cusses as he's hit in the back by a massive tome.

Lucifer comes up next to her. "Lilith, I don't want to sedate you. We need you. Get your shit together."

I watch in horror as Levi breaks away from his protective spot and runs over to Lilith. He slides in between Murmur and Lucifer as Bez comes up to help shield him from the onslaught of debris flying around the room.

Levi doesn't say anything, but his hands start to glow as they touch Lilith, and he rubs her arms. Slowly, the winds die down and the books, knicknacks, and papers fall to the ground.

"Holy shit," I whisper in awe.

Fire erupts in the fireplace, and Lucifer throws a glare in my direction. I shrug and mouth "sorry."

"Was that because of me?" Benny asks from my lap, and I completely forgot she was there. I release her while Zeke continues to hold Reaper so he doesn't get hurt with the aftermath of the destruction.

"Not at all. She's just a little... off her rocker," I guess.

"She was never one to have a rocker," Zeke clarifies.

Slowly standing up, I peer around the room and see it's wrecked. Books, papers, broken glass, a painting, and pieces of wooden furniture lay scattered everywhere.

"Is everyone okay?" Astaroth asks, and we all reply with some type of yes.

"You okay now?" Levi asks Lilith. She grabs ahold of Levi's cheeks and pulls him into a hug. "Thank you, baby. You've always been able to calm me down. Yes. I'm calm enough to go kill some Demons."

That's a scary thought.

She releases Levi, and he backs up to give them room to move.

"We'll clean this mess up later. Or get the servants to do their job while we're away."

We head for the front door, Lilith leading the way, when the room shakes with a jolt. Lucifer throws another glare my way.

"Don't look at me! I didn't think, say, sing, or sneeze a dirty word," I say in my defense.

He narrows his eyes again before the room shudders, toppling a bookcase, and I fall against the bar.

"Fuck!" I yell as I crack my head along the corner.

Screams ring out as we try to brace ourselves from falling and getting hurt from the remnants of Lilith's earlier tantrum.

"What is going on?" Bez growls.

"ASTAROTH!" Zissa screams. She comes running into the parlor with wide eyes, blood dripping down from her hairline, and caked in dirt.

"What is it?" he demands, approaching his pupil.

"An uprising! I don't know who's behind it, but Demons are attacking," she wheezes out.

"Impossible," Bez grunts.

"Shit, did you get the ward fixed from yesterday?" Lynx asks.

Murmur looks at Lucifer, and you can tell the answer by the looks on their faces.

"How many are out there?" Astaroth asks as he starts pulling weapons out of thin air.

Oh, his S.I.N. box in action!

"Too many for me to count," Zissa says as she wipes away the blood that's dripping into her eyes.

"Tell me what you know," Lucifer demands.

"As I was coming up, I heard them behind me, running. I got through the ward and pulled on the defensive measures you showed me, Astaroth. That's when I saw some break away and start to circle the gate. I made it inside the door right as a Demon got to me. I fought him off, Asa. He was just a kid, and I killed him." She swallows heavily and shakes her head, clearing it. "So they are getting through the ward, I just don't know where or how many can cross at a time." She shakes her head in shock as tears start to build in her eyes.

"Zissa, concentrate. This is *not* the time for tears. The Demons you could see, did they have any marks? Colors that looked familiar?" Murmur asks as he starts to pace back and forth.

I'm not the one being questioned, but my heart is pounding out of my chest, and I can't tear my eyes off of Zissa.

She shakes her head back and forth until she freezes and her eyes go wider than I thought possible. "The Demon that almost came in with me, the kid. He was wearing a medallion around his neck. Asmodeus'."

A Demon runs into the Parlor and skids to a halt. "Master. We have Demon's trying to break into the throne room."

"FUCK!" Lucifer yells and turns toward me, his eyes wild with flames. He strides toward me, and I find myself backing up as fast as possible, but there's nowhere to go.

"Take this and the book," Lucifer demands and hands me the map and the small white book I found yesterday. "Take the tunnel and get to the Trail of Worth. Open that Portal so we can pull in the Council and get some help."

He turns to JP, quickly pulling him into a hug and whispers something to him. "Moni, show everyone how to get there. Stop by your rooms and get whatever materials you may need—the bags Lilith made, clothes, food—but make it quick. Love you, my little warrior," he says, giving her a hug and kissing her on her forehead.

"You heard Dad!" Moni yells. "Everyone grab your shit and meet in our hallway in five. We need to roll out."

I don't wait for anyone, I book it down the hall and back to my room, where I quickly grab the bag Lilith gave me yesterday and throw in the book Lucifer just handed me. Thankfully it's already stocked with the vials she gave me and the cheat sheet. Next, I go to the closet and think of extra clothes, underwear especially after remembering what Moni pointed out yesterday, portable stuff for Reaper—who hopefully is still with Zeke—lighters, blankets, pillows, and anything I can shove into my endless bag of crap. Once I jam all of that into my bag, I run out of my room and back to the kitchen. Halfway there, the building gets rocked hard, and I fall to the floor. As I try to pick myself up, hands grasp me under the armpits and pull me to my feet.

Looking back, I give Bez my thanks as he smiles down at me. Movement to my right has me whipping my glaive up and out like muscle memory from practice with Astaroth. The clang from meeting the knife jars me, but Bez's beefy hand engulfs the tiny Demon's face and fire bursts from his palm. The Demon's scream is quickly cut off when I slice his throat.

I can't stand watching him burn to death in front of me.

I look up at Bez just as the realization comes to me that I

intentionally killed someone. It wasn't an accident. I truly killed someone. *By. My. Hand.*

"You saved him from a more gruesome death that I would have given him. You are a true warrior. I am proud. Now go." I can't help but look at the gentle mass murderer in a different light. I don't know when it happened, but this group of Demons have become somewhat like father figures to me. Bez isn't the type to hug, and I give him a slight smile and a nod.

I don't think; I just run to the kitchen, where I find Reaper with everyone else as they are packing drinks, snacks, and whatever they can into their packs.

"Is everyone here?" I ask as I raid the second fridge and grab the leftover meat for Reaper.

"I think so," Zeke calls back. "Moni is in the back of the pantry throwing down the dry goods."

"Smart thinking," Ryker calls out.

"See, I'm good for something," Moni calls out, and I wholeheartedly agree. If someone ever said something different to her, I would slice their neck without a second thought, like I did to the Demon in the hall... Well maybe a second thought, but she'd be worth it to me.

Once everyone is packed, I quickly count and double check everyone is here before we race for our hallway once again.

"Wait," I yell, stopping the group. "Where is Zissa?"

"She's staying behind to help L.A.M.B. with their defenses. She's being groomed for the job, so she's the best to help with it," Ryker announces.

Well shit. That's great and all, but I was hoping she was going to come help us.

"Let's go!" Moni yells.

Did I ever tell you I'm not made for fucking sports? This type of exercise is not for me.

Moni takes the lead, and we go down a hall I've never been down, which takes us to a *dead end.*

"Are you fucking kidding me?" I screech like a damn banshee from Hell.

Moni just smirks at me over her shoulder and presses her hand against the wall. A click sounds and a door swings open.

"Well then," I say begrudgingly, and she just laughs. Reaper barks and darts in before us, the flames from his coat lighting our way.

As we enter the tunnel, there's enough room for two of us to walk side-by-side. The door closes behind us with a swoosh, and Lynx looks at me with wide eyes.

'*Do you feel like we're in a horror movie?*' he asks.

'*Starring in one, more like it,*' I agree.

"How far did you guys get in here?" Ryker asks as we reach some stairs and start to descend a circular staircase.

I reach forward and grab the back of his vest since it's getting harder to see. I wasn't blessed with night vision like some in this group.

It's amazing to think that even in Hell you can get cold, but I find the temperature is falling the lower we get underground. I would have thought it'd get hotter.

"Um, that door," Zeke replies.

"So you have no idea what's down here?" Knox asks.

"That would be correct," Moni says.

Freaking great.

We finally reach the bottom, and it opens up a little bit, but before we continue on, I ask for a minute.

"Guys, give me a moment. I was in such a hurry I stuffed the fucking map in here," I confess.

"We did a shit job packing too," Zeke admits.

So as I try to dig through and find the map, most of the guys rearrange the things in their bags too. I grab the map and something special I conjured up for Reaper before calling him over. He runs over and jumps up on me, giving me kisses.

"Just to make sure you don't get hurt, run away, or someone tries to take you when I'm not watching, okay?" I say, as I place a fire proof collar and leash around him. I know I look silly, but I wrap the end of the leash around the belt of my glaives and make sure I can still pull them out safely.

"Okay, let's head out," I say as calmly as possible, even though my nerves are strung like a hair-trigger.

The tunnel is all dirt, and occasionally, some of it falls down, making me sneeze. It makes me jump, thinking we're about to be buried alive. Checking the map, it shows only one tunnel leading to Lilith's house, but from there, a few tunnels branch out that we'll have to watch out for.

"How far is Lilith's house from L.A.M.B.'s place normally?" I call out to either Levi or Ryker to answer since they've been here before.

"It didn't seem this far when we were little," Levi calls back.

"Then again, we weren't allowed to travel to L.A.M.B.'s house," Ryker admits.

I hear a grunt and look back in time to see Knots stumble into the wall. '*Knots!*' I yell and move toward him. JP and Zeke help him up, but back away when I reach him.

'*What's wrong?*' I peer up into his brown eyes, and all I see is sadness.

He looks over my shoulder, and I follow his gaze to see that our friends are giving us some privacy.

'*I might as well come clean since I can't hide it anymore,*' he says as he leans his head back against the wall. '*When you went to grab the Demstone for the spell to help slow the effects of being down here, I talked with Dr. Steinbeck.*'

'*Let me guess. It wasn't good and you decided to keep it to yourself.*' Even mentally my voice cracks. His bowed head is answer enough, and my eyes start to burn from the unshed tears. *'What did he say?'* I demand more than ask.

Knots reaches for my hand and pulls them to his chest and even though I'm hurt, I allow him to take them. *'His educated guess was that without that spell I was going to slowly waste away and die, or become a true fallen and I could possibly be trapped in Hell.'*

He wipes a tear that falls free and tries to escape down my cheek. *'I'm sorry, Rez. I didn't want to scare you.'*

'That's not an excuse, Knots. You should have told me anyway.'

'Yes I should have, and you're right. There's no excuse for me keeping it from you. But don't worry... I'll make it up to you back home. Maybe a nice bubble bath and a rub down.'

'I'm holding you to that, because I refuse to lose you here.' I admit as I revamp the shield around him. *'Can you at least tell me if this shield is helping at all?'*

'It is. It feels like a warm hug, and it's probably the only thing that's keeping me from deteriorating as fast as Steinbeck gave me,' he reveals.

'It's a good thing I don't always follow doctor's orders,' I say before kissing him and sending up a quick prayer for the Fates to bless him.

With Knots' condition in the front of my mind, we continue on for another hour until I feel a weird sensation that I've felt in the past and pause. "What's wrong, ma chérie?" JP asks, rubbing my shoulder.

"I—It's hard to explain it," I start.

"Shit," Knox says. "Let me take point." Knox switches places with JP and glances at my face. "You feeling a premonition, kitten?" he asks.

"Is that what it is?" I ask with a scowl.

"It's what I'm calling it. Feels like something is going to

happen, like that day we were flying in the woods?" he pushes, and I nod.

"Okay, I'll take point. Be ready to pull your weapons. Remember, we left our allies behind. All that training we just went through is gonna come in handy now; it's about to get real," Knox says.

He drops to all fours and in his place is... I don't know what appears, but it looks lethal. I can only assume it is Slayer, his new form. By the gasps from a few of the guys, they have no idea what he is either, and I would wager a bet that they didn't even know about this new development.

'Hey, gorgeous!' The bat faced, long-ass leopard thing turns his head and winks at me. *'Now you get to see a big boy play properly.'*

"Are my eyes going weird, or does Knox have six legs?" Lynx asks. I check, and sure enough, he's right.

"Nope, your eyes are fine, but did you see the five-foot tentacles from hell reaching above us with fish-hooks dangling out of him?" Zeke responds. I peer up and gasp at the sight.

"Aww shit. Whatever he is, it's the rarest thing I've ever seen. It's never been mentioned in any of the mythical creature books that I've read in the past," Ryker says in awe.

"Well, remember what Knox said, get your weapons ready," Levi reminds us.

I pull my glaives free but don't activate them as I follow behind Slayer.

We quickly follow the tunnel until we come to a fork. To the left, I see stairs leading up, and to the right the tunnel continues on. I squat down close to Reaper to look at the map.

"Guys, I think this is Lilith's house. Right here are the stairs, and if this is correct, that"—I point to the right—"should be the tunnel we would have went down in the first place."

"Okay." Knots nods, and I take stock that his voice sounds stronger but he's still using the wall to rest against. "Let's go." I stand up, and we start to move when the floor above us rumbles and dirt begins to fall.

"What the—"

"Shh..." Lynx says. "I think I hear someone."

'Rezzi, push Reaper behind the stairs. We need to dim his light, just in case.'

Without question, I pull Reaper behind the stairs with me and stand in front of him, trying to hide his flames. Lynx waves for everyone else to spread out, and I lean around to see what's going on. Stepping on a loose rock, I lose my balance and fall against the staircase. That's when I feel the vibrations.

'Shit! Lynx! People are coming down the stairs!!' I scream at him.

'Okay, Rez; I'm shifting,' he calls back.

'Slayer, Demons are coming,' I warn.

'Good,' he purrs back.

"The tunnel is so old they probably forgot about it," a voice calls out, and laughter follows. It sounds like more than just a few people. I quickly wipe my hands off on my pants before gripping my glaives again.

"Pompous assholes."

"What about the other ones? The ones spotted with L.A.M.B.?"

"We really don't have to capture them. Asmodeus won't know either way if they die by accident."

"Yeah, it would just be easier to kill them."

The first one steps off the stairs with one foot raised, and the second one never hits the ground.

Slayer's tentacle reaches out and slaps the Demon in the chest, lifting him off his feet before whipping him back to his mouth for a killing blow at the Demon's throat.

Screams ring out as Lynx—in his tiger form—jumps from

the shadows and takes out the next Demon. Three Demons get past Lynx and turn to circle him, but I activate my glaive and give the one closest to me a kidney shot before he turns and swings. I back up but trip over the fucking leash and land on my back with an oomph.

The Demon smirks down at me as he raises his knife for a killing blow, but Reaper jumps onto my belly, making me cough and my eyes water. The Demon scoffs but doesn't stop the arc of his blade descending. Reaper arches his back and his flames burst higher, burning the Demon's face and making him drop his knife.

Zeke flanks him and grabs the Demon by his head and simply rips it right off of the fucker with a roar.

"My lady." He smiles down at me and helps me up.

"Thanks," I tell him with a curtsy, quickly praising Reaper for saving me before looking around. The five demons that came down the stairs are in pieces, yet we all seem to be fine.

"Is everyone okay?" I check, shaking off my close encounter.

"Yep, just another day's work," Moni says, smiling down at her sai.

"They might have been scouts. We need to move," Knots advises us.

Fuck, he's right.

"How does jogging sound?" JP smiles and gives me a look.

"It sounds like death," I moan. *'Knots? I'm scared to ask. I don't want to put strain on you.'* I reach out while I pull out my map.

'Nonsense. I will not die down here. Lead the way,' he says, and I take off.

We run down the tunnels for about an hour, following the twists and turns before we take a moment to catch our breath in an open cavern and have a drink. I check on Knots and refresh his shield. I almost ask for a longer break when we see lights coming down the tunnel we were just in.

Fuck!

"We know you're there, little ones," a squeaky voice calls out.

'Let me see what's going on,' Slayer says as he slinks back down the tunnel.

'Won't you be seen?' I ask, freaking out just a tad.

'Nah. I can throw my form. If they do see me, it won't be the real me,' he explains.

"Let's pack up and be as quiet as possible. We should be at the door soon," I say as everyone turns back from watching him leave.

"You mean the gatekeeper and the monster," Moni says while sporting her pale white bark and wide eyes. I know she's scared to death, but she's acting so brave.

'We'll meet you down the right-hand tunnel, okay? The other one looks like it leads to a dead end,' I tell Slayer.

'Gotcha.'

We start jogging down the path, and that's when I hear Slayer cuss up a storm.

'We're fucked! I'm a badass and all, but even I know when we need help, and this is it.'

'What?'

'They have a small force coming this way. Maybe thirty or forty Demons, and they are armed,' he explains.

I stop and look back at my friends, my family, and the look on my face must say it all.

"It's bad isn't it?" Ryker asks.

"Slayer—Knox's new form—says there's close to forty Demons on our tail, and they are all armed."

"Well, we obviously can't fight them here, so let's work on finding a position we can defend," Knots says and turns to Moni. "You ready to save us?"

"Me?" she squeaks, pointing to her magenta bark.

"Yeah."

Moni raises her chin, pulls her shoulders back and nods. "What did you have in mind?"

"**I**s that enough room to get through?" I ask after a few minutes. Exhausted, I wipe the sweat off of my forehead with the back of my hand.

"It should be. I'm the widest of us all, and I can go through sideways," Knots confirms as he shuffles out through the passageway. He looks back at us. "Are you girls ready?"

Moni and I share a look and a small smile. "Bosom besties for life," Moni says.

"For Life!" I agree, even though she got the saying wrong once again. I love her, though. *Are you sure you are okay?* I ask Knots.

I am a Door Knight and before that... Guardian. This is what I do.

That's still not an answer.

Yes it was. He smiles.

He glances over at Lynx, Zeke, and JP. "You guys clear on the plan?" They nod, and he takes a deep breath. "Okay, then let's go."

Zeke and Lynx join Knots on the other side of the passageway while JP, Moni, Ryker, Levi, and I stay behind. I hate this plan, but I have to agree with Knots. It is smart, and it's better than fighting them head on, especially since we aren't sure what monster we will be dealing with at the door, and we know we can't fight two enemies at once.

"Go ahead and call Slayer back," Knots says before he disappears on the other side of our wall.

Okay, Slayer, bring home the bacon.

'That's what I'm talking about,' he says.

Before me is a massive pit that would be difficult for a Giant to get out of, it's extremely deep and runs from wall to wall. In front of it is a wall of dirt that was formed with all the loose dirt Moni blasted up from her Sonic Booms. She has focused them down to the precise area to make a trap, where hopefully we can confine the Demons in the pit and make a run for it. My shield is holding the wall of dirt in place, and Ryker is holding the illusion that there is no wall.

The scariest part, sending the guys out there to fight or lure them into the trap. I've tied Reaper up further back so we don't give away our plan too soon. I check around the edge of my wall and see the guys taking their fighting stance as the Demonic horde approaches.

I swear, my breath hitches as I see the first Demon approach. He throws something at Lynx, and I quickly toss up a shield around him. It plinks off of it before Lynx's tiger paw slices through the Demon's gut, ending his life.

Shit, why didn't I throw shields around all of them? I quickly apply shields around Knox and Zeke as they engage the enemy. Slayer creeps along the wall and picks off Demons on his way back to us. All I see is Demons being plucked out of thin air and dropped back down without heads.

"Okay, the platform is built for JP," Levi calls out.

"Go," I urge, and JP climbs the nearly invisible platform where he'll be able to perform his job safely.

I send out a burst of my shield to push the Demons back that are in front of the platform—the signal we agreed on—and Zeke, Knots, and Lynx all pull back. As soon as Lynx crosses the pit using the plank, he turns and digs his claws into it and pulls, keeping the Demon's from crossing over safely. The Demons laugh at our retreat, and they step forward to follow, only to find there is no floor below them.

As soon as they realize their mistake, they try to stop but

with the Demons in the back pushing the mob forward, there's no stopping the mass. They cry out in pain and fear, but they haven't seen anything yet. JP had said he could feel water in the tunnels, so his job is to fill the hole with it. My bet is most of these Demons don't know how to swim.

Water quickly starts to rush into the hole from the bottom and the Demons frantically start to climb over each other to get out. Well, those that didn't die from the fall alone. Those that were the last to fall in, hang on to the edge of the pit or dunk the others to try and survive, but that's where I come in once again.

I take in a deep breath and bring my hands up against my chest, as if I'm about to do a chest press, and push against my shield. The same shield holding up tons of dirt and soil. It crashes over the hole and onto the Demons that are still in the tunnel. Cleaning up my mess, my shield smooths out the top of the hole where it is more watery mud.

"Now, JP!" I yell and follow Knox, Levi, Ryker, Knots, Zeke, and Lynx behind the other wall we had constructed.

If JP can make water fill up, he can also drain water. I watch in sick fascination as the water slowly drains out, and the Demons in the water dry in the mud and die in their solid grave. JP climbs down from the platform Levi made and joins us behind the second trap. We weren't sure if we would need it, but since Slayer was buying us time and led the Demons on a wild goose chase, we took advantage of it.

"Do you think we should do the same to the dirt for the other Demons that were in the tunnel?" I ask, looking up at Knots. His chest is heaving and sweat is pouring down his face. "Knots!" I say, concern lacing my tone. I wipe the sweat from his face as he leans against me, almost crippling me with his weight.

Levi looks at Knots and back at the destruction behind us. "I don't think we have time. Moni, think you can seal up that passage? We can just leave the wall and Rez's shield. If they fall, hopefully it takes them out, but I think we need to move," he says.

And I completely agree with him. Lynx meets my eyes and rolls his, before shifting back to a human and coming over, taking Knots' weight. I give him a quick kiss on the cheek before helping Moni set the last trap, thickening my shields around the trap and Knots before grabbing Reaper.

Please be okay, Knots. I send up a silent plea to the Fates once again.

CHAPTER 51
The Beast

Lynx

I must be crazy to volunteer to help this fool. Nah, not crazy, just fucking in love with my mate, that's what this is. I'm a fool in love.

'You're no fool, Lynx,' Knots declares.

'You got that right; you are. You noob,' I tell Knots.

'Thank you. I know you'll treat her right when the time comes,' he mumbles.

'When what time comes?' I ask. I swear this guy is too heavy to be completely filled with hot air. He's not making any sense. The only good thing about carrying this sack of rocks, or wood in his case, is that I'm up here next to my Rezzi-Bear. She doesn't want him out of her sight, which means she's in my sight.

'I'm not going to last down here, and she's going to need you,' Knots rambles on.

'Well, you're gonna have to. If you break my woman's heart, I'll tear yours in two,' I growl out.

'Can't help it,' he mumbles.

Ugh, this guy is infuriating!

"I think we're almost there," Rez calls out right as we turn a bend.

I almost drop the bastard as the Door comes into view. It's nothing that I would imagine seeing in Hell. It's an all white door with figures moving along the surface.

"Well, I don't see no fucking beast," Ryker scoffs. "So this will be a piece of cake."

"Ryker!" Rez chastises him. "Don't you know you're going to jinx us?" Rez spits out.

Cue karma. The ground starts shaking, and I quickly set down Knots so he doesn't get hurt falling from higher ground. Taking position in front of him, I quickly shift into my tiger form.

A screech rings out from the door, and the sound drops me to the floor. My fucking sensitive ears ring, but I don't cry out like my friends around me.

A spiraling jet of water as thick as a tree trunk shoots out of the ground. Tentacles branch out from the bottom of the water and whip back and forth as the rest of the monster materializes. A watery ribcage forms, and spikes erupt from where the shoulders would be. Out of the water, arms form into solid bone with razor sharp claws at the end, paired with armor over the joints. A head raises out of the water with seaweed draping down the back of its head, resembling hair. As the head turns our way, I get my first look at its face. There's no nose, but a thick metal forms above their mouth, extending over their eyes and down to their neck. I assume it's a protective layer of some sort. Their underbite is impressive, and I wish I could send them to my old dentist.

The monster turns and roars, its earthy breath rolling over us. Digging my nails into the dirt, I'm able to hold my place but something about the smells hits me.

"Fuck!" Ryker yells. "JP, can you suck the water from that thing?"

"Ugh. I'm not that powerful, but I can try," JP says.

JP starts to drain some of the water, and the monster screams before it suddenly shudders and shifts into another creature.

This one is one I know. A Manticore. The body of a Lion, bat wings, and scorpion's tail. Except this one has porcupine quills all over it, so you can't get close. *Shit.* I focus on their eyes, and that's when it dawns on me.

"How the fuck are we going to defeat that?" Knox yells, back in his human form.

I shift back into my human self and quickly sweep the Manticore's image, trusting my instincts. I'm our only chance. Not even Knox's new form can take this on, and who knows what else it has in store for us. With my mind made up, I step before him and shift into a clone of his form. I crouch down to pounce despite Rez's protest in my head to retreat and come up with a plan. The beast's head jerks in my direction, rearing back slightly at the sight of my identical form, and I don't waste a moment. I launch myself at the monster and extend my claws. I have a clear shot when I hear the group scream, "NO!!!"

Movement has me checking to my left, only in time to catch sight of the venomous barb aimed right for my unprotected flank. I was taught better than this, but at least I rocked my woman's world and I'm not going out a virgin.

Glossary

Door Knights

- **Knots-***(follower of War/Rez's Door Knight)*
- **Willow-***(Emer/Angels Door Knight)*

Fates

- *Adalyn*
- *Anwen*
- ~~*Liliwen*~~ *DECEASED*
- *Seren*

Foundlings

- ***Chestnut-*** *(Shifter) Moni's mate*
- **Monikaloy/Moni-***(Pimp-Half Pixie/Imp)* JP's sister
- **Jacques Pierre/JP-***(Demon/Nix/Water Nymph)*

Harpies

- **Angel/*Red-heeled Barbie*-***(Fae/Demon)*
- **Emer Elverson/Queen Harpy**-*(Elf)*-2nd of the Elverson Clan
- ~~**Gertrude/Fish face-** (sea monster)~~*DECEASED*
- **Janika-** (Witch)
- **Karmyn-** (Dragon/Lizard/Troll)
- ~~***Katie May-** (Fire Elemental)*~~ *DECEASED*
- ***Serafin-*** *(Sea Harpy)*
- ***Twilight Twins-*** *(black hair/purple skin-???)*

L.A.M.B

- **Lucifer-**(Pride Demon)
- **Astaroth-** (Wrath Demon)- Weapons Smith
- **Murmur-** (Mischief Demon)- Mental foritude/Shields
- **Belzebub-**(Vengeance Demon)- Wield/Control HellFire

Leaders of Nova

- **Lilith-***(Demon)*- Teacher, fashion designer, mother figure
- **Matthew Caldron**-*(Mage)*- Dean of Purgatory Prep Academy. Levi's Father
- **Jessup Cloak**-(Shifter)- Chief of Police, survival 101 professor, Knox's Father
- **Carl Steinbeck**-(Fae)- Head Physician & Scientist. Ryker's Father
- **Daniel Abernathy**-(Vampire)- Mayor of Nova. Zeke's Father

Princes

- **Ezekiel/Zeke Abernathy-** *(Vampire/Necromancer) Death*
- **Leviathan Caldron-***(Mage/Demon essence) Famine*
- **Knox Cloak-***(Shifter/Demon essence) War*
- **Ryker Steinbeck-***(Fae/Demon essence) Pestilence*

Taylor Household

- **Nerezza/Rez-***(???)*
- **Lynx-***(Storm Shifter)-* Rez's BFF
- **Jillian Taylor-***(Human)* Rez's Mother?

Uncharacterized Supes

- **Asmodeus-(**Demon) Prince of Lust
- **Cpt Brooks-**(Shifter) Officer in Special Ops
- **Gus-***(Sphinx)* Owner of Sparks Coffee Shop
- **King Elverson-** (Elf) King of all the Elves
- **Lyrical-** (unknown) Nurse
- **Ms. Teal/Marjoriekine-** (Hybird) Decorater/ Moni's egg donor

Supernatural Species Guide
Species—Appearance—Powers

- **Arte Demon-** short, wrinkled skin, stubby tail, and wings-harmless, no powers, servants, ugly AF
- **Demon-** varies—possess humans, strength, various powers depending on type of demon.
- **Elf-** tall/long ears-superior hearing, cunning, natural abilities based on their kingdom's element
- **Fae-** generalized name for magical creatures that came from Conquer/Pestilence.

- **Fallen Angel-** varies-original powers from heaven/able to blend magic from heaven and hell. Strongest Demons (Royalty)
- **Hercules Goblin-** varies-produces a poison thru cuts in a targets skin. Makes a profit by selling the antidote.
- **Guardian Angel-** varies- strength, ability to seek charges easily for protection, healing song, shield
- **Illustrious Imp-** long body, whiskers, looks like a Chinese dragon- bends light/shadow, flight. Extremely rare.
- **Imp-** varies- flight, conjure fire, cause chaos
- **Incubus-** varies-controls lust, able to change appearance to seduce.
- **Hellhound-** black/red dipped in flames- urinates acid, strong bite force.
- **Mage-** varies- conjure items, spells, crowd control
- **Netherwraith-** panther body, six legs, bat face, tentacles- blends in w/ darkness, throws projection of self.
- **Nix-** Shape-shifting water spirit. Not much known. Rare.
- **Pixie-** varies-cast charms/blessing to affect humans/nature
- **Pteroraptor-** velociraptors with thin membrane between arms and legs- glide down from trees/open sores that burn prey
- **Shapeshifter-** varies- shift, telepathy w/ animal, abilities from animals
- **Storm shifter-** varies- not limited on animals
- **Vampire-** varies- strength, healing, speed
- **Water Nymph-** varies- control the flow of water, mind reading

- **Withering Sulks-** an oily black strip- death strip that kills all that touches it.

✨ *Moni's Feelings/Color Chart* ✨

- **Normal-** Greenish Brown
- **About to Sonic Boom-** Cycle through colors
- **Angry-** Red
- **Confused-** Seafoam Green
- **Dehydrated-** Black (lack of coffee)
- **Depressed-** Orange
- **Desperate-** Periwinkle
- **Ecstatic-** Neon Green
- **Embarrassed-** Pink
- **Excited-** Neon Green
- **Happy-**Pastel Yellow
- **Horny/Attraction-** Purple
- **Jealous-** Dark Green
- **Loved-** Rose
- **Nervous-** Dark Gray
- **Sad/Upset-** Blue
- **Scared-** Pale White
- **Shock-** Glitter Bomb
- **Sick-** Yellowish-Green
- **Surprised-** Magenta
- **Tired-** Dark Brown
- **Worried-** Light Teal

Places

- **Bazaar-** Hell's version of a market
- **Blood Slick Road-** Road covered w/ dead bodies
- **Crucible-** Meeting hall/ Portals to Purgatory
- **Elite Couture-** Lilith's design studio

- **Hub-** City Hall in Nova
- **Nova-** Capital of Pugatory
- **Onyx's Mort-** Hell's Black Market
- **Pugatory-** Where all Supernatural creatures originated

Words

- **Hrmjc oep** = Thank you
- **Oep'gl lbseal** = You're welcome
- **Ve srlsc ej cmnj** = Go check on Cain
- **Amihlg! Irmwl jli!** = Master! I have news!
- **Aeroportal**= Portal to whisk away someone to a predetermined place.

Afterword

Okay, I know what you're thinking... "How could you?" Simple... It just flowed out of me. Actually, what you just read wasn't the original ending. I changed it after Cassie went through it. But hey, look on the bright side, it wasn't as bad as the first book, right? I promise things will be better in the next book, which will be called *Road of Worth*, and out hopefully in late 2023 but no later than 2024.

Thank you for reading Road to Salvation. I can't tell you how much it means to me that you continued Rez's story. I hope you enjoyed the book. It would mean a lot to me if you could leave a review wherever you bought it, because I love to hear what you thought of the story.

Every time I see you recommend my book in reader groups, on your bookstagrams, your blogs, your TikTok, I see that. Each time you interact with my games or discuss the characters or mention something you think they would do... I SEE THAT. I'm like a creepy Santa Claus (I'm watching you). You guys give me so much joy that I'm busting at the seams and I need new sweats.

I hope you stick with me for the next book and follow Rez and the gang.

Make sure to check out a Purgatory Spin-off series that will be coming out later this year in a Monster anthology. The doors of Purgatory don't simply pull the Supernaturals back to Purgatory; they have some help.

Time is up and overdue, now the Reapers are after you. The prestige agency of Monster Hunters is the only thing keeping Earth from being overrun by Supernatural creatures. But what happens when the Hunters become the Hunted?

Blurb:

When you make your living on the open road fighting monsters, love is barely in the rearview mirror.

With family lore and urban legends as their guide, hunters track banshees through bogs, exorcise demons and try to find the best dry cleaner to get pixie dust out of their favorite jacket.

Finding out you're fated to fall in love with the monsters you're meant to destroy is just adding insult to injury. Falling in love with your best friend who's also a monster hunter is almost as bad, and that incident with the cursed object and the succubus doesn't even bare mentioning.

Follow these hunters in this action packed anthology filled with your favorite authors as they defend humanity from creatures that go bump in the night and find love along the way.

https://www.books2read.com/monsterhunters

Acknowledgments

Buckle up buttercups because this is a long thank you.

First of all, I want to thank Jillian for stepping up and taking over as my PA. You've been keeping me straight when I started to tumble down the rabbit hole. I can't wait to see what we come up with next! I love you to death, bestie!

I also want to thank Kayleigh for being with me this past year as my Social Media PA. I would be lost without you and your advice. Please don't leave me.

To my *Bossy Minion*, thank you for putting up with my past/present writing chaos. One of these days I'll get it right, until then, you get the pleasure of constantly fixing my mess! LOOOVE you!

Kellie, thank you for editing this massive project. Once again, you made my work shine brighter than the stars.

Leanne, you worked magic on this cover and I can't wait to see what you do with book 4. You took my vision and made it come to life, thank you for adding in your own personal touch.

Thank you Hope Brown for the graphics you did for the book. They are gorgeous.

My betas were a beast with this book. Bonnie (Stab a bish) Nyas, Lin (Book dragon) Lasky, Naedrax (Horror queen) Rb, Becca (Cheerleader) Sabala, Tanya (Eagle Eye) Courtney, and Jacquie (Thirsty) Stolz. You girls crack me up, keep me going, and throw out the best ideas. Please don't leave me!

To my ARC team, you guys are the freaking best! You

guys blow me away with your energy and how you're always ready to go at a drop of a hat! Thank you!!

Special Shoutouts to:

Kelly Paez, Heather Rochelle Hoffman, and Lin Lasky for the name ideas for Reaper and other nicknames for him. I wouldn't have been able to come up with him without you all. Kristin Rodriguez for giving me the name for Benny. Ericka Cade for her knowledge and information about Chinese Dragons. I also want to thank my Patrons on my Patreon account.

Amber, your art work is freaking amazing, but I knew that back in grade school! I love the work you did for Rez's tattoo. You whipped that up less than 3 days and blew me away. Yes, I'm putting it in the book so people can see what my vision was at least. Thank you. If you want to check out her work: Website

I also want to thank Rosa Lee, Kira Roman, and Lexie Winston. You guys continue to provide me with a plethora of information and friendship that I don't know what I would do without you.

And finally to my family and friends that have supported me in the process. To my Aunt Patty who has been one of my biggest supporters and is constantly asking me how my book is coming along, thank you. Thank you mom and Nay Nay. I love and miss you both. Fishy kisses. And to the real MVP that pushes me to my computer chair and tells me to write...my Kaeden James. Thank you for being awesome! I love you, little man.

About the Author

Kerry Keller is a RH/ Why choose romance author that has an addiction to caffeine, swearing, and sarcasm that has no filter when talking in public.

As an avid reader to escape the drama the world throws at us, she finally got the bug to write a story she would love to read herself. Being at the mercy of the voices in her head, she plans on writing more than just fantasy. Anything from paranormal to contemporary, to bully romance to best friends turn lovers, she plans on writing it. As long as the characters behave. She's often found yelling back at them and getting strange looks in public.

When not writing books, you can find her working in women's health care, in school, or being a single mother to a very sarcastic pre-teen boy. She swears she's a bad influence to him, so if you guys cross paths in the future.#sorrynotsorry.

She was born and raised in the midwest but has traveled all over the United States and is now currently living in Alaska.

Also by Kerry Keller

World of Purgatory

Road to Redemption

Road to Chaos

Scorned by Hell

Coming Soon

Aliens on Earth: a Limited Edition Sci-Fi Romance Collection

Monster Hunter